Beyond the Treeline

Mark A Ellis

First published in the United Kingdom in 2025

This edition published in 2025

Copyright © [2025] by [Mark A Ellis]

All rights reserved.

The right of Mark A Ellis to be identified as the Author and the Work has been asserted by him in accordance with the Copyright, Design and Patents Act 1988

All rights reserved. No portion of this book may be reproduced or stored in any form without written permission from the publisher or author, except as permitted by copyright law.

All characters in this publication are fictitious and any resemblance to real persons, living or dead, is purely coincidental.

Paperback ISBN 978 1 0683451 1 1
e-book ISBN 978 1 0683451 0 4
Typeset in Atticus

Cover by Miblart

Ananta Publishing

About the author

Mark Ellis lives in Sheffield, England with his wife and two children. When not writing sci-fi he is usually reading it, or climbing/cycling in the nearby Peak District. He is also a University Lecturer and holds a PhD in Responsible Leadership, a field in which he also publishes. Beyond the Treeline is his debut novel.

For those who know the difference between reality and fiction is only time.

Part One

Chapter One

"The questions you have of this world will endure, your faith in the inhabitants will not," says a voice out of nowhere, close enough only I could hear amidst the gaggle of noisy customers jostling in the haphazard queue. All pushing to be served by a solitary overworked teenager dashing about behind the bar.

"Sorry, are you talking to me?" I ask, turning around to see the person attached to the voice. His appearance snatches a double take from me: he is striking, with perfectly groomed snow-white hair, a pointed waxed moustache, a pristine designer three-piece suit and unnerving eyes, black within black.

He replies with a nod and subtle blink, and I go to ask him what he means, but it never reaches my lips. A shadow arrives next to me and as I look to the giant casting it, a hammer blow to my temple takes my vision and my head erupts in agony. The lights of the room dance and the world flips as the force of it bounces me into the surrounding crowd. Somehow, I stay upright, clamping either side of my head in excruciating pain, its like someone's driven a huge nail into my temple. I'm sure I can feel my head swell as the agony grows; like it's about to burst. A second later a powerful hand grabs my shoulder from behind and spins me around, it's the giant. My face is only level with his chest as I look up and see his scarred and weathered face, just as he grabs the lapels of my jacket and hoists me into the air, before launching me backwards across the room. I'm airborne for the briefest of moments and then something whacks the back of my legs hard, glass smashes as I land flat on my back and my head flicks backwards violently, hitting the stone floor hard. Then, nothing.

The growing noise of an excited crowd pulls me back to the room; blackness steadily becomes a blur of shapes and colours that slowly resolve into the world around me. I can feel the weight of him across my chest and my chin, pinning me, I can't move to make out more. There's an overpowering stench of damp leather, tinged with mould and yesterday's beer, invading my senses, smelling salts waking me from a nightmare. Except the nightmare's real and returns with a vengeance. Struggling to breathe with the leather jacket smothering me, I give every ounce of my strength to force the full weight of him off me. My frantic wrestle for freedom forces him to one side and I seize the moment and roll away, desperately sucking in a lung full of air.

Fuelled with adrenalin I'm instantly on my feet. Walking backwards away from him, I scan the room as quickly as I can and spot the door. But he's up and heading at me, his head dipped with intent, his eyes fixed on mine, unblinking, saliva dribbling across his chin. I notice how huge he is: well over six feet tall with an unshaved anvil face, his biceps like footballs bulging in his leather jacket.

"I'm gonna fucking kill you," he mutters with the certainty of experience, teeth clenched, snarling like a rabid dog.

The blood drains from my head and my hands go cold. I'm lost, this is all wrong; the bar is spinning around me and the crowd is staring, some of them shouting. At me, or him? I can't tell, the chaos is overwhelming.

"STOP!" I yell, holding my flat palm towards him, bent over panting, still backing away as he accelerates towards me. "STOP, why are you doing this? I don't understand, what have I done?"

My plea only enrages him further and he ducks his head lower, his pace turning into a run. Charging straight at me, he headbutts me in the chest like a raging bull, launching me backwards. Breath explodes from my mouth, my vision flares bright yellow and then goes altogether. I land on a nearby table and more pain erupts. My whole body screams at me, electricity spiking into my temples, the pain exploding in my chest forcing my eyes wider than they've ever been. My vision returns but with crackling yellows and reds flashing wildly at the side. And... I can't breathe. I can't breathe at all, not a single pant, nothing. I go to suck in air, forcing it, nothing. He must have ruptured something, damaged me, fuck! I stare at the ceiling: is this it, is this how I die?

People are stood around me, upside down and leaning over, all looking down at me, pulling their drinks towards their chests protectively, their mouths moving, angry faces silently shouting. I am the spectacle they'll be telling their friends about tomorrow. I flick my head from one person to the next. Their inverted faces make it hard to tell, but I don't think they're going to help; people don't help people. Bizarrely the thing that I notice out of place is that they are all attentionally present – not one of them is distracted by an AIC. Which is unusual; I spend half my teaching life trying to distract people from their ever-present personal AI devices. Instead, there's a single shared focus: me. The cacophony of noise suddenly grows as their voices return to them, only to go quiet a second later as they look up and back away, which must mean... I look down towards my legs dangling off the end of the table and he's there, coming back at me, his menacing smile more confident than ever.

I'm on my elbows facing him, I still can't breathe. I try to force air in – nothing. Push air out – nothing. I try to say something to him as he leans over me – nothing. You really can't make a sound without air moving over your larynx.

He leans over me, hands outstretched to grab me. Instinctively I roll sideways, across the carnage of spilt beer and broken glass and off the table, only to land on the stone floor knees first. There should be pain, but my panic dominates. Kneeling in the detritus on the floor, I look up at him and raise my hands in surrender, before pointing to my neck, giving the "throat cut" symbol with my flat hand, realising as I do that this might not be the message to send. But it slows him; the menacing eyes open wider, and his eyebrows raise as he stops, towering over me.

Seeing my opportunity, I jump up, both legs in sync, garnering as much power as I can, launching my whole body upright like a jack-in-a-box. My eyes are fixed on his chin as I thrust my head forwards at the last minute before making contact. There's an excruciating hammer blow to the top of my head; I don't care. All I can think is: direct hit. A full body uppercut to his chin.

I lift my head to see him land flat on his back. Shit, he actually left the ground with both feet. I stare at him, trying to make sense of everything, still unable to breathe, and he starts to move.

"SEAN!" somebody shouts from across the room.

What? Quickly looking around, I notice a man frantically waving his arms above his head, staring at me from the other side of the pub. He sees he has my attention and waves me over. He mouths the word "quick" – he's stood next to the door, which is exactly where I need to go.

I dash over, efficiently threading myself through the crowd of bystanders, knowing anvil face won't be far behind. The crowd get the message and soon part, allowing me more speed as my mystery saviour opens the door and I run into the car park and into a sea of MyCars, all perfectly lined up in the well-lit lot.

My saviour follows right behind me and I see him tap his AIC and speak. I stare at him; I have no idea who he is. I don't care.

I still can't breathe.

"Do your best to stay calm Sean, it will help with the breathing. Car's coming now," he says, pointing.

I follow his finger and a silver Jaguar glides to a halt just behind me, out of place amidst the ubiquitous MyCars. How does he know my name?

"Jump in the back," he says, just as the door to the bar slams open behind him.

Anvil face!

I need no encouragement; I leap into the car. He follows almost as quickly.

"Home," he says to the car. The motor clicks and we're away.

My eyes are fixed on anvil face as he races towards us. He has no chance and gives up as the car accelerates away.

Wide eyed and with growing terror, I turn to look at my saviour. I still can't breathe or talk. I desperately mouth "help" and point at my neck, hoping he understands and can do something. Desperation is surely written across my face. I must be close to passing out, or worse. How long has it been since I drew breath? How long can a person go? I stare at him, hands shaking, but still focused.

"I know," he says calmly. "Just try to relax. He's only winded you, severely I grant you, but that's all it is. It will pass. Sit back and relax."

I don't think he gets my reality, but lacking options I do as he suggests. I sit back, close my eyes and try to imagine the breath leaving my body. I crunch my stomach muscles a little, forcing slightly; there's pain from the fight. But a small amount of air also escapes my mouth...

I keep pushing, more comes. Now I suck; it's like breathing through the smallest of straws but air is coming in. I keep going, in... and out... in... and out...

I'm not going to die.

"Who are you?" I croak as I open my eyes.

"Good, you're breathing. How's the rest of you?" he replies.

"What was all that? Did you see it, him? It was just... I don't know, why...? What was that all about? Who was he? Did you see?"

"I just caught the end of it," he replies. "I didn't see how it started, but you gave a good show with that headbutt manoeuvre. Are you hurt?"

"Not sure," I reply, scanning my body. "My stomach feels like I've done a million sit-ups and my knees are painful, but amazingly I think I'm alright. Soaked in beer but no permanent damage."

"That's great an—"

"But, who are you?" I interrupt. "Why did you help?"

"Well..." he replies and looks straight at me with a huge grin, his eyebrows pushing to the top of his forehead.

"Well...?" I repeat back, confusion growing.

"Don't you recognise me?"

"Err... no."

"You are Sean Freeman?" he asks. "Went to Bradshaw Primary School in Halifax?"

"Yes..." I reply, tilting my head sideways and squinting at him, and something twigs in my mind. He is familiar.

"Do you remember a friend there called Mike Swale?"

"What? Yes. No way, Mike Swale!" I squint again, staring at him, thoughtlessly scrutinising his face. "Mike?"

"Yep, that's me," he replies with a beaming smile, like we've just bumped into one another at a party.

Of course, there he is. I see him: my mystery saviour miraculously transforms into an old friend. We were in the same class but didn't really hang out together. He was one of the posh kids, sophisticated, without a regional accent. He wasn't a bully or anyone to stay away from and, now that I think about it, I remember he was one of those kids who you just knew would fare well in life, destined for medicine or law or to be a serial entrepreneur or in some top job. And here he is in his own self-driving car, well-groomed, with just the right mix of smart and casual; a pale blue designer shirt that matches his eyes, khaki loose-fit trousers and brown brogues. I can make out firm muscles beneath the shirt and his posture and physical size give him a presence, which, coupled with his well-groomed appearance, oozes confidence before he says a word.

I recall the skinny kid I used to know, skidding down an ice slide with me and the other boys, during the one and only snowy winter we had. Was it Mike who fell on the slide and chipped a tooth that day, which we all got in trouble for – resulting in us being paraded outside the headteacher's office, where we were all given a thorough dressing down about the dangers of making an ice slide? After which we all ran straight back out and continued the fun before the sun broke up our game.

"Wow, what are the chances…?" I say, still revelling in the memories. "And thank God. Gavin never turned up, so I was on my own there. Some bloke started talking to me at the bar, not the big guy, an older man with a hipster moustache. Then out of nowhere a massive punch in the side of the head and I end up flying across the bar. The big guy, who was he?"

"No idea, but you were in a pickle, he was twice your size."

"Well, thank you Mike. You really saved me there, thanks," I say, letting out a long breath.

"That's alright. You would have done the same."

"It's nice that you think t—"

My words are taken from me by an ear-shattering crash and severe jolt that sees me fly off my seat. I'm violently shoved to one side and a cocoon of white fabric appears from nowhere, smooth and solid, pinning me against the seat. I can't move; a massive bang is quickly overtaken by a piercing screech and I feel the car tipping over sideways. My legs, the only part of me able to move, helplessly kick around wildly in the footwell of the car.

As the realisation of the crash hits me, the airbags soften and start to deflate, releasing me. But only for a moment as the car lurches forwards again and the headrest of the front seat comes straight at me.

"... Sean, SEAN!"

The world fizzes back into reality, dulled at first, like an old photo. The muffled noise grows, outlines of shapes appear and colours fill in what was dark and grey. Someone's calling me?

"Sean, you're back. You K?" asks a man peering into my eyes, his face so close I can smell his breath.

It's... Mike, yes Mike. Car crash, we were in a car crash. But car crashes don't happen, auto drive and radar don't allow it. Except it did, didn't it?

"What, what happened?" I ask, blinking Mike back into focus.

"You're conscious," replies Mike. "You had me worried for a minute. Can you move?"

"Think so," I reply, lifting my arms and sitting up. "My face though, my nose." As I touch it, a spike of pain spears into my forehead. "SHIT! That hurts, shit... Have I broken my nose?"

"Don't know, but we need to get you to hospital, get you checked out. Best stay there for now, back in a mo," he replies, tapping his earpiece AIC and getting out of the car.

I go to open my door, but it won't budge, I push and pull getting nowhere and finally give it a huge shove with my shoulder. It flies open, and I go with it, only just managing to grab the doorframe and prevent another face plant. Can this day get any worse? I clamber out and lean on the back of the car, not sure which parts of me are damaged and which bits still function. My whole body is aching, I need to sit down.

I look around to see we're at the side of a main road, but it's quiet; no cars passing by, grey fields of corn disappearing into darkness and the silhouettes of industrial buildings on the opposite side, all dark, all quiet. Even though Mike's car has been thrown about, it sits neatly straddling the curb and the road. You'd be forgiven for thinking it was badly parked and in need of a paint job. I look around for the other car, but there isn't one. And there's no one else here – how long was I unconscious? Or did Mike's car fail and crash itself. Can that happen?

Mike's still talking and pacing up and down the pavement, leaving me to nurse my injuries. Another car heads our way; I step to the side so it can pass easily but it slows as it approaches. They must have realised something's wrong. The rear window slides down as they near, so I give a smile and raise my hand.

I see the shadow of someone in the rear as they pull to a stop. He leans towards the window and the streetlights bring him to life. My head jerks backwards as I recognise him: it's the guy from the bar, the one who was talking to me when the fight broke out. Definitely him, white hair and a hipster moustache; he's in his seventies and neatly dressed in the same blue suit, a trendy hipster grandad.

"You were in the bar just now, weren't you?" I say.

He doesn't reply and slowly shifts his gaze from me to Mike's car, to Mike then back to me. "Are you injured?" he asks.

"What? No, not really. But... who are you? Have you followed us?" I ask.

He ignores my questions and I follow his gaze as once again he looks from me to Mike on the pavement talking on his AIC.

The click of the car's motor snaps my head back around to him just as the car starts to move away. His window now sliding up, I watch as they disappear into the distance.

"K," says Mike as he walks around to my side of the car. "Long story short, no ambulance. Even though you were unconscious for a short time, you are up and walking so not a priority. Cutbacks eh? Anyway, I've ordered a MyCar. It tells me it will be fifteen minutes; we can head to the hospital ourselves and get you checked out. Alright?"

"Yeah, I guess. What about you, are you alright? Were you hurt at all? Did you see what happened even? There's no other car. And..."

"Yes, the air bags save you, but you can't see a thing. I'm guessing a hit and run, an uninsured driver perhaps? But the diagnostic on the car will be able to tell us later and the cameras will have got them at some point or other."

"Yeah, good point," I say. "You know, you seem remarkably calm about it all."

"Well, I am perplexed. But we're both fine and that's the main thing."

"I guess," I say, nodding. "Did you see the other car, a minute ago, the one who pulled up?"

"I did, were they just seeing if we were alright?

"Err, yeah... I guess so. But it was the bloke from the bar, from earlier."

"What?" replies Mike, shocked.

"No, not him. Not the anvil face thug. The chap I was talking to before the fight happened. No idea who he was. Kinda felt like he was following us though, weird – or I'm just paranoid."

"That would be weird. Anyway, maybe we should sit," he suggests, clearly concerned. "The MyCar will be a little while and you could be more shaken up than you realise."

He goes to sit on a low wall at the side of the pavement. Dutifully I follow. It's late but dry and too warm like always. With no traffic it's actually quite peaceful on the outskirts of town, away from the bars and burbs. As I sit quietly, I notice the tranquil surroundings and feel my body slump, relaxed enough now for the aches and pains to return.

"How come you were at a bar on your own anyway?" asks Mike.

"Oh, that. Yes. Bad day at work, colleague says let's go for a drink, he doesn't turn up and big guy beats me up for no reason whatsoever. All in all, shit day."

"Yeah, that stinks. Will you be alright for work tomorrow?"

"It'll be fine either way. I'm into a big chunk of analysis so home or the Uni is fine."

"Got you. Analysis?" replies Mike.

"Yeah. I'm a researcher these days, solving the problems of the world and all that."

"Interesting. What's your field?"

"Biology," I reply, not in the mood to go into detail.

"K... and?"

"What? Oh yeah... longevity. I'm exploring how we can increase longevity in humans, so we live longer. If we live longer, we'll look after the planet and each other."

"K... Just that then. I thought you were joking when you said you were solving the problems of the world."

"I was. It's gonna be a long journey and, like most research, probably not fully realised in my lifetime. But worthwhile; important. At least I think so."

"I would agree old friend, impressive."

"Thanks. Listen, do we need to go to hospital?" I ask.

"Your choice, but if you've had a head injury it's best, I think."

"Yeah," I reply, knowing he's right but just wanting to be home. "Just being beaten up it's... I don't know."

"Yeah, then a car crash," replies Mike. "Shit day, sorry Sean."

"Yeah, but not your fault Mike, not your fault."

Chapter Two

I discovered the tranquillity of early summer mornings writing up my doctorate; avoidance was the battle. It's a world of blissfully cool, deserted streets, where the gentle murmur of nature reigns from the first light. But all too soon, I know the tranquillity will be shattered as the commuters are released and surge forward like blinkered horses, racing through the streets, desperate to outrun the rising tide of heat. It's hard to imagine a summer day being anything but sunbaked. Not like the old days, before the *melt* made the maps obsolete. You never know what you've got until it's gone.

I take a deep breath on the doorstep and soak it all up as I leave, feeling the stillness of the day. A waft of lavender and the buzzing of bees emanate from my neighbour's garden, putting a smile on my face, and I can feel happiness radiate from me. Renewed, I head off, the echo of my footsteps the only challenge to the dawn chorus. Mornings like this are meditative, a cleansing reminder of what once was. That wonderfully naive world of childhood, where every day was new and exciting and the only people that really counted were you and your friends and the games you played. The summers were endless, and we were always laughing; we just lived for the day, for the fun, our imagination taking us anywhere and everywhere. Simpler times, before the mystifying complexity of teen years and adulthood.

Not for the first time I arrive at work with little recall of the two-mile walk. I head up to the lab. My office is at the other end of the campus, so I use my office as storage and my lab space as my lab-come-office. Of course, this has nothing to do with the lab being allocated energy and an AC unit. Working at a cool twenty degrees every day, well that's just a happy coincidence, lucky me.

It's still early when I arrive so I stop by the canteen and sneak my cup of tea into the lab. These early mornings are great; I get the lab to myself, which transforms the place into a den of serenity, and I can write, think and imagine. But, as I sit and switch on my laptop, a distant rustle tells me, unfortunately, I'm not alone, and my oasis of calm becomes a mirage.

I pop my head up to see beyond the partitions and scan the lab. The place is the size of a tennis court and accommodates six of us, our analytical equipment and storage cupboards, resulting in us being tightly packed into our own little zones surrounded by a chaos of our own design. As I peer past the white melamine jumble, I spot Michelle at the far side, partially hidden by the centrifuge.

I shout a quick, "morning Michelle". She hears me.

"Morning Sean, how are you... cup of tea in the lab? Naughty boy... Did you bring me one?" she says, grinning ear to ear, always happy – how does she do it? Michelle has been resident in this lab much longer than I, during which time she has amassed numerous low-res printed photos of family, friends and motorbikes, all of which adorn her overhead cupboards. These are accompanied by other small ornamental tranklements on most flat surfaces, many of which I can't identify, except the perpetually waving cat. All of which I'm sure contravene lab policies. She also has a ring tone on her phone that shouts at her: *PICK UP THE PHONE! PICK UP THE PHONE!* I think it's a recording by her boyfriend. More than a little annoying when she's left her phone and AIC earpiece in the lab and gone to a meeting and the inevitable happens. She's definitely not a traditional reserved academic; she swears like a trooper and is always her "authentic self".

"You're in early Michelle, and no, sorry, no to the tea, I didn't think there would be anyone in yet".

"Yes, I'm off to Donnington to watch the superbikes this weekend, so need to get a few things sorted before lunch. Exciting!" She exclaims, with a high pitch zing and small clap of her hands. "It's gonna be great and I reckon I might even have a drink or two."

"If it's anything like Godfrey's leaving do then God help Donnington," I say, knowing I couldn't insult Michelle if I wanted to. She loves to party, and I have no doubt she will do just that over the weekend, accompanied by a motley crew of middle aged rockers. Come Monday we will be regaled with tales of derring-do and outrageous mishaps.

"This is a silly question Michelle, but you do know it's Thursday don't you?" I ask.

She rolls her eyes at me. "Yes, of course I do. Packing this afternoon, pre-drinks at mine tonight and then I'm on leave for an early start tomorrow to get there and get a good spot for the weekend. Forward planning maketh a great weekend, Sean." She taps her temple with her finger.

"Nice, enjoy! I look forward to hearing all about it come Monday," I say, dropping back to my seat and laptop.

An hour later, like a tag team, Anthony arrives as Michelle leaves. He says his brief hellos to us both before reviewing ongoing experiments and flicking his laptop on. This is often followed by expletives of disbelief as he reads through demanding email requests. Today is no exception.

"Have these people got no idea at all?" I hear him mutter with disbelief. "I'll bet not one of them has set foot in a lab or a classroom in over twenty years and here they are telling us what works best when it comes to research and teaching. Utterly ridiculous, it really is."

He stops talking and I can feel him looking at the back of my head, waiting for a response, for me to become his co-conspirator in slating the University. Today, I resist the temptation to turn around. Anthony has more than a flair for melodrama, which, if you want to get any work done, is best avoided. The continued silence tells me he's waiting and not giving in so easily today. I submit and spin around on my chair. As predicted, he's sat looking at me; I smile back and nod sympathetically.

"I expect you're right old mate, but what do you do?" I say.

Anthony continues his stare for a moment. "Yep, you're right. You really are, so annoying though, you know…" He sneers, and then with a subtle shake of the head spins himself back around to face his computer.

To many this would come across as rude, but I've known Anthony a long time and I sense something's not right, but I might have to wait for it to come out. He loves a good rant about the University and it's not like him to pass up the opportunity. The interesting thing is he's extremely bright and will often spot the reality behind the façade of a policy long before the rest of us. Like me, he's also quite political and we have some great chats on the manipulations of right-wing governments and their lack of insight into this or that issue and how that has led to disastrous outcomes. But when it comes to the University procedures and policies, the rest of us aren't that bothered and realise the machine of the Uni is too big for us to tackle. So we go along with the system, knowing the machine must be fed and that we ourselves need the machine to enable us to do our research that may in some way contribute to the world, this being a much easier job than changing the University's systems. It smacks of making the change in the enemy's camp from "within" and all that, but until I win that Nobel Prize, I doubt they'll listen to me either.

I now turn Anthony's primary weapon on him and stay facing him in my seat, staring at the back of his head. He holds out longer than I did, so I continue our conversation anyway. "So how are you today Anthony?" I ask, very obviously and deliberately avoiding remonstrations about the Uni. He knows the signal.

"Yes, I know," he replies, spinning back around to face me, "I will reign it in and I'm K, thanks for asking. If I'm honest, I think I'm just pissed off at having to rewrite this annual improvement plan. They changed the format from last year's plan and all the headings have changed. Guess who simply did theirs as a rewrite of last year's in the old format, under the same headings, and will now have to rewrite the whole thing?"

"Really? I hadn't seen that email, thanks for the heads up," I reply, genuinely grateful as I would likely make the same mistake.

We're interrupted by a single loud thump on the door, which is then immediately swung open. When I see who it is, I realise the thump was likely an indignant knock. It's Peter, our illustrious Assistant Dean who enters. I go back to my laptop, hoping he isn't here to see me.

"Where is she?" he asks abruptly, with no attempt to hide his frustration.

I sense the shit's about to hit the fan so I respond. Better me than Anthony – that could become a car crash in no time.

"Michelle?" I say, "are you looking for Michelle, Peter?"

"Yes, where is she?" he demands, looking to me and Anthony. "She's not answering my calls and I'm sick of talking to her AIC."

Experience tells me only exact specific direct responses will suffice here, so I lie.

"She was here earlier, I believe she's gone to a meeting and then is straight to teaching, I think," I reply, carefully, in a way that could be perceived as a mistake if investigated. Others might call it bullshitting with confidence whilst leaving the backdoor open.

"Bloody hell. Knowing her she's probably pissed somewhere having an intimate conversation with her own AIC," he says, scowling at me, desperate for a target. "When she reappears tell her to contact me immediately. I need a set of marks from her for the assessment board tomorrow morning. She knows the ones," he says, teeth still clamped together. Instruction given, he doesn't wait for a reply, turns on his heel and is gone.

"How rude is that man?" says Anthony. "And... did he say what I think he said?"

"You mean the AIC intimacy thing?"

"Well, yeah. I mean, was he implying she, you know. You know, that. Doing, that... with her AIC," says Anthony, his eyes flicking down towards his groin every time he says the word *"that"*.

"Anthony, I believe *that's* exactly what he was getting at," I reply. "As in, Michelle... err, how can I put it... is knocking one off listening to her AIC. Which, as I hear it, can be quite good; that is, they get to know what works for you and either read porn that you like, or make it up based on your preferences. And, if you have your AIC tuned into your vitals, as people do, then the algorithm can really go to work. AICs make you feel clever; your own personalised AI. It knows you and knows what you like and want. If anything's going to tickle your fancy, it's going to be your own AIC."

Anthony nods at me, flicking his eyebrows up, not sure where to look, his cheeks taking on a reddish flush.

"I know," I say, my blood boiling as I focus in on his detestable comment. "It's outrageous. You know, we could get him sacked for that. That guy is a misogynist and bully. In fact, I think we need to talk to Michelle when she's back in the office, see what she wants to do. Although I suspect he'll squirm his way out of it, just like the previous times."

"But he's the Dean," replies Anthony. "How can someone like that end up in that job?"

"Really Anthony? You don't think we have our share of self-interested careerists?"

"Hmm, I suspect you're right. Sad though."

"It is. But let's leave it till she's back, I don't want to ruin her weekend. Although we probably do need to ask her about the outstanding marks. I'll call her." She won't respond to Peter, but she will to me.

"Hey honey, miss me already?" she says as she picks up.

"Hi, yes, listen – Peter's just been in and he's looking for you. He's not happy, which I know is normal. He was after a set of marks for the board tomorrow and I know you're off tomorrow. Are they sorted, or…?"

There's a silent pause from Michelle, followed by, "that fucking grasper! Fuckedy fuckedy fuck. Shit!" Another pause. I hear her breathing; I know she's got the message so I wait. "Can you go to my desk Sean?" she asks politely, regaining her composure.

"K, walking across now. What am I looking for?" I ask as I approach her desk area.

"On the windowsill nearest my seat," she says. "A pile of scripts, perhaps twenty of them, labelled 'Level 4 Introduction to Research Methods'. Are they there?"

I spot them straight away, I can't believe she's actually printed them off. "Yep, they're here. What's the situation?"

"I forgot, I fucking forgot! Shit, there goes Donnington, bollox!" she shouts and I can hear her voice moving from angry to miserable. "And sorry Sean, I printed them off again, sorreee...."

"Hang on, there goes Donnington?" I say. "No way, you can't be cancelling your weekend."

"It's my fault Sean," she replies. "I can always arrive a day late, just means I won't be able to get the camper van in. Which will be shit, but my fault. BOLLOX!"

I know how much the super biking events mean to her and how missing out on the first day will destroy the weekend. I pick up the scripts and have a look at the top one. It's generic stuff around research, we all teach it.

"Don't worry Michelle, I can sort it. I can mark these tonight and have the marks handed into the board first thing tomorrow, Peter will never know. I'll say you left the marks with me and I forgot to pass them on."

"WHAT? No way," she yells. "That's really kind of you Sean, but we both know your super diligence in marking means you ain't that quick, credit to you. But it means your entire evening will be gone. I could probably knock them off in two or three hours. Thanks, but it's alright, I can't ask that of you, it's not fair."

"Fair or not, I'm doing it," I say. "And I will do my best to be tardy in my marking; I may not even read them twice."

"What? Nobody reads them twice!" she yells, her pitch even higher. "Sean, wonderful offer but really it's K, I can come back and sort them. Or... I could get my AIC to do them, there are electronic copies on the system."

"You have got to be kidding, you could lose your job over that," I say. "Look, seriously. If I wasn't doing this I would just be cleaning the house, or some other admin task I dream up. This way I know

I'm being helpful and that's a good thing. Makes me feel I've done my good deed for the day. So, there we have it, sorted. Alright?" There's a pause from Michelle's end. I smile, knowing she's letting me help her.

"Thank you Sean, I owe you. Big time," she replies, returning to her usual upbeat self.

"No problem, you just forget all about these. I will hundred percent get it sorted. You focus on having fun with Carl and the gang and I will see you on Monday."

"Yes sir! Mate, you are a star, love you loads."

"K, see you Monday."

"You will. Byeeee." Then she's gone.

What is she like?" chortles Anthony from behind me, having worked things out from my side of the conversation.

"Yes, I know, she's a bit chaotic, but in the best of ways," I say, and we both of us smile knowing how much Michelle has brought to the department and, if I'm honest, to our lives. She is a joy to be around. Just then my phone rings and I give a knowing nod to Anthony as I take it. It's Jason, one of my research assistants.

"Hi Sean, have you had a look at your email yet?" he asks.

"Some of them, why, what have I missed?"

"Are you by a screen, can you have a look now?"

"Yes, I'm in the lab. Let's have a look," I say, clicking onto my inbox.

"Which one, who's it from?" I ask.

"It's from David, as in Professor Green, sent late last night."

I scroll down and spot an email from David Green, my research mentor and one of the Uni professors. Very handy to have his name included on funding bids and research papers; he knows his stuff, so a great resource for me.

The email is marked urgent and is quite lengthy, so I skim read whilst Jason is on the phone. It's not good news. One of the participants in our trials has found a lump in her neck; it's on her lymph node, so possibly a tumour. They've done a biopsy and are awaiting results. Not that he needed to, but David reminds me that as the primary investigator I now need to put the whole project on hold, pending the outcome of these investigations.

"Shit..." I say, struggling to take it all in. "I take it you've read all this Jason?"

"Yes, what a nightmare. What do we need to do?" he asks, mild panic in his voice.

I re-skim the email. This could be horrendous; the worst news. I feel the blood run from my head, making me dizzy and unable to focus.

"Sean? Are you still there Sean?" asks Jason.

I get a hold of myself, trying to put aside the whirlwind of issues and focus on what needs doing right now.

"Well... first thing, is... I need to get in touch with all the clinical leads and let them know to put everything on hold and inform their teams and the participants. I can get on with that now." I feel a sense of dread at having to make those calls, but I need to remain calm and be seen as calm.

"This is very unfortunate but not that unusual," I say, as much to myself as to Jason. "We have procedures in place for this eventuality. What would be really helpful is for you to find out who has done the biopsy and when we can expect the results, along with any other medical details. I can also contact David and see if he has anything further to tell me. In fact, he will know who's done the biopsy, so I'll text you the name of the clinic and the clinician when I get it and you can follow up, is that alright?"

"Sure, of course, anything else?" asks Jason.

"There will be," I say, thinking on my feet. "But for now don't share this, unless you have to of course, but don't volunteer the information as we don't really know what we're dealing with just yet. You K with that?"

"I think so. You're not asking me to cover this up or anything are you?" he replies nervously.

"No! Of course not," I say. "But these things can get out of hand, with rumours changing the reality and causing all kinds of problems, especially if it gets in the media. So, it's really important to have all the facts before we go public – if we have to go public. Otherwise, we wont be able to answer questions and indicate our way forward, and that can lead to all kinds of other problems. So, for now, don't mention it until we have more clarity. If you have anyone giving you a hard time or you feel uncomfortable dealing with them, then just send them to me. It's not your job to deal with any shit or have to justify anything. Is that alright?"

"Yes, no problem, thanks," he says with obvious relief. "I'll wait to hear and get on with whatever as soon as I do".

I sit back, staring unfocused at the email on the screen, unable to think, with words like tumour and lymph node leaping out of the screen at me.

Anthony breaks my thousand-yard stare. "That all sounds very ominous Sean, are you alright, is there anything I can do?"

"Not at the moment Anthony, but thanks for the offer," I reply. "We've had a trial participant report an illness and it could be linked to the trial itself, but might not be." God, I hope not. "So we need to put everything on hold and investigate."

"Understood, hmmm... that could be pretty serious. I'm here if you need, as you know. I can imagine there's lots on your plate now, so I'll shut up and let you get on. But give me a shout if there's anything, or if you need someone to cover your teaching or whatever."

"Will do, thanks, it's appreciated."

I set to prioritising and emailing the various stakeholders in the first instance to halt the trial and then call David. He's on his way in and we agree to meet in the Uni deli area in twenty minutes. I use the time to finish off sending the few remaining emails, all of which I will need to follow up with a phone call before the end of the day. Putting people at ease, answering questions and maintaining confidence in the project is going to be my mantra for the next few weeks.

I hit the usual wall of heat as I leave the lab and head down to meet David. It gives me time to think, the reality of the situation starting to sink in. This could be the death knell for the project; over eight years of work wasted, gone. My career all but over. And of course, the participants. SHIT! The participants...

Developing a growth or lump in the lymphatic system is exactly the kind of issue that could occur with our approach. If our "wonder drug" Teleopote has led to this, it will be horrific.

My mission is to extend life, not shorten it.

Chapter Three

I spot David sat at a table on the far side of the deli. His complexion is ashen and he looks shattered, hair not brushed and scruffy looking as if he's been up all night. I've never seen him anything less than neat and tidy; there's his usual sweat patches on his shirt, but that's everyone nowadays with the energy rationing and no AC.

"Hi Sean, how are you doing?" he asks as I take a seat opposite, his sombre tone foreshadowing the message.

"I've been better. You?"

"Probably…. much the same as you old chap," he replies, nodding. "Not good news, but no matter what, we'll get through this. We both know research is never straightforward and much of the learning comes from the parts you weren't expecting." He attempts to give me a sympathetic, encouraging smile, but fails.

"How sure are we it's Teleopote?"

"Well, let me share this," he says, passing me his screen.

It has the physician's notes on. I scan them quickly: they're dire.

"The other tab at the bottom has the various test results on too, have a look," he says, leaning over and pointing.

The results are dreadful, even worse than David's sombre tone implied. "Fuck," is all I can say, head between my hands, looking down at the screen.

"Yes, that sums it up," says David.

"What now, where do we go from here?" I ask, hoping for some pearl of wisdom.

"Well we plan for the worst and hope for the best," he replies. "We need to look at all the stakeholders, our commitments, policy, the regs, compliance and so on. But right now we need a plan of action, a plan you can take forward. OK?"

"Yes, my thinking too. I've made a start, with a few priorities," I tell him, and pull out my notes to talk him through my ideas.

I find it tough to focus and it takes us two hours, but we pull together a plan for the coming days and weeks. It's overwhelming and I really need to have a fix on all of this, and there is too much I simply don't know yet, much of which I *can't* know yet. But I know me and my need to know, to get on top of things, to fix it all, to make it right – and my burning need to do that straight away. This drive I have is not always a good thing; it generates results – but at a cost.

The conversation with David becomes draining. Every new issue he wants to discuss pulls energy from me, sapping my strength and will. I know he means well and is doing his best to help, and the million questions are important, but the situation gets too much. I have to look away, to avoid for a moment, to come up for air. It'll seem odd, but I know me and it's all I can do to avoid the crush.

I blank out David and look away, my eyes drawn to a rowdy group of students laughing and joking at the other end of the deli. Carefree lives – lucky them. I see some colleagues I know sat close to them, having a quiet chat, sipping their ice tea, sat back in their chairs, enjoying some time out. Like I've done many times, sat in clusters beneath the ceiling fans. I can't see me there in the future. This could be it, my relatively short research career over. All the work, all these years, just gone. My life upended but no one else knows – and if they did would they care? Why should they? Would I? It's a strange reality, all of these lives in the same space but radically different experiences.

I come back, look at David. He's stopped talking and is sat staring at me, eyebrows raised.

"Sean, you are with me, aren't you?" he asks.

"Yeah, sorry... what were you saying?"

"OK, so we have a plan, *you* have a plan," he replies. "That's good, I know there's a mammoth amount to do and in a short space of time, so you don't need me to tell you to use the research team, do you?".

"Of course not, I'm the PI, I lead and don't take it all on myself, got you. Any other sage-like words of advice, David?" I immediately bite my tongue. I always was good at biting the hand that feeds.

"Well, whatever the outcome," replies David, ignoring my sarcasm. "In time it will all pass and there will be other roads to go down. Don't see this as the end. OK?"

I nod and, at odds with Uni culture, I stand and put out my hand to shake his to show my appreciation. "Thanks for all you have done and are doing David, seriously, thank you," I say, holding his gaze, hoping he recognises my sincerity.

"We'll sort it old chap, don't worry. Play it by the book and all will be well," he says, and gently slaps me on the shoulder.

"The plan" sucks the rest of my day and I have to borrow a coat to walk home. The weather has taken one of its freakish turns and is wild. Wind and sheets of rain have arrived from nowhere despite the forecast. I don't go home to my empty house – I can't. When I get home all the shit will be made real, but if I'm not yet home, then it's not real, it's still only a possibility – Schrodinger's cat. When I do get there, it will just be me rattling around, looking for something to clean or tidy, for what, or who, I don't know – certainly not my non-existent girlfriend. The house is spotless, permanently, but I still clean it, again and again. Perhaps I'm keeping it clean in case I meet someone and in a moment of wild spontaneity I invite them back. But that's not going to happen. It's too stressful, not knowing what to say, pretending to be interested when really you're not, which to me is just dishonest. So I walk and I think, or more accurately, I worry.

I have a habit of catastrophising things in my life. I run movies in my head – they're not planned in anyway, it just happens. They'll start off as real life events, like when I met a girl at a conference in Uxbridge and she gave me her number. Later in the conference hotel room I imagined where things might go to. In my mind I ring her up and she's keen to meet for a drink, so we go out. It's all a bit awkward and the conversation dries up quickly. Then we bump into her old boyfriend. He threatens her and I'm not sure if I'm meant to defend her or not. I don't want to assume as the man that this is my role and that this then detracts from who she is. Also, it's our first date – I don't know her well enough to stand up for her, do I? Does that even matter? Before long, the ex-boyfriend ends up thumping me and we then end up at the hospital with the police involved, and it all ends really badly. I'm just running this all in my head, catastrophising, and I try to snap myself out of it. But I just end up back there five minutes later. It goes away at work, in the lab, or where I can focus on a problem. But people are hard to understand, to know what they really want, despite hearing what they say.

My reality is better than my imagined catastrophising. Although not always – I have a hurdle, and if people can get over it and accept me as I am, then things can work out well, like Michellle and Anthony at work. And Janine, my girlfriend for a whole three months. She was cagey at first, but turned out that was intrigue – she just didn't know how to take me. Like on our third date, when she suggested she stay over at mine after dinner, and I initially said no as I had an early morning meeting the next day. It took me thirty minutes to realise she was suggesting we go to bed for the first time, how did I not spot that? But she got me and saw my cogs catch up and it turned out to be a great night I'll always remember. But even her intrigue had its limits and eventually she tired of my lack of insight, like most of them – she just lasted longer.

Despite all of this, I know I'm not a bad guy. I want the best for people and for myself and will work hard to achieve this. I just see things differently than most.

The rain starts to get really heavy now and runs into my eyes, blurring my vision, and all I can see is a tabloid headline declaring the Uni being sued. I'm out of a job and unemployable. I make the news. People recognise me in the street and know where I live, so I have to move and take a job at McDonald's. Then—

—I catch a reflection of myself in a shop window and stop walking. I stand in the street looking at me, rain drenched, water cascading down my neck and back, the wind whipping me in the face as it switches direction, my hair wet and slicked against my forehead. The coat I borrowed long since soaked through and me with it. I stand there in an empty street, pitying my own image, not knowing which way to go.

Chapter Four

Work becomes a treadmill. Like Sisyphus condemned to push a boulder uphill for eternity I keep going, unable to see if or when the end will ever come. I spend my time on my mobile whilst marching across the campus on the way to meetings, or in meetings trying not to be distracted by calls on my mobile. No one is outwardly panicking, but there's a lot of distancing going on as everyone ensures their back is covered and they're not in the firing line of the press or the research council's ethics committee. I don't blame them.

The biopsy cultures are due to mature, so I head to the hospital and the receptionist ushers me into a small meeting room, one of the soft furnished ones where they deliver bad news to family members. I settle into one of the comfy floral-patterned armchairs and notice the AC unit in the ceiling, silent; I don't warrant the energy allocation. I stew in there for ten minutes before Gary and two of his colleagues squeeze into the room. Their sombre looks tell me all I need to know, but I still cling to hope as Gary starts to read through the results. It takes less than sixty seconds for him to share and as he delivers each point the blood drains from my head, and I sink further and further into the armchair.

"—which tells us the growth is malignant and could have been caused by Teleopote," he says, silencing the room and anesthetising my mind as he looks at me, ensuring the message has sunk in. "Nothing is conclusive of course Sean, after all it's only a single case, but we need to be prudent."

I look at them, but I can't read the team's reaction to the results; they're sombre one minute and upbeat the next. I don't think they can decide to treat me like a patient's family member or another medic. Not that it matters.

"I think I should perhaps talk to the participant," I suggest. "To apologise or something, do you think? Would that be helpful?"

"To be honest at this stage it's best to leave things with us," replies Gary. "It's complicated and as you've never met the patient then it would be a further complication they could do without."

The immediate relief this brings me is quickly overtaken by guilt. I desperately don't want to have to face someone who I might have almost killed, how do you do that anyway? What do you say? *"Sorry, it wasn't on purpose, and we were trying to do the right thing, honest".* But now I don't have to say anything, thank goodness. But *maybe* I should, isn't that my duty? Or am I seeking some kind of clemency? Forgiveness I don't deserve.

I glance up and the team are all looking at me with blank stares. "Well listen, thanks for everything and sorry," I say, standing to leave, needing to leave. "I don't know what to say... we checked for all of this, this shouldn't be happening. It doesn't... sorry."

"We know Sean," replies Gary. "We'll keep you up to speed as we know more K?"

"Yes, please... of course, yes," I reply, shaking his hand and heading for the door. "Thanks again," I say, turning to face them briefly before I march to the exit, desperate for air.

The words "malignant" and "caused by Teleopote" are all I can hear on my journey from the hospital to work, Gary's voice as he reads the results echoing in my head. The guilt builds and I can't solve this; all I can do is walk away and hope. Looking at my fellow passengers on the bus, I start to wonder, if they knew, what would they think? How would they judge me?

And my career, where now? I was targeting a P-Contract on the back of this project, a permanent job, access to the Uni EliteCar pool and all the other perks, no more searching the streets for an available MyCar for me. That's all gone, definitely for now and maybe for ever. Where does that leave me? The researcher who can't do safe research. The researcher who killed people. Standard contracts run out at the end of the academic year. I wouldn't re-hire me, it would be irresponsible to the institute. Will anybody ever trust me again?

The familiarity of my lab brings some relief to the turmoil in my mind. A safe harbour in the chaotic ocean of my life. That is, until I switch on my laptop and the email I was dreading screams at me from the screen. David and I are requested to update senior leadership and the University research ethics committee first thing tomorrow. This has never happened to me before or to anyone I know.

I set too with urgency, collecting and collating the information I have, from early concept, stage 1 and 2 trials, financial approvals, full ethics approval, board minutes, everything I can lay my hands on about the project. I go through the data again and message David with a link for him to check too. It's all I can do. The chips will fall where they may.

Chapter Five

I do my best to stifle a yawn, the early start and sleepless night taking its toll. I'm on fire in my suit and tie and can't stop fidgeting and checking my phone as we sit in awkward antique chairs in an unfamiliar oak-panelled anteroom waiting to be shown into the meeting. The private pre-meeting where the committee is reviewing all the information is overrunning, this is not a good sign. I go to check my phone again. As I do I get a call which I almost a decline until I see who it is.

"Sorry Gary, I'm just about to go into a meeting, can I call you back in an hour or so?" I ask.

"You can Sean, but quickly, you need to know that we have just had another participant from the Teleopote trial present with a similar issue to the existing participant that halted the trials. This is a lump in his axilla, his armpit, near the lymph nodes. We've taken a biopsy and began investigations and will formerly notify you this afternoon, but I wanted to call you as soon as I could. For obvious reasons." Gary stops talking, waiting for a response. The silence goes on – we both know what this means.

"Thank you... for letting me, know... Gary," I reply. The news silences the world around me. "I'll call you back... we're just going in to meet with Uni leadership, to update them... I'll call you... after," I say, my throat so dry I can only just get the last words out.

I end the call pacing a spinning room, my palms wringing wet. That's it, we're sunk, I'm sunk. Teleopote is a failure. The statistical likelihood of this occurring twice within a trial of this size is nil. Wait... shit! There could be more! My mind races down a myriad of outcomes, all of which are disastrous. This really is the end – years of my life wasted and now an uncertain and in all likelihood shitty future. This is as bad as it gets. I breath in deeply, looking around the oak-panelled room at the pictures of famous alumni and researchers. I will not be joining them. But it was never about fame and fortune, it was always about purpose, living a meaningful life.

But I'm still me, I tell myself, I still count. I take a slow breath, stand tall. I'm a good person. I have made a monumental mistake but above all, my intentions were good.

I stop pacing and turn to David, look him straight in the eye and share the news. He listens intently and then walks away and slowly folds into a seat, head in his hands, staring at the floor between his feet. He looks up at me; his lips move slightly but nothing comes out, his face just reddens. He's motionless for nearly a minute and then gets up, only to take another seat a few paces away. He must be going through the same thoughts as me. We both know this is the end.

"What do you think?" I ask, not knowing what else to ask. He looks at me, his face now so pink I start to worry.

"What to say Sean... it's over, most certainly. Damage limitation needs to be the mantra here on in. If the worst happens, you know if someone..." His eyes fix on mine, stopping mid-sentence, skipping the word, the word neither of us want to say, or hear. "Well, that would be... unthinkable."

We stand a few feet apart, facing each other but saying nothing, our brains boiling over with the potentially disastrous ramifications of our situation.

"But..." says David, breaking the silence. "We aren't there yet. We plan for the worse and hope for the best. OK?" he says, placing his hand on my shoulder, offering his support and optimism.

I force an impression of a smile. "Thanks," I say, just as the meeting room door opens and a young lady approaches us.

"Gentlemen I am really sorry," she begins. "But a member of the committee has suddenly been called away on an emergency and we will need to postpone the meeting by one hour. The Vice Chancellor has instructed that you return for a ten-fifteen start, we will see you then. Yes?"

"Err, yes," I reply, uncertain if this is good news. Not that it's possible for things to get any worse.

As David and I look to each other for some kind of solace my phone goes again. It's Mike Swale. We'd swapped numbers to stay in touch. I hang up – a distraction I don't need right now. The phone rings again. Mike not giving up. I hang up and put my phone on silent.

"A stay of execution," says David. "I'll see you back here at ten past ten then?"

"I guess so," I reply, my thinking muffled.

As David leaves, I shuffle to follow, allowing him to leave. No rush – what can I achieve in less than an hour with this hanging over me? I head in the general direction of my lab on autopilot, my mind blank, avoiding the thoughts – the permutations – of what's to come. The now inevitable end of my career, the wasted years, the pointless effort...

Then as I round a corner I see him. I don't realise at first, distracted by the whirlwind in my head, and he's a good fifty feet in front of me at the other end of the corridor. But as he turns, I see his profile and I recognise him. The aging hipster from the pub and car crash. What's he doing here? He's turned off and is instantly out of sight. Am I imagining things now, in some bizarre coping mechanism? Could it be him? It's a big university.

I quicken my pace. That night was all very weird. For him to be here... what can that mean, just a coincidence? I get to the corner, turn, and he's there ahead of me still, maybe thirty feet away.

"EXCUSE ME," I shout, and he and the other people in the corridor turn to look. As he turns, my heart stops. It is him! Without a doubt, hipster moustache and all.

He sees me, and I am sure he recognises me as he immediately turns away, quickens his pace, and disappears around another corner.

I give chase. Too weird, too much of a coincidence – and why is he running away? None of this makes any sense. I follow him into an open atrium next to the main refectory. I stop there, scanning intently like some meerkat: there's lots of people coming and going, but none with white hair. I look at both exits on the far side of the open area; he's nowhere near them and couldn't have made it across the wide expanse of the atrium and out the door in the few seconds it took me to catch up.

I hurry towards the seating area. He could be under a table or behind one of the large plants. I patrol the area, eyes on stalks, weaving in and out of the tables, making sure to keep an eye on all the exits. It takes me ten minutes. Nothing – no sign of him. I start to doubt my sanity. Could I have been mistaken?

Enough, I tell myself. I need to be present, to come back to the now and the harsh reality of my impending doom. I'm minutes away from losing my job and my career and I'm searching for a seventy-year-old under the tables of the refectory. Shit, what's going on with me?

The vibration of my phone distracts me. I take it out – it's Mike again. I'm about to dismiss it and then I remember Mike was there in the pub and at the car crash, he might know something.

"Hi Mike, how are you?"

"I'm good thanks, you?"

"Well... had better days to be honest. But can I ask you a question?" I ask, ignoring the need for pleasantries. "It might sound weird but when we bumped into one another and had the car crash and all that. You remember a car stopped to see if we were alright and then drove off?"

"Yes, I remember."

"Well, the guy in that car was just at my university."

"Was he? Did he say anything?"

"No, in fact I'm pretty sure he ran away from me, which... must sound a little bonkers. *Is* a little bonkers."

Mike doesn't reply, making me think I may have overshared. What must he think?

"It's just he was in the bar before as well," I say. "And I was wondering if you'd seen him, he was very distinctive. An older man with white hair and a white, hipster, waxed moustache."

"Really?" replies Mike, and I hear an element of surprise in his voice, masked but there.

"You know him then?

"Err, no... Sorry. But that does all sounds very odd," he replies. "But listen, the reason I called earlier was to see if you were up for a catch up next week, maybe lunch? I'm near you on Thursday, any good?"

"What? Oh yeah, of course, you rang me earlier," I say, only now recalling. "Well, things are a little crazy right now so maybe not good for me to commit to anything. I might not even have a job tomorrow."

"What? Really? That's sounds terrible Sean. What's happened?"

"Too much to go through right now. I'll tell you some time, but right now I've got to go. I'll call you, K?"

"Understood, speak soon and take care. Here if you need," replies Mike and hangs up.

My stay of execution almost up, I head back to the senior leadership offices and wait for David in the carpeted anteroom. Sat alone my mind is torn between an impossibility and a harsh reality – the disappearing hipster and the firing squad assembling next door. David arrives, we chat for less than a minute and the door to the meeting room opens ominously and we are swept in by the same lady messenger.

The meeting is immediately stuffy and formal. Total silence as we walk in: even the plush red carpet mutes our footsteps. After being directed to our seats, we hang our jackets on the back and sit at a small foldaway table across the room from five middle-aged greying men. They're sat a few feet from one another on ornate velvet seats, spread out along the far side of a grand mahogany table; all that's missing is the courtroom wigs. I don't know any of them, although one says a brief hello to David. The room is one I didn't know existed, tucked away amongst the carpeted corridors of senior leadership. It's wall-to-wall mahogany panelling up to about twenty feet, the final ten feet pale, off-blue, Uni colours, adorned with heraldry from who knows when.

"Thank you for joining us this morning gentlemen, allow me to make introductions," says the man in the middle, assumedly the chair.

He then introduces two professors, the head of research ethics and also a rep from the research council who has part funded the work. Our chair, it turns out, is the deputy vice chancellor, whose name I recognise but have never met. It's an all star cast.

He kicks off the meeting with background information for the minutes and the main reasons why we are here, not that anyone was unsure. At this point I raise my hand slightly, finger pointed. He notices.

"Dr Freeman, we will get to you soon enough," he says and continues with his formal diatribe. I keep my hand in the air, feeling like a schoolboy who desperately needs the toilet. He sees me, notices I'm sure, but simply keeps reading from a pre-prepared script.

"—Sorry, sorry to interrupt..." I say, raising my voice as I do, trying to be heard above the deputy VC, my hand still in the air. I now have everyone's attention, but he keeps bloody reading. "It's important," I say, near shouting.

The other four committee members look to the Deputy VC, who relents. He turns to me with slits for eyes and deep furrows in his brow.

"Very well Dr Freeman, it seems that you have something urgent to say, do enlighten us," he says, sarcasm dripping from every word and then entreating me to comment by opening his palms towards me, as if carrying an invisible bowl of fruit. All of which confuses me, probably his intention.

"Yes, perhaps more important than urgent, a recent development," I say.

"Very well, and..." He makes no attempt to hide his frustration.

"I've just, this morning, received a call from one of the clinicians working on the project. He's just reported in, it's not good," I say, glancing across the panel as they look on, waiting. If there's a way to soft-soap what I am about to tell them, it's beyond me, so I just say it. "There's a second participant in the Teleopote trials reporting an abnormal growth, not dissimilar to the existing case." I stop there and give no more details, waiting for it to sink in.

There's a couple of seconds of silence as the bomb slowly detonates. It turns out surprises at meetings like this are not welcome, especially ones of this magnitude. My news turns the meeting into a free for all, like some parliamentary enquiry. The questions come thick and fast, and we're drilled on every aspect of the project. It's clear the panel are concerned for the University's reputation first and then the participants.

I'm reminded several times by the Deputy VC that, "this is not good Dr Freeman, not good at all". All this serves to do is put me on the defensive and make me feel on edge. Fortunately, we can respond positively to most questions. Yes, we have complied with policy and all safety protocols and yes, we have auditable evidence of this. Yes, we have full consenting participants. Yes, all our paperwork is up to date.

After what feels like an age the questions steadily dry up.

"Well gentlemen, it seems you have been above board. All ethical policies adhered to and your clinical processes compliant with policy and practice, at least within the scope of your responses. I suspect the fundamental here is your science. The premise you are working under, that is, if it's not stating the obvious... it is flawed... clearly, *bad science*, Dr Freeman," he says, looking directly at me. "So, your responsibility is to make good the current situation. Dr Freeman, you will work with Roger on this," he says, looking across to the head of ethics, "and report to him. You can discuss this after the meeting. Agreed?" he says, looking to me. I nod my acceptance just as he looks away, not waiting. "Very well, everyone, thank you for—"

"— It's not *bad* science," I say, interrupting.

"Excuse me?" replies the Deputy VC, his face flushing.

"You said the flaw is bad science," I reply, raising my voice and sitting myself upright. "That's not the case. Our scientific method was fine, it's just the outcome was not what we expected. This is the norm within research, as we all know," I say, looking around the room for support.

"You are in no place to be splitting hairs, Dr Freeman," replies the Deputy VC. "If I were you, I would quietly get back to my work and hope that things don't deteriorate further."

"Perhaps, but you're not me. And the scientific method was sound, we simply arrived at a null hypothesis, as do scientists all over the world every day. I just think it's important to be accurate here as the record of the meeting may well be used to inform future investigations, so accuracy is key. Would you not agree Sir Richard?" I say, not wavering from my stare.

At this point he knows my argument is solid, he can't not. He looks at those around him, his face now heading towards a shade of purple. Their silence endorses all I've just said. "Jenny, make the amends to the record to reflect Dr Freeman's comments," he says, with a heavy sigh. "Now, if there's nothing else? We can adjourn," he announces and looks to David and I, a clear sign for us to exit.

As we leave the antiquated oak-panelled room and my mini victory, the portal of the doorway delivers me into a new world. In this new world I'm not the celebrated bright young thing with great prospects anymore, I'm the has-been, the failure. The one that when he walks into a busy room halts conversations and can feel eyes burning into the back of his head, the same eyes that will refuse to meet his. The one that when he leaves the room, hushed conversations ensue. The one that everyone knows, but no one wants to.

David pulls me to one side and starts saying something. I don't know what, I don't care. It can't matter, not now, how can it? I stand facing him, only a few feet away, watching his mouth open and close, hearing nothing, just watching. I feel a warm uneasiness in my stomach. My mouth starts to salivate. Jesus, I'm going to be sick. I swallow, and again and again; I need water. David's mouth is still moving, more quickly now, and a small spit bubble forms in the corner of his mouth, only for a second, and then it pops and some of the spittle sprays me. I look down at my shirt to see if it's noticeable. I can taste the vomit.

"—so all in all, not too bad, eh?" says David.

"WHAT? Really?" I yell, feeling like I've just left the boxing ring after twelve rounds. "What would bad look like David, do you think, eh?" I ask, not holding back.

"Yes, and Roger's a good man," he continues. "So, work with him on the best way forward from here and of course include me where you need to. OK?"

Before I know it, David's patting me on the back with a reassuring smile and walking away; he doesn't turn around. Why would he? It's on me now, it always was. At a snail's pace I return to my office, knowing I can't put off dealing with the mountain of shit that needs shovelling.

Then reality slaps me. I stop walking – what am I thinking? Where's my guilt? There are now two participants who are ill and the potential for more to become ill. Some could be terminal. People could die because of *me*. I feel sorry for these people. But I don't feel the guilt like I should, why not? Where's my empathy? It's like witnessing atrocious war-torn scenes on the news – terrible, but not here, so not real. Very sad and all, but that's what you see on the news and life here goes on. I want to feel for them more – perhaps I should have visited them, perhaps now I should? But would that be helping them, or just be an empty gesture to help me? Am I rationalising not visiting them because it will be too hard to do, to cope with and manage the emotions? I might make things worse. I'm not intuitive with people's emotions. I could easily say the wrong thing.

I spend the rest of the day in my office, avoiding the lab. Thankfully, no one thinks to find me there. I know well-meaning colleagues will commiserate and tell me this is part of the process and cite instances of great scientific breakthroughs that came after failed attempts like mine. They will be right. But when I say I've wasted years of my life and this could be the end of my career, I'll be right too.

The piles of files on my desk and post-it notes on the side of my screen grow steadily across the day as I attempt to fix that which cannot be fixed. I realise it must be late when I can no longer read the words on the screen. I give in.

By the time I arrive home, my back thinks I've been crushed into a small box for days and is refusing to straighten without intense pain. The sweat patches dominate more of my shirt than the clean patches. I haven't eaten since breakfast, but a fridge nibble is all I can manage with my whole-body throbbing like a hammered thumb. I collapse onto the bed, staring at the ceiling, broken.

Chapter Six

Killing time is not as easy as you think. Great if you go off on an exciting holiday, but not so good if you have no focus and your only real aim is to simply *not* be somewhere. Nobody calls to ask where I am, or how I am; in fact, nobody calls. And I *know* hiding won't' help me. I *know* I need to move forward and stop feeling sorry for myself. I *know* this. But it's not so easy when your life's work is being bulldozed and all you can do is watch.

I catch myself in the mirror as I pace around the house. I stand there for a moment, looking at my reflection. He's almost unrecognisable; he looks older, weary, spent.

He stares back at me, saying nothing, his eyes bloodshot and squinting now which grows his crow's feet, youthful vigour long gone. I know what he's thinking and I know he's right. His advice is solid. I need to move on. The milk is spilt, deal with it... His posture straightens. I will go into work tomorrow and be as optimistic as I can, remembering to be empathetic about the sick participants. Empathy is not a natural bedfellow for me. I wish it were – my intentions are good, it just doesn't flow like it does for others. I've always been very pragmatic, "robot like" my mother would say. It's how I dealt with bad news or being bullied at school, not that I liked it, just it was what it was, so I dealt with it and moved on. You get slapped around a bit by the bigger boys, you take the hits, pick up your stuff and walk away, hoping they get bored. Fighting back doesn't work, running off makes it worse. I worked all this out early on.

My mother saw my robot pragmatism and disengaged with me emotionally when I was about eight. It's a sharp memory I still have, realising one day that running to her for a hug to make something better was not an option anymore. Those days were for toddlers, not for kids in primary school. That's how it was, part of growing up. Things are often shit, tuff, deal with it, move on. And right now that's what's needed. So that is what I'll do. His eyes widen in the mirror, and he gives me a curt nod of agreement: we are on the same page.

As I hoped, the Uni is deserted when I arrive just after nine. Then I get to the lab and, sod's law, everyone is in, and as I enter a deathly silence descends. I offer a general "morning" as usual and this is met with the same, the morning routine, but today with a sombre tone and quickly cut short. They're playing it cool. It's no surprise: everyone knows of my catastrophic failure. I wouldn't know what to say either. I settle into my seat and open up my laptop, sticking to routine. But the elephant doesn't leave the room and it's making it feel like somebody died which, as I think it, sends a shiver down my spine.

The awkward silence continues, with everyone busying themselves quietly until the needs of the day prevail and the volume of the lab slowly increases as people settle back into their usual selves. I know as soon as I say anything that everyone will stop what they're doing and be super attentive and concerned. I've caused enough devastation recently; removing the elephant from the room is the least I can do. So I walk to the middle of the lab and attempt but fail to lean casually on a filing cabinet, looking around to gather people's attention.

"Guys," I say, and as if the almighty himself had spoken, everyone stops and you can hear a pin drop, including Michelle hanging up on some poor soul. "Guys... I'm thinking you all know that my project has failed and people are ill." I look around and am met with unchanging expressions and slight nods. "K, so it's shit, there is no silver lining. But it's important to say that the participants who have become ill are receiving the best of care and the prognosis is positive, that's the important thing."

As I say this my mind wanders and I start to breath heavily and faster. A realisation hits me: I can't be a researcher anymore no matter what. I do not have a career. Nobody in their right mind will give me the work. If it went wrong again, it would implicate me as being the point of failure – and they hired me, so their poor decision would implicate them. They can't take the risk; I wouldn't. Shit, I really am screwed.

Everyone is looking at me now as internally I descend into despair. I look at them, from one to the other, my eyes wide as the full extent of my realisation lands. They are doleful and patient, waiting, giving me space. The anxiety coursing through my veins is making it hard for me to stand normally and whatever I was about to say has gone. My mind's in turmoil, a hall of mirrors reflecting every disastrous future I can imagine.

I close my eyes, breath slowly in and out. I know they'll all be watching me, I can't care about that. I just need to be me. To find my way, here and now. I take another breath and another. I am not the issue here, I am one of billions, just a person. A speck of sand on one of a million beaches. I am not what is important... The failure to increase the longevity of the species is the real loss here. Individual lives are important, but the human race going off the rails doesn't bare thinking about. Longevity is the key. Certainty hits me; sure as night follows day, I cannot quit.

Michelle comes to my rescue, "Sean you're right, of course it's shit. But! It's not your fault mate, its not. We all know this – research goes wrong all the time; it's just if it's further down the road there can be casualties. I know I'm stating the obvious, but I think it's easy to lose sight of that. It's not your fault mate, it's not."

"Michelle is absolutely right," joins in Anthony. "And what is key here is that you don't lose hope and give up. I don't mean you need to ignore the casualties and simply pick up where you left off or anything like that. But the last thing that needs to come out of this is for the world to lose the talents and brilliance of an excellent researcher – you, Sean." He pauses and clears his throat, looking directly at me. "I know I don't often speak highly of other people, perhaps I should try to more often. But you are a cut above Sean and your mind and your capability have huge potential".

I stare slack-jawed at Anthony; the whole room is stunned into silence. Anthony doesn't suffer fools and never offers praise. I look around supressing a smile, waiting for a witty comment from Michelle, but none come. The usual banter is replaced by a quiet sincerity. Our group have entered new ground, sharing emotions, being open and honest. It feels odd but nice; supportive. I shake my head, smiling at Anthony.

"Thanks for that Anthony, not sure I agree with your assessment but nice of you to say."

They all continue to stare at me in silence, including Michelle's lab assistants Janine and Peter, who say little at the best of times and right now are two rabbits caught in the headlights. The warmth of the emotions in the room flows into me, and I feel a new openness, an acceptance of support now my defences have dropped.

I look from Michelle to Anthony. "Thanks guys, I really appreciate that, I really do, it means a lot. Thanks."

I feel my throat tighten and the welling of a tear as my emotions start to get the better of me. I push it back and stand tall, looking around our small group, "K... so, that's it from me," I say, wincing as I swallow to ease my throat. "I just wanted to be sure you knew where things are at... but best get back to it for now, ey?"

Normal business resumed I continue to work through the backlog of emails, only to be interrupted by a call from Mike Swale.

"Hi Mike, how are you?" I say, picking up.

"I'm having a good day today thanks, I hope you're having a better one than when we last spoke," he replies.

"Well, things have moved on. I'm still in gainful employment, if that's what you're asking?"

"Good to hear. So, lunch? I'm here on campus, you free?"

"What? Err, shit. Lots on to be honest."

"Come on, 'lots on' needs a break too. Shall I meet you in reception?"

"K... right, you're actually here on campus... you know what, yes," I reply, realising how much I need a distraction. "I'll be ten minutes."

I head down to the reception atrium. I see Mike and he greets me warmly, hand outstretched to shake mine with his winning smile.

"Great to see you again Mike and, of course, thanks again for coming to my rescue," I say.

"Anytime Sean, anytime," he replies with a subtle nod and slow blink.

"We have a healthy options deli nearby, that suit you?"

"Yep," he replies, and I lead us off.

We can't have been sat for more than five minutes before he asks the obvious question, "how is my research going and do I still have a job?"

I don't know what to say. It's a can of worms that I would like to avoid for a moment – naive of me to think Mike might be a distraction from the chaos.

"Long story short, it's over. We've hit a brick wall," I say.

He stops eating and places his knife and fork against each side of the plate, then slowly places his hands in his lap and just looks at me. The kind of look you get when you tell someone your pet has just died. Is it pity? I don't want pity.

"Sounds like you've had a rough time. How long have you had this current project on the go?" he asks.

"Over eight years now." I reply, stirring my coffee, even though I don't take sugar.

"That's a huge amount of work. I'm thinking setbacks are part of the process? If this is new science then finding out what works and what doesn't is the game you're in, right?"

"True, but there are setbacks and there are setbacks. This is a major setback, this is the end of the project."

Mike looks at me, saying nothing for a moment, eyes narrow, pensive. "So that's it – no more searching for the elixir of life you told me about after the crash?"

"That's about the size of it; this is science. I know it makes me sound pathetic, but it's important to know when to quit, especially when your research is funded. Funders don't like research that fails, they like the odds stacked in their favour and that's no longer the case. In fact... no, never mind." I resist an urge to share with him my decision to continue. I don't know what that looks like yet and it would be too hard to explain a future I can't see myself.

"So will you start down a new avenue of exploration then?" he asks.

"I don't know. To be honest I just need to stop for a while. Maybe go back to teaching, simplify things."

"Sounds tough. Sounds to me like funders and others are seeing this as a failure and the end of the project and that longevity is not worth the risks or the challenge. Perhaps they really do see it as the elixir to life, mythical and impossible to achieve."

"You might be right, but it can work, longevity. It's only as mythical as flying must have been before the Wright brothers."

"Right, then what needs to happen?"

"What?" I frown as I ponder his surprisingly forthright question. "Err... the same as the Wright brothers I guess: keep going even if there are risks."

"Interesting. Are your risks more severe than the Wright brothers?"

"To me personally? No, not nearly. I don't have to fly an aeroplane made of wood, canvas and glue. But the participants in the trials, they take risks and professionally we do too."

Mike nods slowly, "So best not to take those risks?"

"Perhaps..." I pause for a moment as I realise. "I see what you're doing here, Mike. You're flipping the conversation so I have to say it's worth the risk and thus I start to accept that. I get it, and I know you mean well, and it's appreciated, I think. But I'm not in the place to pick up the project and without funding, there is no project."

Mike gives me an earnest flat smile and nods. He sits back in his chair, looks up at the ceiling, then at me. "Interesting, interesting," he says, way too dramatically.

"What is Mike, what's interesting?" I ask, playing along.

"Well, it just occurred to me," he says, leaning in, his eyes now burrowing into mine. "How many scientific breakthroughs in history has humanity missed out on? You know, where the challenges were just so big the scientists decided not to pursue things. They quit because it was just too hard?"

"Mike, this is not making things any easier or making me feel any better."

"Sorry, just thinking out loud. It's just the man I took to the hospital, well he was going to change the world. I believed him. Now it seems like yesterday's bad news has deleted his tomorrows."

"Err, thanks," I reply. "Listen, Mike, I need to be heading back quite soon. But I wanted to ask you about the guy from the car crash again, the white-haired hipster. You sure you don't recognise the description? It's just on the phone the other day I kind of felt maybe you did, or weren't sure?"

Mike shrugs. "It sounds like someone I used to work with, a long time ago. But I can't see it being him, he must be long gone now. It was over twenty years ago, just a similar description. That's all."

"Well. It's possible it was just a coincidence I guess," I reply.

"Oh, sorry Sean," says Mike, raising his hand next to the AIC interface in his ear. "Just getting a call I've been waiting for. Do you mind if I take it?" he asks, hand poised.

"Sure, of course," I reply.

He gets up, taps his earpiece and strolls towards the doors, chatting as he goes, only to turn and return a few seconds later. "Really sorry Sean, something has come up and I need to go," he announces. "So sorry, we can catch up again I'm sure. But listen, don't think that an individual can't change the world. In human history it's the only thing that ever has."

"What?" I reply.

"Bye for now Sean," he replies with a nod and heads off across the cafeteria.

I watch him weave his way towards the door and he's gone. What was all that about? Did he know who I was talking about? And it just ended our lunch?

Chapter Seven

Returning to the lab, I'm greeted by a note and a business card on my keyboard, from Anthony:

This lady dropped by to see you as she's here visiting someone in the physics dept and a mutual friend said it would be good for you to meet, something about sharing research... not really sure tbh. Anyway she seemed really nice and left her business card here.

P.S. Why don't we have business cards?

I pull the stapled card from the note. She's Dr Jessica Hart, a researcher from Cambridge Uni, Trinity College, Department of Physics. Impressive, but not my area at all. I give the number a call, expecting to get her AIC, but she answers.

"Oh hi, yes... it's Sean Freeman here, you left your card with a colleague for me to give you a call?

"Dr Freeman, yes. Thanks for calling and sorry for the unsolicited visit, I suspect your AIC is on do not disturb so I thought it was as good a way as any, I hope you don't mind." Her voice is direct, but also open, serious whilst being non-judgemental.

"No, that's fine. I don't have an AIC; not a fan, I stick with my mobile."

"Oh, really. But what about your ghost?"

"You mean my AIC remnant?" I say, knowing what's coming next.

"Well, yes. For your friends and family, you know, after your gone."

"There isn't anyone to leave it to, not really. And if I'm honest I'm a bit sceptical about how an AI copy of me might be used, or abused, after my death. Let alone having the thing listening to your every move 24/7 year after year."

"Yes, I've heard of AIC remnant abuse cases," she replies, her voice quieter.

But, how can I help?" I say, giving a more upbeat tone, moving us both on from the sombre note this conversation always leads to.

"Well, I'm not sure if I'm honest. I recently met David Wright from Imperial at a conference, and he suggested I drop you a message as our research overlapped and there might be scope for collaboration. Have you worked with David before?" she asks.

"Err, no. I don't recognise the name. Maybe he's read one of my papers?"

"He didn't say," she replies, her voice less sure.

"Are you still on campus?" I ask. "We can meet for a quick coffee if you like?"

I head back to reception for my second visitor of the day. I don't get many visitors at the Uni which is probably why I made the error of arranging to meet her in a large busy public area without knowing what she looks like. Not the first time I've made this mistake.

I scan the reception atrium for middle-aged female physicists. None being immediately apparent, I downgrade this for women over the age of twenty five who don't look like students and are on their own. I spot one sat near the windows; she too is looking around for someone. As I approach she sees me and stands to greet me.

"Dr Freeman?" she asks. "Yes, Dr Hart I presume?" I say, holding out my hand to shake hers. She either misses, or decides to ignore my joke.

"Yes, it's just Jessica though, or Jess," she replies.

"And I'm Sean, nice to meet you." I say, doing my best not to stare or be awkward. She's beautiful, remarkably and effortlessly so. She has shoulder length tousled blond hair, large brown eyes, an almost angelic face and a playful smile that makes me think she doesn't take herself too seriously. And a scar I notice, sat on her left cheek, pure white so old, about an inch long, small but obvious. It gives her an air of mystery. I catch myself staring at it and quickly look away.

"Coffee?" I ask, keeping my sentence short.

"Yes, that would be great, thanks. Decaf if they have it?"

"They do, there's a cafeteria just down here", I say pointing, and we head off.

"Are you K for time?" she asks. "I realise you weren't expecting me and I just thought I would stop by on the off chance."

"I'm fine for half an hour or so, no problem," I say, giving myself an exit. "So, tell me again who was it said we should have a chat?"

"Yes, it was David Wright. He's a professor at Imperial, at least that's where he was presenting a couple of weeks ago. We got chatting after his talk; he'd read one of my papers and was keen to know what I was currently up to, which I told him about and he immediately suggested I talk with you." She's so focused on talking she almost walks into someone but swerves at the last moment. "He was really, really insistent. It was a little embarrassing. He actually made me *promise* I would call you – strange, especially considering I don't know him. And you say you don't know him either, now that is odd."

"It is, and I'm sure I don't know him. I guess he could have read about my research but I don't recognise his name as an author in my field. I'll have a look online later and it might bring up something. Which paper of yours had he read – what was the area he was interested in?"

"It was some research I published on a few years back on quantum entanglement. Is this something you touch on in your research?"

"No, not at all," I say, as we enter the cafeteria and I gesture for Jess to take a seat while I head over to get the drinks.

Thankfully there's a queue, which gives me a minute to remind myself to see her as a colleague, not to stare and just be at ease. Not be the goggle-eyed schoolboy I feel like right now.

I return with coffees and a smile, and take a seat. "So, quantum entanglement – sounds interesting, can you tell me more?"

"Sure, quantum entanglement, or QE as it's often called, is relatively new knew in the world of physics. It involves subatomic particles so is not the easiest of things to study, but some of the key properties are easy to understand, as are the potential applications. The key point is that when you have two entangled particles, such as electrons or photons, and you separate them, they can communicate with each other across any distance instantaneously, effectively faster than light speed." Except I know that's not possible – nothing travels faster than light

"So, two particles can communicate with each other, got that," I say. "Across any distance, impressive. When you say instantaneously, do you really mean that? Surely that's impossible as the information would need to flow from one place to the other and no matter how quickly that is, even if it is faster than light speed, which isn't possible, it will still require some time."

Her eyes narrow slightly as she listens. Like I do when I'm politely waiting for people to catch up.

"That would be a logical conclusion to draw, however you would be wrong," she replies. "It really is instantaneous. Let me explain. This is because the two entangled particles must exist in one of two states; for example, being either green or red, and if one is green the other must be red and vice versa. It's like a pair of gloves; if you have one that is right-handed the other must be left-handed, that's how pairs of gloves work. It's the same for the particles they effectively co-exist or are entangled and within that, one must be green and the other red. With me?"

"Yeah..." I say, nodding as she looks to me for confirmation.

"Of significance here is that the state, or colour, can be changed and if that is done to one of the entangled particles then the colour of the other entangled particle will also instantaneously change. So the two entangled particles must always be one green and one red – you change one, the other changes."

"So, if I have one entangled particle and you have the other and we are miles apart, I know that if mine is green then yours must be red, correct?" I say.

"Exactly." She gives me a warm smile; her student having caught up.

"And if I change my particle from green to red, then yours must do the opposite, instantaneously?"

"That's right," she says.

"So you can communicate information across vast distances in an instant," I say. "Even if it was with morse code you could have green and red instead of dot and dash and from that you can form any sentence at all. In fact, binary code is only a one or a zero and that can be complex computer code. Wow! That's fascinating, the potential must be huge, I mean really huge."

"It is. But what is really exciting is," she says, leaning forwards and lowering her voice. "We're now trying to manipulate matter through QE. At the atomic level – early days and experimental but still thrilling stuff, you can imagine."

She lights up as she tells me. There's a sparkle in her eyes and an energy pulsing from her. Its captivating. I just nod, letting her tell me more. I could listen to her all day; she has no ego, but I suspect she's a world leader in what she does. She's amazing, the beautiful girl next door who just happens to be a quantum physicist.

"And, what about you and your research?" she asks, bringing me back. "Can you tell me about it? David didn't say much."

"Yeah, for sure," I say. "I'm trying to significantly increase human longevity. When people live longer they're more invested in the world, in society. You know, if you live for three hundred years the climate crisis will really be *your* crisis and the social challenges we face will be yours too – you know, economic inequality, the public health crisis, homelessness, food shortages. So you do something about it because you're not just passing through anymore, you're here to stay."

"Fascinating, so what's the science then? Give me your elevator pitch."

"Sorry?"

"You know, you've stepped into an elevator to find a Nobel laureate in medicine, and you have her attention for sixty seconds after she asks you, 'what's your research about?'"

She gives me an encouraging smile, lifting her eyebrows, and for the briefest of moments my eyes are again drawn to the tiny scar. I start to guess the story behind the scar, wanting to know her more, knowing that knowledge would mean a deeper connection.

"Interesting, well... My research is to understand, limit, or prevent the process of ageing. The three main areas of focus for us right now are preventing telomere depletion, pushing suicide principles into senescent cells, getting them to die when they reach the end of their useful life and DNA reprofiling."

"Interesting, and now for the other people in the elevator?" she says, with a wry smile.

"Well..." I say, thinking it through again. "When it comes to limiting ageing there are many gains to be had from lifestyle choices, you know around diet and exercise, this can have a significant impact. But the project I'm leading is all around cellular response to a new drug, one that tells the cells within the body to act in different ways from how they were programmed to act. Like the senescent cells' suicide and synthesising telomerase to prevent telomere loss."

She raises her eyebrows at my not-so-simplified explanation.

"...which in layman's terms... is enabling certain cells in the body to renew themselves indefinitely through the production of a chemical. And for those that don't fully get this message, we tell them to self-terminate because them hanging around when they have ended their useful life is not good for the body."

She nods and smiles, holding a palm up in acceptance. "Got you, makes sense, and the link between longevity and climate change, people addressing long term issues, because they have become long term themselves. Not an obvious link, but I can see where you're going and boy do we need it, sea level creep is getting faster every week." She pauses, holding my gaze and squinting slightly, quizzical. "But... the social, economic and political impact... pensions would be unfunded, housing and resources demand for a continually growing population would be unsustainable, and you could end up with a two-tier world – those who can afford longevity and those who can't. That could lead to a revolution; wars. Wow. Scary. Sorry... sorry, getting carried away there," she says, frowning.

"Don't apologise," I reply. "It's not without major challenges. A paradigm shift from the world we know... but the climate crisis is upon us and radical situations require radical responses. And you're not wrong, there's much to be 'managed' if we're successful, and it's still an 'if' of course. And the changes won't be overnight, it's big picture stuff."

She nods slowly, soaking it up.

"Just imagine," she says, "from a personal perspective – quite selfishly really, as a researcher – you could take your research into so many new areas and just keep going. You know, not just nudging the field you're researching forwards and then leaving it to whoever follows to pick things up. But concluding your research. And even live many lives; you know, go off and be a farmer for fifty years, then become a musician, or something crazy like a travelling performer and who knows what else. How exciting would that be!"

Mike was right, the project is contagious.

"It's a fascinating concept isn't it," I say, grinning. "You know Jess, even now after years of thinking about it I still come up with new ideas and avenues; the potential, it's just mind boggling," I say, more openly than I'm used to. As I realise this, I push myself to the back of my seat.

Then it happens. I look over to Jess as she goes to take a sip of her coffee. As she takes a drink she looks up and her beautiful brown eyes meet mine. She pulls the cup away, pauses for a moment and shares a private smile with me. A smile that's more than a smile, like she's a little embarrassed or shy, different, not the kind of smile you expect at work. I feel a glow in my cheeks.

We've made a connection; she gets it and maybe even gets me a little? She's so interesting and interested, I hope she thinks the same of me. She's beautiful, striking and the occasional glances from passersby tell me this is not just my opinion. And... she's genuinely interested in my work. Or is that just wishful thinking? But I need to stay on track, ignore her beauty, her intrigue, her insight, focus back on the conversation.

It's not easy.

"So, where is the crossover, do you think?" she asks, "you know, between our work?"

"I've been thinking just that same thing. I have to be honest, it hasn't leapt out at me. You?"

"Nothing obvious, on the face of it. But that's not unusual, it might be worth touching base with David from Imperial to see what he was thinking. Do you think so?" she suggests.

"Yes, I guess. Whoever he is. Let me have a look online and I'll be able to find out. Is it K if you leave it with me?" I ask, needing to solve the mystery.

"Of course. And now we know each other's research there might well be things that come up in the future – that's happened to me lots of times. But what about right now, what's the next big milestone for you – you near writing up and publishing at all?'"

And with a simple well-intentioned question my heart sinks – the party is over.

"Well, we've hit some unexpected results recently. We don't yet know the implications as yet, we're looking into it."

"Oh, nothing too serious?"

"I hope not," I say, desperately seeking a way out, not wanting to lie, but also not wanting to share the nightmare. "The drug trials have seen one or two participants react badly, so we're investigating and for safety reasons put the trial on hold. So, we'll see. There are always set backs, it's part of the process." I take a drink from my now-empty coffee cup.

Have I just lied? I don't want to. But, in my defence, I can't report on this out of official circulation. Those are the rules. The rules I ignore all the time.

"K, understood. Well, listen, thanks for the coffee and for your time. I'll have to get going I'm afraid, my AIC tells me the train's on time, so… It's been really interesting hearing about your research and, who knows, I'll put my thinking cap on and come back to you if anything occurs to me."

"Of course, and I'll let you know about David Wright when I make contact with him."

Did she already know about the trials and was testing me? To see if I would tell the truth. And now I've failed the test, she's leaving? How could she know? I push my paranoia back into the shadows and walk her to reception. I shake her hand and our eyes meet again. The connection holds me: the touch of her hand, looking into her eyes; I feel it again. Lost in the moment, a contented smile grows on my face, only to be extinguished a second later as I realise and release her hand. It feels awkward… hopefully that's just me.

"It's been really interesting to meet you Sean, really it has," she says, moving effortlessly beyond any awkwardness.

"Likewise, of course, I really hope there's scope for us to collaborate. You never know."

"Definitely," she replies. "Let's see where your investigation takes us."

I watch her walk away, longer than I should. I can't help myself and I don't care if others notice. She's everything I would want in a partner and the reality is I will probably never see her again. Perhaps when I've contacted this David Wright it could give me a reason to contact her again, or email her to suggest coffee if she's ever near the Uni. Or if I'm near Cambridge, could I drop in and say hi? Although I have no plans to visit Cambridge, or at least I didn't... But, if we had a reason to chat again... Who knows? Or, am I just kidding myself? She's out of my league, probably has a partner, is likely not interested. But when she smiled... it was different, I felt it, there was something.

I return to my desk, task focused, and search online. There is no David Wright at Imperial. I phone them and there is no one by that name working there now or recently. I find a couple of Professor David Wrights at other institutes, but nobody I recognise and not in QE or my area of research. All very odd. A professor that doesn't exist *insists* that Jess meet with me to explore how we can collaborate, of which there is little chance. She then just happens to be in my building a couple of weeks later and we get on better than I have with anyone in years. But all leading to nothing. Strange doesn't cover it.

I need to go back to Jess to check this all out. I pull together an email with the links to the two professors' profiles to see if either of them are the person Jess met. As I'm about to send I stop myself. I need to play it cool. Not be a stalker.

I'll send it tomorrow.

Chapter Eight

The chaos of my project rages, but life goes back to a modest form of normality. I still have my teaching commitments and there are numerous tasks around the project that need attending too. But the sleepless nights are behind me and the elephants have left the room. Both the Uni and the funders are giving me some space and not making any demands, although I doubt that will last. I get positive reports from the physicians looking after the participants… simply taking them off Teleopote is sufficient to see marked improvements. This is great to hear, of course, but also final confirmation of what we suspected.

Take enough of it, and Teleopote can kill you.

Then a spring breeze wafts in. I get a call. It's Jess, and I turn back into a nervous schoolboy, delaying accepting the call for a couple of rings, getting my head in the right space.

"Hi Sean, how are you?"

"I'm good thanks, and you?" I reply, self-consciously.

"Me? Oh, I'm fine thanks. Listen, great to chat last week and thanks for the email on David Wright. Neither of those two people are who I met and I can't find anyone else on the internet. Very strange… I wrote his name down at the time and he pointed me to you and you are exactly where he said you would be. So not sure on that, very odd. But that's not why I called."

My heart races, why has she called? "K..." I say, listening intently, my heart in my mouth.

"It's more on an idea I had following our chat. I know when we talked about our research there were no obvious areas of synergy, or at least that's what we thought. Well, you mentioned that you'd come up against a challenge of participants rejecting Teleopote, right?"

Of course, she's called about work. I pull my heart back into my chest and return to the conversation.

"Yes, that's right, and to be honest it's a bit more than simply rejecting, but go on, what was your idea?"

"Well, tell me if I get this right. You inject Teleopote to instruct the telomeres not to deplete right? And Teleopote is a synthetic form of telomerase and the participants' bodies seem to be able to distinguish between the two and are rejecting Teleopote yes?"

"Yes, spot on. What were you thinking?"

"It occurred to me on the way home last week that you will know how the cell creates telomerase, and I think you said this occurs only in stem cells – and that's part of the challenge."

"That's right," I say.

"What if you could instruct a regular cell to create telomerase; you know, if you were able to instruct it to do so, or stimulate it to do so."

"Well... that's an interesting idea, but it doesn't really work like that. Although I have to say I'm impressed on your knowledge of all this, but there are complexities within this that aren't that easy to quickly explain. But theoretically, if you could do that it would be great, but senescent cells simply don't do that, that's why they're senescent cells; senescence means to deteriorate with age."

"I know that Sean," she says, almost masking her irritation. "But what if you could, theoretically?"

"That would be a game changer. But I don't see how we are even close to that as it would be an entirely new approach, developing a drug to force cells to do what they were never designed for... and, not wanting to be negative, but there could be all manner of untold side effects to a drug like that, pushing against nature, so to speak."

Do I share with her the failure we've had? It might help her understand the issues with what she's suggesting, and it would bring her up to date. But the last thing I want to do is push back on her enthusiasm and interest.

"That's not what I'm suggesting," she replies, and I cringe, sensing more exasperation. "I'll explain. You remember how in QE you can have entangled particles that remain connected even when separated, the red and the green? And when you knew the colour of one it informed the colour of the other? And if you changed the colour of one of the particles then the other particle must change in accordance, so there is always one red and one green in a pair of entangled particles?"

"Yes, I remember that... say more."

"K, so what is a cell made up of?

I reply, keeping it simple. "The basics? Membrane, cytoplasm, nucleus, lipids and a range of organic molecules."

"Great, so molecules in a range of forms. Next question, what are molecules made of?"

"Atoms and electrons," I say. "Varying in number of course, dependent upon the molecule."

"And, once more, what are atoms made up of?"

We're moving into the subatomic world and my excitement is pricked. We are approaching the realm of QE, perhaps there is something?

"That would be subatomic particles, protons and neutrons I think, then quarks, but we're moving into your area of expertise now not mine. I'm intrigued... where are you taking me, Jess?"

"I can influence subatomic particles to act in certain ways, this is QE remember. If I scale this up to the level of two cells and the subatomic particles within are entangled across both cells then I can effectively instruct one cell by changing the other. So if we know the DNA sequence of the part of the stem cell that produces Telomerase, we can instruct a normal, senescent cell to change its DNA to that code and it will then produce Telomerase."

Jess pauses to let me take this in. There could be all kinds of problems with this, but it could also be phenomenal. If it really did work Jess might have just changed the world; she may have solved longevity and a host of other issues too. Theoretically I can't fault it. It's too good to be true, which usually means one thing.

"I think I follow Jess..." I say, keeping my excitement in check. "And yes, this sounds, well, amazing. If this worked, it would solve the challenge I have. And there could be a host of other applications, cures for cancer, all sorts, but I imagine you've spotted that?"

"I did."

"And... I'm thinking this is done with two cells in the lab and you could then reintroduce the cell that's entangled and control it externally through the other cell?"

"Something along those lines, yes. What do you think?"

I rub my jaw, my pulse racing, dozens of questions competing for attention in my mind. "Have you done this before, with other cells in experiments in your lab?"

"Not with a full cell no, but with organic matter at the subatomic level, yes. Scaling up would take some doing, but I'm thinking as we've developed most of the tech that should be doable, we understand the key principles. It's probably more ensuring the constituent parts of the cell continue to function as a cell when they are created or grown, and once entangled. But in theory I think it should work, but I don't know enough about the functions of cells and the biology behind that. But... you do!" she says, suddenly excited, and I hear the smile in her voice.

"I do, yes."

This could be something. But it is all too good to be true, or is that just me? But... this could be fantastic. Save the world and get to work with Jess. I'm not even sure which is the best. The hairs on my arms are stood on end and I feel the tingling across my whole body; it's like the room temperature has just plummeted. Could this really be it? I stay with reality, ignoring the dream that's materialising around me.

"K, now this could be huge, but it could also not work at all," I say, clunking into project mode. "Are you happy to meet up and we can chat further? Can I come and visit you at your lab? It would be good to see the tech and the processes involved in QE."

"Yes, of course, when, when? This is exciting!" she replies, singing the end of her sentence. I feel her smile again and I wonder whose is biggest.

I arrange to head down to Cambridge the following week. I know my uni will be keen for me to rescue something from the Teleopote trials. If this comes good it will blow their socks off and then some. As for the funders, I will have to be careful with that one – this is not my project anymore, this is something new. My face flushes and I can't stop smiling. I haven't been this excited since I was a kid expecting Father Christmas.

"I only heard snippets," says Anthony from nowhere. "And wasn't really listening but that all sounds very exciting Sean, was that the lady who popped in to see you last week when I left a note for you?"

"Oh, what? Yes," I reply, hoping I haven't let anything slip. "Yes it was, she's called Jess and I'm heading down to meet her at Cambridge next week, to explore some collaborative research. Could be something really meaningful."

"Ahh, that's why the smile, yes, her appearance hadn't escaped me when she dropped in. Well good luck on your collaboration," he replies, fingering speech marks around the word and grinning like a Cheshire cat.

"Its nothing like that, genuine shared interest and loads of potential," I respond, a little too earnestly.

"Absolutely old chap, I wouldn't suggest otherwise." He holds up both hands in mock surrender, still with the fixed grin.

Chapter Nine

Like a babe in arms, I'm coddled by the gentle rocking of the train, sinking me into my seat with a blanket of excitement covering me, shielding me from any negativity the world cares to throw at me. Even the packed carriage, the heat of the day and the lack of AC can't dampen my spirits. Life is good.

It's all very reminiscent of when I left home to start uni. My excitement of the three years to come was palpable but overshadowed by my anxiety of the unknown. Excitement and fear mixed into a heady cocktail of potential.

True adventure.

There I was, only nineteen years old, standing on the platform with a backpack and suitcase, worrying about being able to get them near my seat on the train so no one could steal them, all whilst trying to look like a seasoned traveller and not a vulnerable unsuspecting kid heading off to live on his own for the first time. I remember it being an overcapacity London bound train on which two old men sat opposite me, slipping me glances and eventually coaxing me into talking to them, despite my initial one-word responses and eye-contact avoidance. They were kindly, and I found out as we neared the end of our journey that they'd thought I was a runaway heading to London, at the mercy of the likes of Fagin and the Artful Dodger, or worse. I often wonder what they would have done if that had been the case, would they have taken me in? Tried to talk me into going back home? Or maybe they were Fagins recruiting? You never can tell.

That cocktail of potential was firmly with me once more as I head to see Jess, butterflies in my stomach, mind awash with dreams of what might be and what this could mean for me, and for Jess, and for the world. But I'm conflicted. Am I doing this for my own interests, or for the world? I know it's both, but in what balance? The dreams swimming in my mind are all focused on me. Daydreams of being interviewed by major news channels, invited to be the keynote speaker at global conferences, government committees inviting me to participate and even chair key decision-making bodies – even being a guest on chat shows. It's all about me and I'm loving it. Except for the fatal floor in that fantasy... would I really want that level of attention and responsibility?

Of course, Jess is going to be a key partner in this, and the real outcomes is for society, not my personal gratification. I know this. But right now, I'm a kid in a sweet shop and it's hard not to get carried away, just to dream. After all, the stark reality is there's more likelihood of nothing coming from this, especially at such an early stage. This could be a few days away leading to nought.

But... I know it's important to be honest with myself on how I feel about all this, not openly share it. Others wouldn't understand. Life's hard lessons have taught me that open, honest sharing is not always a good idea, which seems odd, but that's how it is. Like when I blurted ... my ex-girlfriend Mariella that I didn't love her and just saw us ... nd boyfriend and that I had no long-term aspirations for ... d in her brandishing a knife from her kitchen cupboard...

thankfully I knew her well enough to know it was for dramatic effect. It ended badly, there and then.

I snap out of my revere, shaking my head chuckling, briefly drawing other passengers' attention. I'm getting carried away with myself, catastrophising in reverse. This is a first meeting on what will likely be a long road, with many pitfalls, and may eventually come to very little, or nothing. But... it could be a change for all of mankind, a brave new world; a solution to the climate crisis and much, much more.

I subtly look around at my fellow passengers, they have no idea of course. Not that they're sat amongst greatness or anything egocentric like that, but that there is hope, things could get better. We might not be as doomed as we all feel, with the polar caps melting, the collapse of the Gulf Stream, megastorms raging and unemployment rampant. If I told them, they wouldn't believe me, and I wouldn't blame them. I have the Cassandra Complex, where the Greek god Apollo, struck by her beauty, gave Cassandra the gift of prophecy. Then, when she refused his advances, he cursed her so that no one would believe her prophecies.

Jess's building is surprisingly modern; it being Cambridge I was expecting lots of old sandstone, gargoyles and mullion windows. But I'm greeted by an extended entrance garden walkway and dynamic-flowing glass and steel. The facility centrepiece is a large curved roof atrium with lots of light and space, this is flanked by numerous interconnected "pavilions" of the same style, each with a large glass turret dotting the skyline of rooftops surrounding the central atrium, all quite futuristic and, I bet, carbon negative. A cool place to work, literally.

As I enter the building and head to the reception, my heart skips a beat when I spot Jess sat nearby waiting for me. She comes over to greet me, looking effortlessly beautiful, her smile so contagious I can't help but grin right back at her.

"Welcome to Cambridge," she says, managing the friendly yet professional balance as she shakes my hand. "Shall we get a coffee?" she asks.

"Sounds good," I say and follow her lead.

"So how was your journey? Did you come by train?"

"It was fine, nice hotel too, thanks for the suggestion. Great building," I say, looking around as we're served our coffee. "I imagine there have been many hallowed footsteps in this place over the years."

"I guess, but it's a big sprawling metropolis Cambridge, pretty disconnected from itself as well. Everyone tends to be focused on doing their own thing. But they leave us alone to get on with our work, which is great of course. I can show you as we head over to the labs." We head off, coffees in hand.

We leave the main building we're in and head out across the campus, with Jess pointing out various sights of interest. Looking at my eMap as we go, I see how vast and varied Cambridge Uni is. Just as Jess said there are departments and faculties dotted all around the city and I notice mixed in are a series of empty sections of map, white space here and there.

"What's this Jess?" I ask, showing Jess the map on my phone.

"What? Ahh, those. That's a low-lying area that's permanently flooded, but with infrastructure on it. You know, like the London dispersal areas."

"Got you, no pump out then?"

"No. If it's blank they've let it go and it's not accessible, at least not legally."

"Has it hit you, the flooding?"

"Not yet, we're deemed a strategic body so they've upped the defences. Which you can see over there," she says, pointing in the distance to a continuous dyke, some twelve feet high, parallel to the road we're heading towards. "But we're not going that far, we're just down here." She directs us through more of the cycle route, which then opens up to a central courtyard surrounded by large newbuild sandstone buildings.

"That's us," she says, pointing across to one of the buildings, signed Cavendish Laboratories. It's an ordinary-looking affair, until we enter the physics labs and I have a feeling we've just entered a James Bond set. The classic scene where Q introduces Bond to a range of spy gadgets being worked on or tested by people in lab coats. Except here the lab is an order of magnitude bigger and the machines and experiments seem incredibly complex and, simply, huge.

I examine one of the setups and realise I have no idea what I'm looking at. It's just tubes interconnecting with large vats, many wires and occasional screens; it could be for brewing beer for all I know. Jess notices this and is great, she pitches her explanations at my level and walks me around most of the facility. I can't begin to imagine the cost of some of this. We finish off in a large, dedicated lab about half the size of a football pitch. This, it turns out, is where Jess and her team are based.

"And this is me," she says as we enter. "Welcome to my lair."

"It's very impressive Jess, although I have to be honest, I'm feeling a strong sense of imposter syndrome being here."

"I can see why. But then what you bring is mostly in your head, whereas we physicists have lots of equipment, we love kit. Like CERN, now *that's* impressive."

"I guess you're right. My lab is pretty simple and compact compared to all this," I say scanning the lab and taking in the numerous sets of clusters of pipes, frames, electronics and screens that could be anything.

"Come over here, this is what you need to start familiarising yourself with," she says, weaving her way amongst what must be individual experiments set inside white lined areas of the floor. "This," she says, pausing briefly for me to catch up and then panning her hand across an expanse of interconnected equipment, "this is QE in action."

I look over the rigging of complex stainless-steel boxes and interconnected wiring and readouts held together by a large scaffold frame. It seems to focus on a central copper cylinder. But all pipes, tubes and wiring seem to go to the drum or come out of it; the complexity of it all is staggering. As a whole unit it's the size of a small car and it must have taken an age to assemble, let alone for it to actually operate and produce something. As I step back to take it all in it's mystifying, like looking at modern art. I have no real idea what it is or what to say about it.

"Impressive," I say.

"Really?" replies Jess with a checky smile.

"K, you got me. I have no idea what I'm looking at, but, in my defence, the whole place is impressive."

"Nice come back, let me talk you through it," she says walking over to one end of the kit.

She goes through the various apparatus and how it links together to become a process that enables QE. The names of most of the equipment are new to me, but I resist asking lots of questions, I just need to soak things up for a while. Essentially, she and the team have achieved quantum entanglement at a macro level at room temperature. Big deal[1] featured in the journal Nature, no less. Currently, the focus mental applications is all on electronic devices, quantum g.

"I realise you wont be taking this all in Sean and most of what I'm showing you is probably new to you, but hey, we have to start somewhere. What do you think? You must have questions?"

"Lots, and yes, it's very new to me. But I think I get the layman's interpretation, you know, without understanding the practicalities or science behind it. I'm thinking because QE is instantaneous then the processing speed of quantum computing must be increased by an order of magnitude, is that the essence of it?"

"Spot on, although an order of magnitude doesn't cover it. We've manged to increase the processing speed one hundred and fifty-eight million times faster than IBM's supercomputer Peak. The QE device processed in two hundred seconds what it would take Peak ten thousand years to do. Something I can't quite get my head around."

"Holy shit! That's incredible – that's more than a game changer."

"I know, that's why we get the space and the funding, the potential is... well I don't think we've even scratched the surface of that yet."

An hour later we settle into a booth in a nearby coffee shop. I'm in awe of Jess and her achievements. She needs who I might become in ten years, a more experienced me, further down the road with the research, more confident in myself.

"So, where do we start?" I say, pulling out my writing pad and pen. Jess pulls out her screen pad.

"Well, the focus at this point has to be proof of concept. Can it be done? QE with organics," suggests Jess.

"I agree and I suspect that's going to take a considerable amount of time, money and effort."

"No doubt, in fact I think we will be into seven figure sums, just off the top of my head."

"Wow, really?" I blow my cheeks out. "I had no idea."

"I think the real challenge will be the scaling up – that's when we have proof of concept, and we want to create something meaningful."

"You think? Can you tell me more on that?"

"Well, the two key phases will be entangling complex mater and it remaining stable, our proof-of-concept phase. Then growing the volume of this to encompass enough of the atoms in a single cell so that we can instruct that cell to do as we wish. How many atoms in a single cell?"

I scratch my head for a moment. "It differs of course depending on the cell, but we are talking perhaps a hundred trillion… I see what you mean, how do we overcome that hurdle?"

"Hard to say," she replies pensively, "but my thinking at this stage is that quantum computing may well come in. Theoretically it will be able to control and manage this process so that it can be done in days rather than years. Interestingly, QE will be enabling further development and application of QE – it's chicken and egg all over again."

"Machines creating machines, just like the Von Neumann prophecy?" I say, not really expecting a reply.

"Yes, of course, could be! I'm guessing you're a sci-fi reader Sean?"

"I am, you too?" I reply.

"Not so much, but I'm familiar with Von Neumann's ideas."

"You know Jess, I have to stop myself now and again. It's just like, well, we're chatting on this project here in this lovely coffee shop in Cambridge. And we could be embarking on one of the most significant scientific breakthroughs… ever. I mean, if this comes off it can, no it *will*, change the world. If we're successful the ripples of this will change everything for humanity, everything. Where death is chance, ʾill become choice. It will change our whole paradigm in ways we ɳ't yet begun to imagine."

She looks at me with her beautiful brown eyes, nodding, agreeing. She sees it too.

"I know, it's been keeping me awake," she replies. "The implications, good and bad. You could end up with a two-tier state, where the wealthy were long-lived and the poor who couldn't afford it were left with standard lifetimes, serving the needs of the long-lived. The wealthy would become the new aristocracy, or rather the aristocracy would become the long-lived and maintain a dominance over the working classes, even more so than now. It could be really bad."

It's my turn to nod agreement and cringe. She's right, we both know this. But we can't let that stop us.

"I've had that thought too and am worried about the collapse of economic systems around pension funds and population challenges. The catastrophe list gets bigger all the time. But we can't not do this. Can we? Surely, we must?"

"I agree Sean, where would we be if we didn't try to advance science because of what might happen. Which is possibly a moral convenience for us. But it's not like we're faced with Oppenheimer's dilemma when he invented the atom bomb; we're trying to create not destroy."

"And, you know what? This might sound a bit cloak and dagger, but I think we need to be covert about our work."

"Really, why?" Jess lowers her voice and leans in closer.

"Well, just the potential of what we might create. I've been searching for the elixir to life for years, and once people know you're serious, the interest is huge. Too huge, commercial pharma – well, you can imagine if you had a drug that helped people live for longer.

"My thinking is that we position our proposal as replacing my Teleopote drug with a substitute approach that doesn't use drugs, essentially redirecting my existing funding and research. That way we have cash quickly and can get going and we aren't lying, just maybe not sharing everything. Essentially, hiding in plain sight, as just another project that may well be decades in the making. So we don't get too excited publicly and that way the misdirection gives us time to generate repeatable results. Meaning—"

"We're protected," says Jess, interrupting and smiling. "Nice Sean, I didn't have you down as such a politician, but I'm impressed. Makes lots of sense."

We finalise our proposal the next morning. Everything falls into place and before we know it, we're good to go. The whirlwind has yet to start but the wind is picking up. I pinch myself again.

"You could get an earlier train, you know," suggests Jess as I close up my laptop.

"Yeah, although I've never seen Cambridge. So I might spend the afternoon as a tourist, see one or two of the sights."

"Good idea, fancy some company?" she replies.

"Err, y-yes," I reply, my schoolboy crush rushing in on me.

With Jess as my tour guide, I see both sides of Cambridge, not just the usual tourist stuff, like shops in quiet alleyways and ancient buildings, but also the lesser-known sights like the mathematical bridge. Its only for a few hours but it feels like I'm on holiday and I love it. Eventually we land in yet another coffee shop with Jess quizzing me lots on the biology and functionality of cells.

Then, out of nowhere, the conversation stops, with Jess, poker-faced, holding my gaze. I start to worry just as a smile grows on her face and she raises her hand, finger pointed upward, eyes narrowing, and says, "we should punt".

"What?" I say. "Punt?"

"Yes, we need to punt," she says.

"You mean like out on a river with a boat and a stick?"

"Exactly, out on the Cam."

"Don't we have bigger things to deal with?"

"Yes. But look at the bigger picture. We're about to start working on a project that may well last years, possibly consume the rest of our careers. This could lead to the biggest discovery since... since Darwin. We don't know, but it could, and we hardly know each other. We need to get to know one another, we need a team-building activity, and punting will be great." She pauses, looking at me quizzically, waiting for my response.

"K," I say, drawing out the letter, my head tilting.

"Besides, you can't come to Cambridge and *not* punt, that would be rude," she says with feigned seriousness, and then stands to leave. She looks at me. "And, 'get it while you can on the cam'. The river levels dropped so low last year there was no punting for most of the summer. So, we go, yes?"

"Yes." I start to collect my papers and gulp down my coffee. This girl is something else, she's amazing.

Is it endearing to disguise your weakness or to be open and honest about it, or both? I can't be sure. My mother always told me to hide my ignorance as a child. But it turned out my mother was ignorant of a great many things, including the value of being open and honest.

I'm so relaxed in Jess's company it doesn't even occur to me to need to be good at punting, which I'm not. For my first attempt I stab the pole hard into the bottom of the river and push hard against it as I walk a couple of paces towards the rear of the boat to see us off, only to get the pole stuck solid in the mud and need to give a frantic wiggle and huge tug to pull it out just before I topple into the water. My pathetic attempt is so bad I end up sat on the rear of the boat, doubled over with laughter. And I love it. Jess's reaction tells me this is a good thing; for the first ten minutes she can't stop laughing either.

"You've got to ssss, got to, sto... stop, please," she cries out, holding her sides, tears running down her face, lying across the seat, incapacitated through laughter.

"But I won't learn if I don't keep trying," I reply, a huge grin on my face.

"K, K," she says, raising a hand, still breathing hard and struggling to speak. "Just wait, please... I need to, to get my breath back. It's just, just. Sorry Sean, but you are so... shit!" she cries out and rolls back into the seat, screeching with laughter again.

I stand there, looking down on her, wobbling on the stern of the punt, pole in hand, the happiest shit punter in the world. If my punting can make Jess this happy, may I never improve.

It takes her a good five minutes to calm down. At which point I hand her the pole and with a sardonic wink she tells me she will show me how it's done. I soon realise this is self-deprecation and not arrogance as she is nearly as bad as me and we very nearly take out another couple who make it clear that ramming is, "just not on my dear".

"I'm going to take us over to that pool near the trees," she says, pointing across to a shaded part of the river. "There's a kiosk there and it looks to be open, we can get a drink and hide from the sun for a while."

And so we sit with our ice-cold drinks, bobbing up and down with the mild ripples of the river as boaters pass by, shaded from the sun by a patch of large poplar trees, our boat gently nudging up against the shore line. The whole scene is idyllic, bird song surrounding us as we sit in a comfortable silence, just enjoying being right here, right now.

"So where did it all begin for you Sean?" asks Jess. "Being a researcher, a biologist."

"Yeah. Well, at school, I guess. I enjoyed science, was good at it, got good grades and all that. Uni seemed like the next obvious step. Which of course I took and then never left, you know, the usual, do your degree, stay on and do a Masters and then get sucked into being a research assistant and doing a PhD. I guess it's a well-worn path for lots of us. Was it the same for you?"

"No. I suspect for me it was the men in my life," she says. To which I quizzically raise my eyebrows. "Not like that," she replies. "I have five brothers and a father who was a mechanical engineer. He was great and was constantly inventing stuff and building stuff for us to play on as we grew up – the back garden was like a scene from Willy Wonka's factory. We all loved it and we all got into it, you know, building stuff with Dad, it was great. Except I was the one that wanted to know everything: why this will work and that won't, what will happen if we try this way or that way. Experimenting and learning at every opportunity, I guess. Still doing it now in many ways."

"Sounds blissful," I say.

"And the longevity research, how did you make that leap? It's not an obvious one."

"No, I guess not. But I think it's something I've always had in me from as far back as I can remember… a need to fix things, kind of like you I guess. Except this was a need to fix… well, the world I suppose. I realise how that must sound. But, you know… the climate crisis, the selfish pursuit of the wealthy to manipulate others so they stay wealthy whilst millions are starving and homeless, all of that. It's just wrong.

I don't mean I've sat down and thought what is right and wrong and what can I do about that. I mean it's like there's a flood coming, and we must build a barrier. You don't need to evaluate that, you see the water rising and you know you've got to do something. It's like that, we all need to do something, we can't just watch the water rise and complain if we get wet. And if we live longer, I mean hundreds of years longer, we will, because the scary future that is on our doorstep will not just be our children's future, it will be ours too. And that is when people will be driven to act, to make the changes we need. They have to; it will be do or die."

She studies me, her lips pursed, her face emotionless, clearly thinking, but thinking what? "Sorry," I say, cringing. "Gone on a bit of a rant there."

"Don't apologise Sean," she replies, shaking her head. "It's great to see someone with passion and belief in what they're doing."

"Thanks," I say. "You're kind."

She replies with a brief smile and stands, grabbing the punt pole. "Probably time to head back, we only had an hour." She gives a stab into the bank to set us on our way. I sit back in the middle of the two-person seat, lounging and relaxed, a blissful smile on my face, hands behind my head as I watch Jess avoiding the other punters, carefully steering us back to base.

"That's weird," she says. "That's the third time I've seen him today. If I didn't know better, I'd say he was following us."

"What, who?" I reply, sitting up to scan the riverbanks.

"There," she says pointing. "He was looking at us again. He's just walking off the bridge now, can you see?"

I scan the bridge ahead; it's maybe a hundred feet away, busy with pedestrians.

"The one with white hair," she says.

I'm on my feet in an instant, nearly capsizing us both. I steady my feet, squinting the scrum of people on the bridge into focus. My heart stops as I see him, the white-haired hipster. It can't be, not here in Cambridge. He's off the bridge quickly and heading across the open-grassed area towards a college building.

"Jess, quick, please. Take us to the bank, I know him. Well I don't, but he shouldn't be here. If it's him."

"What? You know him? You mean he is following us, Sean?" replies Jess, a note of panic in her voice.

"Well, maybe. If it's him. I can explain, sorry, but just get me to the bank, I need to find out. To catch him," I say, injecting as much urgency as I can.

"K, doing my best." She gives a big push sideways, redirecting us towards the bank. I stand in the middle of the punt, ready to jump and run, urging the bank towards us. We glide closer; one more stab will see us in. I look at Jess. "Big push Jess," I urge.

"Doing my best," she replies as she grunts a little, giving us a mighty heave towards the bank.

Fast approaching, I reach over and grab the bank to pull the punt alongside.

"NO SEAN," she shouts, and I instantly realise why. I have both hands on the stone plinth that is the river bank and my feet, still in the boat, start to move away from me. I'm pushing the boat back out into the river and I'm suddenly doing a plank manoeuvre between the punt and the bank. My stomach muscles lock on, holding the boat steady now, but the punt must be near my full body length away from the bank and my arms start to stretch out further. I can't hold it. My outstretched body collapses and I splash into the cold murky water. With the noise of the bubbling, splashing water all around, I do my best to get my feet on the bottom and stand, which I manage with the water up to my waist.

"SEAN! Are you alright?" shouts Jess.

"Yeah. Just wet," I reply and start to wade the few feet to the bank and claw my way out as quickly as I can, to cheers from nearby onlookers. Ignoring them, I scan all around to where he last was, back to the bridge to the entrance of the college buildings. I can't see him anywhere... he's gone. Was it even him? How is that possible?

"Sean," says Jess and I turn to her as she sits on the bank with her feet still in the punt, holding it in place. "You sure you're alright? You're soaked."

"Yes, but I've lost him. If it was him."

"Who?"

"The white-haired guy you saw."

"Yes, but who is he?"

"That's the thing – I don't know. But he keeps, kind of, popping up. And now here in Cambridge? That's just too much of a coincidence. If it was him? Did you say you saw him a few times?"

"Well, yes. What was weird is he was watching us or looking our way. That's why I noticed him. If it's the same man. What does that mean?"

"I don't know Jess. But it can't be good. Unless it wasn't the same man and I'm just being paranoid, maybe that's it?"

"Well, whatever it is," she says, "let's get you into some dry clothing. Jump in, or maybe not... just step, one swim's enough for today," Her smile grows and my feelings for her rush back in.

We return to the rental hut, the return of stability beneath my feet bringing with it the return of reality. No matter my feelings I can't risk a relationship interfering with the project. She might not even be interested, and if she wasn't, and turned me down, that would still be there in the background and there would be an awkwardness. And if we did get together, how long could it last, with all that we're about to get involved in? But if the project fails, there might be a chance? But what am I talking about – it won't fail, it can't fail, it mustn't fail.

The next two weeks go quickly as Jess and I shuttle the proposal between us and pull together a rationale for the changes to the Teleopote project and write a compelling narrative of the plan and outcomes. We position the next stage of the project as cost neutral. We know that when we ask for more money there will be greater scrutiny.

We're ready to submit the proposal when I get a call from Jess. Her abrupt tone tells me she's not herself. "Sean, I was chatting with a colleague here today who happened to know about your research and the Teleopote trials."

As she says the words the reality of the situation hits me like a slap to the face. I'm a grasper, I've fucked up. I haven't gone into any real details on the project failure with Jess. Thinking back, I can't recall giving her any details at all. Idiot.

"Ahh, yes you're right. I should have gone through that with you, sorry," I say, squeezing my fist and clenching my teeth, hoping against hope this doesn't get in the way. How did I miss this?

"Before you apologise just let me check. As I hear it your volunteer participants developed a cancerous growth as a result of the trial drug, is that true?"

"...yes," I say quietly, like a sorry schoolboy. "I know I should have mentioned it, I was just so excited and focused on where we're going. I don't know, it never really came up. Sorry."

"WHAT?" She yells and stops abruptly, breathing short sharp breaths down her nose. I can feel the anger in her. "Really, people could have died; it sounds like they may have health issues for years or even a shorter life because they took part in your project. This is a big deal. 'Never really coming up' is not an excuse. Sean... I thought I was getting to know you and now. Now I don't feel like I know who I'm talking to. We spent so much time on this, I just can't—"

Silence descends as she stops talking again, I can still hear her breathing. It's fast, she's pissed off and nothing I say will change that.

"I'm so sorry, my mistake. Really, sorry," I say, desperately searching for something more insightful or meaningful to say, but nothing comes.

"But this was only weeks ago Sean. You've never once mentioned this in all our discussion. Why?"

"Well, I'm not really sure. My focus has all been on the future and the potential there. I don't know, it was distressing when it all happened and maybe I was subconsciously avoiding it?"

"How did you feel about it at the time?" Jess asks, her tone calmer.

I bow my head and breathe out, looking to the floor. I hate being reminded of this. "It was devastating, years of work swept away in an instant. And the participants... well thankfully all on the road to recovery."

"How many were affected?"

"Only three."

"Only three, what are their names?" she asks.

"What? I don't know, participant information is intentionally separated from the trial data, standard practice."

She pauses again. "You didn't go to see them, did you? When they were taken ill."

"No. I offered but the consultant said it wasn't needed."

"Didn't you want to? Didn't you want to say sorry to them, see how they were doing, offer to help. Did you have no empathy for what they were going through?"

A sudden awareness smacks me in the face. She's right, I didn't, but I should have. How can I have missed that? What's wrong with me? What can I say to her? Lost, I say nothing. I feel the heat grow in my face, my head. I begin to sweat, how did it come to this?

"And for me Sean, as your research partner. Don't you think I should know key history on a project I'm about to join, did this not occur to you either? What else has not occurred to you Sean?"

Is she out? Just doing it gently? I really need this to work. "There's nothing else, *really*," I say. "I just get too focused sometimes and that can mean I miss things. It's a strength and a weakness and if I'm honest. Empathy is not a strength either. What can I say, I'm sorry, I really am."

"Oh, I believe you Sean, but..."

"But what?" I ask, cringing, waiting for her to tell me what I can't bear to hear.

"But it's not alright. The lack of empathy for people you nearly... that's more than a concern Sean, I'm not really sure what that means, but it's not good."

"You're right, I agree. And not making excuses, but I've long suspected I'm neurodivergent." I cringe as I say it, desperate to dig myself out of the hole, feeling like I'm playing some trump card that's not appropriate.

"You mean you're autistic? Wasn't that picked up through standardised screening at school?"

"No. Well, you see. My mum. She kept me off school on the screening days. Which at the time I didn't even know they were going on, I was only a little kid. You just do what you're told. Having said that, I've suspected it since my teens. But I don't know that I subscribe to labels around neurodiversity, I think I'm just an A-typical human. But then aren't we all, you know... individuals."

"What do you mean by suspected?"

"You know, how I see things and feel about things compared to most people. Which if you think about it I can only suspect as I can't know what it's like to be somebody else, so can't be sure and thus it's a suspicion. I've never felt the need to have it confirmed through formal testing or anything. It can make things difficult at times, but it's a superpower too."

"Sean, if that's your answer, *I suspect* you're right. But, correct me if I'm wrong, but autism doesn't affect your memory does it?"

"Err, no."

"So you not telling me, wasn't because you forgot? Was it?"

"...I don't know. No?"

"It was because you thought I might leave the project, wasn't it. Be honest with me Sean."

"I don't think so... It, well we were riding high, everything was just going so well. There was never a good time and it kept getting further away."

She sighs and I can feel the room temperature drop as she stops trying to hide any disappointment. "Really? That's it, that's the best you can do?" she replies, disappointment in every word. "So, I can't trust you can I? This is... significant. How can I have a lab partner I can't trust?"

"...Jess," I say, hoping she's still there. Needing her to know.

"Yes?"

"Not, sure," I say, lost.

"Sean, I'm going to have to think about this. I'll be in touch."

"I understand," I reply, my knees starting to fail me.

"Bye Sean," she says flatly and is gone.

I'm left clasping my phone in both hands against my chest, staring across the lab at nothing. I could have told her at any time – the trials going wrong is not my error here. It's not telling Jess, that's where I fucked up. *IDIOT!*

I hear a rustling of movement behind me and remember Anthony's in. Thankfully he's saying nothing, although he will have overheard,

I know. I get up and walk to the door, ready to punch the wall or something, but I don't. I simply leave and walk, out of the building and across the town, stewing, wanting to blame someone else and them suffer the result, leaving me to carry on unaffected. Back to my near-perfect world.

Jess doesn't call for the rest of the day. I continually check my phone: no message, no emails, nothing. A sleepless night sees me into work early the next day and as I click on my laptop I go cold as I see there's an email from her. Maybe...? I open it with my heart racing, ready to scan it rapidly. I don't need to. The first words are "*Sorry Sean*". I read on: she's out, hopes I can understand why, nothing personal...

How can it not be grasping personal?

Chapter Ten

Work is pointless, so I don't do any. I make up some bullshit illness and email in sick. I can go five days before they'll ask for an official Wellness Plan. Besides, there is no work without Jess's expertise: no project, no future, no hope. No point. I've single handedly managed to screw up the biggest opportunity of my life. With one of the most wonderful people I've ever met. There is no silver lining here, just a valley of shit.

The worst thing is it needn't have happened. Why did I not mention it? Why did I avoid telling Jess about the Teleopote failure. Lying by omission... I don't blame her for not wanting to work with me. What else might I not be telling her? Something that could ruin her career? Something that could lead to people dying... fuck's sake! Idiot.

After another night spiralling into oblivion in bed it occurs to me, this is just another problem within the project, and I solve problems, that's what I do. I need to fix this. How do I fix this? I need to solve *me*. To work out why. Why this happened. So I can prevent it from happening again and make good on now.

I repeatedly scour the past few weeks... and learn nothing. Then I look further back and realise there's a pattern... me allowing others to think favourably of me. In fact, even facilitating another's positive view of my knowledge and skills, but never by directly lying. Just hinting at knowledge I might have, *"oh yes I heard about that, interesting stuff"* or hinting at things I can do and then letting the listener put the rest together and assume more of me than I am and not challenging this.

I think it started in school, certainly in my childhood, where any sign of weakness was preyed upon. Where being the one who was crap at sport was weak and thus you became prey, easy pickings for casual bullying. Hiding your weaknesses or your ignorance was survival mode. Even with friends, the piss-taking culture was rampant, the likes of, *"what you don't know who so and so is, have you been living under a rock you freak?"* Although that was everyone – people were just unkind to one another. Most of them simply owned up to it and didn't really care too much if they didn't know something or couldn't do something, they just insulted others right back. But I cared and wasn't about to start insulting people, so I hid it, or managed it through saying very little or just enough not to implicate me. All in an attempt to avoid being the butt of the joke.

But I can't do this anymore, I need to be more open with those who I trust. Actually *trust* them, although that won't be easy after a lifetime of having my trust betrayed. This is the fodder you take to counselling, work through over months or even years. But I don't have that luxury; I need to grow out of this and quickly if I want to move forward.

If I want my world to be different, I first need to think differently. Then to act differently.

The following morning, I'm on the train to Cambridge. Despite my grasping fuck up, which I am desperate to repair, it's also not about me. At least not just about me, or Jess, it's way bigger than us. Together we might change the world, improve the wellbeing of millions and help create a better future for mankind. We might not as well. But if you don't try, you'll never know. So I head to Jess, cap in hand, not really sure what tack to take with her. But I am compelled and a certainty burns within me, this is the right thing to do.

When I get to her Uni I decide that surprising her might appear a little stalker-like, so I go to reception and get them to tell her I'm here, which they dutifully do.

Twenty minutes later she appears. She's emotionless as she approaches me across the foyer.

"Hello Sean, I wasn't expecting *you*," she says.

"No, sorry about that. But, well, it's really important. Can we talk?"

"You've come all this way, I can hardly say no, now can I?" she replies gesturing towards the exit, and we head off, away from the prying ears of the receptionists.

"Can I just say again how sorry I am," I say as we head off across the campus. "And that I really didn't mean to keep things from you. Seriously, it was my mistake, I get that one hundred percent, but well, sorry."

"I know, Sean. But you have to see my issue with this. It's serious, not to be briefed an all aspects of a project I'm signing up to. And then to find this out from a colleague... also very embarrassing, not that that's the issue."

"Can I explain please?" I ask.

"I think you already have Sean – we did this already, on the phone."

"I know, but there are a couple of really important things I should mention."

"Well, you have my attention." She replies, not slowing her pace as we march on toward the labs.

"It's not been easy, the project failure. You know, I thought my career was over. Years wasted; it's been tough, really tough. And then... you came along, bright and brilliant and full of optimism and... well, pretty amazing all round, to be honest. You were the other side of the coin. And talking with you, being with you, focusing on the project, you seeing the potential, all of it... it brought me back to life, made me realise the potential and how important this is. It's not about me. It's about what this might bring, for everyone. And... well, I guess I just got lost in all that. And flipping the coin to look at the other side, I avoided it. It was a mistake, a big one. And I am sorry Jess, I am."

She doesn't respond but keeps walking. It's enough for now, so I keep pace and avoid filling the silence. Giving her space to think.

"But Sean, how can I trust you? How can I know this won't happen again? I don't think I can?"

"Yes. I understand, I've been thinking about this a lot too. The lying by omission, not sharing and allowing others to think more positively than maybe is accurate. I've reflected on this lots over the last few days. I'm sure it's born of my school days and hiding any ignorance from bullies and so-called friends, a coping mechanism, or something along those lines. Which I know doesn't excuse it, but perhaps explains it."

She studies me as we walk, her eyes doleful and beautiful. I can sense something, maybe sorrow. I hope it's not pity. I don't want pity.

"Please don't feel sorry for me," I add. "I'm being honest and open with you to try and demonstrate the new me. The open, sharing me. Not so you'll reconsider because you feel sorry for me."

"K," replies Jess and we continue walking.

"I may be sensitive to things too, if I'm honest," she announces after a while. "I've had unscrupulous lab partners in the past. Men who have written up my work as their own where there had been ambiguity in their mind. They simply claimed the credit and forgot to mention this until it was too late, and the paper was published. So I'm wary of people who keep things hidden."

"Really? I'm sorry to hear about that. That's awful and I can see why you would be careful. But that is *not* me, I think you know that. I'm more likely to shoot myself in the foot than anyone else."

She gives me a knowing smile and a nod. "I've also been thinking about the project itself," she says. "The potential and the loss of this and what that might mean, or not mean."

"Have you?" I reply, wanting more. Optimism filling my heart, she's seen it too.

"I have," she says and stops walking, turning to face me. "And you're right, it's bigger than us and I really don't think we can simply hand it over to someone else, or walk away in good conscience. So Sean... I agree. We must go on. BUT how we do that is important."

"Of course, Jess," I say, suppressing a smile, breathing a sigh of relief. A not guilty verdict has been passed, but by a slim majority.

"Let's keep moving forwards and see how things go," she says. "I know you're great at seeing the big picture, but don't forget all the individuals that make up that picture. And transparency, being open and honest, this is a given. Yes?"

"Jess, this won't happen again. You have my word and if you ever suspect I've overlooked anything, please just say. Don't feel you have to be sensitive to my needs, tell me straight or whatever works. It won't ever be intentional." My words are sincere, and I desperately need Jess to know this. I just hope I live up to my responsibility. It may not be easy, it's not my default, but my motivation to learn is immense.

"K Sean, let's see how we go."

I stop now and she follows suit as I turn to her. We stand facing one another, removed from the students and cyclists weaving their way past us on the busy pathway. I look into her eyes, "and Jess, believe me when I say I will *never* betray your trust. Professionally or personally, this not who I am or have ever been."

"I know Sean," she says and raises her hand towards me. Maybe to take mine? I do the same and take it in a half-hearted handshake, unsure what this means. For a moment there's an awkwardness as I hold her hand. She smiles, seeing the moment for what it is and clasps both her hands around mine. I catch her eye and she mine and for the briefest of instances there's a connection. I'm looking into the eyes of one of the most wonderful women I've ever met and holding her hand. My whole body glows.

"I suspect we will be fine Sean, I really hope so," she says, releasing my hand and breaking the spell.

The following week I present our proposal to the University and funders and everyone is so overjoyed that we have identified a way forward at no additional cost they are more than happy for us to continue the research. They ask one or two leading questions around QE. But, as planned, Jess is not there so I fudge my answers and make excuses as this is not my area of expertise.

They release the funds for twelve months of planned work. Jess thinks it will be gone in three at the outside, the plan being that we'll have early results that are so ground-breaking that accessing funds won't be an issue, which is just as well as Jess's estimates of scale-up costs are into eight figures. Remarkably she doesn't seem too phased by this, but she has worked at CERN and it takes five countries to come together to fund their research.

Chapter Eleven

No matter how many stupid questions I ask and how many mistakes I make, my new boss is amazing; she just listens, watches and guides me. She has the patience of a saint and suffers me without compliant. I have to remind myself on a daily basis that this is not a dream, albeit a dream come true. That which was lost has not just been salvaged but enhanced one hundred-fold. I am living my best life.

I fall into a routine of supporting Jess, learning on the job, making tea, moving kit and the basic assembly of equipment, during which Jess takes the time to explain to me the "why" behind the task and where we are going – except for the making tea, I have that one nailed. But after a couple of weeks we've not moved forwards – zero progress from what I can tell. I don't say this to Jess and put it down to my lack of appreciation of the nature of physics labs, which to me are more like clean factories than laboratories. But I follow Jess's instruction without question; my faith in her is unwavering and I soon realise she's a workaholic. No surprise really considering what she's achieved in such a short time; most of her contemporaries at Cambridge are grey and wrinkled.

After the initial weeks of preparation without progress, we begin to actually build something when we start to cannibalise existing rigs in Jess's lab. I see Jess's face light up when we take delivery of the specialist equipment she designed, although I have to hide my disappointment and ignorance when we unpack a plain, large stainless-steel cylinder from the shipping crate. This single item has swallowed nearly all of our budget and it looks like a silver bass drum. But my lack of confidence is washed away when only days later Jess has wired it into the main rig and we have a working prototype designed to entangle molecules.

"This is a first Sean," says Jess, beaming with pride as she steps back from the rig, rubbing her hands together and turning to me. "There are a few more connections to pull together and we are good to go. Look out hydrogen, we're coming for you!"

The rig is primarily the large stainless-steel bass drum cylinder the size of a washing machine, mounted three feet above the ground on small-scale scaffolding. The wiring packets that go into it are phenomenally complex, like a tidy nest of multicoloured arteries feeding a silver giant egg from all angles. These are each connected to a range of apparatus I still don't understand but are a mix of stainless-steel tubes, measuring devices and screens. The whole thing looks like the inner working of a computer wired up to a shiny cement mixer.

"Alright, first full test. Ready Sean?" says Jess and I see the excitement in her eyes. She stands at one end of the rig, her finger poised above the keyboard controller.

I'm stood back out of the way, towards the other end of the rig, slightly concerned that the thing might blow up. "Don't be daft," she said, when I voiced my concerns. We'll see.

"Yep, fire away," I reply, holding up my crossed fingers. Jess ceremoniously clicks the button at her end of the rig.

Nothing.

"K..., not what was expected. Let me have a look," she calls across and starts to check the rig.

"Anything I can do?" I ask.

"Not really, just hang on, I think I know what it is."

Ninety minutes later we're good to go again.

"K, firing," says Jess. There's a thunderous hum across the rig, followed by a barely audible whistle that fades to nothing.

"Is that how it should sound?" I ask.

"Not sure, let's look at the results," replies Jess, hesitantly. "Hmm, not really understanding the data," she says looking at the screen. "We need to set up and go again, after a minor tweak."

"Anything I can do?"

"No, you might as well get yourself a drink, this might take a while."

When I return, she's laid under the rig like a car mechanic. I watch for a while but she doesn't come out. A hand appears at one point with a request for tea. But after an hour or so she's not moved and suggests I head off.

Weeks pass as we use trial and error to get the rig operational. Meanwhile I build my knowledge of physics and Cambridge. I read most nights and Jess is great as my own personal tutor. We spend lots of time together, but she seems keen to retain her social life outside of work and not include me in this. I know she plays badminton on Tuesdays and belongs to a reading group, which seems to be dominated by someone called Barry, and I know she volunteers for Shelter at Christmas. But that's about it and all picked up from incidental comments.

I don't blame her for not introducing me to her social group, but I've grown to see us as friends before colleagues, making me feel left out. I suspect it's the reverse for her. Which is as it should be, but it's important I'm honest with myself. I've learnt that as well as being fun, creative and spontaneous, she's also very rational, so I can imagine she has weighed this all up and made an informed decision, or she's just not interested. I try not to think about it too much; it's a distraction and not helpful. But when I forget myself and watch her working across the lab, the whole of her is all I see.

Despite the setbacks, Jess's confidence is good. "This is normal"; "it's new science"; "there's no manual to follow" are the phrases she throws my way when she senses my concerns on progress. But I'm happy regardless, I even feel I am contributing as my knowledge grows, though I worry I'm just loving being on the project.

"Jess?"

"Yeah, what is it?" she replies, emerging from under the rig, hair ruffled, sweating, more like a car mechanic with each passing day.

"How far do we go, do you think?"

"What do you mean?" she replies, wiping her sleeve across her forehead.

"You know, if it doesn't work. How long do we go on for?"

"I don't know, until nobody gives us money to continue?" She gives a quizzical frown and I can't tell if this is serious or not.

"Aren't we already there then?" I reply.

"Sean. Really? No. Not for me. You serious?" she replies, as if suffering some injustice. "We have time, we have the kit, we keep going. You alright? It was never going to be easy. We knew that. Setbacks will always happen, but we go again, this is how it is. Not giving up is part of the deal."

"Sure, I guess. Well, I just don't feel I'm contributing as much as you. You know."

"Yeah, I get that. But you can't, not at this stage, not more than you are doing to be honest. Things are moving forward, it's just not that obvious to you as you aren't living inside this thing." She slaps the shiny cement mixer. "My head is in here all the time, literally," she says, laughing at her own joke.

I smile with her she's right, but to me our world-changing results seem no closer now than when Jess and I met.

Then as each day becomes each day, from nowhere, something.

I have a dream. In the dream, Jess and I are trying to QE-print a virus that will kill another virus infecting a host, which is a rabbit in my dream. We're testing how much virus we need to infect the host with but not kill it, and the experiment we're doing is all about the amount of the viral load we administer and a range of other variables such as room temperature and energy.

The next morning, I sit staring at my breakfast, reflecting on the dream, and the potential unravels in my mind like a ball of string. We're going about things all wrong. We shouldn't be experimenting on a single molecule, we should be experimenting on large groups of molecules in the knowledge that some may fail but some may be successfully QE-printed, and the variables of heat, energy and so on may well influence the yield and can be experimented with to test for the optimum output.

I arrive at the lab full of excitement but keep it bottled in front of Jess. Can a dream really be so helpful? Is Jess going to see me as clutching at straws, losing faith? No, the woman I have come to know... that's not her. Carefully, I share my dream and idea with her and, as ever, she is patience personified and listens quietly as I explain.

"Interesting... I can see where you're going," she tells me as she looks to the ceiling, deep in thought.

"It will be a challenge," I say. "As we'll be scaling up without our proof of concept and that way we will need more funding with no real proof to demonstrate the potential."

She stares at me for a brief moment. "You know Mendeleev dreamt of the periodic table? That's how he created it," she says. "And Ramanujan, a great mathematician, had lots of his ideas in his dreams... he actually dreamt the solutions to classic maths problems, and they were right. He said a Hindu God gave him the answers in his dreams and he wrote them down when he woke. You know what?" She nods. "If it worked for them, maybe it will work for us?"

"So do we need to go public and start with funding bids?" I suggest.

"You think?" she replies. "There's nothing to go public with, not really."

"No, but the intent, we can be transparent on where we think this will go. Share the potential."

"Perhaps, or I have an idea," says Jess, her tone more optimistic. "We can do a half-way scale up and we can do that here with what we've got. At least we can if I acquire equipment from some other ongoing experiments."

"Really?" I say, like I'm five and I've been told I'm going to Disneyland.

It's my turn to spend time lying on my back tools in hand, now underneath a much bigger rig. It's ten metres in length, still with the central silver cylinder, where the magic happens. But with a significantly increased level of input and output functions, it will run longer and louder, Jess tells me. Which means we will consume significantly more resources and power.

"Will we get noticed?" I ask. "Stealing all this kit and now needing to install new power couplings. Surely someone is going to start asking questions?"

"Sean, compared to some of what goes on here, we really are small fry," she replies, shrugging. "Don't worry, even if they did, I can explain it away, if needed."

The re-build consumes three weeks of intense activity and then, almost by surprise, its ready.

"Alrighty, déjà vu and take two, we ready to go?" says Jess.

"Yes, fire away," I yell, smiling from the other end of the room, well back from the rig.

Jess clicks the keyboard and the usual warmup hum is replaced by a deafening roar. I can feel the vibration through the floor, all of which builds for a few seconds, and then the whistle and wind down is so loud we both rush to cover our ears. As silence falls, I'm left with a tinnitus buzz.

We both glance at each other and I can see the worry in Jess's face; she was not expecting that. I then look at the lab door, waiting in the buzzing silence for someone to come rushing in. Thankfully we're not disturbed.

"YES!" shouts Jess and I turn to see her looking at the results screen.

"Results?" I say.

"Yes, lots of failed particles but also loads that are now paired and, from what I can tell, stable. Yesss!" She pumps her fist joyfully as she leans over the screen.

"Fantastic," I reply as I arrive to look at the screen and we high five, huge grins the pair of us.

"How many did we get?" I ask.

"I think perhaps a fraction of one percent, so a few hundred," she replies. "But that we can work on, the thing is it works, it works Sean. It works!"

Just like my dream, Jess repeats the experiment, adjusting the various settings on the rig. It has an impact and when we get the mix right, improves the success rate to almost fifteen percent of the sample.

We can create stable QE-printed pairs of hydrogen molecules, and the process is repeatable. This is a first in the world.

We have arrived.

"K. Lets go for it," says Jess. Staring straight at me. "You up for that? Increase volume by two thousand percent, let's really see if she flies. Yes?"

"Let's do it," I say, gritting my teeth excitedly.

The now familiar noise comes and goes and as we remove our recently acquired ear defenders, Jess squeals.

"Yes Sean! We've got the same yield. Fantastic!" she yells as the results screen fills with data.

"No way," I say, squeezing in to look at the screen with her. "That's amazing." I turn to her, she's beaming. Caught in the moment, I give her a smothering hug. I pick her up, spinning us both around. "I can't believe it Jess, this could be it," I say, lost in the joy of our success.

"I know," she replies giddily. "But listen," she says, "put me down, listen. Let's go for it, let's go for living tissue. That's the real test." She looks at me, willing my agreement.

We do. It works, and neither of us can believe it – the yield is actually improved. We adjust the settings again... the yield on live cells is again improved. In fact, the results with live cells are the best we have had across all our experiments.

"You know Sean, I don't really swear, but you are a FUCKING GENIUS!" she shouts, clenching a fist and elbow pumping into her side with a muted "Yessss!" It's Jess's turn to grab me in a huge bear hug. Feeling her in my arms, her scent washing over me, my heart races, I can feel my cheeks glow, and I'm lost in all that is her. Still holding me by the waist she leans back. As she does our hips press together, our eyes meet and something inside me pushes me to lean in and kiss her. She kisses me back; the smallest of kisses but the most amazing of moments. Then she pulls away, releasing me, avoiding my gaze, looking to the floor.

"Sorry Sean," she says, her cheeks ruby red, stepping back.

"Don't be sorry, it was me too and... well it was nice," I say.

"Not very professional though," she replies, raising her eyebrows now as she catches my eye. "But... you solved it Sean, *you* solved it. We have living tissue QE entangled and stable. The first ever!"

"Me? No way, this is so much down to you," I reply, respecting her need to move beyond the intimacy. "I had a dream, which wasn't even really any effort on my part; all I had to do was remember it and suggest it. You made it a reality Jess. You designed the rig, all based on your research. You're the brilliant one Jess, it's your name history will recall and rightly so."

With the biggest of grins, Jess turns to look at the rig. "So, we have repeatable results. We can publish and we can demonstrate to the scientific community," she says.

"We have arrived," I say ceremoniously. "Time to celebrate?"

"Yes, good idea. Pizza at Carluccio's?" suggests Jess.

"Of course, where else?" I reply and take a breath. The dream is back on track, we might just make this happen, we *will* make this happen.

"Jess?"

"Yes."

"I know we've talked on this before, but more than ever I really feel we might just be about to change the world. I really do. Do you?"

"Well, yes, maybe. But I don't want to count my chickens and all that, there are still many hurdles. Long term entanglement stability for starters."

I nod, understanding, but unable to suppress my excitement and my grin. "I know, but I just have this inner confidence. I can't say why, it just feels like, I don't know, like destiny. Which sounds silly, I know. I wonder is this how other scientists felt as they saw the potential in what they were doing, you know like Louis Pasteur, or Marie Curie. Don't you feel like that?"

"I think that we're positioned as well as anyone can be. But it's still not a given, you know that. Nothing is. So as excited as I am, no, I don't think I'm totally there yet, but things are going as well as they could. So I couldn't be happier, really." She catches my eye and shares a smile. "But we haven't crossed the finish line yet. I don't think your confidence is misplaced, I think that's part of what you bring to the project, the vision, the drive, the energy, the passion. It all means a great deal to me – we wouldn't be here now without it."

"Thanks, that's nice of you to say. Shall I stop writing my Nobel Prize speech and we get off for some food?"

"Sure, but... you know, there is still one thing that bothers me, amidst all of this. I'm not even sure it is a thing, but I can't let it go."

"That is...?" I ask.

"How we met, you know. Me being approached by the ghost that is David Wright from Imperial, or not as the case may be. I can't stop thinking about it, or him and the *coincidence* of me being at your university two weeks later. It all seems, well... odd, like someone behind the scenes making things happen."

We could have a fresh look, try and go wider in our search," I suggest.

"I already have, I left an AIC on it for two days, but nothing has come up, at least not someone with that name who looks anything like the man I met. Odd, odd, odd," she says, wistfully shaking her head.

"Was he Dutch?"

"What?" she replies, raising an eyebrow.

"You know, the Breach. Millions were displaced."

"Yeah. But I don't get what you mean? Ninety-nine percent of the population survived the Dutch Breach, in fact didn't the London Breach kill nearly as many?"

"Yes, but I'm thinking records, data, lots of that was lost when the infrastructure was destroyed with the flood. He could have been a Dutch refugee with no records, we had several of them working at my Uni."

Her brow furrows as she looks up for a moment. "Maybe... But remember, he said he was from Imperial, and we now know that was a lie."

"Hmm, you're right... well, let's not let it take away from the now. We can look at it another day. Right now, Carluccio's!"

"Yes, let's," she replies, her eyes smiling once more, and like a chameleon she's back in celebration mode and taking me with her.

Part Two

Chapter Twelve

My phone wakes me from deep sleep. It's the only thing lighting the room as I scramble across the bed to pick up. I see it's Mike and pause for a second before deciding to answer.

"Sean, sorry for the early call," he says. "I wanted to catch you before you went to work."

"Well, you managed that. What is it that couldn't wait?"

"It's complicated, so I wanted to show you if I can. I'm on my way to yours, I'll be with you in twenty minutes, can you be ready for then?"

The unusual request wakes me, and I pause, trying to work out where this is going. I can't even turn him away; he's already on his way.

"Yeah. Well, really? I'll put the kettle on then, see you in a bit I guess," I reply, not trying to hide my annoyance

"Don't do that, meet me outside. The thing I need to show you is elsewhere."

"Really? At this time, can't it wait?"

"Be good to get on, you'll see," he says,

"Well, yeah, k. Twenty minutes, right."

On cue, I'm standing outside my door, looking up and down the street for Mike. It's eerily quiet, deserted, dawn just breaking, still cool and... no Mike. Then I hear a distant whisper and his Jag floats around the corner at the far end of my road. It glides down the street, pulling up next to me. I squat to look through the opened passenger window; he's at the wheel, smart jeans, blazer and sunglasses on, beaming at me.

"It's me, get in old chap," he says, as if this is a regular morning pick up.

I get in and close the car door, "Mike, what the h—"

"—Did you manage to get anything to eat?" he asks.

"No, just got dressed, had a wash and stuff. But never mind that. What are you doing in Cambridge, in fact how did you get a car in the city and how did you get my address? In fact, no. More to the point, why the hell are you waking me up at, what time is it?" I look at my watch. "At FIVE AM! And then whisking me off to who knows where. What's going on?"

"I can see why you're confused, who wouldn't be. I'll explain on the way," he says, sat bolt upright, almost hugging the steering wheel, focused on the road ahead as we zip through the deserted streets.

"On the way?" I reply, "to where? Where are you taking me?"

"It should be where are you taking us? You know, in the bigger picture and all that," he replies, drumming his hands on the steering wheel excitedly, his eyes focused on the road ahead, nodding his head, appreciating his own wit.

"MIKE!" I shout.

"K, sorry. Yes. I can explain but first, reach behind my seat," he says. "There's a brown paper bag if you can grab it."

I reach behind his seat and grab the bag.

"What is it?" I ask.

"Breakfast. I suspected you might not have had time to eat. So I stopped off, have a look."

I open the bag. There's a fresh almond croissant, along with a sandwich and a small clear box of Suckeez. "Thanks," I say, "Suckeez?"

He shrugs in response.

"I appreciate the breakfast Mike, but can you just tell me what's going on?"

He takes his eyes off the road to glance at me, giving me a reassuring smile. "Something has happened which is quite significant," he says. "But is also quite complex and you really need to understand the background before anything else."

"Alright, so tell me the background," I say.

"When people quote Darwin and the theory of evolution they say 'survival of the fittest', which is not wrong, but doesn't capture the key point. What is really meant by Darwin and was published in his later work was the phrase 'to be better designed for the environment'. Meaning those that are best adapted to their environment will fare the best, and he was right."

"Mike, is there a point to this?"

"Yes... people are going to try and interfere in your research."

"WHAT!" I cry, shocked. "Who is? How do they know about it, and more to the point, how do *you* know this?"

Mike's voice is calm and frustratingly patient when he replies. "You are bound to have lots of questions and the answers are complicated, hence the background information. Can I go on?"

"Yes, but get to the point, and I still don't see the need for the dawn raid melodrama."

"You will. But rest assured, you're safe."

"What the fuck, Mike! I didn't think I wasn't!" I yell in response. "Now you've got me worried. How am I safe? Why do I need to be safe?"

I stare at Mike, no longer sure of anything. Is he even who he says he is? For all I know he could be a spy or something and that's why he avoids questions all the time. Is that why he just reappeared in my life after all these years? Shit, is he spying on me – does someone know what Jess and I are up to?

"Mike, just tell me what's going on and what I need to know."

"Thanks. Well... your research could very well change the world, as you and Jess have no doubt surmised."

How the hell does he know about Jess? And what else does he know, that he can't or shouldn't know? Confused, I stare out of the window, we're almost at the edge of the city now, amongst the modernist housing built for the displaced after the floods. The roads are straight here, and we whizz along with not a sole to be seen. With all that Mike's throwing at me it's like some bad dream.

"And there are those who would support you in that and there are those who would not. I myself would always want to support someone to be the best they can be. If you have a friend who's struggling with life, do you just leave them to fend for themselves, or do you support them to enable them to move forward?" I almost go to answer him, but he carries on quickly, picking up speed. "The thing is, natural selection is not the survival of the fittest or the best adapted, because others might come in to help. This ensures the whole pool of the population survive as a community. If it were survival of the fittest you would end up with a small pool of genes that would become less and less adaptive. There can only be *one* fittest. So maintaining variety, adaptation, treating others as you would wish to be treated, and the survival of the species go hand in hand. This is one view, a view I hold. Make sense?"

"Yes," I reply, my exasperation growing with Mike's ill-timed lecture. "The point being?"

"Stay with me," he says. "The other view is leaving a species to the vagaries of natural selection. Any interference and you are not allowing natural selection to function and what evolves will not be sustainable as it has not adapted, it has been helped, and will need that help to survive. Thus, the resources that would have supported the evolution of the fittest are now diverted to a wider community and may compromise the survival of the species."

I open my mouth to speak, but Mike interrupts.

"But..." he says, raising his voice and a finger. "I would argue that theory is flawed. If it were *you*, you wouldn't want it, so why allow it to happen to others?"

"K," I say, realising as out of place as this conversation seems I'm going to have to go along to get to the bottom of things. "We're talking right-wing versus left-wing politics here, aren't we?"

"In simple terms, yes."

"Understood, then are you saying there are some right-wing radicals trying to interfere with our research?"

"Of a sort, yes, and I will come to that, I promise. The background is really important, you'll see, stay with me." He glances across again as he drives, to check my agreement.

"K..." I reply, nodding.

"Now, as a species evolves it does so along different aspects. These aspects often move forwards in tandem, like technologically, socially, politically and so on. But although all these different aspects are progressing at the same time, they seldom move forwards at the same rate. So you might make huge leaps technologically during war time but hardly move forwards at all politically. But overtime, like a child in school, the lessons all move forwards to develop a rounded child who can perform in maths, drama, geography, etc."

Mike looks to me, "You with me?"

"Yes. But please get to the point."

He smiles. "Getting there. Now, within the process of evolution there are milestones, or hurdles, where species go extinct. This is natural selection at work. Humanity is at a hurdle now, where technological evolution is progressing but social and political evolution is not. You can imagine how this might turn out. If a politically and socially unstable country managed to get hold of functioning nuclear weapons; well, we know the probable consequences. It's not good. So the more socially and politically advanced may well try to prevent this occurring. They see this as their responsibility for the greater good."

"Are you saying our progress is too fast and people want to stop it?"

"That is a factor, yes. The choice for me and for the Ananta is do we leave you to it and see what happens, or do we support you to give you the best chance of success? I'm all for supporting. These are our values. These values give us purpose, and purpose is life, and life is purpose."

My head spins. Is Mike really telling me there are people out there wanting to interfere in our work? People who know what's going on when neither I nor Jess have told anyone – which isn't possible. Who could know? Has Jess talked to people? I can't believe that. But... she could have. I don't really know her that well, not really. Beyond work, I know hardly anything about her.

"That's a lot to take in Mike," I say, trying my best to keep a level head. How can this be, no one should know? Except Mike clearly knows. I can't believe its Jess. There must be some covert surveillance or something. "And who are the Ananta?"

"They're another group. Or rather, a self-interested faction, they focus only on the survival of the fittest."

"Right, so let me speak," I say, taking a slow breath to calm myself as the car speeds along to God knows where. "Putting aside you somehow know lots about me, Jess and our research, just putting that *little* point aside, you're saying there's some radical right-wing group out to put a stop to our research and that the tech advancement of QE is too soon for us and we need to stop?"

He shakes his head, keeping his eyes on the road. We're in rural Cambridgeshire now, mostly fields with the occasional quaint village. "Not quite. I doubt that will work. QE is around the corner no matter what. It's better that you and Jess are the ones to continue your work and not others who may not have the responsible values you share. My role here is to support you in leading the change."

Fear creeps in. I don't really know Mike, or where he's driving me to – and someone has been spying on us! "What! You have a role...? To support me...? Something you just happened *not* to have mentioned," I say, flabbergasted, staring at Mike. "Right..." I continue, needing to keep moving forward, desperate for clarity before the quicksand swallows me. "You're telling me there are people out to stop our research and you are here to protect me from them. Pulling me out of bed at five AM like this tells me there's a threat. Have you been assigned to protect me or something?"

"No, and not really. That is, protection is not my brief. Support, mentoring, subtle guidance is my brief. Our focus is on supporting others, enabling – not doing it for them, that would be self-defeating."

I think on this. "Makes sense, but how can you help me, us? Shit, Jess! Is Jess alright? Is she not implicated here too?"

Mike lifts a hand from the steering wheel, raising it to calm me. "Don't worry, she's fine, there's no threat to her."

"You sure of this? I'm still in the dark and all of this is pretty incredible. You must see that. So I'm not really buying into all you tell me here. In fact how can you be sure she's fine and I'm not?"

"It's complicated."

"What?" I say, clenching my fists, my temper rising. "Mike, that's not an answer, enough now, enough... just stop."

"Alright," he replies, and the car starts to slow.

"What are you doing now?" I ask, becoming more confused and frustrated by the second.

"Stopping, like you asked," he replies.

"What? No! I mean stop with the meandering and avoiding my questions. Get to the grasping point man! That's what I mean."

"You're worried about Jess, I get it."

"Do you?" I say.

"Listen, I can promise you nobody is under any immediate threat. I'm certain of this."

His confident tone somehow reassures me, but there's a niggle... what is he *not* telling me? I could call Jess, just to be sure. Make sure she's safe. But then... what would I say? I'd end up scaring the shit out of her.

"So... next question Mike, how are you *supporting* me and also who are you working for, is it the government?"

"I will come to that, I promise. But it's important for me to wrap up what I was saying," he says, looking across for my permission.

"Quickly," I reply, desperate for clarity.

"If you achieve longevity, which as you have already realised QE can enable, then this will take you to the next level of evolution as a species. It's a big leap and species often fail here. They fail because they lack the responsibility that is needed to ensure they go down a social, environmental and politically sustainable road."

"Sorry, did you just say *other species*?"

"Yes."

This blows me away and I take a few moments to try and process that which can't be processed. My head starts to throb with the possibility. "Other species that make it to longevity. We're not talking about wildlife here are we?"

"No, beyond Earth," replies Mike, as smooth as you like.

The mild fissure Mike has created in my mind tears wide open. Beyond Earth! What the hell is he talking about? I need to stop this, it's too ridiculous. If I believe what he's saying then, then what? Then the world stops turning. He's talking about... other species! Like he's met them. Mike has got himself mixed up in something and is living out some delusion. I was struggling to keep up and now, I can't believe anything. Getting me out of bed at five AM and heading off to who knows where, with no credible explanation – this is all in his head. There's no evidence for any of this, just his words.

I look across to Mike, and I can't decide whether to worry about him or be scared. How far does his delusion go? Is he as harmless as he seems? Is that the thing with psychopaths, they seem perfectly normal until they kill you? But, Mike *being* at my Cambridge house and he knows about Jess and our research. I can't explain any of that. And now aliens! It makes no sense. Unless... I'm the delusional one?

I need to work this out, there has to be a logical explanation.

"Mike... that's pretty, massive..." I say, working hard to maintain a calm facade. "And what does failure look like, that sounds pretty final?"

"It is. Like all species that fail as a result of natural selection, they make choices that are not aligned with their environment, and they fall into decline and become extinct."

"Yep, that's final alright."

"I know this is hard for you to believe," says Mike. "You probably think I've lost it. But this conversation, like most things, this is part of a process, which will lead to your belief and then to action."

I meet Mike's gaze. He gives me an understanding, almost parental, smile before refocusing on the road. All I can do is look ahead again, say nothing. I need to work this out and I still don't know where the hell we're going. Although that's not so important now – I guess I'll find out when we get there, unless... no, can't think like that yet.

I sit in silence. The dry pastures, corn fields and occasional farms in the distance all seem like a movie scrolling past my window. But only the view makes sense to me now as we zip past on this merry-go-round, lost in my own mind, desperately trying and failing to make sense of all that Mike's told me. The car's silence starts to become oppressive, suffocating me. Neither of us talking and I desperately need answers and the deeper I go the further away they are. Who knows what crazy shit is going on in Mike's head. Every time he speaks the situation descends into more chaos. One of us has lost it.

"Mike, the other species you mentioned. Have you met them?" I ask calmly, playing along.

"I can give you more on that, but just pass me the Suckeez will you?"

"What?"

"The Suckeez, they were in the bag with the breakfast I bought you."

I reach for the bag on the floor between my legs, open it and grab the Suckeez. I pass them to Mike.

"Those aren't Suckeez," he says, looking at the packet in my hand.

"What?" I hold them up in front of me to look closer. He's right; they don't look like sweets at all. I can't make out exactly what they are. Then I see they're moving – they look like small beetles. I hold them closer... they are beetles! I throw the pack into the car's centre console; it lands, opening slightly. The beetles crawl out, loads of them, and they're fast. They quickly scamper into the footwell and disappear in the darkness.

I quickly pull my feet up onto the seat. "For fuck's sake Mike! What is this, what are you playing at?"

"Sorry Sean, it's part of my demonstration, apologies. I'm in the process of asking you to make a paradigm shift in your thinking and that takes quite a bit of doing. It will all be clear soon, I promise."

"What?" I say, confused and now scared. I look again at the pack of beetles: they're Suckeez. I pick the pack up, clicking the lid closed. They stay as Suckeez. I hold them up and turn the pack around, upside down. I open it and take a sniff. It's just a pack of Suckeez. I don't eat one.

"Mike, these are Suckeez again, please explain? One of us is losing their mind and I'm starting to worry it's me."

Mike gives an empathetic frown and nods. "Yeah, sorry. I will give you one more clue... it's important you work this out for yourself, it's the only way you'll believe. Take a look ahead. As we round this next bend there will be a structure in the distance. It's a big one and recognisable. I know you've seen it before. Let's see if you can recognise it now?"

We round the next bend and there, on the skyline, I can clearly see the Eiffel Tower, probably ten miles away. Shit! Impossible... My mind shatters. We've covered a seven-hour journey in half an hour, and we've not gone through the tunnel. My stress rockets into full blown panic, my palms start to sweat and my mind races, nothing makes sense. Drugged, I've been drugged; too much is wrong.

"Mike, what's going on?" I say, pleading now, desperate for answers. "Is any of this real, is this a dream?"

"You're on the right track," he replies calmly. "But it is real, sort of. But then you have to ask yourself how I know about Jess and your research?"

He's right. Being drugged or delusional would not allow for that, unless he doesn't really know... but he does, he just mentioned it. I fold, sink in my seat with the world closing in around me. I say nothing, looking at everything and seeing nothing. I have to push through this, whatever *this* is. I pull myself back, look at the Tower, then at Mike and then I glance at the Suckeez. None of this is real; Mike is not real. Did I ever really meet Mike? Was the whole bar fight and car crash in my head?

"None of this is real Mike," I say. "It can't be. I've lost it, or I'm dreaming and can't wake myself up. In fact, I suspect *you're* not here, or real."

"Jackpot!" he replies, giving me his beaming smile as he looks across. "Good work, Sean. Dreaming is as accurate as you can be, with the knowledge you have. The reality is you're asleep, and we are having this conversation, but this is me, not a construct of me made by you. When you talk to someone else, you make noises in your throat and the other person interprets them as meaning, so you are communicating with noise vibrations in the air. What you are experiencing right now is simply another form of communication, and it's a mechanism that can work whilst you're asleep. The fundamentals are the same as talking and listening, just your state of consciousness is different, and that means it's possible to input other information into the communication, such as the experience and view of driving along a road, as we are now. Is this making sense?"

"Well... sort of, yes," I reply, swallowing deeply, trying to ease my cracked throat. I take a deep breath, clench my teeth and hold it. I need to be rational, stay the course, wherever he's taking me. I need to find out what's going on.

"So what's the emergency?" I ask, trying to keep my focus and not let my emotions overwhelm me.

"Things have escalated with your recent breakthrough. It's been noticed."

"Noticed by the Ananta, the right-wing extremists?"

"By everyone that matters, Sean. Nobody knew for sure that you would get there at all, let alone this quickly. So that's good in some ways and less good in others. I thought it was important to let you in on all that's going on, it's only fair. It's the responsible thing to do. Things may evolve quickly here on in. But I assure you, neither you nor Jess are in any danger, just things are less predictable than they were."

"Understood," I say, although I don't understand any of this, it's blowing my mind.

"I still can't figure out how you know about our research – and what about when I met you in the bar? Was that a dream?"

"That was real life, no comms, and I knew you would be there. And... this is going to take some believing... but to ensure we got talking and continued our relationship after I rescued you, I had to assume a familiar identity. So there's a lot to take in here. I know it must all seem incredible, because it is. But in essence it's just advanced tech, you know, like showing someone from the Middle Ages a film on a screen."

"K, with you, I think," I say. "So right now I'm asleep and you have created this fictional world for us to meet and talk in?"

"Yes, spot on," replies Mike.

"Amazing. If that's the case, who developed this?" I ask, holding up my hands to inspect them, trying to spot pixels or something. "This will shatter the telecoms and entertainment industry," I say, continuing to wave and examine my hands, looking for the cracks.

"We've had it for some time, but that's not important right now. But who *we* are is. I'll talk to you about that tomorrow, and I can update you on how we know about your research; how I know where you live and all that. But you need to prepare yourself, be open minded, and listen before you judge – and you need to call me. K?

"Sure, when do I call you?"

Mike smiles enigmatically. "You'll know."

Chapter Thirteen

My wind-up alarm clock wakes me. Autopilot flicks the bed covers off and I walk across the room to silence it. As the echo of the ringing bell fades, a memory edges its way into my reality, halting my progress towards the shower. A day out with Mike yesterday... except I wasn't with Mike yesterday, I think... but. I scan the room and peek through the curtains; all I see is the empty street.

That was the most bizarre of dreams. Vivid, so real, in fact wasn't that part of it? Real, but not real. Suckeez spiders, or beetles? Weird upon weird. I shake it off; my autopilot re-engages and takes me to my morning shower.

With the hot water cascading over me I relax, half asleep, leaning against the wall. Then, from nowhere, I'm hit with an adrenalin shot. My eyes widen, my pulse races and bolt upright I stare straight ahead. I'm wide awake. Steam surrounds me and water pours over me, but I'm back in the Jag with Mike. Unlike a moment ago, there is no fog to my recall; everything is crystal clear in my mind, all of it: the dream that's not a dream, aliens, the right-wing extremists gunning for me and Jess.

I don't know how much time passes as I re-live the dream again in the shower, it's like watching the same movie two days running. It's real, there are too many details. But, shit, it's too fantastical to be real. It has to be a dream. It's too ridiculous to be anything else. If it was what Mike said...

Ten minutes later, I've transferred my fixed stare to the kitchen wall, with the kettle bubbling away beside me. Do I call Mike? He said I would know and right now I'm certain of nothing. I feel drugged, de-realised; the world isn't what it was yesterday. And yesterday wasn't even yesterday.

The answer is staring me in the face... I need to call Mike. And when I call him, I can say very little and wait for him to speak. He will confirm what happened or simply think I'm bonkers when I start talking about yesterday's trip to Paris. It's that simple.

Except no... because... there was something else, something I'm missing, some other clue or piece of information. I have the feeling I get when I've missed something in an experiment, usually something obvious that has passed me by. What was it? Mike is real, but not everything we have done together is. What does that tell me? Hang on, that's it. Not what, but who. Who is Mike? That's it! He said he'd assumed a familiar identity when we met at the bar and that was in the real world.

I sprint up the stairs to my office and grab my laptop; it can't be too hard to find out something about Mike Swale from Halifax, same year of birth as me. I get to work, try the obvious Tyax and AIC-online searches but draw a blank. It was all twenty years ago when I last saw him, what social media will he have been on back then? I flick to my VMe account and locate my old school friends. I go to their list of friends and on my third attempt I find him – Mike Swale – there he is.

I click through to his page, the image could have been a younger Mike. I scroll down through his timeline. There are numerous annualised comments remembering good times past and how Mike is missed but not forgotten. No entries from Mike, just from friends commemorating. I've seen entries like this before; it was another old school friend from way back who died of cancer. I keep scrolling down, there are more condolences; after a long list it seems they started well over ten years ago. This is a dead person's timeline, the Mike Swale I went to school with is dead.

I pick up the phone to call Mike.

He said I would know when to call. Did he factor in my digging into his past and discovering his secret, and that that would be the trigger? With the tech he has access to, I can't believe he wasn't able to manipulate a VMe page if he wanted to. But he hasn't. Is this part of yet another reveal – he said I needed to keep an open mind? The phone starts to ring... down the rabbit hole I go.

"Hi Sean, I've been waiting for your call. How are you feeling?" says Mike cheerily.

"Confused," and then hesitantly I say, "you did say I would know when to call."

"I did, and you did."

A swell of relief passes through my body. I'm not going nuts, we did share a journey yesterday. Although it might be better if I was going nuts and it was all a dream, with all that Mike has shown and told me, if it's all true... where do you go with that? Aliens existing – how can anyone get their head around that?

"So, my dream last night was not a dream at all but you communicating with me through some device, that, well, acts like telepathy or a version of VR beyond anything ever seen."

"That's about the size of it, yes."

Stunned, I listen to Mike's breathing, my heart pounding in my ears. Both are deafening, and my mouth dries as I stand there trying to digest that which can't be swallowed.

"I ta—" I try to speak, but my voice drains to nothing except air expelling from my mouth, my throat too dry to speak. I force a painful swallow, take a breath.

"I take it the tech used does no harm? There was no equipment in my room when I woke."

"There is hardware involved but it's remote so you wouldn't see it and there are no side effects using the tech. Just like a phone or AIC."

I notice Mike's answers are more direct, sterner even. This is not the Mike of old. He knows. He knows. I know he's not Mike; he's waiting.

"Mike?"

"Yes."

"That's not really your name, is it?"

"Yes and no. It's the name I've adopted for this mission, which means I've had it for some time. So it is my name, that is I don't have an alternative one or a 'real' one for you to use. I suspect the question you want to ask me is, am I the Mike Swale you went to school with? But you know the answer to that."

I hold my head with my free hand, struggling to contain my frustration. "Jesus Mike, nothing is ever straightforward with you is it? Not even you being you! I take it you didn't bump off the real Mike Swale and assume his identity?"

"No, he died some time ago. Nothing to do with us, but he was convenient in having had a past with you and no surviving relatives."

My thoughts fracture once more; there are too many impossibilities. Everything I know could be wrong, or different, or something else, something I can't even imagine. Not what I know, what I know to be reality, is not what it is. There's more out there, way more. We are just specks of sand in a huge cosmos.

"Look, I know you have lots of questions and understandably so," says Mike, as if reading my mind. "I think it's better for us to talk in person. Shall I drop by yours and I can explain? Remember our chat yesterday, when I said there was more to know and it was important for you to be open minded about it?"

"I remember," I say, cautiously.

"Well, I'll explain after I pick you up. Twenty minutes alright, and I'll be outside?"

"Err. Yes fine. See you then," I say, hanging up the phone and starting to pace the room. I need to work this out. What do I really *know*? Not what have I been *told* by Mike. Mike has access to super-advanced tech and is able to assume a false identity, and he knows more than he should about me, Jess and our research. There's lots of evidence for that.

And, of course, there's the Ananta, the right-wing extremists. I have an enemy. Shit, *we* have an enemy. I need to bring Jess in on this today. The only thing that makes sense is Mike being the same person in both dreams and reality. Mike is still Mike, although he isn't. The truth *is* Mike. Which makes Mike a government spy, or something like that. Which is cool, but not cool: spies die. Shit, I was right about the rabbit hole.

Chapter Fourteen

Scanning the empty street, I hear a whisper and turn to see a familiar Jag round the corner. It's got diplomatic plates on it; that's how he got a car into a traffic-free zone. It glides to a halt in front of me with the passenger window down. Mike leans across, dressed identically to last time. "It's me, get in old chap," he says.

"This is not by chance, is it?" I say, as I slide into the passenger seat.

"What, I'm not sure I follow?"

"This replay of yesterday's dream, the dream that wasn't a dream. The only thing that's different is my clothes and... there's more background noise today. Yesterday it was silent and unusually cool," I say, noticing the difference.

"Well spotted. The thing is, it's easier to base QE Comms as close to reality as possible, it makes the whole thing more acceptable to your psyche."

"QE Comms? Is that what it's called, what I've been calling dreams?"

"Yep," he replies, nodding.

"And stop me if I'm wrong, but does QE stand for quantum entanglement?"

"Sure does Sean," he replies, turning to me, his eyes bright, eyebrows raised and giving me his widest grin.

"So... the fact that we're researching QE is not by chance?"

Grin still in place, he flicks his eyebrows.

"You know it," he replies.

"So, Mike," I say, siting myself upright. "Can we have a change of approach from yesterday? Where I ask questions and you answer them? And you're straight with me, open and honest?" I ask as we drive away.

"I'll do my best," he replies.

"Is Jess in any danger, at all?"

"No."

"K, are you a spy or working for the government in some way?"

"No."

Alright, so open questions.

"Who do you work for, Mike?"

"Easiest explanation is that I belong to a group which I've told you about before. We are the ones who believe in equality of opportunity. That resources should only be disproportionately shared when someone is more in need than others. And that only together as a united interdependent community can we hope to prosper in the longer term. We accept responsibility for ourselves and each other."

"That sounds rehearsed, like the company values."

He shrugs. "It is."

"What? No, never mind... how come you look so alike, like Mike? In fact, no, let's come back to that, why do I need to be open minded?"

"Because things are not going according to plan and I need to give you the full picture of what's going on. This is the most responsible thing to do right now."

"K, one more question before you fill me in. Are *we* in any danger?"

"I don't think so."

"Seriously, is that it. You're not sure?"

He lifts a finger as a reminder. "Open and honest."

"Who might we be in danger from?"

"The Ananta."

"How?"

"Not sure, sorry," he says, and I see him wincing.

"But you seem relaxed about it all, so my guess is that I shouldn't worry about it?"

"Yeessss…" he replies, the most non-reassuring *yes* possible.

"Mike, really? That's the best you can do?" I say, any confidence in Mike I had fading fast. "In fact you know what, just pull over, now."

We slow to a stop at the side of a busy main road and Mike kerbs the car in response to a horn blare from the car behind as they go to overtake us. Parked up with just the noise of the traffic, I calmly turn to face him, holding back my frustration at his continued avoidance.

"You need to stop messing with me, Mike. I've had enough now. Straight answers to straight questions, K?"

"Yes, sorry."

"Let's start with who are *you* Mike?"

"Good question," he replies, only to then twist his face into another question. "Sorry, but can I give you a bit of background and how *who* I am is linked to QE? It will help if I do."

"Are you taking the piss?" I say, not holding back.

"No, really. It will all start to fall into place, there's a lot and it's complex."

I simply look at him for a moment, weighing things up and getting nowhere. "Fine, but don't go around the houses."

He clears his throat, coughing into his hand. "Well, QE as you are researching and as you know about from our chat on the beach, it is *the* mechanism for communication. Once you have two entangled particles, if you know what one is doing then you know what the other is doing – red and green, etc. This is what you're doing in your research, entangling two particles so you can instruct one remotely, yes?

"Yes, that's right. Get to the point Mike," I reply, as he stokes the fires of my frustration.

"This principle, instantaneous remote communication through quantum entanglement, this is a key to many leaps in science, which you already know. But what you don't know is that this is the mechanism for... interstellar travel."

He stops talking and looks across to me, stone faced, expressionless. Giving space for the message to hit. I look right back at him. My mind wanders off in a dozen new directions, each having twenty questions and more new directions. In that moment, with our eyes locked, I feel an awakening of who Mike is. I know him but have no idea who he really is. It's knowledge I have born of an emotion and not facts or information, a vital feeling. Looking into his eyes, there's a gulf between us. I can *never* know him, not truly, yet I feel a real connection to him. I see it and feel it; we exist on the same planet but in different realities. The peculiar intimacy fades as Mike turns away to set off again. Smoothly pulling out and driving us away, relaxed, like he's just told me the time.

"Mike, just repeat that last sentence," I say.

"Sure, what you don't know is that QE is the mechanism behind interstellar travel."

"Well... that's just, incredible. Have we used it? Successfully that is?"

"Who's we?"

"What do you mean who's we, you know us, humans, probably the Chinese or maybe the Americans?"

"No, they haven't, they aren't aware of it yet."

"Then *who* is?" I say, suspecting the worst.

"My group, as you're probably working out, and others, like the Ananta."

He's doing it again. Pulling the rug of the world from under me, so I don't know which way is up and which way is down. I can't fight him for information and answers, as much as I feel the need to. I just have to drink from the tap as it flows.

"Mike, just tell me what you are here to tell me, and I will deal with it. No easing me in with tortuous tales and trips to France."

"Interstellar travel is the key," he begins. "I say this as you are still pursuing this through chemical propulsion. This will never get you to the stars, they are too far away and even if you start to approach light speed, which you can't get close to with traditional methods, even then the universe is simply too big. You would be trundling around sloth-like for an eternity. The key to interstellar travel is not to send matter, but to send information."

Mike takes his eyes off the road and looks across at me again, his ever-present smile long gone. He nods slightly, I reply with the same. Scarily, we're on the same page. It's obvious now he says it; matter is limiting in many ways, information is not.

"And the only effective way to send information across the vastness of space is through QE. In simple terms you entangle two particles, separate them and you have instantaneous comms. Exactly as QE works within your experiments."

"Got you, are you saying this works at any distance?

"Yes, any distance. We have yet to find its limit and we have tried and continue to."

"But, hang on. You separate the entangled particles. And they can be as far apart as you want and they remain entangled – got that and I buy it. But how do you get the remote entangled particle to the other location, wherever that might be? If you want to send an instantaneous email across any distance you need something, probably made from matter, to be on the receiving end?"

"Correct. To set this up between two points you do need to send something physical in the first instance; however, it need only be very small and thus easy to propel at close to light speed. The first time you go anywhere new this is the limitation – you have to send physical matter first. The matter you send is a probe and it's pretty special. It can utilise the source material, the matter, at the destination and reconstitute it into anything on the periodic table and use this to create anything you might want. A Von Neumann device that utilising the local resources and with enough time could build a city. And guess what? It does all this through a wider application of QE, not dissimilar to what you are attempting in the lab with Jess."

I can see it; theoretically what he says is solid. Again my mind reels: the possibilities, the implications and applications of the technology.

"And w—"

"Stop, Mike," I say, holding up a hand towards him, blocking off further hammer blows to my reality. I need to digest, to understand what he's just said. The human mind is not built for explosions of information like this. Information like this should evolve as we do; it should emerge as we make progressive discoveries, so we can learn what it means and adapt... cope. But right now, if I'm right, I can see where this is going. If what he's saying is true, it can only mean one thing.

"Mike, there's wider implications here aren't there?"

"Yes," he replies earnestly, meeting my eyes. "I'm not the same as you Sean... a medic would never know, but strictly speaking I'm not human. I'm from another place, light years from Earth."

I was right. I grasping knew it. I sit gawking at Mike, slack-jawed; no words exist to make this acceptable or sortable. But... I believe him.

"As I said before, I'm here to help," he says. "All I have said previously is accurate; my subterfuge is pretending to be your old friend from school. You can imagine why that was necessary now that you know the truth."

With all that has gone on in the last twenty-four hours, in the last few months, this makes sense of all that, in a bizarre, twisted way. There's logic to what Mike is saying. I think I'm not surprised, though another part of me is shocked to the core and another part confused as hell and doubting my sanity. My derealisation is palpable, like I'm on hallucinogenic drugs and reality isn't recognisable, or I'm still in a dream, another dream.

What I know to be real has been smashed against the rocks. I feel my increasing fragility, struggling to cope, the foundations of my world steadily torn down. And now, I'm completely adrift. He who was becoming an inspirational mentor is an *alien*! From another world, for fuck's sake, what do you do with that? I have no experience to draw from to deal with this.

The storm in my mind rages; the solid granite cliff I had to protect me against these colossal waves has turned to clay. And each wave, as it batters the cliff, smashes my reality and carries it in pieces back out to sea, lost forever, the waves returning seconds later to continue the destruction, steadily eroding my understanding of our shared reality. Should I be frightened of Mike? Shit, should I be running away? Where do I go with this?

I have to believe, that's all there is. Not because the evidence stacks up, but because my alternative is head-in-the-sand, in the hope that there is no one out there wanting to stop me, this Ananta. That would leave me growing increasingly paranoid, then ditching my work with Jess, maybe having to quit my job and literally running away and hiding. And if I'm hiding, then I'm accepting that there are people out to get me and that means what Mike says is real. Which puts me back here. So... do I have a choice? My choice is I believe everything that Mike says or I believe nothing and nothing leads me nowhere.

"Mike?"

He looks at me with the same empty look, bereft of emotion. This might be a tipping point for him too.

"Mike, I believe you. At least, I do for now," I say.

The beginnings of a smile returns to his face, but different, more discerning now I see it, more genuine.

"Great," he says with relief. "I wasn't sure how you would take it. I've not had to share that before, so this is new country for me too. It feels good to be able to tell you, so I suspect we've done the responsible thing."

I nod in agreement, then take a breath and run my hands through my hair. "K, what now Mike, where do we go from here? Should I still be calling you Mike?"

"Yes. I've had the name for many years now so I identify with it. And where do we go from here? Well, now that we've opened Pandora's box, I should give you the full picture and take you to my office, which is a little more than an office."

We drive, with a destination now what Mike has shared feels more real. He tells me more about QE and how this is also a naturally occurring phenomenon that we all have within our cells. We all use it to communicate but don't recognise it. We put our communication down to words, intonation, body language and so on, but the reality is QE is playing a part and as we evolve, it will become more so. He gives me the example of metaphors in language, where we have a deeper understanding of what the other person means, even with less accurate words. This is because it forces our QE system to work harder to compensate and thus we share a deeper understanding, beyond words. The QE connection is strong in families, where we often know what our children are thinking and feeling with no words, and where there are instances of identical twins it's really prevalent.

"You see, it's all part of your genes," he says. "You inherit the ability but you can also get lucky. Like a random genius or Olympic athlete in the family. The leaders that have steered your world have strong QE, you know, like Obama and Deakin, and great actors; all have the power of influence through QE."

"That would make sense," I reply. "I'm thinking we might call it charisma or some such."

"You're on the right lines. You see my role is to identify these individuals and then facilitate their progress in moving humanity towards being responsible. But this has to be subtle – a nudge here and there."

"So this is what you did for our research. What else? What or who else have you *nudged*?"

"The idea of superheroes in comics and film during the last century is a good example; it worked so well we moved it onto this century too. You've seen the old Star Wars films as a boy, remember the Force? Remind you of anything?"

My eyes go wide, I loved those films. "No way. I've seen all those old movies, their classics. But wouldn't it be better to buddy up with national leaders and whisper ideas to them?"

"You might think so, but for cultural change you need more. You need hearts and minds of the masses. Remember the Wright brothers?" he asks.

"As in the ones who built and flew the first aeroplane?"

He nods. "Yes... a fantastic technological leap for mankind. How did they get there?"

I take a moment to think. "Well, I imagine they saw birds flying and thought that it's possible, so experimented to find out how."

"Exactly, but the key thing is that they *imagined* it first. They saw the birds fly and their imagination carried them away and inspired them to want to do the same. It was the imagination and the inspiration that carried them forward, not an alien leaving some blueprints around for them to copy. That doesn't work."

"Got you. You're inspiring storytellers to tell tales that will light our imagination?"

"Yes. To want to be something better, to dream, to have a vision of what might be, so you can work towards this."

"We can all be Jedis, one day?" I say, raising my eyebrows.

"Perhaps you already are," he replies, glancing across mischievously.

"Seriously?" I say, unsure of the game here. "But how many of you are there, how long has this been going on?" I ask.

"The wider story is for another time, probably best for us to focus on now. The really significant thing here is that you now know *who* I am. Remember this is a first. Also remember we didn't instigate the current situation and, perhaps more importantly, we don't know why the Ananta did."

"But we're not in danger are we?"

"We're pretty sure that's the case."

"Hang on Mike, I need more than that. Jess needs more than that" I say, sitting forwards in my seat and turning to him. "Mike, we need to tell Jess. She's implicated in all of this and if I have a right to know, so does she."

"I don't agree. She's only implicated through you; our intervention with Jess was miniscule. Your activities have influenced lots of people and we aren't about to go around revealing ourselves to everyone you've affected. That's the whole point in having a focused intervention with one individual, who themselves has the capability to go on to influence others. This is what we do."

"So, I'm the influencer?"

"Yes, of course."

"So... from your earlier comment. Does that mean I have strong QE capabilities?"

By the speed with which he flicks his head from the road to look at me, I see I've hit on something. He holds my gaze. "Yes, yes you do," he replies slowly, reluctantly.

I smile, like a proud parent. Am I special? *Jedi I am?* Is this why he chose me? Is this my neurodiversity? "But why me, there must be more like me?" I say.

Mike continues to drive, ignoring me.

"Mike, why me? Why have you chosen me?" I repeat, raising my voice.

He pans across to look at me, thinking, but not saying.

"Well?" I say, raising my eyebrows.

"It had to be you," he replies, only just audible.

"And the reason for that is...?"

"It had to be you, and, that's all I can say... for now."

"What? You can't do that. Implicate me and then not tell me why."

"I know, sorry. But that's how it's got to be. For now."

"Mike, come on," I say.

"I can't. The thing is... you wouldn't believe me if I did. I wouldn't believe me if it were me. Sorry."

"You don't know that. These days I'm pretty open minded," I reply.

"Perhaps, but it's a non-negotiable, sorry."

I breathe out and rub my forehead, thinking on my options. "K then, for now. But what do we do about Jess Mike, can you protect her?"

"Not in the way I think you mean. But she should be fine, the Ananta won't get involved, that's against their ideology."

"Unless... they wanted to stop this experiment in its tracks," I say. "Which to me sounds like they do." My heart leaps into overdrive – Jess isn't safe. Mike's confidence seems to come and go and my faith in him with it. For all we know they could be heading her way right now.

"Call her," suggests Mike, reading my thoughts again.

I fumble my phone out, and it rings and rings. *Pick up Jess, pick up, not your grasping AIC.*

I push out a long slow breath as she finally answers. "Hey you, how are things?" she says. Her words are a spring breeze washing over me; they immediately transport me from this chaos back to the lab and I feel a smile tighten my face. "I'm... I'm good thanks. I was... I was just looking for my... notebook, you know the hard back blue one I always use. I can't seem to find it. I didn't leave it in the lab did I?"

"I've not seen it, no. It doesn't have anything sensitive on it does it? If you know what I mean."

"Err, not really. Hang on, it's here, found it. All good. Sorry to bother you Jess. Listen, got to dash, I'll catch you later, K?"

"Sure, bye for now," she says and hangs up.

"So she's fine, for now. But we need to bring her in. It's just... Mike, you're not in control of things, are you?" I say,

He responds with silence.

"If I'm responsible for bringing Jess into this then I'm responsible for her now," I say. "So we go to her now and I tell her everything. Right?"

Mike continues driving. He's thinking, ignoring me, or maybe communicating with someone else? His QE connectivity is likely way beyond our AICs, he could have countless capabilities I'm not aware of. Can I trust him? He doesn't seem concerned for Jess and I know he hasn't told me everything.

"We can go to Jess," Mike announces. "But I think telling her might not be in anyone's best interests. You simply don't know how she will react; she may well think you're insane, wouldn't you?"

"Perhaps, but that's what we're going to do," I say, focused, determined.

He nods, accepting my stubbornness. "Very well, where will she be?"

"Hmm, I should have asked her. But anyway, she will definitely be at the lab in an hour or so, so we head there."

"You're the boss. I'll spin us around."

I know I'm right – the secret to a good relationship is to have no secrets. I bring Jess in and we face this together, anything else and I'm hanging her out to dry. But how do I bring her in? How hard was it for me to believe Mike? And that took time. Mike could be right, she could think I'm nuts?

We speed down the A1 returning to Cambridge, the road's quiet. The only traffic is a mix of slow moving auto freight trudging along and manned lorries zipping past them, with the yellow fields of parched earth surrounding us all. As I start to factor in how to sensibly bring Jess on board, my eyes are drawn to a bright dot in the sky. Initially I dismiss it, but a niggle tells me something's not right. It's not moving and its only small, so must be way off. But it's dead ahead, and now I focus on it I realise its growing ever so slightly. Squinting doesn't bring it into clearer focus. Then it really starts to grow, increasing in speed. My pulse quickens, and I push myself back in my seat.

"Mike, what the hell is that?" I shout, pointing ahead.

"No idea," he replies, leaning in towards the windscreen, sounding more perplexed than scared.

It comes straight towards the car, a direct line, growing still, and the brightness so intense I have to shade my eyes. It leaps at us from several hundred metres away in an instant, accelerating hard. It strikes the front of the car with a mammoth crash; the sound is deafening. I'm thrown into my seat belt with the air bags smothering me on all sides as the car crashes to a dead stop and I feel my spine compress into my chest. It feels like the rear of the car is lifted up in that moment, only to be immediately dropped back down again. We've gone from forty miles per hour to zero in a second.

The air bags droop to empty sacks and I look across to Mike, only for my neck to spasm, and I wince in pain, I try again, this time rotating my body stiffly without moving my neck.

"Mike, you alright?" I call.

"No. Yes, I think," he replies, exchanging a look of disbelief with me. "GET OUT!" he yells, "there could be more."

My door doesn't budge. I give it an almighty shove with my shoulder... my neck screams in agony but nothing moves.

"Mike, my door's jammed, I can't open it," I yell, still pulling on the handle and shoulder barging it again, adrenalin now deadening the pain in my neck.

"Mine too, try the window," he barks and I hear the desperation in his voice. Now I'm scared – nothing shakes Mike.

The window slides down steadily. I watch it every inch of the way, willing it to open all the way. Which it does. I unclip my seatbelt and wriggle through the opening, landing unceremoniously on the road just as two pairs of hands take my arms and sit me up.

"Are ya right?" asks one of the pair of hands, which as I look up I see are attached to a burly bearded man. "That were crazy, yer car just exploded and stopped dead."

"What?" I mumble, looking up to my rescuers, two of them, both wearing checked shirts, jeans and baseball caps, their truck sat behind us blocking the road. I wriggle free of their support to stand.

"Thanks fellas, thanks. I think I'm alright," I say, stepping back from them, demonstrating my lack of injury.

I look around to see the car is a wreck and I see a neat ten-centimetre hole in the centre of the bonnet. The surrounding edge of the hole is discoloured in that peculiar mix of purple and copper caused by intense heat. The whole front end of the car is bent upwards so that the front wheels are off the floor, it's like the whole car has been snapped and pushed up at an angle by an enormous force.

Mike's head appears at the other side of the car, "Mike, you alright?" I shout over. He replies with a nod, rubbing his neck as he heads towards the three of us.

"Is it a Jaguar thing, d'ya recon?" one of the rescuers asks. "Do they blow up?"

"What? No," I reply, attempting to stretch and mobilise my back as I walk over to Mike. "We hit something. Not sure what, but. But, I'm alright, Mike you?"

"Shaken, but I'll be fine," he replies, and I see the look in his eyes. We need to go.

"Listen gents, thanks for stopping, really," I say. "The car's a right-off, but we're both fine. Yes Mike?"

"Yes, we can take it from here," he says, looking to our two rescuers, "thanks for stopping, it's much appreciated, but I can make some calls now and get this moved."

"Ya sure?" replies one of them, the other just shaking his head, not on board with our claim to be fine.

"Gents, we are fine. All is well thanks, we can take if from here, really, thank you," replies Mike, ushering our two rescuers back towards their lorry. But neither of them move, they just exchange a quizzical look.

"Stu," says one of them, drawing the other's attention as he nods towards the rear of the car. "You see it?" he says, looking at the license plate.

"What? Oh yeah," replies Stu, "best get on ay," he says and cocks his head towards the truck.

"We'll leave ya to it then gents," says Stu as they head over to their truck.

"We need to go, now!" whispers Mike through clenched teeth and he starts speed-walking away along the pavement.

I chase after him. "What the hell was that Mike, a missile?"

"I don't know, maybe."

"And this is us, *not* in danger?"

"Yes, I see that. I was in the car with you," he replies.

"But Mike, you said we were safe, that Jess was safe. You were wrong, very wrong."

"I know, I know. It'll be alright. It will. If they had wanted us gone, we would be."

I stop walking, my fear and anger briming over.

"Mike, for fuck's sake be real. You don't know what's going on, do you?" I call, raising my voice as he continues to walk away.

"It'll be fine," he replies over his shoulder, still not stopping.

"NO, MIKE," I scream after him.

"STOP THIS," he yells at me, "it's not helpful."

"I don't care... THAT'S NOT THE POINT," I bark, my blood boiling. Even now he's not taking responsibility.

He stops now and turns to me, ruddy faced. "IT'S NOT MY FAULT, this is not how I remember it—" he yells, only to cut his own words short.

"What? Remember what? This? This whole thing?" I say, looking around me.

I stare at him, waiting for something. Standing on the narrow pavement at the side of the road he looks anywhere but at me.

"MIKE!" I shout, pulling him back.

"Look, it was a warning shot, alright," he replies. "No doubt targeted at *me*, to warn *me* off helping you. If they had wanted to they could have sent ten missiles and laid waste to us both. But right now we just need to focus, I can explain more later. But this, *this,*" he says, waving his hands at me and the car wreck, "is not helping,"

This is a new side to Mike: vulnerable, fallible, maybe dangerous.

"Just give me a minute," he says, walking ahead again, tapping and then talking to his AIC.

My nerves are fried and my confidence in Mike is gone. He's bluffing or clueless or out of his depth, or all of the above, none of it's good. I need to get to Jess and get help.

Get help... who do I go to for help? Who is there for this kind of situation? There's no one, no Men in Black agency for alien intervention management, certainly no one who isn't going to want to lock me up.

"—better than that, if possible," I hear, as I increase my pace to catch up to Mike walking away from the scene of the crash.

"A car is on it's way, so we keep walking," he says. "We can then resume our drive and go to see Jess. I've sent a probe to monitor her for now."

"I'm calling her, just in case," I say, taking out my phone and hitting her speed dial.

"Hey there Jess, you K?" I'm not really sure what else to say.

"Err, yes, still fine. Have you misplaced something else?"

"No, all good. Just seeing where you are, are you in the lab?"

"Yes, just arrived and here all day, like every day. Why?"

"I'm... dropping in later and just wanted to be sure you would be in."

"I'll see you then, then. Just in the middle of something, so bye for now, K?" she replies and hangs up.

As soon I get off the phone Mike puts his hand on my shoulder, grabbing my full attention. "There's something else you need to know, just in case," he says. "It's important, so please listen carefully."

"Right, go on." I say, not able to imagine what more there could be to say that could possibly shock me.

"It's the function of interstellar travel... you need to understand how it works."

"Err, sure. But is that really important right now?"

He ignores my question. "You understand you have a terminal at the start point and at the destination. So you have a person at one location and you send them to the other. Yes?"

"Yes."

"Except you don't. Remember, you only send information, and you do that via QE. So nothing physical goes once the two points are set up. You only send information, computer code, and because it's QE information then it's instantaneous, faster-than-light travel across the stars. But only information. With me?"

"Yes."

"Do you see the implications of this?" he asks. There's something in his tone, the way he asks, something fundamental.

"Not sure? So... a person steps into the transporter at point A, then it must map who they are in some way, using QE. And then sends the map of that person to point B, and at point B, they build that person from the map?" I suggest.

"Spot on," replies Mike.

"But hang on, that means there are now two of you. The person at point A and a duplicate person at point B. Is that right?"

"Nail on the head, Sean."

Then it hits me. "Mike," I say, unsure if I want to ask my question. "How did you get here?"

"The same way as everything else. I suspect your next question is what you really want to know?"

Is he that smart, that quick? "I have to ask... well, there must be two of *you* then? Or maybe more, how do you cope with that?"

"I am a copy of a former me, you're right, and over time there has been and still are several variations of the original me, although we look at this concept quite differently to how you do."

"K..." I say, waiting for more.

"Well, you have short lives, so your perspective is as limited as your lifespan. But then you of all people appreciate this, Sean. To us, having another version made of you is something not to be taken lightly, like humans having a baby. Bringing new life into the universe caries responsibility. Granted, our new life is usually a mature adult with all the capabilities and knowledge of the sponsor. But the two will immediately start to become different entities, or people, and as time goes by the differences will become increasingly apparent. The sum of our experiences is a large part of who we are."

"That's remarkable," I say, shaking my head, the hairs on the back of my neck firmly upright. "It must cause all kinds of philosophical and ethical dilemmas? You know, like If you have a partner, how will they feel, parents, friends? You can't both go back to the same job and carry on the same life as before. Where does the new person live. In fact, how do you know which one of you is the new person?"

"You hit upon some of the challenges there. But you have to remember our social systems are different from yours. Remember, I was transported here as information, that's me. At the end of the day you are the same, as is your life, your existence. Granted some of it is complex, such as love, relationships, trust, but it's all information. Lots of us stay as information for all time. So our needs are quite limited and very different; our society is very, very different to yours."

How can I have been so blind? Mike's not human. He's an alien from another planet. He might not even have a physical form, but just takes on those that are useful. He's doing a good job of being a human, so I keep seeing him as that.

"I hear all you say Mike, but what about Jess, and the thing that hit the car? I'm very worried, aren't you?"

"Yes, but there's no way the Ananta would approach Jess in a public place like the University and if they had wanted us dead, well, we would be. So although it might seem otherwise, we really are safe for now, it was a warning shot. And a car is on its way."

"There's a logic there," I reply, but my confidence is shot. Trusting Mike, that's gone. But he's my only way out of here. I need to get to Jess.

"You see I'm only a limited copy of my original self," continues Mike, carrying on our conversation. "Fully autonomous but not linked back to my origins. That way I can fully integrate and thus seem human. If I came as the whole me, I might well look at you all as children and fail to appreciate who you really are. My perspective would limit my understanding and integration would not happen."

I look at him for a moment, taking in what he's saying. "Sorry Mike, are you saying you've dumbed yourself down to blend in?"

"You could say that," he replies, stopping and tapping his AIC. As he does, a silver Jag approaches on the other side of the road, executes a neat U-turn and pulls alongside us. It's identical to our previous one. "Our ride awaits," he says, gesturing to the car with his hand, and we're back on the road. The coolness of the car's AC brings much relief, until fresh sunburn on my face and neck stings as I sit back.

"My AIC tells me Jess is fine and there is no cause for alarm," says Mike. "And weighing up the options, I think turning up and just telling her everything could lead to all kinds of problems. So I have another solution. It will bring better results and will be lower risk."

"Is she safe, really safe?"

"She's at the lab and her diary has her there all day," he replies. "She couldn't be any safer."

"Then tell me more."

Chapter Fifteen

I can't keep my eyes off Jess as she approaches the car; hidden behind the windscreen it feels OK to stare, to admire. She looks amazing for sixty. When I see her at a distance like this, I can't help but look and appreciate her. Not just how she carries herself, effortlessly beautiful in every step she takes, but also for the inner beauty of the person she is. How could anyone not fall for her?

"Morning Sean," she says as she drops her bag in the back seat and then jumps in beside me.

"Morning. How've you been, I haven't seen you for over a week?" I ask, wincing inside. That might not be a good question, I need to be more careful than that. Don't initiate.

I quickly follow up. "Nice dress, is it new?" I ask, eyebrows raised, hoping my acting ability is better than it feels. I start driving as well, adding further distraction.

"This? Gosh, can't remember to be honest," she replies. "I think I've had it for a while. Anyway, how are you, ready for the conference, presentation sorted?"

"Yes, all good and you?"

"Fine, and you know what Sean? Heading to this conference I feel so much more relaxed, it feels more like a celebration of the successes of our work rather than when we were out presenting our early findings, with everyone sceptical and critical. Do you remember?"

"Yes, challenging times. But we got through in the end," I reply.

Good response: answer-focused, ambiguous and short.

"And here we are," she says. "I never dreamt that things would move so quickly and that we would be able to personally benefit from longevity treatment."

"Me too, me too."

We continue our drive, mostly just chit-chatting or sitting quietly. I soon learn that as long as I don't elicit too much conversation and just respond to what Jess says then things move along smoothly. No awkward questions with me unsure on what I can and can't say.

We get to the driveway of the hotel; it's raining and there's a group of people on either side of the gate. Nearly all of them have a placard with various slogans on. One says, "Three score years and ten = 70!"; another says "No Death, No Heaven!".

They seem well-ordered and aren't blocking the road, but I can't figure out who put them there. It wasn't me, at least not consciously. I go with it and focus on driving smoothly and swiftly through the gates, hoping none of them recognise us. We're semi-famous here, and I don't have the skills to predict how things will go.

I notice Jess looking around as we queue to check in, probably for some familiar faces as tends to be the case at academic conferences. "You know I can't recall where this conference is, which is odd?" she says. "I haven't seen any of the usual crowd either."

"Devizes, in Wiltshire," I reply. "At least that's the nearest town. Nice hotel don't you think?" I say, looking around.

"I guess, are we early? What time was check-in for the conference?"

"I don't think so... oh look, he's free," I say, pointing to a member of the exquisitely tailored staff behind the ridiculously expansive obsidian marble reception desk. Minutes later we're heading to our rooms and simultaneously receive a message from the conference team with our timings for the tether lift. Departure is in two hours, so we agree to meet back in the lobby before that.

I decide in my room I might as well change. Jess will do and I need to play along. I open my bag to see what options I have. It's empty. This messes with my mind; it had the weight of a full bag when it was closed, but the weight of an empty bag now it's open. I check the wardrobe and as suspected, it's full of clothes. Not only that but a wide selection all my size, nothing too outlandish, all items I would have likely chosen and perfectly prepared and presented. I could get used to this. I go a little more daring than usual and opt for a blazer with shirt and no tie – living on the edge, that's me.

I arrive in the lounge just before Jess. She's wearing a pastel and floral summer dress; it's a very lightweight fabric that leaves little to the imagination. I smile as I notice she's still drawing the attention of those around her, just like the early days at my Uni. She's still got it. In settings like this she reminds me of a movie star, sophisticated, confident, capable and beautiful, and... out of my league. She spots me, lights up the room with her smile and heads over.

"I feel I'm travelling very light, considering where we're going," she says.

"I know. But in reality, the distance is only a few kilometres. It's a first for me too."

"You nervous?" she asks.

"Yes, but excited too. You?"

"Absolutely, no one could have predicted all this. It's just, well, out of this world!" she says with a dry smile.

Twenty minutes later we're aboard the hotel's hyperloop connection, silently speeding along at close to Mach One, tether bound. The initial acceleration was impressive, with all passengers locked into their compression seats, like an Apollo launch. Now at cruising speed, we move around freely. The eye height letter box windows give a view of the immediate landscape, which is a blur. Only as you look to the distance does it resolve into the world we know. I stop and stare, with entire hills passing by like cars in the opposite lane, its dizzying.

"Looking out of the window's making me a bit nauseous," I say.

"Yes, I noticed that too," replies Jess. "I guess that's why they're so small. That and keeping the vacuum out."

"Yes, that old one. Getting pulled into a vacuum at six hundred miles per hour must suck," I say. Jess gives me her slight-frown-and-head-cocked look. The one that tells me: she got the joke, it just wasn't funny.

The conference reception is being held at the end of the tether in low Earth orbit, hosted by our newfound friends the ambassadorial contingent of the local Galactic Community: Mike's friends, who formerly revealed themselves to us not long after our longevity treatment was proven. And who look just like us as they don't have a specific form themselves, being a mix of many origin species and only occasionally having to engage in physical existence, such as early contact like this. To help us out, they always wear a small red sash around their waist or neck to denote who they are, the intention being *"integrate not imitate"*. It's early days, so few people have met them in person. Jess and I are the keynote speakers for the conference on sustainable longevity.

As amazing as the hyperloop is, other worldly and beyond smooth, this pales as we emerge from a tunnel and have a distant view of the Tether. I can't believe the vastness of the engineering, it's huge, an elevator to the stars. But I shouldn't be surprised.

The central column looks impossibly thin, a pin stuck into the planet, too narrow to stay upright. My eyes follow the never-ending slender chimney upwards, squinting to trace the line of it as far as I can, before it blends into the sky and evaporates. At the speed we're travelling we soon get closer and I can just about discern the wires holding it in place, they splay out to distant anchors that must be many miles away from the tether's base. Like a suspension bridge they gradually curve as they ascend to meet the central shaft at a range of intervals far above the ground. I turn to see Jess also craning her head to see the top. I catch her eye and feel her awe.

"How far away do you think we are?" she asks.

"My guess is... five miles?"

"And we can see the cable... can you imagine the diameter? Amazing."

Our moment of wonder is cut short as all passengers are instructed to take their seats for deceleration. After we lock in, the seat rotates, putting our back to the destination. Our weight increases as we start to sink into the padding. It's an odd feeling and I test the system and can only just lift my head from the chair. The locking in your limbs makes sense now. Soon enough the "free to move about" sign is on and we prepare to disembark.

We follow the signed route, taking us from the hyperloop station to the base of the tether. This takes ten minutes of walking well-polished corridors with pristine white walls and white marble floors. Every inch is exquisitely clean, giving you the space age feel it was designed to.

The corridor widens and opens up to become an elevated viewing area set a few floors above the tether departure lounge. Jess and I both halt as the vista emerges, clearly designed to give new arrivals an instant impression of the immense size and complexity of the tether building. The lounge itself is vast; it's larger than the biggest of sports arenas and is wholly open plan, pierced at its centre by the tether, the centre to everything. This is surrounded by a grassed area with walkways and trees, a small park, which itself is surrounded by a circle of low-level buildings, shops and restaurants, from what I can make out. Moving out from the shops is yet another grassed park area, adjoining the circle of shops, which then leads to yet another circuit of low-level buildings. This pattern continues, like onion layers spanning out from the tether until it meets the outer edge of the arena, which has shops, gyms, cinemas and all you could want from a medium-size city. There's even a small river flowing through the park areas. It's an architect's utopian dream.

The vista is all lit by an immense harlequin glazed roof, an array of multi-coloured diamond shaped panels of glass spanning the entire lounge, with the sun beating through. This creates an amazing rainbow effect across large sections of the floor space. The roof, gradually rising up from its circumference, is centrally penetrated by the tether, a jade green transparent crystal tube some thirty metres in diameter. I spy numerous other tubes inside, spiralling upwards like a DNA helix. Towards the ground the tether penetrates what looks like a giant, gleaming-white tortoise shell. Each section of the shell is as white as snow, opaque and diamond-shaped, complementing the roof. This must be the boarding point for passengers, but with no obvious entry point I guess this is accessed from below, like the Louvre. The whole scene is amazing, like we walked onto a movie set. I turn to Jess, who notices and returns my glance with a beaming, childlike grin.

"Exciting!" she says, setting off to explore, her eyes enticing me to join her as she starts to walk away.

We wander through the parks and shopping areas. There are people, but the place is so large it feels deserted as we window-shop our way through the lounge. Finding your way couldn't be easier as we simply head towards the ever present tether, eventually finding our departure gate.

From the outside, the shuttle looks lacklustre and unimpressive, like an erect aeroplane fuselage. It's a silky white and perfectly clean cylinder the height of a three-story building, dotted here and there with windows. As we walk through the entry door I feel I've suddenly gone deaf as the background noise dissipates to nothing and there are just a few hushed voices from fellow passengers. The luxury furnished seating could account for this, but there's more at work here, some high-tech sound proofing, and it's relaxing me, just as well.

The seats are sumptuous and large, set in groups of five all facing in on each other, with a small central table. It has the feel of a cocktail lounge rather than space flight. Sooner than I would have liked there's a brief notification before we start to ascend, with our pilots and crew on the floor above us accessed by a curving staircase set against the outer walls of our cylinder. There are only half of the guest seats occupied, the five sets of seat clusters making up yet another circle formation around the central column of our vehicle. The other passengers are all quiet and self-contained, I'm relieved to see.

We start to ascend, slowly at first, and my knuckles turn white as I crush the arms of my seat, my body locked solid, only now realising what I've set myself up for. I hope Jess doesn't notice. The ride is so smooth I can only tell we're moving by looking through the window at the crystal walls as they fall away around us. Then brightness illuminates the windows as we pop out above the tortoise shell, with a panorama of the departure lounge; this shrinks below us and as soon as we emerge from the harlequin crystal roof, Jess is up.

"Come on," she says, leaping from her seat and heading to the nearest window.

The outer edge of the shuttle's cylinder is made up of a mix of luggage compartments, stairs and, to my horror, the occasional floor-to-ceiling window, which is exactly where Jess beelines to.

I do not like heights. Jess obviously doesn't have the same affliction. She leans against the bar that sits horizontally across the centre of the window, head almost toughing the glass, peering down towards the base of the tether. Reluctantly, I get up and join her. I strategically place myself against the luggage compartment adjoining the glazed section and lean against this whilst looking inwards towards the seating and my fellow passengers.

"Amazing technology and so exciting," she says, eyes fixed on the view.

"Sure is, I wonder if they give us an indication of speed anywhere," I say, looking for instruments.

"I've not seen one, but I think we must already be quite a way up and accelerating."

"Wow! Look at that, Sean. The splay of the cables must be miles apart. This is big stuff, it must be anchored well into the bedrock."

"No doubt," I reply.

"And where is that? I can't see the hyperloop but that town over there, where is that would you say?" she asks, turning to me. "Sean, what's wrong, are you alright? There's plenty of room for you to look too," she says, moving to create more space at the window.

"Sure," I say, delaying. "How far up would you say we are?"

"Perhaps eight hundred metres, maybe, but climbing fast now?"

"K," I reply, hoping to sound much more confident than I feel.

I turn to face the compartment I'm leaning against, staring close range at someone's luggage. I slowly move my hand out towards Jess and grab the rail. I then steadily move sideways, crablike, to join Jess, eyes fixed on the distant horizon.

As I slide in front of the window I swallow and wince at the pain in my throat. I feel the sweat form on my forehead. I know all is well, I also know that when we get to aeroplane cruising height, I'll be fine, but when you can see the fall... the drop. It's hard not to be scared, totally illogical, but I can't ignore it... I've tried, it doesn't work.

I feel Jess's eyes burrowing into me, analysing. "You're not comfortable with heights are you Sean?" she says.

"I'll be alright," I say, my body frozen, focused on the horizon.

"Sean, let's sit down. It's alright, sorry I didn't know."

"It's fine, really," I say, willing us to gain more height so I can look down and not vomit.

"Come on," she says, grabbing my arm and pulling me towards the seating area.

"No, really, I'll be fine. We must be quite high now." I risk a glance down towards the ground. It's almost a patchwork quilt, interspersed with the grey sprawl of urbanisation and road arteries. I feel my soggy grip on the bar loosen and my body relax a little and I breath again, we're approaching cruising altitude, must be.

I slowly turn towards Jess, my body still rigid, "I'll be alright now, it's just taking off I struggle with."

"You sure? I'm more than happy for us to sit."

"No, it's fine and a great view," I say hesitantly.

"As you wish," she says, my discomfort no doubt still obvious. "You know, we must sound like some old couple," she continues in a hushed voice, looking around at our companions, "faffing about at the window, marvelling at the world below."

I nod in agreement, catching her eye as I do and a gush of emotion and love for Jess floods my head. If only that were so, to have lived a life with Jess as my partner. The emotional overload makes it difficult to keep up with the situation, but I must. I push it back, I can't manage that right now. Especially when I hadn't counted on my physical reaction being the same as when flying in the real. An oversight on my part, a distraction I need to overcome and quickly.

Jess and I stay by the window for much of the rest of the journey. I tell myself we're standing next to a scrolling movie screen and by the time we arrive I nearly believe it. She's fascinated by all this new tech and the experience. I play my part and join in our discussion. Over the course of the journey we decide there are only three heights. The initial "I am off the ground and if I fall will likely die", perhaps a hundred metres plus; I'm petrified at this point. Then we have second height, we call this "omnipotent overview" at around a kilometre. Here we can oversee the world, towns and villages as shapes; fields as a mix of perfect green circles of irrigated crops, with yellowing patchwork quilts filling in the gaps. This I can just about cope with, although it's quite different from an aircraft as the view doesn't change it just continually shrinks, imperceptible from second to second, but obvious from minute to minute.

Then there's height three, where you can just begin to see the curvature of the earth. This is easy, like watching a film The altimeter reads just past ten kilometres at this point and is where our world view changes, literally. You stop looking down at the Earth and start to look to the stars, physically and metaphorically.

"I think this is why they've chosen to have an off-world location for their ambassadors," Jess comments, as we fine-tune our three heights theory.

"So, we meet them halfway. They're not coming to us and we're not going to them. But we're making huge leaps off planet for us, challenging our perspective and pushing us to think in wider terms. Do you think?"

"An interesting theory Jess, I see where you're going. We could ask them when we meet them?"

"No, we will not ask them Sean!" exclaims Jess, supressing her raised voice.

I smile.

"You're winding me up aren't you?"

"Sorry," I say and mean it. "You know, I do love our chats and how we seem to be able to find science and a theory in most things," I share, savouring the moment with Jess.

"Yes... it's amazing how distracting that can be isn't it," she replies, giving me the smallest of winks.

Aha... nice one Jess, I hadn't realised. "Thanks," I say, knowing our conversation is real, even though nothing else is.

I had struck a deal with Mike. To bring Jess in, my responsibility, my decision. I don't know that I left much option for Mike to decline, not if he wants my continued involvement in his plans. Although, the suggestion of using QE comms to achieve this was his. But the reality of managing this fictional world I've created whilst simultaneously existing in it is way more difficult than I'd thought.

Mike spent time with me on this, with me hooked up to his laptop via QE – only then did I realise his laptop is an interface to some super-computer location unknown. He talked me through the principles: imagination is what creates the world and a calm zen-like subtle focus is that which controls it. Being relaxed, but not forcing relaxation. Making the car go where you want but without steering it. Easier said than done.

I spent an afternoon dreaming up what the future might hold for Jess and I and how things might roll out with the world linking up with other sentient life and longevity becoming a reality. It was amazing fun, making your dreams come true, until I understood that imagining the world was only the first part. When I then put myself in it, I had the challenge of serious multi-tasking.

I have to keep the dream alive in my imagination and keep in my mind's eye the "story" I've created. If I do this right we stay on track and as long as I don't allow stray thoughts to take us down unexpected new avenues, we're good. This is hard, like when someone tells you not to think of a pink elephant and of course you immediately think of just that. Trusting myself to the flow of my own imagination was the way, like floating down a river and not panicking but allowing it to take you and having faith in the invisible current that is your subconscious.

I then need to simultaneously interact with Jess and not let the complexity of it all consume my whole attentional capacity. To keep it real for her, I need to be able to respond to her and her unpredictable reactions to both my comments and this new world, all while not allowing this to take me too far off track or give the game away to Jess. Exhausting does not cover it, thank God for hyperfocus.

So here we are, in the future, heading into space to meet the Galactic Community. Too much by Mike's judgement, but then he doesn't know Jess, and this is all about her.

My confidence growing, I slipstream us through a brief moment of haze and we are at the end of the tether on the platform in a reception area, drinks in hand. I surreptitiously check on Jess – she seems oblivious to the whole change in scene and is taking in the new venue. The place is like an enormous goldfish bowl, the size of a football pitch. The giant disc we stand on is the size of a football field with a wall-to-wall obsidian marble floor; surgically clean, it reflects the subtle lighting with glints of quarts winking back at us as we move. The deep marble meets the floor-to-ceiling window encircling the whole platform. This is broken by a single set of double doors on the other side. The platform has been designed for the view, to look across Earth and to the stars. I didn't have this in my imagination when I dreamt up the end of the tether, but I can't think what I had instead.

Towards the other side of the platform there's the low-level hum of chatting in a bar area, with high level standing tables of the same black marble, seemingly extruded from the floor, and a few clusters of well-attired human guests, drinks in hand. Perhaps twenty of them, near a small circular bar, with a perfectly neat, middle-aged bartender seeing to their needs. All of them designed to be grey-haired middle class ambassadorial types, deep in conversations, not easily approachable. I look around and Jess has quietly shuffled off towards the window. I tentatively approach and realise it's bowed outward. That could be my fault, likening it to a goldfish bowl in my head. It's amazing, an astronaut's view, and as I look down on the Earth an emptiness grows in my stomach; I'm humbled. I love this world, and here it is precariously floating in the nothing of space and just one of billions. If I didn't know it before, I do now. We're not that significant, it's just very comforting to *think* we are.

"Looks like someone has spotted us," says Jess, looking across to the bar area. I follow her gaze to see Mike heading over to us; his smile and outstretched arms draw us in as he approaches. Ever the ringmaster, he has our undivided attention.

"Welcome to the habitat," he says, sweeping an arm off to one side, panning across the room and then returning his gaze to us.

I feel a huge sense of relief. My shoulders slump and the weight returns to my feet. Mike is now running the show. I knew it would be hard, but the level of concentration needed to manage the construct leaves me mentally exhausted. The pressure to maintain the environment and keep Jess in the moment, whilst not being overawed at the power I was wielding, gave me a continual adrenalin rush that has sucked me dry. Now, as Mike takes the reigns, I realise this and as I relax, I become a couple of inches smaller. I give an internal sigh of relief and look to Mike to fill the silence, which he does effortlessly.

"Sean, it's great to see you, and this must be Professor Hart?" Mike gives a small bow and shakes Jess's hand, playing the diplomatic host to the full. He might even have clicked his heels together, but Jess is taking it all in her stride. I sense no doubt in her over where we are and what we're doing.

"I'm Mike Swale, part of the ambassadorial team here on the tether," he says.

"The two of you have already met?" asks Jess. I hear the surprise in her voice, masked to keep up appearances, but it's there.

I look to Mike and leave space for him to reply, he's the professional at this game of emergent reality. I don't have the focus to create what's happening next whilst knitting some level of subterfuge so as not to give the game away, only for Jess to slip from the dream while I'm not looking.

"Yes," says Mike. "Although I asked Sean not to mention it as we know that he'll be interrogated on all sides from friends, family and the press alike. Experience tells us that early on in contact situations it's best to keep things moderately low key for as long as is practicable."

"I see," says Jess. "I can imagine that there are many challenges in situations like this and that diplomacy must be at the heart of your decisions."

"You are quite right, Professor," affirms Mike with a nod.

"I imagine misinterpretation born of cultural differences are bound to occur, it must be quite challenging," says Jess, looking to the both of us. "You mention previous experience in these situations, can I ask how many other species you have made contact with? And why us now?"

Mike nods sage-like, eyes half closed. "Very perceptive and good questions Professor, or may I call you Jess?"

"Please."

"Jess, your question on why now is relevant and is linked to your work with Sean and the reason we are all here: reaching the milestone of longevity and becoming sustainable longevity. You see, the long-lived have a responsibility to those that join them; to those that follow. Our responsibility extends to you, as you are following us, you in turn need to consider to whom you are responsible to and for what?"

"That's a big question, I imagine the answer isn't so straightforward," replies Jess.

"No, the answers are never straightforward in these matters, however *intent* is. Your intentions are what make you who you are."

I see Mike slipping into teacher mode with Jess, do I stop it? It could go one of two ways. Jess is sharp, she'll spot any trickery on Mike's part.

"You see, perfection is an aspiration and never a reality," says Mike. "And if your intention is to do the right thing, but you don't quite hit the mark, then that's alright, we all do this. If we do what we think is the responsible act and then learn from any mistakes, then we improve for next time and thus we are progressing as individuals and as a collective. We are working towards a better version of us."

Jess nods agreement. "It's all about the journey, not the destination."

"Exactly," says Mike, as he looks from Jess to me for confirmation – today's lesson is for both of us.

"Once you realise that death is not around the corner then life becomes a journey. The previous focus on making tomorrow better, well that will change and you will become more connected with today and those around you now. And if you build well for today and be your most responsible self, then the outcomes, your tomorrows, they will look after themselves."

"An interesting notion, Mike," replies Jess. "It feels counter-intuitive. Although I like the idea of simply doing your best, learning from it and keep moving forwards – no judgment on whether it was good enough, simply accepting that it was best efforts."

"Glad you like it," say Mike. "The thing is, once you remove death, life is only a journey, you've just removed the destination. However..." he says, lowering his voice and pausing to look at each of us, "let us cut to the chase. Pop your drinks down and let me show you both something."

We follow Mike as he places his glass on a nearby table and heads off across the platform, weaving his way through the guests. We get to the far side where there are significantly less people around and the set of large double doors, made from the same obsidian material as the floor. Mike stops abruptly and turns on his heel to face us; we only just avoid bumping into him. With a grin on his face, Mike rubs his hands together.

"So, Jess."

"Yes?" she replies.

"What's missing?"

"I'm sorry. What do you mean?"

"Our little habitat here, what are we missing?"

"Oh that. Do you mean what's here, rather than what's missing?"

"Brilliant, you are on to us! Sean, do you know what she's referring to?"

"Err no, I'm not sure what either of you are talking about?"

"Gravity," replies Jess. "We have gravity, I was putting it down to some advanced tech."

Jess is right, of course, I'd missed it. But reality has become a stranger lately, so I'm not surprised. Where is Mike taking us?

"There is Jess, let me show you more, come on."

As Mike turns on his heel again and strides out towards the double doors, I see he's enjoying the theatrics of all this. Jess and I struggle to keep up as he quickly slips through. Side by side, we approach the doors and simultaneously push on a door each and walk through. We don't make it all the way.

We're confronted by a familiar view for me and most certainly a shock for Jess. It's a wind-swept beach that I've walked on before with Mike – it's our practice construct where l learnt to control the imagined world around me. The dunes go off into the distance as far as we can see, not a single building or tree, and the shoreline too stretches off way into the distance, with a slow curve taking it out to a spur some five miles or so to the horizon. Jess and I stand on top of the shoreline dune, each with the opposite arm outstretched, flat palm against the wind, where a second before there was a door. We both look behind us, only to see the dunes stretching off into the distance. Jess is visibly shocked, her brow furrowed, eyes squinting, trying to re-focus the scene back into reality.

"What?" she exclaims, but says no more. Lowering her arm, she rotates steadily, taking in her new surroundings. I lower my own arm and take back my balance from leaning into the door that isn't there. I'm unsure how to support her, or what to tell her. Where the hell is Mike?

I wipe my eyes against the wind; the last thing I need her to think is that I'm crying. Our clothing has changed... Jess just now realises this as she pats her bulky duffle coat and visually inspects herself, lifting her arms, scanning herself. She turns her attention to me, picking up on my lack of panic.

"Sean, what's going on? Where are we? How is this possible?" she asks, fear creeping into her voice, seeking help, seeking reality. Shaking her head, she looks again from one side to the other, behind her, twisting in the sand, back at me, eyes wide. "Sean!"

"It's alright. It's just VR, virtual reality. No cause for alarm, really, its K," I say, willing her to be alright and accept.

"What? But I didn't put on a headset or anything. What's the interface?"

"Well beyond our tech capabilities, you can eat and drink, pick stuff up. It's more reality than virtual."

She continues her self-inspection, waving and watching her hands in the air, which seems to be the standard response to being in this place. She sniffs, turns, looks to the distance, bends down and picks up some sand, lets it fall through her fingers. I relax as she looks up to me with a huge smile on her face.

"Amazing, this is amazing, this will change the world. And they have this here up on the habitat?"

"Ahh, the habitat.," I say. "Yes, well, that's part of it too."

"Part of what too?"

"The VR, we've been in it for some time."

Jess's smile slips and is replaced with confusion, that slowly morphs into annoyance or anger, I can't tell. She's waiting for me to follow up. I don't know what to say.

"And you didn't tell me this... for what reason?" she asks, raising her eyebrows and her voice.

"So you can have firsthand appreciation of what might be. Also, it was the way I was introduced to this, and it seemed to work."

"Where are we now? In the real world that is. Where am I?" demands Jess, a stern look forming and intensifying.

"You are at home, asleep in your bed. There is no one in the house with you. Everything is exactly as it would be if were you not connected to the VR. The connection is remote so you don't have any equipment attached to you or anything like that. All is well." I say this as passively as I can, hoping it will reassure her enough to not break the connection.

Jess continues to stare at me. She doesn't blink, her eyes penetrating my soul. All I can do is meet her gaze, I'm lost for any other response. I start to feel like I've violated her in some way, her privacy broken without consent. Is this wrong, if it's just a phone call?

"Why Sean?" she asks, her disappointment tangible.

All I can do is look at her, my lips pressed together, lost for how to make this better.

"TRUST Sean! Remember that? The conversation we had. Trust Sean, this is NOT trust. For fuck's sake!

"I'm sorry Jess, it seemed the best way."

"It's not. And how do you know so much about all this?"

"Because although this setting may not be real, well... the situation with Mike is. And yes, Mike is an... alien. Although that does sound negative now I say it out loud, it's important to say that he is a good guy and he's here to help." I look around; I know Mike will be listening in on all of this, even though he's not visibly with us.

"Mike, can you join us please?" I say.

"Of course," replies Mike from behind us. We spin around to face him. He stands a few feet away wearing the same heavy clothing as Jess and I. "How can I help?" he asks, eyebrows raised and head cocked, a warm smile to greet us.

"Are you able to update Jess on the real situation please, from your perspective, not ours."

"Yes, of course. Let's walk shall we?"

As we drop down the dune towards the sea the wind calms to a faint breeze, although the waves continue to crash and their spill shoots up the beach towards us. We walk the line of where the ocean meets the shore, the easy-going path of hardened sand, just beyond the reach of the waves.

"Jess," says Mike, "there is much to know about us and why we are here. And I can only apologise for the nature of our introduction, but I feel experience is a great teacher. Can you imagine if Sean had simply told you about me, us, this," he says, looking out to sea. "What might your response have been to that?"

"Yes..." she replies, reservedly.

"Well, let me give you some background," he says and starts to walk the shoreline with Jess at his side. "We are on your side; that is, the side of communitarianism, the side of equality of opportunity, the side of transparency, open and honest information. The side of being responsible for one another, for helping humanity prosper and move forward, not the side who would sit on the fringe and watch you drown, although... they are out there."

I follow the two of them, a couple of metres behind. Jess is super attentive, soaking it all up. "So why us, Sean and Me?" she asks.

"You are the researchers behind QE and QE is the key to your future. All that you see here, as you look around and listen and smell and feel, all this is QE tech. Interstellar travel is based on QE technology; humanity's evolution as a species is linked to QE."

Jess slows to a halt, bringing us all to a stop. "That's a hell of a lot of responsibility Mike."

He looks at Jess for a moment, unblinking, his head nodding ever so slightly, as if he knows her of old. "It is, Jess. But the thing right now is, when you wake up, will this all be a dream? Is it too much to take in? I suspect so. What do you think?"

"I can't be sure, but I feel I know what I have heard and seen, so in all likelihood I will accept it, I think."

"Understood. What might also help is the logic of your situation, as this will remain. That is, let me ask you a question. Do you believe in life after death?"

Jess thinks for a moment. "Logic says to me there is nothing, however emotionally I can't help but feel there has to be more than this, there has to be a purpose."

"Good points, so there might be something but not sure what?"

"Yes," she replies, nodding.

"K, but I take it you also believe in evolution?"

Jess nods again.

"And thus at one time you were a microscopic organism and, following that, an early aquatic form of life, progressing to amphibian, ape and so on?"

"Yes, that makes sense to me," replies Jess.

"And as a micro-organism was there something after death?"

"Hmm, unlikely."

"What about the aquatic life forms, did they have purpose of some sort or life after death?" asks Mike.

"Also unlikely. But," she says, pausing, "how come now we have a belief in an afterlife and yet it wasn't there in our earlier evolution, when did this start to happen? The comforting miracle of an afterlife."

Mike smiles and nods his agreement. "Exactly. Also, lets look to the future. If in say a million years mankind has ceased to exist, for whatever reason, what would happen to the various deities, would they still exist with no worshipers?"

"Interesting point," replies Jess, raising her eyebrows.

"Let me offer you another perspective," says Mike, now looking to us both. "Try to see your species as a collective who are evolving and not individuals. Imagine you are looking down on Earth and you can see the evolution process take place over many millennia. You would notice that with sentience comes complexity and with that lots of positives like art and philosophy. But you still have the need for safety, so when you understand that death is inevitable you devise philosophies to cope with this. You see where I'm going?"

Jess looks at him, twisting her head slightly with one eye half closed, her "not sure" stance. "I understand what you are saying but I'm not sure of the point."

"Well as you move forwards from here you realise with science you can negate death. You and Sean are on the cusp of extending life and this is a key step. This is an evolutionary milestone. All those that have come before you: great scientists, cave men and early life on earth from which you evolved; all of these people, animals, organisms; their purpose was to take the species as a whole to the next stage of evolution. And you are now at a significant point on that continued journey, a vulnerable point, hence my involvement to support you to be the best you can be. So you can take the next step in humanity's journey."

Mike looks to each of us for confirmation; we nod slightly, the enormity of Mike's words starting to hit home.

"Through QE there is no need for death, even total destruction of your physical form can be compensated for with a remote back-up. You need not die!" he says, eyes wide as he looks from Jess to me, pushing his words, his truth. "There is no need for an afterlife, you have evolved. For the wider Galactic Community, *you* have arrived – most do not. And I might add that this, too, is not the end of the journey; remember there is no end, especially not now. The journey goes on; there is only journey."

Mike looks to Jess, saying nothing, waiting patiently for her to reply.

"Fascinating," she says. "I see your logic. But I'm not sure it makes the whole thing more believable to be honest – perhaps the opposite."

Mike remains silent, tight-lipped, nodding an understanding.

"Where do we go from here?" Jess asks.

"My suggestion is back to reality, and then Sean can talk to you more and see how you feel."

"That makes sense," says Jess. "Can we meet again, you and I, in the *real* world?"

"Yes, Sean can arrange that," he says, looking to me. I nod.

"Very well. Shall we end our little get together?" suggests Mike.

As Jess's eyes meet mine I sense a deep uncertainty. She's lost, but coping.

"We can chat as soon as you wake up and call me Jess, I'll come straight over. K?" I say.

"Sure," she says, coping.

I wake in my bed and I feel the session with Jess went well. Not quite as intended what with Mike disappearing, but we seem to have got her to a point of understanding. I get dressed and grab something to eat whilst monitoring my phone for any incoming calls and then set off to Jess's.

I arrive and as I approach I see movement inside, which is worrying as she hasn't called me. Has she put it all down to a dream and dismissed it?

She answers the door looking visibly shaken, like some poor earthquake victim in a live news report. She's still in her night clothes and dressing gown and her hair's not been touched. She has worry lines on her forehead, her eyes are slits and she looks exhausted. She's been waiting. Unblinking, she looks into my eyes, saying nothing. No hello, not a word. She just stares.

"It was real," I say.

She continues to look at me in silence for what seems like an age. "Sorry," I say, unsure what I'm apologising for.

She doesn't reply, just turns and walks back into the house, leaving me to make my way in. I sense a deep sadness within her; I've not seen this Jess before. I shouldn't have brought her in, it's too much, Mike was right. I follow her to the kitchen, where she picks up a half-empty cup of coffee and takes a seat in her comfy chair in the corner, folding her legs into the seat. She continues to look at me, not offering me a drink or a seat.

"I can see you're upset Jess. I know it's a lot to take in. I couldn't believe it all at first either."

I wait for a response, but none comes. She just sits staring into her coffee cup.

"I guess my question at this stage is do you *believe*, or do *you* have questions. What can I tell you?"

"Sean, your question at this point is, 'how do you feel Jess, are you alright?', don't you think?" she replies sternly, eyes once again fixed on mine.

"Sorry, yes, of course, that's a given. How are you feeling, how are you coping with knowing all this?"

"Not good. You may have noticed. I can't decide if I feel violated because you and Mike have invaded my head without my consent or elated that we are on the cusp of something amazing with our work. Perhaps both, perhaps neither. Right now, right now..." she says, raising her voice and looking to the floor, "I don't know what to think."

Silence descends and I'm scared to say anything.

"Sorry, I'm still processing all this," she says eventually. "SHIT, and now I'm apologising to *you!*"

"I understand. I think for Mike it's just a form of communication, like talking to someone on your AIC. And I think that's how I've come to see it, you know like a phone call."

"Seriously Sean, a grasping phone call? The robot returns, eh? she says, leaning forwards in her chair and holding her head between her hands. "You're not the person to help me with this Sean and right now I need you to leave. I'll call you later and we can talk more on what there is to know... I know I'll have questions, but right now I need to digest what I've just been through and heard. I was on a space station twenty minutes ago, talking to a fucking alien about the future of our species and my involvement in that."

"Sorry Jess," I reply, wanting to give her more, to take the pain away.

"It's a lot to take in Sean!" she announces as she stands and marches to the door, opening it, showing me out.

My heart sinks, and my skin goes cold. I wasn't expecting this. I've made a mess of the whole situation, scared the shit out of Jess, and done who knows what damage to our relationship and the project. How could I not see this? She's right to be upset, I see it now. How can I have been so blind?

I leave, turning to Jess before I step through the doorway. "I am here for you, you know, no matter what. I know all this will change things, but I couldn't allow you to be involved unwittingly, that wouldn't have been fair either. Neither of us asked for this."

Jess's face relaxes a little and her stare becomes less intense. She takes a step closer to me, wraps her arms around me and lays her head on my shoulder, giving me a hug. I hug her right back, savouring the moment. I haven't lost her. We stand, in each other's arms, saying nothing. My world is at peace and something inside me changes: a positivity, something new.

"I don't blame *you*, Sean," she says as she pulls away.

I nod as her eyes meet mine.

"We can talk later," she adds, tilting her head to look up at me, seeking agreement. "It's just... well, it's all so much. Like a bad dream that'll go away, but it doesn't. I'm not sure how to deal with it... keep moving forwards I guess, just keep walking."

"I understand, I've been down the same road," I say, still savouring the intimacy and trying to suppress my grin. "Call me?"

"Yes, of course." She closes the door behind me.

Chapter Sixteen

Playing high stakes poker with Jess's emotions is like riding a roller coaster, a combination of fear and trepidation of what might be, mixed with the euphoria of living my best life: an intense hug with Jess. I'm elated and exhausted at the same time, and I'm still not sure of any of this, or where we're going.

I *think* bringing Jess in was the right thing – that was my intent – but certainty is a stranger these days. Which means? Which means... I chalk up the learning and keep moving forward, I *think*... I so miss certainty in my life.

My smile born of her hug is still with me when I arrive home. I feel a warmth within me, it radiates, making me more content and relaxed than I have been for a long time. I celebrate our hug with a cup of South American coffee and drop myself into my screen armchair. The sun beaming in through the window pulls my attention. It's different, enhanced; the colours of the room are more vibrant and the world seems brighter. Hypnotised by the dust motes caught in the sunlight I once again feel Jess's warm arms holding me. Like footprints in the sand, she's left the imprint of a hug wrapped around me. I close my eyes and I'm breathing in the sweet smell of her breath as she rests her head on my shoulder.

My phone rings, tearing me from my daydream. It's Mike.

"How you feeling?" he asks before I say anything.

"I'm good, thanks. It went... wellish, and Jess is, Jess is... well... I think. She's processing it all and working things through, sensemaking, you know. I'll check on her later, but the key thing is she seems to have accepted things, and I think that makes her part of the team?"

"Hmmm... You're probably right there, certainly we can't make her unknow now."

"I'd never thought of that, so you can't erase memory?"

"No, far too complex and our comms-link with you is only a computer that has a QE interface, similar to your own work."

"Our QE experiments you mean?"

"Yes," he replies, and right away something clicks in me, a feeling of... discomfort.

"Sounds interesting, can you tell me more?" I say, listening to my feelings, which have evolved an ability to spot things I miss.

"Well... not why I called. But we have a QE interface with you and for that to happen we have our version of you on the computer and this is what we talk too, it's a QE copy of you. Our computer can read what you say and do, and also say and do things to you. But memories scattered across your mind – thoughts, emotions – all of these are much more complex and not always accurately interpreted. It's why we interface with you when you're asleep. Much easier, much safer."

The hairs on the back of my neck twitch. "*Much safer*, Mike. What does that mean? Are their risks which you failed to mention before?"

"Its fine, it's just there's no real competition from your conscious mind when you're asleep. So we can talk to you and push situational constructs onto you, and you readily accept them. If I whisked you away into a strange environment right now, you would be lost and start to question your sanity. Your subconscious mind is a different thing, it's very accepting. Just like when you dream, you go on all kinds of crazy adventures and never question the possibility of it all."

"You could do that? You could change what I see and feel right now?"

"I could, but as I explained. I'm not about to, it's not good and—"

Does he have a permanent link with my mind? If he does, what does that mean – where does the control stop? Can they get me to do things against my will? Shit, can they get me to do things and simultaneously influence me, so I believe it's my will and I believe I'm in charge? Am I a puppet? A puppet blind to the strings? But... I'm seeing the strings now. They wouldn't allow *these* thoughts, would they? Do they know what I'm thinking now?

Mike are you listening to this...? I say in my head. No. Mike said they monitor and interact with talking, listening, and touch, and what I see. But Mike doesn't tell me everything.

"Mike."

"Yeah, what is it?"

"Tell me how the comms link works."

"I did for the most part. What do you need to know?" he replies.

"Is this link you've established with me – is that permanent and can you control my thinking and actions?"

"Well, our copy of you is linked to you of course, but we can turn it off and on, or if we wanted delete it entirely. But it's useful to maintain the link so it's up to date."

"Up to date with what?" I ask.

"With you – it's a copy of you on a QE substrate. Like a biography, it needs updating as you continue to live your life and who you are is continuously updated by your lived experiences. So for us to have an up-to-date version of you, we leave the link in place."

I try to stay calm as the horrifying truth creeps up on me, needing clarity of focus, needing to know. "Mike. Sorry if I'm being slow here, but... are you saying you have a copy of me, and Jess too, now. Is that right?"

"Yes, that's how the interface works. Its QE remember, there has to be a linked external aspect for us to interface with, just like your experiments. You communicate with the entangled cells to make them change; we communicate with an entangled version of you."

"But you have a full copy of me and Jess, not a link with a bunch of cells that form a hormone. This is not the same," I bark, the realisation drowning me.

My feelings serve me well, this can only mean one thing. The duplication of individuals for interstellar travel, how his people travel across the stars. This must be what he's done to allow him to communicate with me. He's created another me, a copy of me that constantly updates as I live my life. He talks to the copy version of me which is QE linked to me – it's the same as talking directly to me.

Shit! There are two Me's.

"MIKE," I yell. "For fuck's sake, you've never mentioned this. There are two version of me? Shit. Oh my God, Jess, she will hit the roof when she finds out. Do you do this with everyone you have QE comms with?"

"Yes, it's how the technology works, it's that or being on the phone, AIC or in person of course. This is how we influence, but only in a passive, positive way. Responsibility is our mantra, remember. Although subjects don't find this out, ordinarily. In fact, it would be good to get your thoughts on all this."

"Are you fucking shitting me, *good to get my thoughts*, seriously?" I yell down the phone, seething, my anger raw. "You don't see it do you? And making us sound like lab rats in an experiment is not helping either."

What the hell is Jess going to say about this? Shit, shit, shit.

"Yes, well, sorry... it's not my intention to upset you. I'm not sure what you're suggesting we do here?"

I hear Mike's plaintive tone – he really doesn't get what he's done. Why is such an advanced species not able to see this? Not able to resolve it? How can I be more informed than Mike? That can't be right?

"Let me ask you this, Mike. Can you build another me? As I understand it, you have me as computer code, right? Can this be made into another me?"

"Yep, you are held as code and yes we can, make another you."

I fucking knew it! Shit, this is not good. Jess will totally freak. I hold the phone to my chest and start pacing, looking around. I need a solution. What the fuck, how can he just tell me this now. The implications of there being multiple copies of a person, we even talked about this. Mike is out of control, we really are lab rats.

"Mike, how the..." I stop myself. Do I want to know the answer to the questions I am about to ask, really? Of course I do, there's a chance I could be wrong. "Mike, how did you get all the data in the first place, how have you got a map of me and now Jess?"

"We send in a probe whilst you sleep. It takes a few hours but it is totally non-invasive, physically," he says, confirming my worst fears.

Grasping fuck! Talk about invasion of privacy without consent? And that's just for starters. And... shit, they must know everything about me, fuck, where does that stop? No, not everything... memories and emotions are too complex he said, but not too complex they can't be recreated. They are our overseers. Making us toys of the Gods, like ancient Greece... This gets worse and worse. What am I going to tell

Jess? It was me who brought her in on this. No more hugs for me. Mike didn't say anything about probes and scans, what else is he not telling me? Christ, just the words "alien" and "probes" is enough to send anyone screaming to the hills.

"Non-invasive physically!" I yell back at Mike. "What the... what does that mean? So where is it invasive?" I'm bordering on losing it, but I need the information. I need to know.

"We establish QE links across your cells, like I said, similar to your own experiments but at a significantly more complex level. You and Jess have just invented the system that we're using."

"Not the same Mike, not the same," I reply.

"I'm sorry you feel this way Sean. But can we continue this discussion another time? I need to update you on other issues?"

"Delete Jess's file," I say.

"What? But you only just brought her in. We will lose our comms link with her. She will be on her own. And when I tell you what I have to tell you, you'll realise now is not the time to be on your own."

"Alright, what? What's the update?"

"The Ananta. We have reports, intelligence, that they know of our current situation, your QE experiment's success. And that we have made contact with you and now shared with you the true nature of our intervention. If the reports are accurate, *they* have made contact with you or are about to."

"WHAT?" I shout, disbelieving.

"I know, I know," he replies, but I feel no empathy here, just platitudes. "Has anyone new come into your life in recent months, since the night we bumped into each other in the bar?" he asks.

"Seriously? That was ages ago," I say, taking a moment to think. "YOU Mike, you're the new person in my life," I say, pointing and waving my finger at no one. "And Jess of course, but it can't be her.

But... hang on, what about the guy who put her in touch with me, we never got to the bottom of that one."

"Do you mean David Wright from Imperial?" asks Mike.

"Yes! How did you know?"

"That was me, sorry. Necessary nudge."

"Really, wow. Right," I say, the pieces falling into place. "Hang on, hang on," I say as a chill washes over me and his image appears in my mind. "What about the hipster guy in the bar, who also stopped at the crash after, and... I am sure it was him at my University, and... shit, he was spying on me and Jess in Cambridge when we first got together on the project."

"Older man, white hair and neat white moustache?" asks Mike.

"YES!" I scream, my eyes bulging from their sockets.

"Ananta. He's with the Ananta," Mike replies.

"Meaning?" I say, needing to know as the terror grips me and I feel myself sliding deeper and deeper into this shitshow I never signed up to.

"Meaning they know who you are and are likely tracking you, which means..."

"Means... what Mike? Means what?" I say, scared witless.

"Means... they likely have a QE copy of you too," replies Mike, his voice tapering off.

"What? FUCK!" I scream, burying my head in my hands. What has Mike got me into? This can't be happening. "They have me too?" Fuck. I take a breath, slowly, and a necessary calm descends. "Are you saying, the Ananta, the right-wing extremists, have a map of me as well?"

"It's a possibility, sorry Sean."

"But, then... hang on. That means they're fucking aliens too, right?"

"Yes, yes they are," replies Mike coolly.

The world spins. My thoughts burst into a million tiny pieces. I stare into space, my eyes locked on nothing. I'm no longer present in the room, my mind too occupied with chaos to process information from my surroundings. My reality is not my reality. What is my reality, now? What am I now? Who am I now, a pawn? Mixed up in some alien invasion set to destroy us? Fuck!

"This all started back in that bar. You were in that bar Mike. The hipster was in the bar. You saved me from that thug. What was going on? That night was full of craziness. Mike, what *aren't* you telling me?

"They must have been following me that night, I can't see how else they would know where you were," he replies.

"But he spoke to me, the hipster. He identified me in the crowd. Shit. What did he say? Something about *faith in the world,* and... *not being able to trust the inhabitants,* that was it. Seemed a really weird thing to say, but... now, now..." I say, my trust in Mike in its death throes. "Mike, was he talking about you?"

"Impossible to say, who knows what he was up to?" he replies, a suspiciously cool tone in his voice. "He was probably just trying to distract you from me or something."

"That makes no sense," I reply. "The distraction was me being beaten up by anvil face. Wait, Anvil face. *He* was the distraction, a totally unprovoked attack. Why would the hipster want to distract me from himself?" I stop talking as the penny drops. He wouldn't. But... someone else might. Who would not want me talking to the Ananta? There's only one other player on the board.

"Mike, did you set me up in the bar? Did you get the thug to beat me up?" I ask as coolly as I can. I don't want my suspicions to be true, and I can't second guess, this could change everything.

Mike replies with silence. I hear him breathing. I wait, forcing him to fill the void. "It was a last resort Sean," he replies in a small voice. "An emergency action. I am sorry. But it worked, it got you away from them, the Ananta. In the bigger picture, you know, the whole scheme of things, it was not that big of a deal, you know, a few bruises. But look now at where you are, what you and Jess have achieved. It's a small price."

I feel my head swell with outrage, a pressure cooker needing release or it will explode. Knowing the seriousness of my situation I channel it – raw anger will not help me or Jess. My fury is so unyielding it takes me to a place of calm calculating focus I did not know I had. How much has Mike lied to me, how much subterfuge is there? How much has he *not* told me, I cannot know. But I do know this thing is huge and right now, Jess and I are on our own.

"Mike... I thought I could trust you. I thought you were here to help. I thought you were my friend. I was wrong," I say, dispassionately. "Please don't call me back or make further contact with me," I add, and close the call.

Chapter Seventeen

"Hey it's you, back so soon... should I be worried?" says Jess as she opens her door, her face morphing from surprise to troubled.

"Can I come in?" I reply, forcing myself to keep solid eye contact, something I have struggled with all my life, but now glaring at her, pushing my thoughts towards her through my fixed stare, pursing my lips. She needs to understand and quickly.

"Sure," she replies, frowning, and stands aside to let me enter.

I walk through to the kitchen and take a seat at the table. As she sits opposite me I continue my silent stare, hoping she gets me. Knowing the Ananta can monitor everything I say and see, but not what I think, not the unspoken.

"K..." she says, drawing out the letter. "Something has changed, I think?"

I continue my stare and give a small, almost imperceptible, nod.

"Right..." she replies, cocking her head to one side, and then I see her face sag, the life of it taken by the realisation of what I mean. She knows something is amiss and I'm not talking for a reason.

I nod again, she replies with the same, then we both sit and watch each other for a few brief moments, the reality of our situation settling between us.

"Shall I put the kettle on?" says Jess, breaking the silence. Message received, I hope.

"Yes please," I reply, playing along. I think we are on the same page. She knows someone is watching or monitoring in some way, but she won't know the full implications, how deep the invasion is.

"What's new then?" she asks calmly, playing her part.

"I've had a fall out with Mike," I say, confused as to what I can say to let Jess in on what's happening whilst not scaring the shit out of her. Knowing the Ananta know pretty much everything that's gone on, so there's only my thoughts and plans I need to keep from them, they've seen and heard everything else. "Which isn't good, because, well he's... meant to be here to help. But..."

"Right, that's a problem," says Jess, her eyes widening, at odds with her calm words.

"Yes," I reply. I forage through my mind on what I can say. What can I tell her? What can't I tell her? "It's difficult, his ways are different to ours... It feels, well, wrong." Do I tell her about my QE copy? "You know, his approach."

"Really? In what way?" she replies, with a slight shrug, uncertain.

I try to work out how I tell her what's going on in some form of code or slang that the Ananta can't understand. But they know I know. Just keep it about me, see how she feels about this – if it's just me who's been copied. But if she finds out that Mike has a copy of me and this is how the QE comms construct works then she will figure out in no time that Mike also has a copy of her. And that will lead onto how and when did this happen – and a world of other painful questions.

"He doesn't tell you everything," I say. "We can't trust him. I'm not sure who we can trust."

"Yes," she replies with a nod. "I can see why you would say that and I agree, but at the moment, with all that we now know, surely, we've got to stay close to him – we can't not? Unless you know something I don't?"

And there it is. Now it's on me to lie by omission, and to Jess of all people. But I can't tell her about our duplicates or about the Ananta, not just because of the pain it will cause, but the Ananta will know I've told her and their interest in her will change. Right now, as she is, they probably see her as a bystander and that's how it needs to stay. Giving her more information involves her more and that can't improve things, in fact it can only make things worse.

And then it hits me like a slap in the face and I can feel my hands go numb. Is this what Mike is doing with *me*? Protecting me by *not* giving me information? Is this what's going on? He's doing what I have just decided to do for Jess, to protect her.

"Jess," I say standing from the table. "Really sorry, but I need to go. I can explain later, I know it must look weird. But I have to ask you to trust me right now. Can you do that? It's just, something's just occurred to me, and I think I have what I need and... Can I tell you later?

"Well, sure. If that's for the best, is it?" she asks, not sure if the game is over or not. "But, *you can* imagine how I feel right now Sean, *can't you*?" she continues, clearly sharing her distress, with me at least.

"I do, *really* I do. And it is for the best, it will all make sense, I just need to clear something up with Mike. I'll call you later. Sorry."

"Alright, then," she replies, and I see the anguish in her eyes. She's putting her trust in me. I have to honour that and live up to it.

I take a small step towards her as we get to the front door, as lovers do for a parting kiss or hug, but I stop myself. I feel we've moved beyond colleagues, but I'm not sure she does, and the Ananta need nothing more on Jess than they already have. Awkwardly I step back and give her a tight-lipped smile. "Thanks Jess, I'll be in touch soon, thanks," I say. I turn and am gone.

I have to get back to Mike. I don't need to trust him to work with him. Or do I? Do I just need to trust him blindly, just as Jess is doing with me? I grab a nearby MyCar and call him as soon as it sets off. "Mike I need to know for sure, do the Ananta have a QE copy of me?"

"Almost certainly. It's easily done and they seem to know where you are, so my assumption has to be yes."

"And Jess? Do they have a copy of her?"

"There's no reason for them to pursue that. The only reason we did it was at your insistence and that was only days ago."

"How did the Ananta get a copy of me, the same as you did?"

"That's the most likely, if they have a copy, of course."

"How else?" I ask. "What other ways are there?"

He doesn't answer, "Mike, did you get that? What other ways are there?" I repeat louder.

"I heard you," he replies quietly.

"And?"

Again silence. Why is he not answering? Because the Ananta could be listening. How else could the Ananta create a QE copy of me? A question he can't answer. It must be a way that Mike doesn't want them to know he knows. What does he need to keep from the Ananta? If the Ananta didn't create a copy of me, how else could they get it? If you don't write the programme, how else do you get a copy of it? A copy of it... Yes!

They have a copy of me, but not directly from me... from an existing copy of me. They've hacked an existing copy of me. The only copy that's out there is on Mike's computer system. And he doesn't want them to know he knows. This makes sense with everything Mike's *not* saying.

Another battering ram hits me in the face. Jess's QE copy is on Mike's system, and we've just been talking about Jess, and the Ananta are listening!

"Delete Jess's file, Mike," I say.

"This is not a good idea, Sean," he replies

"Delete it now." I repeat. "No more chat, no negotiation, delete it or I walk and this time for good. Got me?"

I hear Mike's breathing. After a few seconds he responds. "You will be leaving her isolated at a time when she may need us. This is not a good idea."

"Mike, we will be putting her back to how she was before I pushed you to bring her in, which *you* didn't even want. So taking her back a week and taking her off the radar of..." I stall for a moment. I'm giving the game away, got to be more careful. "When I see her next, I will explain the link used was temporary and if she wants to re-establish the link going forwards she can and it will be with her full knowledge and consent. As it should have been in the first place."

"I don't think this is a good idea, Sean."

"Delete her fucking file, Mike. Now!"

I sit silently, again listening to Mike's breathing. A few seconds later he replies, "K... It's done." Relief washes over me.

"Thanks Mike, I appreciate you trusting me. We can bring her back in, but under her own terms and when we know it's safe. It will be for the best," I say, feeling we've pulled her from the rails just before the train hits. A weight is lifted from my shoulders. I've made good on my mistake, but it's a minor victory quickly overshadowed by the impending doom of an all-seeing alien in my head.

"Be that as it may, Sean, but right now we have bigger problems. We're on new ground here remember, us letting you know the true nature of who we are and what we're doing. Well, now they know this and the Ananta may look to intervene, and I don't mean just via QE comms. I mean intervene to bring this whole thing to a halt."

"How? How would they bring things to a halt? Destroy our research, discredit us, *kill* us? You don't mean kill us, do you?"

"I don't know. But killing you won't be on the cards, otherwise you'd already be dead. Plus, you're too important now."

I look behind the MyCar as I head towards my house. There's no other traffic, just some pedestrians and cyclists. They could be waiting for me at home? Except they don't need to, they know exactly where I am and what I am doing and saying, at all times...

"Mike, you're scaring the shit out of me here. I don't think you're getting it, don't you see? They wouldn't be breaking their own rules, they would be re-setting things to how they were before you intervened. They would be putting things back to how they were without you and your group. Do you not see this?"

"No," he replies sternly. "You would likely have made the discovery with someone else or someone else would have read a publication of your work and added that to their own work to come up with a similar outcome. Perhaps some years from now, but that's a drop in the ocean in galactic timeframes. You are the key, they won't touch you."

"What about Jess?" I yell, panic again surging through my mind, blocking my thinking. "Now we've removed her from the system is she safe? You know, the success of our work is more her than it is me, right? She must be as important as me, surely?"

"She's safe. But going forwards we really don't know how things will play out. We're in new territory here. And, there's more, but not for now. You know why. Think man, think," he says.

Chillingly the implications of all this, what it means beyond what Mike is saying, start to make sense. More importantly what is Mike not saying? Because he can't, because the Ananta are listening. I can't rely on him anymore, if I ever could. He's compromised and out of his depth and I suspect he's making this up as he goes along. I have to save myself and Jess here. I need to get to the bottom of this, I need to work it all out. Sort it. But I have no idea how.

"—SEAN! Are you listening?" Mike yells down the phone.

"What? Yes, what?"

"I'm on my way to your house – looks like you are too. Now listen to me Sean, please try to calm down. This is really key, they can't read your mind, remember? I know you're pissed off, understandably, but think about this. Right now, it's best to keep quiet and listen – remember, they can hear everything you say. Understand this, it's important. I'll get there a little while after you arrive. For now, just hang up and I'll be with you in no time, we can talk then. Understood?"

"Alright," I reply, biting my lip, uncertainty boiling within me, I'm relying on Mike again. What choice do I have?

I sit back and collect myself. I know my thoughts are free of the Ananta, so I plan. I can't write it down, but I can think, prepare. I arrive home and stand at the window waiting for Mike, there's no hiding now. Before long I see him approaching and purse my lips together.

I get to the door as he does and let him in; meeting his steady stare we communicate, but not with words. Our every move's being watched, at least that's how I feel, and if my suspicions are correct then the spying is more invasive than that. I feel violated. I have little men in my skull taking notes on everything I say and do and I have no idea how long they've been there for. Shit, what have they witnessed?

Mike looks at me. "Take a seat" he says, coolly and calmly as he takes out his laptop. I do as he asks. I'm in his hands now; against my better judgement I have to trust him. I sit, watching, as he takes a seat facing me and opens up his laptop, clicks on a few keys, then looks to me with a brief, forced smile. He holds the palm of his hand up, high-fiving the air between us, then his hand drops as he says, "We're good, for now. I'm running interference of sorts, that is I'm pushing another situation on your QE self as well as the 'real' one we are in now. So it will be hard for anyone to make sense of what we do here and now. We have about thirty minutes."

"And then what?" I ask, sitting forward, elbows on knees, needing more. I can't see a way out of this. "And why only thirty minutes, why not always?"

"All encryptions can be broken eventually – enough processing power and time, that's all it takes. But... I have a plan. It will sever their connection with you."

"Great, sounds good, tell me more," I say, glimpsing a ray of hope.

"So, what we do is... We reconstitute your atomic structure, so that the QE links are severed. That is, we disconnect you from *every* QE version of you. The link will be cut between you and any other version or copy. The copies will still exist but will be disconnected from you so of little use to the Ananta; yesterday's news so to speak. We can't get them to delete your file but we can disconnect it from the real you. What do you think?"

My eyes go wide and my jaw drops. "Reconstitute my atomic structure, what the hell does that mean? Are you talking about lobotomising me or some other radical procedure? It sounds, well, like brain surgery. Not to be entered into lightly, you know."

"It's alright, you will be exactly the same person. We kind of take you apart and put you back together again, which I know sounds like a big deal, but we do it all the time. Seriously, it's quick and you don't even notice. We have done it with lots of others in the past; they never knew and never noticed. It's simple, for us at least, and very safe."

Lost, I look at Mike, feeling more alone than ever. How can I trust a man, no, how can I trust this *alien*, who has lost control of the situation and makes mistakes. And who now wants to disassemble me like a car and then put me back together, rebuild me. But... do I have a choice?

"Mike, with all that has gone on... how can I trust you? If I'm understanding this correctly, you and the Ananta have been in my head for months, able to monitor everything I see, say and do. I need to think about this. It's hard to get your head around and you keep introducing new... stuff, that makes it even more complicated."

"Understood, you've got about twenty minutes. Then you're back online. Sorry," he replies flatly.

Shit, I can't win. I can't trust Mike and I can't do nothing. Inaction gives me back to the Ananta, going along with Mike, who the hell knows where that leads? I need to solve this, for Jess and for me, I need to calm myself, allow my thinking to function. I stand again, looking out of the window, watching my breathing, slowing it. I only see one way.

"How did they get a copy of me anyway?" I ask, knowing Mike can tell me the truth now.

"We don't know, we really don't," replies Mike. "It could have been a hack on my system, or they could have gone in and copied you. But when we sever you from the system it will resolve all of that."

"And if we sever the connection then what's to stop them re-establishing a new one?"

"We will re-establish our connection with you and monitor through that. We will be doing a full system re-boot so if there are any grubs in the system they will be cleared out too. That way they will need to do a full scan to make the initial link and we can monitor and protect you from that."

"But then you are in my head all the time, can't I just get rid of both of you?"

"You could but then we wouldn't be able to monitor and protect you."

"What, like you have done so far? Shit job there, old friend..." I reply, laying on the sarcasm thick. "I have no doubt my life would be immeasurable better had we not met. No offence."

Mike shows no emotion, no response to my anger. He simply sits, watching, waiting for my decision.

I turn back to the view from my window. My small path leads to an empty street and an ancient dry-stone wall opposite with poplar trees peeking over the top. All is still and quiet, a serenity I miss. I'm a problem solver, this is what I do. There must be another way. There's always another way. The root issue for Mike is the advancement of the human race and for that he needs me. Or does he? He actually needs the science behind longevity to come from me, or someone like me, and for this to be done in a socially responsible way. For the good of all humanity, *responsibly*. That's his mantra.

"Mike, do you have any plans for me beyond the QE longevity science?"

"No, surely that's enough."

A smile erupts on my face. I see it. A third way. I have a plan, which if it stays in my head can't be known by anyone, except me, or someone like me. Someone so like me you couldn't tell us apart.

"Right, let's sever the connection with the Ananta," I say.

"Great, it really will be for the best. Pack an overnight bag and meet me in the car, you have just under ten minutes."

Within the allotted time I'm throwing my bag in the back of the car and dropping myself into the passenger seat breathing heavily. I turn to Mike, "now what?"

"You go to sleep. It will keep our activity and location hidden from the Ananta. When you wake the link will be severed and it will just be us again."

"Alright but how do I go to sleep, are you planning on drugging me?"

"No, we can do it via the established QE link. All very safe." He gives a supportive nod.

"K," I say, and immediately I notice a coldness come from my feet and grow to wrap my legs and waist, I look to Mike and start to shiver... he meets my gaze. I search for reassurance in his eyes; I think I find it. I'm transported back to the operating theatre five years ago, about to undergo surgery for my shoulder, putting all my trust in a man I don't know and know nothing about. I'm the patient, he the surgeon... the social system we live in tells me it's fine, so I go along and it all turns out well. I'm here again, about to be anaesthetised, relinquishing control of my body, but to an alien whose intentions I don't know. The social systems I know and trust don't function here, there is no norm, no rock I can cling to. I have to let go and the river will take me, to where, I can't know.

My whole self becomes cold and rigid; I'm scared, this could be a mistake. But the alternative is worse... I have to see this through. Then from nowhere a calming comes over me, a heaviness. I know I've decided, at least I think *I've* decided. Still looking to Mike I give a slight nod. He returns the same.

"Just try to relax," he says soothingly, and the darkness takes me.

Chapter Eighteen

I try to open my eyes, but it takes a few attempts with a cluster of lights shining down on me. My eyes slowly adapt and it's not so bright it hurts but it does blank out any peripheral vision. Shading my eyes, I roll onto my side and see an empty bed a few feet away. It's a narrow light brown, faux leather affair, wipe down or easy clean with a raised head section, like a medical couch. Which, as my hand brushes against the bed I'm in, I realise is identical to the one I'm laid on.

"Ah, you're back, excellent," says Mike from somewhere in the shadows, and the overhead lights dim to show I'm in a small, panelled room, with Mike sat at a bench attached to the far wall. He's sat at his laptop, smiling at me across the room.

Aside from that, the place is spartan. What looks like some kind of plastic formed panelling goes across the walls and the ceiling. "How did you get me into here?" I ask, propping myself up on my elbows.

"That would be Eric. Eric, introduce yourself," replies Mike, and a section of the ceiling clicks and one of the panels drops down. It's circular, about the size of a car wheel, and drops lower still so it separates from the ceiling all together and simply floats down to silently hover about six feet from the floor. I see no mechanism for it to stay afloat, it's like a drone without propellers. Then a small section on the side wall of the tyre-shaped object changes into a small screen and a cartoon set of eyes appear. "Very pleased to meet you, Dr Freeman," it says in a cheerful, almost childlike, voice. I don't reply, still unsure of what I'm looking at.

"Eric helps out with the heavy lifting," says Mike, walking the few feet towards Eric, "don't you old chap."

"If that's what's needed," replies Eric, rotating through ninety degrees so his eyes are almost level and looking at Mike.

"But Eric is not that good at fine motor control; he's strong but not taking up knitting anytime soon. Which is why we are where we are. Next steps now – and we do need some haste here as the Ananta will have you on their radar again now you are conscious. But they won't know where we are without visual clues.

"Got you, right," I say, as Eric rises up and conjoins with the ceiling again. "What now?"

"You change into this," says Mike, as a section of the wall near me clicks open and a drawer section extends out. On it is a neatly folded item of clothing. "This helps in the procedure, it will keep you stable and easy to map."

"Right," I reply, reminding myself of how important this is. No turning back.

"I will leave you to it to get changed, if you get into the one piece and then pop your clothes on the chair and yourself back on the couch. Alright?"

"Yep, fine," I reply and start to change. There's a voice in my head telling me this is dangerous, don't do it. But I can't listen to it, Jess needs me. I need to be free of the Ananta; if not, all is lost. Jess will be at their mercy, I can't allow that.

The one piece itself is made of a silky fabric which seems to stretch forever, which is just as well as when I pull it off the shelf it looks like it's for a small child. I pull it with either hand to the max of my reach and it stretches almost effortlessly. As I put it on it moulds to my body shape, with a thoughtful section on my groin which toughens into a discreet triangle-shaped box. When I touch my arm, it feels like the suit's not there, like I am touching my skin directly. I must look like one of the superhero comic characters from the last century, but without the super muscles.

Mike reappears just as I hop up on the couch, my legs dangling down the side.

"Ready?" he says as he approaches.

"I guess," is all I can say. I'm nervous as hell.

"Don't worry, you go back to sleep now and it's quick. We've done it hundreds of times, all is well. So just sit back on the couch as you were when you woke up and we'll get on. The Ananta are with us, remember."

I do as Mike says and try to relax. The suit seems to have made the couch super comfortable but my nerves are on edge.

"So, what will happen is the suit will tighten on you a little bit and you will fall asleep. It will happen quite quickly. You ready?"

"Yes. Let's do it." I reply, trying to galvanise my commitment through an assertive voice.

"Commencing," says Mike. He looks towards his laptop just as the suit stiffens, and I realise I can't move my arms.

A moment later I open my eyes to the same lighting cluster as before. "Are we good?" I ask propping myself up on one elbow and shielding my eyes to see Mike still on his laptop. Except he's moved or... the room's moved, or no... I've moved. I'm in the other bed looking at

Mike from a different angle. "Are we done?" I ask. "That was really quick."

"Nearly," says Mike, standing from his laptop and walking over to me. "Just a quick check. And all is good, excellent. Can you lay back down, and we can finish the process?"

I do as instructed and feel the suit constrict again.

Seconds later I open my eyes to a view of the street I live on, which completely throws me. I quickly look around. I'm back in Mike's car, with Mike, parked outside my house. Exactly where we began. "What the... how? That was too quick," I say to Mike, struggling to accept the speed of the change. "Is everything K? Did it work? Is this real?"

"Yes, everything went as planned. You're all good, we are where you think we are. The link with the Ananta is severed, job done. How are you feeling?" he asks, his eyebrows raised with an expectant smile. He's back to his old self, the confident, in-control Mike. The worried, losing-his-grip Mike is gone.

"Well, like nothing's happened." I lift my arms, press my hands against my chest and thighs, checking for something, but not sure what. "I'm fine, it's like... How long? How long did it take?"

Mike nods. "It's been just over twenty hours but will feel much quicker to you. As I said, it's safe and all went as planned."

"Right," I say, gathering myself. Am I all good? How do I check that? Would I know? "If it was so easy, why didn't we do it before?"

"Well, there are ethical issues and it's getting harder to predict what the Ananta are intending. We've crossed the Rubicon here. We needed to, but it's not something we do lightly and not something we've done before. But then people have never known we exist, so it's never been needed."

"Are you sure it worked? Is there a way to test it?" I ask.

"No, as what we've done is take something away, your connection with the Ananta's QE copy of you. Which of course still exists at their end, but is now redundant. We've already established a new QE link with the new you, so you're still monitored by us. However, we realise how much you value your privacy, so the link will be there but not monitored directly. It will respond to you if you need help and we will let you know if we need to communicate with you, like making a phone or AIC call. We'll call you."

"Thanks, that sounds better, I think. Why did you sever your connection with me too? We only needed to lose the Ananta?"

"True, but there's no choice on that one. It's all or nothing."

"K...?" I turn to Mike, raising my eyebrows, expecting more. He's holding back, "because...?" I say.

"We terminate the existing link and set up a new one with new matter so that the existing QE links are still in place but with the old matter, which is repurposed so of no use to anyone."

I get a sinking feeling. The "*new me*"; the "*new matter*".

"The old matter, *Mike*," I say, closing my eyes, head in hands, preparing myself before tackling him. "That was me, wasn't it? And the new matter is the 'new me', am I right?" I turn to face Mike, keeping my eyes fixed firmly on his.

"That's right," he says.

My mind explodes.

"YOU KILLED ME!" I scream, my eyes lasering in to his, my hands gripping into the sides of my seat. I hold myself there, doing my best not to lose it and just lay into Mike, fists and all. My need to know overriding my need for revenge.

"YOU..." I bark, pointing. "How could you not tell me? Mike, how?" I look around, for what I don't know. I want to throw something at him, punch him. I put my hands over my face and scream through my fingers. "I should never have trusted you, never. FUCK!" I shout, smashing my fist into the dashboard.

"You're you. And you're free of the Ananta, all is well," he tells me, eyebrows raised with a forced grin on his face. He's actually seeing this as a positive. "Surely you knew from our conversations, I've kept nothing from you."

"WHAT? NO!" I yell, the blood draining from my head, needing this not to be true, but knowing it is. "No grasping way. How could I have known. I'm not me, am I? I am a copy of me. You have copied me and then deleted, or should I say *killed*, the original me. Haven't you? Just fucking say it."

"It's not that simple," he replies defensively.

Then I realise why I was on the other couch, why there were two couches. The *real* me was on the other coach, and shit... "Mike, was the other me, the original me, on... the other couch, the one I started off on?"

"Well, yes, you know you were."

"And this me," I say, padding my chest with both hands, "this me was then on the other couch... at the same time?"

"For a short time, yes," he says, with an echo of solemnity. And I start to think he gets it, what he's putting me through, right now.

"So for a short time... let me be clear, for a short time there were two me's? That is what you are saying, isn't it?"

"Briefly... it's part of the process," he replies, like he's talking me through how to cook a meal. "We don't dispose of the original until we know the duplicate is fully functional, for obvious reasons."

"Disposed of the original! You mean... killed me. You really have FUCKING KILLED ME, you grasping fucker," I shriek. Only now does the full force of realisation hit me, a realisation of so many nightmare issues I can't hope to resolve or manage now, and maybe never.

We're not built for this, humans; this is not who we are, this is not how we work. We live, we die, the end.

"Well, hang on," says Mike. "The who that is you – the thoughts and feelings you have and what you do – none of that has changed. You are still the same person – same thoughts, ideas, values – you're just as much you as you've ever been. What did you think we were going to do?"

Shit. Is he right, did I know? What was I expecting? Was this predictable and I'm blinding myself from the obvious? Right now I can't think of another way he could do what he's done, so...

"Mike, the matter that makes up my body is not what it was last week, is it?"

"No, but then it wouldn't be anyway. Your body is in constant renewal, that's how it works. Do you really think you have the same bone tissue you had when you were a child? We simply did the same thing in one go rather than over a period of years. The essence that is you is still you."

Shit! Am I complicit? Kidding myself? Mike could definitely have been more explicit, clearer on what we were doing, what I was letting myself in for. But...

Wordlessly, I storm out of the car and, leaving the door open, head back to my house. Fuck Mike. I march up the path and into the house, I walk into my lounge and stand and stare out of the window to where Mike's parked. How can I have been so naïve? I know he talks in riddles and half truths. Idiot!

I walk to the hall and nervously look in the mirror. I look like me, I feel like me and – I think – I think like me. Then I would, wouldn't I? How would I know if I didn't? Shit, has Mike made any adjustments? And the real me, now dead, did he have something about him that is now lost and the new me is a lesser version? How can I ever know?

I'm a new me, but I can't accept that, how can I, how could anyone? If you build a house exactly the same as an existing one, it's not the same house. This is not who we are. Shit, this stuff is going to drive me mad. Will Jess be able to tell?

FUCK, Jess! I've been gone for a day and just left her, after a bizarre cloak and dagger conversation. Shit, shit, shit... I pull my phone from my pocket, two missed calls from Jess and a voice mail:

"Sean where the hell are you? I know I asked you to leave and give me some space but I did say I would call you later and you're not picking up and then you turn up again acting weird like we're being watched, are we being watched? Are we under surveillance Sean? You need to call me, right away Sean. And when I think about what we've just been through I'm really worried something has happened to you. Well, if you get this I'm on my way to yours, just in case your phone is out or something. See you in a while. Ohh, if you pick this up and I haven't caught you then call me. Straight away, K?"

I'm not the only one facing a new reality today. I call Jess, she picks up straight away.

"Its me sor—"

"SEAN! Where the hell have you been? I've been worried sick. You can't just introduce me to an alien and then leave me to ponder the nature of reality, then turn up and say nothing about it and act all weird like my house is bugged. It's not, is it? I'm starting to doubt the whole thing ever happened or even that you came round to confirm it did happen and that it wasn't real, but the situation is real. It is, isn't it? Still? Arggh, you know what I mean."

To hear her panic like this is new and it hits me hard. My eyes start to well with tears, what have I done?

"Yes," I say, croaking. I swallow, what to say? "It's all true. What you remember is all true, all accurate, a hundred percent. Don't doubt your sanity, I know too well how easy it is to fall into that one. The house is not bugged; there was something but it's sorted. I'm so sorry I haven't been in touch sooner, something came up, an emergency. Are you home, shall I come over, it might be best?"

"Yes, do. We need to talk," she replies, her voice small, even timid, not the Jess I know.

I hang up and I'm about to head out the door. Do I need a shower? I need to eat, I'm starving. Jesus, has this body ever eaten anything before? Is that why I'm so hungry? No time to ponder – Jess needs me, I have to take Mike at his word and accept things. Except I can't do that, how could anyone? Every time I trust Mike I end up further down the rabbit hole. I grab a quick snack and drink. All seems well and as I head out of the house, I notice Mike's gone – not that I care.

Jess opens the door before I reach it. So much has happened in the last forty-eight hours I suddenly feel unsure and I stand looking at her in the doorway. I don't know where *we* are at, but I'm sure we're still friends. She looks lost. Her hair's a mess, she's dressed in an oversized sweatshirt and jogging pants, and her eyes are red and puffy. I step inside and give her a hug. She needs me and I'm lost myself.

"How are you feeling?" I ask, pulling away.

"To be honest... I don't think I have the words to describe it. There are too many levels of change and they're very conflicted. It's great to think we're not alone in the galaxy. But people wandering around inside my head, that's just too much. As for where the project's going, well..." She pauses and looks to me. I see a tear starting to form. "How did you cope with all this Sean?" she asks, her voice quivering.

I look at her, desperately wanting to wind back the clock and take this all back. This is not how I imagined things would go. This assertive, capable woman who I have fallen for is in pieces. Because of me.

"I don't think I have," I say. "The difference is that Mike introduced me to things in stages, so it's perhaps easier to swallow. I'm not sure. I feel in a state of constant shock. It's brutal, but almost becoming normal now. Christ, what does that say about me?"

"What now?" she asks.

"We talk and I answer your questions and fill you in on the full picture. How does that sound?"

We sit across the ancient farmhouse table in Jess's kitchen, each nursing a large coffee in Jess's oversized mugs. I talk her through my experiences and what I've learned so far in this escapade. I don't mention that Mike has killed me and that we have an enemy at the gate. One step at a time. The shared experience we have had, I know, has brought me closer to Jess, at least that's how I feel. I desperately want her to feel the same way too. But I suspect we've gone too far down another road and missed that turning, perhaps avoiding rejection, failure of the project, who knows?

Jess starts to ask me questions. I don't hear her, I'm adrift looking at her eyes, her face, her beauty, her. We've come so far, so quickly, but I am who I am, I can't just ignore how I feel. Amidst this chaos I found the time to fall for her.

"Sean!?"

"What, yes, sorry. Sorry, can you say that again?"

"Do we continue our work, the project? Surely that's what this is all about?"

"I guess so."

"And I'm thinking Mike is some sort of partner in all this now. So, setting up a meeting with him ASAP, do you think?"

Jess is back on track and focusing on the road ahead.

"Yes, meeting up with Mike is a good idea. We do need to be careful with him though, at the end of the day we know very little about him and his motives. Like I said before, we can't trust him."

"K, you have a point. Like you said, he's not human, he's bound to be different in ways we don't recognise."

"Yeah, I agree. It is all pretty fantastical and getting my head back into reality now and again I think is helping me cope. I think…" I trail off, getting up to rinse my cup and stare out of the window. I need to tell her everything. She will find out; it's better to come from me in a calm place.

Jess sits quietly, my back is to her but I feel her watching me. "There's more isn't there?" she says.

I turn to face her. I nod, frowning, lips tight.

As I do my phone rings, it's Mike. Fuck Mike. I hang up and sit down opposite Jess, taking her hands in mine across the table. She looks at me, head cocked slightly, inquisitive, unsure. My hands are shacking ever so slightly.

"What?" she asks as her brow furrows, and I see the concern in her face.

"SEAN, we need to talk now!" barks Mike in my head, and I leap backwards, releasing Jess's hands and knocking over my chair.

My head flicks left and right as I stand, poised for action and feeling my ears for an AIC that's not there. "Mike?" I call out.

"Sean, what's going on? Are you OK?" asks Jess, clearly concerned.

Mike's in my head, the QE connection. What the fuck!

Jess continues to stare at me as she gets up and walks towards me. "Sean?".

"Not now Mike, not now," I say still staring at Jess. She looks at me, eyes narrowing in confusion.

"What's going on, are you alright Sean?" she asks. "Have you got an AIC? I thought you were against them. But I don't see one," she says, scanning either side of my head. "Unless... it's an SI-AIC? I can't believe you would go for a surgical AIC?"

Before I can answer Jess, Mike's voice cuts into my thinking again, urgent, pointed. "You need to leave Jess's house *now* Sean, both of you. The Ananta are en route to you right now. You need to leave NOW."

"Shit! What? What, do you mean? What does that mean? What do they want? Why?" I yell, and rush to the window, scanning the garden and street beyond.

"Sean?" calls Jess.

"Sorry, Jess, just a minute. I'm talking to Mike."

"What? ... ahh, right. What is it? Is everything alright?" she asks, and I hear the rising panic in her voice.

Mike continues with a petrifying urgency. "Sean, you need to focus. Listen carefully, you both need to leave right now and head for a destination I've just put in your phone, the route will take you through the middle of Cambridge and without their QE link in place you should be able to lose them. We will pick you up at the destination. Understood?"

"Seriously?" I reply, needing this not to be my reality.

"Yes, right now. GO!"

"K, understood. We're on our way," I say and turn to Jess.

"We need to leave now, and quickly. Coat and shoes and let's go, NOW," I say, injecting urgency whilst trying my best to avoid panic in my voice.

"What's going on Sean? I don't like this, where do we need to go in such a hurry?"

"I can explain on the way, but we really do need to leave, now. Please just trust me, I'll explain once we are on our way. I promise."

"K, K," replies Jess, heading towards the hallway and grabbing her shoes.

We're heading towards central Cambridge in less than two minutes. The sat nav on my phone is set up for a thirty-minute walk through Cambridge to some park. No one's on Jess's street, just an old lady with a dog. We set off walking, at a pace. I can't decide if we need to run or not... there's no one around, we might be running towards them! Fast walk and follow the phone, I tell myself, follow the phone. I turn to Jess, she stares at me, eyebrows raised, teeth clenched, needing answers. "So?" she says, a little out of breath.

We take the corner at the bottom of her street, now heading down a much bigger main road with lots of traffic and more people. "That was Mike on the phone, who I hung up on. He then contacted me via QE, which is why I was talking to myself, but not, you know what I mean. Anyway, the thing is... the bit that I was not telling you, sorry... that I had not yet got to telling you yet, was..."

How the hell do I make this sound acceptable and not shit arse scarry?

"Sean, just tell me. I'm a big girl," urges Jess.

"K, there are some people who don't want us to progress our research. At least that's how I understand it. I think, they think, that Mike has helped us and as a result we now have a scientific breakthrough we shouldn't have." I turn to Jess as we fast walk down the street side by side, trying to get a feel on how she's taking this. "They are the same... species, if that's the right word, as Mike. At least I think they are, they're certainly not humans."

I'm talking fast, and we're walking fast as we round the next corner to enter a busy shopping area. It's a cobbled market square with lots of canvas-covered market stalls with local produce for sale. It's busy, lots of shoppers milling about amongst the stalls and the surrounding shops. Intuitively, we both slow to the pace of those around us and look around. I don't see anything unusual, but then, would I? We're blind, we have no idea who or what we're looking for or running from.

"And what? Sean, you're scaring me. Are we running from aliens here? Are aliens on their way to *my* house? They know where I live?" Jess stops and two steps later so do I. I look back, holding out my hand, as if encouraging a petulant child.

"Come on Jess, we need to move. You're right, they are on our trail. Mike is going to pick us up, here," I say, holding up my phone with the sat nav showing. We stand facing each other for a moment, people moving about us in their safe world. I can't drag her.

"Please Jess," I say. "Mike is picking us up there, he will be able to fill us in, come on!"

"OK. But call him now. He clearly knows what's going on. Get an update. Do we need to be running? Who is following us, what should we be looking out for?"

"Good point, although I also need to see the sat nav to keep us moving."

"Use your QE link, like you did at my house," she says, frustrated at my lack of insight.

"Oh yeah. But he hasn't told me how to yet. It's kind of new... Mike, are you there?" I say addressing the busy high street.

"Yes Sean, you're making good progress. They seem to be able to track you, not sure how, but they've bypassed Jess's house and are five minutes behind you. They're also on foot in the pedestrianised areas. I'm guessing they intercepted my message to your phone and know your route. So, change of plan."

As Mike talks I give a thumbs up to Jess. "Mike," I say, pointing to my ear. I pass her the phone, whispering, "you do the nav". She takes the phone and we're off again.

"Ask Jess if she knows where the University punting rental is near Peterhouse Library," says Mike.

I ask; she nods. "You mean the tours run by the students?" she asks.

I hear her, so Mike hears her. "Yes great" he replies, and I nod to Jess. "Head there, get a punt and cross the river. Dump the boat and then head to Granta Moorings. From there go to the Gonville and Caius cricket ground. The detour and punt across the river will slow them down." As Mike says this I relay it directly to Jess, simultaneously listening and repeating so she gets the full message. She nods to me as I mention the various landmarks.

"Let's go" I say, and Jess is off at a haring pace, me following.

In under ten minutes we're next to the river approaching the punt rental. I'm breathing hard and sweating. Our pace has been part jog, part Olympic walking. I just hope we're putting distance between ourselves and whoever's following us.

"Sean, I see where you are," announces Mike in my head. "Just get on a punt as quickly as you can, get across the river and run. They're moving towards you now."

I share this with Jess and we both realise neither of us have any credit cards with us and I've never set up my phone or watch for payment.

"Hang on," says Jess. "I've got an idea. Just keep close and when I get in a boat you follow me, K?"

"Yeah, alright," I reply.

We approach the busy launch area and see a couple alighting their boat. Jess quickly goes to help them.

"Have you enjoyed yourselves?" she asks politely, taking the pole and using it to hold the boat in.

"Yes thanks," they say, "thanks very much, great fun."

With this they walk away and Jess turns to me, giving me a wink and a sideways nod towards the boat.

"Get in," she says through clamped teeth.

I jump aboard and fall into the seat as she immediately pushes away from the bank. It takes her three stabs on the bottom and we are across. I leap out of the boat as does Jess. We abandon it and immediately hear a shout from the other bank.

"WRONG SIDE, you can't leave it there." We both turn to the person shouting, assumedly staff at the punting shed. I'm about to ignore him and run but my eyes are drawn to the three men just arriving next to him.

My body goes cold as I recognise one of them. He's staring straight at me across the water. The hipster, the Ananta. I'm frozen, as is he. Time stops for us. I would hear a shout from here, but he says nothing. I realise his colleagues are talking with the punting staff and I feel someone pulling at my arm.

"Come on Sean, COME ON!" Jess shouts at me, pulling me away from my unspoken conversation with the hipster. I turn to her, blink, and the noise of the world comes alive again.

"That's them," I yell, "RUN!"

Jess immediately hits a sprint and I'm struggling to keep up. As we round a corner, I take a last look to the river and can't see anyone crossing. We head through urban areas and Jess slows to a jog, giving me a chance to catch up. She stops and leans on a wall, head down, panting.

"Did we... lose them?" she asks.

"For now, but we need to keep going," I reply, breathing hard.

"K, but let's walk for a minute, just whilst... whilst I get my breath back."

"Sure, I'm knackered," I say.

"Mike are you there, at the meeting point?" I ask, as we walk up the street.

"Nearly, I see where you are. We should arrive at the same time. They've crossed the river, you need to run Sean," he says, the urgency clear in his voice. "It's only a few minutes away."

I relay this to Jess, and we're running again, not a full sprint. But hopefully fast enough.

"Mike says... we're nearly there," I call out to Jess, between breaths, as we run side by side.

"Yes, just around the corner," she replies, pointing.

Seconds later we arrive at the sports ground. Ignoring the "Private Grounds Members Only" sign we head through the gravel car park, scanning left and right for Mike. Nothing. A van and a car, both empty, and neither are Mike's Jag. Beyond this there is an extensive park area, mostly dry grassed, with the occasional ancient oak tree – and no sign of Mike.

"Mike, where are you?" I call.

"Seconds away. Head towards the cricket square. We're flying in."

As Mike finishes his sentence, Jess pulls at my sleeve. "Well?" she asks.

I don't respond; instead I look to the sky. I can just make out the sound of an omnithopter above the white noise of suburbia. "Hang on, hang on," I say, scanning the horizon. "He's there," I call out, pointing towards the inbound craft.

"Wow, wasn't expecting that," replies Jess. She looks to me, her mouth still open, gobsmacked, and for a brief instant I'm transported from the chaos.

We keep moving towards the open ground, scanning for our pursuers as we go. We're not out of the woods yet. I walk backwards across the baked dirt of what once were playing fields, still scanning for our pursuers, steadily moving towards an extensive treeless area which I see has a meticulously manicured green cricket square at its centre.

The noise of the omnithopter grows, quickly becoming deafening as it descends, set to land in the middle of the grass square. The down draft pulls at our clothes and wave after wave of loose dirt is picked up and thrown at us. We squat, leaning into it like a sea cliff gale, shielding our faces as best we can. The thopter lands and awkwardly we run towards it, hands still shielding our faces, stooped like a pair of hunchbacks.

I look up to see where we're going and realise it's a police omnithopter. The colours give it away and the four rotors and main body are bigger than the commercial thopters you see in films. It might not be for us. Or... it's the least inconspicuous approach. I feel a huge sense of relief as the rear door opens and Mike appears. He waves us over. I take a look back and see no one. We jog, hunched, to the open door and climb in. With the engine noise it's impossible to talk. Mike mimes the putting on of seat belts as we sit. Belts on, Mike speaks into his headphone set and the engines starts to scream.

I look to Jess sat next to me and take her hand. She smiles and leans across. Putting her hand around my head she pulls me in close and kisses my cheek. My heart misses a beat and a smile erupts on my face. As she pulls away, I see the colour of her eyes and every wrinkle as she smiles back at me and I feel it there and then. I love her; I feel it, in a way I don't understand. And her eyes tell me, amidst the noise and the chaos, that she cares deeply for me too.

"We're away," Mike says in my head and the thopter tilts forwards as we take off.

'We made it,' I mouth to Jess, giving her a thumbs up.

As the thopter lifts, from nowhere, there's an ear-piercing bang and my head is thrust violently to the side and smashes into the window. I see bright lights for a moment but manage to lift my head to look up again. Shuddering from the pain and holding the side of my head, my vision returns, but only as shadows. Then an excruciating screeching drills into my ears and the whole thopter is thrown backwards.

I'm thrown forward, pushed brutally against my seat belt webbing, which feels like it will cut into me at any moment. I look down to the seatbelt release button and try to press it, but I miss. I grab for it again, but things are not where they seem to be. I can't focus; my hands are not going where I want them to.

The thopter starts to shake violently. The noise of alarms and the screeching of metal against metal is ear-splitting.

I turn to Jess, trying to focus my vision on her as my body is thrown about like a rag doll. She's looking to me, eyes wide with panic. I see her mouth shouting my name as she reaches out a hand towards me.

Then a jerk on my arm near dislocates it as the horizon flips and I feel my shoulders crushing into the seat belt and my knees fall towards my face. My left eye is too blurred to see anything, and I feel blood rushing to my head. The engine continues its deafening screech and then as quickly as it began it stops, with the alarms quietening one after another, leaving a buzzing tinnitus of deafened silence in my ears.

Dangling upside down in my seatbelt, pain screaming at me from across my body, I twist myself sideways to look at Jess. Still in her seatbelt, she's semi-conscious, moving her head a little, and then I see it. A rapidly growing red stain on her stomach. Looking at her face, I see the blood running from her stomach to her neck, parting across her chin, running into her ears and dripping from the top of her head. Lots of blood, too much blood!

"JESS!" I scream. "JESS!" I do my best to reach across whilst still upside down, fighting against my seat belt to get to her. "Shit, we've got to get you out. FUCK! JESS, CAN YOU HEAR ME?"

She looks to me, less dazed now, head covered in blood. She mouths something but I can't make it out. She tries again.

"Sorry... sorry Sean" she whispers, with much effort, opening and closing her eyes, fading in and out of consciousness. "Sorry, so sorry."

Tears blur what's left of my vision. I reach across, pulling against my seat belt at it holds me back. I stretch out to put my hand on her stomach to hold back the blood, twist her head to face me,

"JESS STAY WITH ME, I'M GOING TO GET YOU OUT," I yell.

I can't stop the bleeding. I can't even make out where it's coming from. I scramble for my seat belt release button. I have to get free to pull her out. As I claw at my seat belt again, I feel her grab at my frantic hands.

"Sean" she says, struggling to speak, blood gurgling from her mouth, her hand reaching out to me. "I love you." And I see it in her eyes, a deep understanding. My soul mate, but only for a second as her focus shifts to nowhere and her whole body sags. She's let go, let go of life.

I see it and my world collapses.

Chapter Nineteen

"Sean... Sean..." This brings me from somewhere, and I blink myself into the here and now to find Mike sat next to me, whispering my name. "How are you feeling?" he asks.

I push myself up on my elbows. I'm back on one of the brown couches at Mike's installation, although this time there's lots of machines with screens.

"Are we—" is as far as I get before the door of my memory slams open and everything inside me comes to a halt. I see Jess hanging upside down, like a rag doll, her lifeless limbs dangling towards the floor, pushed into her seat belt, blood streaming across her chin, flowing from the top of her head. The waves of the memory slam into me: omnithopter crash, chaos, pain, deafening screeching of metal, upside down, blinded in one eye... helplessly scrambling to help Jess as she...

"NO! Mike, Mike!" I yell, pleadingly, my knuckles turning white as I grab either side of the couch. Sat bolt upright I look to him for something. He meets my stare: grim, serious, empty.

"Tell me it was a dream. Mike, the omnithopter crashing. Jess..." I can't say the word, I can't. If I do it might be true. Unblinking, I stare at Mike. Tears well in my eyes and run down my cheeks.

"I'm so sorry Sean," he replies, slowly shaking his head. "There was nothing we could do. They came from nowhere, we had no idea there were two teams."

"But Jess, is she. Is she, is— gone?" I ask, my final word just audible, knowing there's still a chance. There is – she could have gone into shock and then been rescued. There is a chance. There has to be.

"She died at the scene Sean, nothing we could do. I'm so sorry."

I hear Mike's words, but they don't work. There's still a chance, I know it. I can't have lost her, I've only just found her. That can't be right, the universe wouldn't allow that, there's no purpose in that, no need. It's just wrong, cruel.

I fall back on the couch and stare at the ceiling. My senses are numb to the world and I feel a deep hollowness within my chest, my life purpose ripped from me. I start to sob, my breath coming in fits and starts. My stomach curls in on itself, pulls me into a ball and that's how I stay, with the sobs sending juddering waves through my body. Mike continues talking, but I hear nothing. Eventually he walks away, leaving me, mute, inconsolable, separate from the world around me. The world that took Jess, a world without Jess.

I see her, laughing at me on our punting team builder, getting too drunk at Carluccio's, absorbed in her work in the lab. And... her telling me she *loved* me, covered in blood. We could have been...

I sit up abruptly. Mike notices and turns to me. "Mike, her QE copy. You had her QE copy. We can recover that, and you can create a new Jess!" I look to Mike, hope in my eyes. "Yes," I say, nodding, willing him to agree.

His expression remains the same.

"Sorry Sean, we deleted it, you know we did. It can't be recovered; when we delete something, we don't leave a chance of recovery, otherwise it's not really deleted."

"Wait, what? No, that can't..."

"I'm sorry Sean"

"FUCK! fuck, grasping, fuck," my head is in my hands. "No!" What have I done? I could have saved her, she could be here now with us. Safe. Recovered. With me. Together. She's dead because I second-guessed her wanting privacy – how do I know what she wants? I knew things were getting risky... I should have kept a copy because of that. Mike should have told me how dangerous things could get.

Through my tears, I turn to face Mike. "MIKE, why didn't you tell us things were so dangerous?" I roar, the accusation clear. "We could have kept the back-up for Jess. I could have told her about the option, she could have made her own choice. If she knew things were so dangerous, she would have chosen to have a backup. Why are you not protecting us Mike? Why have you let her die?"

Mike's only response is a soulful look as he purses his lips.

"MIKE!"

"Sean, I'm so sorry. I really am. There was nothing we could do, we never foresaw this. No one has ever resorted to anything physical before. I don't know why they did. It was wrong, unpredictable."

"That's not enough Mike, not nearly," I yell. "It's your fault, you're responsible for her death." My final word *death* echoes louder and louder in my mind. I need it to register, to sink in, for him to feel, something. I swing my legs over the side of the bed and point at him, "You can't be trusted." I walk towards him, finger waving. "You're reckless with our lives and you don't see it, do you?"

He raises his hands in surrender. "I really am sorry Sean, I know how much she meant to you," he replies, with the same passive voice.

"No you fucking don't, not even close!" I bawl, now only inches away from his face, eye to eye. I feel my hands forming into fists.

Replying only with a small nod, Mike turns and leaves the room. I'm left, but not alone. I'm surrounded, suffocated with the knowledge that Jess is gone, gone *forever*. Nothing can be done to reverse that, nothing. I return to my bed, curl up and cry.

I wake sometime later. I can't be sure if it's been minutes or hours. My face is stiff with dried tears. Mike is sat nearby, watching over me. I roll over, turning my back to him.

"It's not over Sean."

I hear but don't reply.

"They're still out there," he says, "looking for us."

I don't care anymore; maybe them finding us would end this. *You can't trust the inhabitants.* That damned hipster, damn right you can't.

"Sean I know you aren't in a place to want to hear this, I really do. But we need to leave. To keep running."

"What?" I say, sitting up, turning to face Mike, noticing lots of changes in the room. The machines I saw earlier are screens near the head of my bed. They're all attached to or extruded from the ceiling, ready to retract back up. I have no idea what the readout says on them, its like nothing I've ever seen in a hospital. But I quickly recognise a shallow thump beating every second or so, in time with a small pulsing light on the bottom of the screen. It's my heart rate.

There's the other couch nearby, and above that there's an unevenness in the ceiling where I suspect another bank of machines sit. I don't remember it being so on my previous visit but the part of the room I'm in seems to be a medical area, with its neatly aligned wipe clean beds and linoleum floor, and it has the hospital disinfectant smell.

The walls opposite consists of a large bank of drawers of varying sizes, some well-thumbed from use. The white panelling on the walls looks medical too. There're still no windows but now the place has the ground-in dirt of much use. It's similar, but not the same place Mike killed me and copied me.

Mike sits across from me with his back to a worksurface that spans a large section of that wall of many drawers, his laptop the only item on it. The flooring and panelling continue around the whole room, broken only by two doors. My eyes are drawn to the far side of the room, only now do I realise it's bigger than the other place and there's a piece of equipment on the far side, the likes of which I've never seen. It's the size of a large car, with a central plinth about waist height the size of a double bed in the centre. This is covered by a large, rounded glass bubble. Attached to one side of the plinth there's a large area of bulk covered by panelling that curves around to become a series of screens, all blank. The whole thing looks high tech and, unlike the rest of the place, it's sparkling clean.

"Where are we Mike?" I ask.

"This is our facility, built by the early probe, remember?"

"Is this where you, you, you re-grew me?" I look around for evidence, not knowing what I'm looking for.

"Yes, same facility, different room."

"And..." I ask impatiently.

"And we need to leave here. We can't risk losing you too. Things have got out of hand and our capacity to predict the Ananta's actions has become too unreliable. We need to take you somewhere safe. You're our responsibility, *my* responsibility."

"Somewhere safe Mike? You mean your facility isn't safe? Then where is safe? In fact, where are we, I mean geographically, where are we?"

"We're about twenty miles from Cambridge, located next to a military base, which is very well protected. But they don't know we're here, the military that is. Our location will buy us some time, assuming the worst-case scenario and the Ananta has located us. But, sorry, we need to get to somewhere one hundred percent safe. That leaves us with one option – we go home, my home."

I've never been to Mike's house before, how can it be safer than where we are now? Then I realise. "You don't mean a house in the UK or something like that, do you?"

"No, I mean that place from which I have travelled. So, not on Earth, no."

"You want me to leave Earth?" I ask, disbelieving. "Mike... you can't just do this. It's just too.... You. But... You've just killed the person I most care about in the world and now you're asking me to leave the fucking planet? Can you not see how this is, just... too much."

I stare at him. If it wasn't for him Jess would be alive. I will him to say something, anything. Even though I know it will be more lies, more manipulation. He doesn't respond. He simply waits, waits patiently for me, a sympathetic smile and a furrowed brow his only response.

"Anyway, how can we just leave Earth, how do we even get to your home?" I ask. But of course, I know. Mike's teaching on interstellar travel has sunk in. And that would mean, killing me again after we leave? Or will there be two me's? Which me will be me, the real me, the original me? The *real* me can't travel beyond the planet, so it can't be me going with him. But if it's a direct copy, will it be me? It has to be me... I'm a direct copy already and I'm the *real* me. I have to be, otherwise...

"You know how interstellar travel works, remember?" he says, looking at me for confirmation. "Perhaps more importantly I should be telling you about my home planet, which is not a planet. The key point is there is no *We* or, there is only *We*. That is, we don't exist as single entities as you currently do. We don't exist in a single place and when you no longer have mortality as an issue *time* also becomes a different construct. So lots of what you accept as fundamental truths to the human condition are no longer the case for us."

He pauses for a moment, looking at me. Uncertain if I'm taking this in, understandably. But now she's gone, none of this matters. Nothing matters.

"Is this making sense Sean?" he asks.

I nod, not caring.

"So, we physically exist in more than one location and not as a physical entity. But, what is really important in all of this Sean is QE. Quantum entanglement is the technological keystone of the bridge that will take your species here, eventually. Where you become a member of the galactic community. That's how important your work is. Do you understand Sean?"

I look at Mike and I hear what he says, but I can't cope with all this now. I simply nod.

"Sean?" says Mike, looking at me for a response, expectant, eyebrows lifted.

"Mike, Jess is... gone. And it's my fault, your fault... our fault," I say, pulling in the guilt, the responsibility that I deserve. "She's dead and we killed her." My anger and frustration with Mike grows – how can he just move on?

"I realise it must be very difficult for your Sean, but the enemy is here. We must do something."

"Yes Mike, I hear you. Don't put this all on me, it can't be just down to me. What happens if I decide I've had enough, I opt out, or even, what if I die? You know at the hands of the Ananta or from a heart attack or traffic accident or something. What then?"

"That would not be good. But if it were to happen, in time someone would go down the road you have been down and make similar discoveries, but that might not be for many years and timing is everything. You see if you don't begin to realise the reality of longevity soon then there is an ever-increasing risk of self-annihilation. Your technological advances will soon outstrip your social capabilities and essentially you won't evolve to become *responsible* for one another. The thing is, when you don't have to die, you see the universe in a whole different way. You have the time to learn, to live, to appreciate one another."

"Jesus Mike. I've just lost my gir–". She wasn't my girlfriend, we'd never even kissed, not properly. Tears well up again, a lump in my throat. I fight them back. "Go on," I say.

"I know this is all a huge burden, Sean, and that you and Jess were very close. But we do need to leave, to keep you safe and think about the best way forward. I'm sorry, I really am, but there are bigger things at stake here."

What would Jess have me do? I know the answer, there's no doubt in my mind. I put my head in my hands, allowing the knowledge of Jess's choices to settle. Then, sitting up straight, I brush back the remnants of tears and blink away my self-pity. We need to leave, hide away for now. Through QE and interstellar travel! Which means... Jesus, I can't even answer that. How much faith can I put in a man that I don't trust? He's killed me once and I'm about to let him do it again. Or am I? I could stay here and another me would appear elsewhere and start to live a new life, but then the Ananta might find me, and all the hiding would be pointless. Shit, this stuff will send you insane.

"Alright, so my guess is that we *delete* this version of me and then QE me to your home world? Is that the plan? We kill me again?"

"Almost... at least, the plan is for us both to return to my home. We'll be safe and I can seek help and guidance. We've come a long way down a road that, to my knowledge, hasn't been travelled before. So yes, we go home. But we don't need to delete you, as I never *printed* you after the omnithopter crash."

I stare at Mike, my temper rising, even now more deceit. "You haven't printed me? You haven't re-created me? So, hang on…" I say, giving myself a moment. "We're in a QE dream thing and none of this is real, is that what you're saying? For fuck's sake Mike! What are you up to? Why don't you tell me the truth? How do you expect me to trust you when you keep lying to me?"

"We are on a substrate, yes, both you and I. It's an exact duplicate of the real installation and the physical substrate we are in is at the installation you see around you. As you know from experience it's easier to base things on reality and this is what I have done with good reason. This affords us a choice. I have not yet printed you as a physical entity, but we can, should we wish. But this way, we don't have the decision of *killing* you again, as we have yet to re-animate you. From here we can go directly to my home, regroup and replan."

"That does make sense." I say, although it doesn't. "Did I die in the thopter crash?"

"You died. But of course the Ananta know we have your QE copy and mine of course. I *died* too. To them it's not the same as killing someone, because its not, not if they're backed up. They took out the omnithopter, I suspect to slow us down, for reasons unknown."

I let the fact I died sink in. It almost seems usual now, what with all the other revelations, but still… I died! "Did they know we've made a QE copy of Jess?"

Mike looks at me for a moment, "it's likely, yes."

He knows where my thinking is going. The Ananta thought all three of us were backed up and thus could be re-printed. No-one intended to kill Jess. The Ananta removed a version of her for their reasons, as they did Mike and myself. Which means… it really was my fault, making Mike delete her file. I'm the cause of her no longer being here. It's down to me. Me and me alone.

"Do we go?" asks Mike.

"What? Yes. Maybe. I don't know," I say. "I'm in no state to make important decisions... Is it simple to get back?"

"Yes, you won't take on a corporeal form at the destination. So when we return there will be no need to *kill* the old you. It's like catching an aeroplane."

I look at him. What is he telling me and what is he *not* telling me? Here I am again, asking myself if I can trust Mike. I can't. *You can't trust the inhabitants.* The hipster was right, except Mike's not *really* an inhabitant. But with Jess gone, I'm not even sure what matters anymore.

"K then," I say.

Chapter Twenty

Time has passed. I sense this, but it could be minutes or weeks. I'm awake and I wasn't a moment ago. I screw my eyes shut and open again to clear my vision in the surrounding darkness, squinting and searching in the pitch black for a shadow, something to orientate myself. It's so black I lift my hands in front of my face, but alarmingly I can't see them either. I bring them close, still nothing. I touch my hand against my face, except I don't I miss. What!

Trying not to panic, I carefully move my hand to touch my face again. It's not there, or my hand's not there. Shit! What's going on? I try again, nothing. My heart goes into overdrive, I try elsewhere, to pad my chest, my thigh – nothing. Shit! I can't find my body, clap my hands, no. Nothing is here. How can nothing be here?

"MIKE!" I call out desperately. Did I even make a noise, or was that in my head? I don't know – did I actually speak or just think I did? I have nothing, no body; I'm blind, I can't touch. I can't breathe. NO! I go to gulp in air, but there's nothing to gulp in with, and nothing to gulp. FUCK!

I close my eyes and slow my breathing. Neither happen but I pretend they do – panic will not serve me well. Calm, calm, calm... I'm not gasping for breath, I'm not in pain. My thoughts are my own, but there's nothing else. There is nothing here, not even a *here*. This is a dream, but my awareness of it being a dream tells me it can't be one. This has to be QE, a construct of some sort. That makes sense. I'm thought, nothing more...

"*Sean?*" I hear Mike's voice in my head, except it's not Mike's *voice*. It's Mike's thought, in my head. Like my own self talk when I'm thinking, except it's Mike's thinking that has appeared in my head, but not through my ears.

I attempt to reply, intending to speak, but before I can get the words out Mike responds to what I was about to say.

"*It will be disorientating for a while, but you'll find it second nature quickly,*" I hear from Mike, responding to my alarm around where we are and what's going on. He's replying to the frightened thoughts that I was about to talk about but didn't get as far as voicing. Mike is reading my mind. *NO, I don't want that. And now you know, Mike.*

"*I realise you're not happy about this form of communication, Sean. But rest assured I can only access the thoughts you want me to. Just as when you speak you decide what to say, so the same system controls your thoughts in this domain. Yet... already I sense you're not convinced by this and that you're worried you might share more than you intend. Understandable – can I suggest that for anything you intentionally want to share you imagine looking at my face; for anything you want to keep private, imagine being turned away from me. This will ensure your control.*"

I visualise Mike and think "*Alright, understood.*"

"*Great,*" replies Mike.

"*Where are we, are we neither real nor in a substrate?*" I think to Mike.

"*Practicalities, Sean. We are on the run to keep you safe whilst we work out next steps. I could effectively leave you asleep, or inactive, but *time would still be moving forwards and when I brought you back, I'm sure you wouldn't be happy. So, here we are at a midway station—"*

Without warning, Mike's voice in my head is washed away by a vision of Jess dying, the blood running over her face, pouring from the top of her scalp. I can't stop the vision, can't stop watching her die again. She's dead, and she died in pain, and it was my fault. Grief overwhelms me once again. I am consumed with loss and guilt. But I have to be here, wherever here is. The intensity of the last twenty-four hours has been too much already and now this... I have to go on, go on for Jess. Surely, otherwise... But how can it be for Jess? She's gone. For me, then? For humanity?

"Sean," I hear in my head, and something else: a feeling, empathy, sorrow. It's Mike. He's sad, worried about... me. I can feel his concern for my wellbeing, like it was my concern, but at a distance. I sense it; he really is worried for me and deeply concerned, he sees my loss. And there's something else, it's... *hope* and... something more, something elusive... a better tomorrow, a future. Me happy again, but different to who I was before, a different me, a fulfilled, better me. Is that a future copy of me, something Mike wants? Is this my replacement or me? But then I'm already my replacement. Shit...

"Mike, what's that? These emotions, are you messing with my mind?"

"How we communicate here is different, more complex on many more levels than you are used to or aware of. In my last thought I also allowed myself to share my emotions simultaneously. It facilitates a deeper level of connection and mutual awareness, more than words. For you it will attach to a memory where that particular emotion was acute. It will make it easier for you to interpret. Otherwise the emotions can be complex and hard to understand without context."

"I see. Can I do it?"

"*Given time. Would you like me to tell you a little more on where we are?*"

In my mind *I nod*... it seems to work.

Suddenly I'm surrounded by the vastness of space, stars twinkling at me from every direction. I turn my head to look around in wonder at the amazing view, despite having no body, or head. But I still see as if I had, giving me much needed comfort.

"*We're still in the Milky Way but many light years from Earth,* shares Mike. "*Let's get a little closer.*" With this thought we start to fly rapidly towards what appears to be a large star, which soon becomes a sun. We slow down and I see we're now approaching a moon in orbit around the sun. I can't tell the size as there's nothing to compare it against, and as we get closer I see the moon itself is not solid. Some of it is like a cloudy rainbow, but other parts are so black there is no discernible depth to them, nothing even slightly reflected to indicate texture or shape. Pure black. And there's a glow emanating from within, a growing light, like stained glass but moving and dynamic, like a river of kaleidoscopic multi-coloured patterns swirling and mixing. We continue to approach and only now do I start to appreciate the vast size of the moon as it continues to grow and more details become apparent as we get closer. The sections of dark obsidian material, the pure black, seem to swallow all light, like a massive infinite sink hole. This is interspersed with smaller sections of the fluid rainbow light. The whole thing was spherical from a distance but as we get closer it's uneven and made up of geodesic forms that I now notice are also not stationary. They are slowly moving and changing shape. It looks like a fluid planet; I still can't gauge the size, but it must bigger than our moon.

"*What am I looking at?*" I think to Mike.

"*A world, would be the best descriptor in words,*" shares Mike, and with these thoughts comes something else, a memory, one of my memories. A feeling of returning home after a hard day's work and it's raining and dark outside but the house is cosy and warm. You hang your wet coat up and settle in front of an open fire, snug. I feel this as a flash, but without urgency. What am I looking at? The answer is home.

"*That's right... at the moment our view is about five hundred kilometres out from a Node, of which there are many. This is an infrastructure where we exist, although it's not designed to support significant levels of corporeal life. The star is Betelgeuse, we're six hundred and eighty light years from Earth.*"

My God, 680 light years in an instant. "*Can we go in?*" I ask.

"*We already are,*" replies Mike, and my view of Node dims and is replaced by a view of the insides of a perfectly square white box, surrounding me on all sides, like a white, exquisitely clean, well-lit prison cell with no window or door and me stood exactly in the centre. Except when I look down, my body is not there, nor are my arms when I wave them. I'm floating in the middle of the box. I feel a surge of adrenalin, which I manage to calm with my breathing. My mind is not designed to cope with these radical transitions.

"*Is this the inside?*" I ask.

"*Of a fashion. This is a viewing platform. We can move quite freely within Node from here. Let's start with the core,*" he thinks, and one of the walls directly in front of me fades away to nothing and I have a spectacular view of a glowing sun, exceptionally bright but not painful to the eye. A number of small spheres are rotating around the sun at an amazing speed, like Bohr's classic diagram of an atom with the electrons orbiting the nucleus. Pulsing out from the core are bursts of light, a heartbeat, which sets off a shell of white light that expands, washing over everything it passes, repeated again and again.

"*This is the core. All are welcome to the core, but it is mostly the ancients who dwell here, the early builders of the core who are now the foundation of our collective. The complexity of existence within the core is... sublime.*"

"*Amazing,*" I say to Mike, not really able to take in what I'm seeing, let alone understand it on any meaningful level.

"*Yes. If we move out from the core,*" he shares, and the view from my white cube rotates and we fly off away from the sun at the centre, moving with one of the light pulses, like we're surfing a wave. Now I see blackness with many points of light spheres doted across my view. Beyond them, I think I see the edge of the structure. It looks metallic or similar, but it's so distant it's hard to tell. Then I realise it's a Dyson sphere – or I suspect that's how it started out. A huge moon sized shell, harbouring life within. Except, as we approach, I see the outer shell is moving, just perceptible, or my vision is playing tricks on me in this alien environment.

"*This,*" says Mike as we turn and start heading towards one of the distant balls of light, "*is a periphery. It's a place of shared understanding and interest, where the like-minded come together to be one and to be with one another. The periphery is where many new species enter into Node, to conjoin in the early days. This enables them to come and go and to slowly adapt and become part of Node on their own terms. They enrich Node and Node enriches them as they begin their journey to the core.*"

As Mike speaks we fly straight at the ball of light and it grows steadily to occupy the whole of the view from my cube, making my wall-window completely white again before flicking into an entirely new scene. It's like the wall was a screen and someone simply switched the channel and flicked to a new show, the new show being a view of a woodland, except the trees are like nothing I've ever seen before. The size of them is impossible to grasp as there is no grass or other plants to compare to, just a mossy floor across the whole forest. None of the trees have leaves; the trunks are as thick as they are tall, with thousands of spindly branches sticking out of the top, like a bizarre spikey crown. The moss that covers the forest floor creeps up and covers the trees, like a huge blanket laid across the whole scene.

I look up to the overcast grey sky. I can't see a sun or clouds, just a grey mist across everything, slightly higher than the tops of the trees. The place is in twilight and resembles a scene from a horror story. As the thought crosses my mind, I see a huge spider in the distance. It must be the size of a human child, maybe larger. As scary as it looks, I don't feel threatened with my box view, suspended in the air well out of it's reach. There's something not right about the spider – it's too slow, almost cumbersome, and then I see a number of smaller spiders following it; they're a little quicker in their movement but not much, it's like they're all in slow-motion replay. Not like any scurrying spider I've ever seen.

"*This periphery is home to an arachnid species, as you can see,*" announces Mike. "*They still exist as their original form and will come and go towards the core as entities when they feel this is beneficial. A steady and purposeful integration at their own pace, likely across millennia. What you see, of course, is a construct of their home planet, not the real thing itself. They exist as data here, as does everyone. And don't let your unconscious bias fool you, this species is far more technologically and socially advanced than humans. A mother taking the kids to explore in the woods is still a meaningful activity.*"

What Mike is showing me makes all the sense in the world, but it's also too surreal to be real, to take in, to accept. The leap from what I know is beyond measure. All I can do is marvel at the view of the smaller spiders in the distance, clearly interacting with each other and playing, running about, as they follow on behind mum.

My view fades and is replaced by our external view of Node again.

"So you can see Node itself is a complex collective of life that is steadily conjoining to become more. If we were to join the main population or the core, it would make no sense to you. Analogously we are in an airlock, so we are no longer in your world, and not completely in mine.

Imagine my species were water dwellers. You're dipping your head in a small rockpool to see what things are like, rather than being dropped in the middle of the ocean. Add to this that you can't swim, in fact you don't even know what swimming is as you've never seen water before. That world would be completely alien to you and your understanding of society and life. So rockpool is good enough for now."

I nod the head I no longer have. Strangely, I *feel* Mike smile.

"How many people, errr... entities, live here?" I ask.

"*One, or many,*" replies Mike.

"*What?*" I think and turn to Mike, except I don't. I have no physical presence; there is no Mike to see.

"*Yes, I thought that might surprise you,*" shares Mike. "*The thing is you are here trying to make sense of a radically different existence based on your own human existence. It's how we make sense of that which we experience, we can only use our existing schemas.*" A sense of compassion and nurturing comes with this; mum smiling at me.

"*Imagine I asked you to think of a new colour,*" says Mike. "*Can you do that?*"

"*What? Probably not, can I?*"

Suddenly, I see Jess upside down, blood dripping from the top of her head, her final breath leaving her mouth and stroking my cheek as tears blur my vision. The image of her dying just appears in my head, eclipsing all other thoughts. I shouldn't be interested and focused on anything other than my grief for Jess, how can I? That would be forgetting Jess and that's not acceptable. How could anything distract me from Jess's going, no matter how fantastical it is. I miss her so much and she would be able to make much more sense of all this. I mentally blink and the image fades to my view of Node and the surrounding stars and I remember where we are, *"sorry Mike,"* I say. *"That was unintentional."*

"I didn't experience anything, Sean. Whatever you thought, it must have been private."

I don't share the image that's in my head, but I allow the grief to flow, hoping the decision will be enough for Mike to understand. It is.

"Ahh, yes I see now," shares Mike. *"It must be very hard for you right now, I can't imagine. Intrusive thoughts are not uncommon in Post-Traumatic Stress, which you are bound to experience and when coupled with your own grief, well..."*

The memory and emotion of being a toddler comes to me. In my father's arms, I've just fallen off my bike having learnt to ride it for the very first time. I'm crying, but Dad's comforting me, holding me tight, telling me it will be alright, but right now the pain is raw. He tells me I just need to hold on, time will heal, hold on. The memory morphs to an image of Mike with a concerned forced smile. We're on the remote seashore again, where we introduced Jess to QE comms. Then that memory slips away. The emotions fade, we're back. Back to here, back to nowhere. Floating amongst the stars as nothing but thought.

The silence grows around me. I'm more alone than I thought was possible. No one can fix what has been broken, that's not how things work. I can't dwell here. I need to focus on the road ahead, be practical. Much is at stake, far bigger than Jess or I. This grief will consume me if I let it, I need to manage it somehow. Am I trying to solve that which cannot be solved, Jess's death? This is not a scientific conundrum – not all things can be solved. A world without Jess is my life now.

"*Mike. You still here?*" I ask.

"*Yes, you were engaged in a private thought, so I didn't intrude.*"

"*Thanks, I appreciate that,*" I share. "*Can you tell me more about the; the entities who live on this Node?*"

"*Of course,*" replies Mike. "*This is a Node of many factions, species, groups, or a Node of one, depending on how you measure this. I exist here. You see, either I live here with lots of other entities, and we are all conjoined as one. Or one entity lives here and a small piece of that entity is currently separate from the whole, that would be me and others like me. Beyond the periphery you just witnessed, we don't exist as humans do, not even close. Our origins are similar, that is we evolved from physical beings to who we are now. Except we are interconnected on every level, so much so that we are effectively one.*"

"*That's hard to get your head around,*" I share. "*So no privacy, no independence, no personal interests, no relationships?*"

"*Yes and no,*" replies Mike. "*You see things are different, very different, you can't measure them on a human socially constructed interpretation of reality. We are a new colour, remember, one you can't imagine and will likely never be able to, we are simply too far removed. No matter the mixing of colours you make to understand us, the primary colours you are starting out with are insufficient.*" As Mike shares this, a forgotten memory and its emotion return. I'm stood atop a cliff, the wind wiping around me, watching the waves steadily calm after a huge storm has battered the cliffs. There's a serenity to it, having weathered the storm. I see it. The journey at Node has not always been an easy one.

"*So now you know a little about us,*" shares Mike. "*But for now, the Mike you know, he is separate from the community. I am me. Like in the periphery. When I return to the main community, I will re-join the whole that is all of us. As a result, the me you know will cease to exist." The feeling of moving away from home for the first time returns to me.

"*You mean they won't let you out again?*"

"*Remember, there is no they,*" shares Mike. "*Only I or we. They are me and I am they. I could return, but I would have reconnected with all of me, my community, and as a result I will view our experiences and friendship in a different way. I will be joining an entity that concerns itself with others in the galaxy, but not at the level we are interacting at. I would not likely return, as my view would be changed and I would not be the concerned friend I am now, far from it. If I did return, I would be reshaped significantly. I would be a small pinch of salt re-entering the soup, I would add to the flavour, but at the same time I would be dominated by the whole and become the soup. I can't then return as salt.*"

"*So, is this goodbye?*" I ask, alarmed. "*You brought me here to say goodbye? What about me?*" Fear grips me, and I don't try to hide it.

Instantly a warmth of reassurance washes over me. It's Mike's emotional response to my worry and with it I know it's not goodbye. I need not panic. It feels like Mum putting an extra blanket on my bed and settling me down to sleep on a winter's night.

"*We have choices to make Sean,*" shares Mike. "*There are options open to us. I'm not about to just leave you on the doorstep whilst I disappear inside.*" Another old memory and feelings pop into my head, the uncertainty I felt at the job interview question I hated. 'Are you honest about your failings or do you play them down?'

"*A key choice here is do you want to know more?*" shares Mike. "*That is about the community, who I am, who we are?*" I'm Alice peering down the rabbit hole.

"*Well, yes of course,*" I reply. "*It's fascinating, amazing. Who wouldn't want to know more. But is that what's important right now?*"

"*I thought so,*" shares Mike. "*This is early for your species, but it's not unusual for the community to get to know new species... volunteers join a Node early on after initial contact. That is the purpose of the periphery. However, there's a catch. If you choose to join Node it's one way, you can't come back.*" Drunk as a teenager, going down the playground slide in the dark at midnight.

What kind of opportunity is this? Going into the unknown and experiencing that which can't even be described. To give up myself, to no longer be a single person, to become part of something, something, out of this world. That could be amazing, or scary as hell, probably both. And one way? That has to mean no way. Although... now that Jess has gone does it matter? There's no one else, and it might take away the pain. But I can't, Mike knows this, the bigger project on Earth. I can't just abandon my whole species to overcome my personal grief. Jess would turn in her grave.

"*That's too much Mike,*" I share. "*And surely we need to go back to Earth, to finish my work, Jess's work?*"

"*We do,*" he replies. "*But those options are not mutually exclusive. You can continue here and we can send a copy of you back to Earth.*" A beautifully wrapped unopened gift.

"*I would rather be the one to go back to Earth and we send in the copy,*" I share with Mike.

"*It doesn't matter which way around,*" replies Mike. "*Both choices are the same. Where there are two versions of you, initially they are identical in every way and will each feel that they are the original and the other is the copy. Both will be wrong and both will be right.*" Looking at myself in the mirror with regret, after telling Wendy Marshall I didn't love her anymore.

"So, I'm almost donating a version of me?"

"No," replies Mike. "<u>You</u> will walk through the door, you will be burning the bridge back to Earth. The copy of you will return to Earth and pick up where you left off." Feeling sick on an antique merry-go-round.

"But you said I would be both—" I share, before stopping myself. "I get you. Each version will only have their perspective, their view."

"Do I have to decide now?" I ask.

"Soon," shares Mike. "You see, we've travelled a long way from Earth, but time is still moving forwards. So back on Earth we are still hunted. I plan to send a version of me, back into the main community of Node, along with a version of you, if you consent. Then hopefully they can update us or influence what's going on at Earth from Node. We two can then return to Earth and continue the mission." The starting pistol firing and me anxiously setting off on the 1500m final on school sports day.

"But why can't you ask them now?" I ask. "The community, and get the answers to those questions now?"

"They don't know I'm here," replies Mike. "Not until I enter, until I join the soup." The time I saw a blind man struggling to get on a bus and me unsure whether to try and help or not.

"But don't they have systems and rules and police?" I share. "How can we just sneak up on them?"

"We are all responsible adults," replies Mike. "Some of us tens of thousands of years old. Laws and rules are no longer needed, mature societies beyond that." Trying to solve the prisoner's dilemma in my economics class at uni.

"Really?" I reply. But I stop there as another memory grabs my attention – it's the hipster. *You can't trust the inhabitants.* Which inhabitants was he talking about? Because he's right, I don't believe

Mike right now, how can you have some omnipotent species just leaving itself undefended, open to any attack or whatever other threats lurk in the galaxy? It doesn't make sense.

The nothingness around me that I had forgotten springs back to life, but only because it starts to fade. It becomes mist, and slowly resolves itself into a familiar shoreline and sand dunes. It's warm, no wind, and I look down at my now-present body. I search for Mike and see a figure heading down a dune, straight for me. He's his old self, beaming and striding towards me with purpose.

"If you are to join me, us," calls Mike, "you deserve to know a little more about us first." He places his hand across my back and gestures for us to start walking. First day at high school.

We walk. Mike gives me lots of background and history of the Nodes, not his species, as the Nodes are many species, most of whom have very limited recollections of their physical origins as this was so long ago and is not seen as who they now are. At the periphery, all responsible species are welcome and over many years assimilate to join the wider community.

"Do humans look to their evolutionary predecessors to support their knowledge base or identity?" says Mike. As always, he has a point.

There are many Nodes across the galaxy, all interconnected via QE. No one knows where they all are, so it would be impossible to eliminate his group as the removal of any one Node will lose nothing and will alert the group of Nodes. Which, given the vastness of space and infinite time to prepare, means this kind of threat was eliminated many millennia ago. However, it doesn't mean everyone gets along.

There are many other types of Nodes within the galactic community. They interact, some more than others, but the galactic community is just that and has infinite variety and movement. Nodes move across factions and back again, across thousands of years. Some also chose to colonise planets, but few settle there.

"More likely a faction would send a probe," says Mike. "Such as myself."

I think for a moment, rewinding what Mike has ever so subtly announced. "What? You're a probe?"

"That would be as good a descriptor as any," replies Mike. "Remember the Von-Neumann machine? Well that would be me, or other entities like me. Think about it. A Von-Neuman machine can re-create itself, which is what we've talked about before."

"So, you're not human?" I say, realising the idiocy of my question as it falls from my mouth. Mike simply looks at me, head tilted, raised eyebrows. He's in teacher mode. I know the reality, but my emotions tell me he's my friend and I only have human friends, therefore...

Mike sets off again and I follow. He tells me more about the nature of being "one" that is built of many and that his Node thinks as a unit, but just like a human walking and talking much of this is autonomic and requires little effort. Where a human might multitask across four or five tasks, his Node does this across many thousands of tasks continually. This is QE in action, and QE is a naturally occurring phenomena. The connections between individuals that can't be explained – mother and child, identical twins, the capacity to influence by significant leaders, the Jedi connection. This is how it begins, the coming together as a single community.

"Humans are on this path Sean," he says. "*You* are on this path Sean, I suspect you realise this now. And like all evolutionary advancements, your QE capability can be enhanced and augmented with technology. Think about the growth in connectivity on Earth facilitated by the internet. In principle, QE is an extension of that."

"But I always thought social media was a bad thing," I say. "Mis- and dis-information abound."

"A knife is both a tool and a weapon," replies Mike. "Gaia theory is a reality Sean. Humans are part of the eco-sphere, just like bacteria are part of humans. You know this, your research is attempting to stop humans from becoming a cancer that kills its host through global warming. And although you are a community, individuals have influence. Sometimes a single person can bring down a society; throughout human history this has often been the case. However, a single person can also bring hope, unite; champion a vision others will share."

I turn to face him, my back to the sea as it gently laps up behind me, the salty air surrounding us, the dunes rolling off into the distance. His eyes fix on mine, silent and unblinking after his little speech. He can't be talking about me? Can he? Best not to ask, he might say yes.

"Of importance in all of this Sean is the me," continues Mike. "Because I am me, not we. As a probe or entity, or whatever descriptor you wish to use, I am a singular sentient individual. And, following the mission, I will take back the experiences to the whole and this will contribute to who we, or I, the community, are. This, of course, is a benefit to our existence, but the primary aim is to support the development of responsible life across the galaxy. Life which is progressive and values others as much as itself and does not see itself as aloof or superior. It's a huge responsibility, to be responsible. And the question is Sean. Will you help, will you join us?"

What is he asking? Does he want my support with the mission or is he asking me to join the community? Wait ... he's asking both. There are two outcomes to his single question. This is why the tour of Node, the briefing on its beginnings and values, who he is and what he stands for – it's a sales pitch.

I get it, except I don't. I'm not about to sign up to living a life of splendid isolation amongst a sea of superior beings who I probably can't even relate to at any significant level. I'm not about to volunteer myself as a lab rat, for them to observe and question and determine my suitability as a potential member. Shit, they might even turn me down, turn us down, humanity. I could end up being the test subject for the whole of my species and fail!

A pulse of heat washes over us as a cloud moves away from the setting sun. I shield my eyes looking out to sea, to the distant horizon. The breeze is cooling, the sounds of the small waves and the herring gulls reminds me of childhood trips to the seaside. The whole scene is tranquil and soothing. I know it's created. But it works; in my soul I am at the seaside.

"Sorry Mike, but the answer is a firm no. It's not for me and I really don't see how it would benefit humanity."

"As I said before, I, Mike, will no longer remain when I re-enter. However, a new species will, in the periphery, and the periphery has access to both the outside worlds and inside Node. So you would become the conduit for support to the Sean back on Earth. Do you see?"

I see where he's going, but my resolve won't change. I shake my head. "But... well, I'll be a prisoner. Captive at Node forever. You must see how unappealing that is."

Mike emphatically shakes his head, patient expression fixed. "That's not the case. The world you would access is beyond your imagination. You could even re-create part of Earth and live that life, here at Node. There are many options. You could even split, go in and do what is needed to support the Sean on Earth and then self terminate. The choices are vast."

"Maybe, but none of them appeal to me. Suicide's just not that high on my list, you know what I mean?" I reply, not believing that Mike sees this as an attractive option.

"I understand, but, the thing is Sean, it's the only way we move forwards. Otherwise, we return to Earth the same as we left and the Ananta have the upper hand. We lose, one way or another."

He's right, rock meets hard place. Or is there more he's not telling me? How can I know? Can I know? Or do I have to go with what I have now. I have to trust him, as much as that has failed me so far. But then, what would Jess do? She would know what was for the best... She would see it as an experiment, she would be fascinated and then when it comes to the little matter of saving humanity. I know what she would do. She would split, definitely – it's in the best interests of humanity and science. And... I can play a role here, more than just Mike's sidekick at Node. I can be in charge of my own destiny; this can play into my plan. I know what I need to do and the me that wakes in Node will know this just as much as I do now.

"If we do this," I say. "Can I enter with you, as you are now?" As I ask the question the beach fades, back to our emptiness.

"*Yes,*" shares Mike. The feeling of abandonment I got on my second date with Deborah, when she made no response to me telling her I was still a virgin.

"*And how do we do it, if we aren't physical?*" I ask. "*I imagine it might be easier?*"

"*In a way it is,*" replies Mike. "*You will wake with me, both here and back on Earth.*" The strange tingling I got all over my body that time I was interviewed on national news.

"*Understood,*" I share, and I feel the confidence of my decision grow. I think that means I've made the right choice. "*Let's do it. And Mike... thanks.*" I allow the sweet melancholy I feel to seep into my thoughts with the hope that Mike can access this, although I know he will still be with me after, but also that a version of him won't and this emotion is for him. I allow this duality, this confusion, to bleed into my emotions that Mike can access. He'll understand. Immediately I feel a smile form on his face, which like a magical Cheshire cat appears before me and fills my vision. He gives me a brief nod. I too feel a smile break on my face as I sense breath returning to me.

Chapter Twenty-One

Thud-thud... thud-thud... every thud is a jolt, the vibration prodding my body, the noise bounding around my mind. I feel the pulsation in my head, my shoulder, my thigh, every point of contact. Despite the sensation the noise is dull, far away – a pile driver in the distance maybe? But I can still feel it; it must be one hell of a pile driver. I open my eyes and lazily stretch as I sit up.

As tired as I was, I'm wide awake the instant my eyes open, my head flicking left and right, like some hunted convict. I have no idea where I am. What is this place? What's going on? The questions in my mind come all at once, vying for attention, like a baited crowd at the gallows. This place is wrong, I can feel it, I don't know it at all. My heart pounds against the cage of my chest. This is not good, this is not good! Where the hell am I? Why am I here?

The room is well-lit, empty and spotless. I'm sat on a padded slab, where I was sleeping a moment ago. I squint my eyes to help me focus on the featureless walls around me. It's no help – the walls are fuzzy or I'm not able to focus on them, like the effect you get when you stand a few inches away from a blank wall and your eyes have nothing to focus on. But these featureless walls are metres away and still blurred. The squinting starts to hurt my face.

I look around: every wall is identical – no windows. The room is more like a cell than anything else. It's about three metres by six, the only feature a single brown wooden door at the far end. The padded plinth I'm sat on is just high enough for my toes to touch the floor and as I look up there's no obvious light source, with the ceiling the same fuzzy, pale, off white as the walls.

Panic surges through me again. What am I doing here? Where am I? I look down – I'm wearing a hospital gown. Have I been in an accident? I don't remember that, and this is not like any hospital I've ever seen. No machines, chairs, screens, windows and a poor excuse for a bed, so no clues. Other than the absence of clues – is that a clue?

Suddenly my whole-body spasms, electrocuted by a deep baritone voice as it shatters the silence. "Hello Sean, how are you today?" it asks.

Unseen people talking to me... or voices in my head? Or an AIC? I stroke both of my ears – nothing. It has to be a speaker, somewhere. Are people afraid to be in the same room as me? Do I have a disease, and this is the quarantine?

"I'm feeling... well, thanks," I reply, warily.

"We are sorry to contact you this way, Sean," says the voice. "It is seldom needed. We realise this must be very disorienting and even frightening, but our choices are limited. We realise you don't know why you are here or indeed where here is, and naturally you are curious. You will not be able to determine this I am afraid, but when I have told you a little more you will understand why."

As he speaks I look around, angling my head to get a sense of where the voice is coming from, trying to find the hidden speaker. There's nothing on the walls or ceiling, and the voice is so clear and close it's like I'm wearing an AIC. I stroke my ears again – still nothing.

"Does what I am saying make sense to you Sean?" the voice asks.

"Yes," I reply, as I pick up the courage to explore and walk towards the door at the far side. As I get closer, I see there's no handle, and the seam of the door is flush with the surrounding wall, with no gap. It could even be a good piece of trompe l'oeil. I resist the urge to press against the door so as not to seem too distressed, but I do run my fingers over the seam, which appears real, and I secretly press the door a little, just to check if it will give. It's solid. As I turn back to face my plinth at the other end of the room, I realise the voice has been waiting for me.

"Sean, it is important that we make contact with you and discuss the current situation. You have been led astray. We suspect that you know this, but have not had other choices from which to go down a different path. Right now we bring you those choices. Do you understand?"

"Who are you?" I ask. There is only one group who could know about my current situation.

"I believe we have met, if you recall?" replies the voice

Surely not, it can't be. "Then at least have the decency to show yourself," I yell. My blood is boiling; an angry glow on my face as I stand up. I clench both of my hands: tight fists, body rigid, adrenalin coursing through me, ready. I face the door, teeth clenched, breathing heavily down my nose. The façade of the cell fades and we're in something similar to Mike's installation. There are three of them facing me now on the opposite side of a small room – the middle one I recognise, the trendy pensioner with the hipster moustache, Jess's killer!

Wrath takes me. I power across the room with all my strength, legs pumping, anger giving me the brawn of ten men, charging straight for him, fists drawn. I swing for the hipster with all my might, and I see the startled look on his face as he realises, as he begins to lift his arms in defence.

Then, everything stops and all I can see is the image of my fist about to make contact with the hipster's face, like someone paused the playback. Then blackness. Nothing – a nothing I know – the nothing that exists on a substrate with no context. The nothing of only existing as thought. I know where we are, sort of, and I know who I am with, sort of. But with Jess gone, none of this scares me anymore. These fucking graspers killed her, and I will, I will... do whatever is needed to fuck them over.

But right now, I'm helpless. Adrift in the nothing.

The bully has me in a headlock and he's much stronger than me. No matter how much I hate him and know he's wrong, I can't break free. I'm impotent in this world of non-physical. I'm a sheet of paper dropped in the ocean, at the ravages of the sea. Or am I? Non-physical... that's got to be it. This is a place of the mind, the game here is cerebral. I need to outwit them, not hit them.

Maybe a minute passes with me in the nothing and my initial anger subsides as I switch to plotting how I can hurt these grasping motherfuckers. The mist returns and condenses. I'm alone in the installation we were just in.

"Sean, we trust you realise the futility of physical violence in this space," says the soft voice, followed by the three of them reappearing, seemingly teleporting in, like the old Star Trek shows. The hipster guy is in the middle again, flanked by the other two, who now I see them could be his twin brothers, but without the moustache. As the hipster starts to talk the soft voice has gone – was that even him? He gives a stern order, not that I give a shit. "You will refrain from a repeat of the actions you just took. Physical violence is not acceptable in any context," he orders.

"Why did you kill Jess?" I ask cooly, pushing my anger down. If this is what is needed, then so be it. But I still need to know why.

"That was unintentional," replies the hipster. "The second team who were brought in to apprehend Mike, they were overzealous, and the vehicle they were in connected with the omnithopter as it took off. This initiated events which caused the crash. It was not our intention. However, we knew the occupants were recorded on a QE substrate."

"NO THEY WEREN'T!" I scream. "JESS WASN'T... and now she's DEAD! You killed her, you arrogant fuckers."

My hands become fists once more, ready for the fight. They don't get it, they don't care. I need to hurt them, for them to know, to know what they've done... My instincts drive me to violence, despite myself. I know it's useless, this anger, this need for revenge. I stop myself and look at the floor, close my eyes, take a deep breath; this will not bring her back. I ignore the three of them even though the Hipster is talking.

Suddenly the room moves. Or I move? I'm sat on the bed, and I haven't moved. How am I sat on the bed? I was standing a few feet away, facing off against the hipster and now, without moving I'm sat on the edge of the bed. And weirdly, my anger is suddenly gone, my heart rate normal. And one of the hipster's men has disappeared.

"What game are you playing now?" I demand, knowing the infinite possibilities of a substrate.

"You are too trusting of Mike," replies the hipster, ignoring my question. "You must surely realise this now – you did not heed my warning. Mike is a rogue agent, not to be trusted; he has no concern for you. If he had, would he have let Dr Hart die? You must see the reason in this. He is not what he appears to be or says he is; you cannot trust him."

I don't reply, I just stare. What do they want from me? The adrenaline gone, exhaustion bleeds into me. I can't keep going like this, from frying pan, to fire, to furnace, to hell.

"Are you aware he orchestrated the bar brawl you found yourself in? Do you know he has interfered in your work, your accessing of funds, being left alone at the University, meeting Dr Hart. If he had not pulled you out in the omnithopter she would still be alive. He has lied to you repeatedly, omits information he has to gain your confidence, and then simply does what is in his interests and not yours."

I look at the hipster as he makes his little speech. I don't want to admit it, but there's truth in what he says. Mike's cavalier with my life and Jess's and makes mistakes, which, if he's some omnipotent super species, does not stack up. But if he's working in isolation, as the hipster seems to think, this makes some sense and does tally with what Mike has said. But that doesn't make the Ananta the good guys either.

"Why are you trying to turn me against Mike, what makes him so bad?" I ask.

"He killed Dr Hart," replies the hipster. "Is that not enough?"

"No. As devastating as that was, it was a mistake, but that doesn't make him bad, just careless. And the reality is, if blame is to be allocated, I should be taking the lion's share." My head dips to look at the floor.

"His interference with your species is not sanctioned," states the hipster.

"By who, you?" I ask.

"We require your cooperation," he says. "When we say this, we ask for it willingly. Mike is a mistake, he is dysfunctional. You must realise that interference with a developing species is wrong. The evolutionary principles of the galaxy must be maintained; as humans say, the laws of nature must be respected. All we have ever done is try to contact you. You must see that at every turn Mike has prevented this. He has poisoned your mind against us, and you have not had the opportunity to hear the other side of the story."

"Well, you have my undivided attention now, so speak," I say.

"Very well," replies the hipster and walks over to the couch adjacent to mine and sits on it facing me, giving me what I think is an attempt at a smile before he continues. "Humans are a species with potential Sean. I don't doubt you will agree. Where did this potential come from, you might ask? Well it came from humans. Your ancestors, your forebears, those who came before. Not from the stars, not from interventionists seeking to manipulate the course of your development to their own ends. You must see, all that you are now, all the potential you have, this is all your doing, humanity's doing. You have pulled yourself from the primordial soup and steadily evolved into a sentient species that may well in time join the galactic community. This was achieved unfettered by others. So why would it be logical to assume that one individual can improve on this, the evolutionary principles of millions of lives evolving as they always have. Surely, as a man of science, you can see this?"

He makes a strong case. Mike has been erratic and cavalier from the outset. It's all been on his terms: him in charge, him making the mistakes, his interests first. The hipster's case stacks up, but for some reason I also believe Mike. Can they both be right? Are their paths mutually exclusive? I can't rationalise this; there's simply too much going on for me to think straight, too much crazy alien shit.

"Do we have your understanding Dr Freeman, do we have your cooperation?" he asks, taking a step towards me, bringing me back to the room.

I meet his gaze. My cooperation? They need me. They don't just want to pull me to their side, they need me for something. I don't need any Jedi sense to tell me something is off; all too easy, too convenient, what's the cost? Can I trust these guys, at any level? How can I know? Can I know, for certain? Probably not, but...

"First let me ask you this," I say, feeling my way. "Should an advanced species support a less advanced species?"

"Most likely no, but there are few certainties," he replies. "However, this is not relevant. Do we have your cooperation?" he asks again, his voice more insistent.

"Why not, why not support a lesser species?"

"Because this will interfere with natural development," replies the hipster. "And lead to uncertain outcomes, caused by the more advanced species. They would be playing God. If you support an endangered species to survive you will be interfering with natural selection."

"But if I help a member of my own species this is fine?" I suggest.

"Yes."

"So, interspecies interaction is not?"

"We require—"

"Another question," I say interrupting. "My guess is that there are lots of different Nodes out there and that each of these Nodes belongs to a group of Nodes, like countries with lots of satellite colonies. Yes?

"Yes," replies the hipster.

"I have a question for you personally," I say. "If you were about to be born into the galaxy and there were a huge number of different Nodes and factions to be born into, and if some of these had a better quality of existence than others – would you want to be born into a higher quality existence Node?"

"Naturally, but this is—"

"K," I say interrupting again, holding my hand up. "Now consider that the Node or faction you are about to be born into is random. So there's as much chance of being born to a poor quality Node as there is to a high quality Node. Under these conditions would you prefer for all Nodes to be equal?"

"Under those conditions, yes," he replies, his tone more abrupt. "But those are not the conditions."

"Only you know this," I say. "But... from what you have said, you want equality if it's in your interests, but *not* if it isn't. Do you agree?"

"I agree that your philosophical argument is limited to a human interpretation of reality and as a result simplifies a far more complex situation," he says, becoming more agitated with each sentence. "Moreover, we do not have time for this philosophical debate. Mike is dangerous and needs to be stopped. You must see this, if it were not for our intervention—" He cuts himself short.

"What? What if it were not for your intervention?" I ask.

"The manipulations brought about by Mike Swale would be endemic across the planet, leading to chaos."

He might be right. Mike is all over the place, but I suspect well intentioned. Whereas hipster, the "Ananta" – something was always amiss with them. And now I see where their true values lie. They only want equality when it's in their interests, which is not equality at all. Mike was right. Mike is the good guy.

"So, what do you need from me?" I ask, playing along, understanding a deeper level of the game.

"Simply to stop working with Mike. Go back to your life, continue the project as you might have done had Mike not interfered. We will remove Mike from the picture."

How can I go back to the project without Jess? There may well be others who can pick up where she left off. But I can't, how can they not see that? "You're going to kill Mike aren't you?" I say.

"Mike is a probe, an independent entity, but he is also linked with a backup. We will remove him, not end him. When this is done, all entities can return to their Node and faction. You will be free to continue your life as you see fit."

As the hipster says this, I notice the corners of his mouth lift up slightly. Is he trying to smile? It doesn't work, it just makes him look like a poor actor. He's a robot. He has nothing like the human lived experience Mike has, he doesn't know us at all.

"The only reason I'm not at my lab working with Jess and enjoying life is because I'm on the run from you. If you weren't around then all would be well. *You* are the aggressor here," I say, now pointing at the hipster. There's not the slightest response to my accusation, he just continues to stare at me, no sign of emotion, a robot.

"Mike is the cause of this situation Dr Freeman," he states. "He is the reason Jess Hart is dead. Nevertheless, we do not have time for this. Let me keep the question simple. You must appreciate that our approach is in the best interests of humanity, leaving you alone. To this end, will you assist us in returning Mike to Node?"

Is that all they want, to get rid of Mike and leave us too it? I find that hard to believe. The reality is Mike has done all he can for us. We are fine to continue on our own, the breakthrough has been made. Mike would even support that. He returns to Node from where he comes from, and humanity takes forward QE for longevity and all that comes after. So the hipster would be happy too. Everybody goes home, all is well. Except – that's not what's on the table, there is more here. Plans within plans.

Hipster continues to stare. "I'm thinking," I say, playing for time.

But… as much as I want to, I don't believe them. Why do they want Mike so badly? They know where we are with our research, they know we have QE. They must think Mike has more to give, otherwise why remove him? And Mike was right, they have no interest in helping us, the hipster just demonstrated that. They don't believe in equality. But if I decline, shit, do they just remove me from the picture, kill me? Or… all this, it could all be bullshit and one big lie to get me to give up Mike… and then they kill me and take away QE from humanity.

"How would it work?" I ask.

"We will give you a device, one that once activated in Mike's presence will automatically return him to Node. There and then. His corporeal form on Earth will remain, but it will be severed and thus be harmless."

And we all live happily ever after. Very convenient. But Mike's corporeal form is a probe, disconnected from anything and can simply start again, like he did the first time he arrived. He could reboot, and we are back to square one. Lies – it doesn't work like that. And if they're lying then… the device just wipes him out entirely. That would work for them. That fits with everything. But they don't seem to expect me to see this, to see through their lies, which is odd, or I'm wrong. Unless… they're robot like in thought as well as action and don't really get "us" at all. They see us as a lesser species; they don't have Mike's experience of human interactions and they're assuming we're dumb mammals. They may be right, but we're not quite as dumb as they think…

"How will that work? Mike might be suspicious If I start acting differently."

"We will approach you on Earth, and pass to you the physical device," says the hipster. "For the immediate future, this conversation will be deleted from your memory. When we contact you on Earth, we will return the memory of this conversation to you. You will then seek out the next opportunity to attach our device to Mike's laptop. Understood?"

"And if I say no?" I reply.

The hipster takes a few steps towards me, so he's only inches from my face. He leans in close, next to my ear, so close I would feel his breath, but there is none. "Know this *Sean*, know this and remember," he whispers. "If you do not comply, you will die a painful death, as will your colleagues Anthony and Michelle. Three deaths among eleven billion is of no consequence. You will do as we instruct."

Shocked at this Machiavelli turn and the mention of Anthony and Michelle I can only stare back at the hipster, slack jawed, as he continues to hold my gaze. I can risk my own life, but to have more people I care about risk theirs – I can't allow that, and he knows it. His eyes slice into mine, unblinking, I stop myself from looking away and hold my own. He knows he has me but I'm not surrendering.

Then I see it: there is menace behind his eyes but no passion, nothing so human. He is a cold-blooded killer and will dispatch us without a second thought. That decision is already made.

Part Three

Chapter Twenty-Two

A churning in my stomach – excitement, a separation, a sadness, emotions overlapping and contradicting – combine and a fog I can't see dissipates into consciousness. I'm here, which me am I? I'm surrounded by Mike's installation and relief washes over me; I'm the back-on-Earth me. Which means right now, there's another me about to join the Node collective. How scared must he be? I just hope he can cope and sticks with the plan... he must stick with the plan. I need to trust myself, my other self now. My plan is our plan. Right now, he's still me and I would definitely stick with the plan.

"Sean?"

I look around to see Mike standing up from a desk at the other end of the room. He heads over, his brow furrowed, looking at me like I'm a naughty puppy.

"How do you feel?" he asks, concern in his voice.

I swing my feet over the edge of the couch and stand up, scan my body. "Err, fine. I think." I walk a few paces past Mike, padding myself up and down. He watches me intently. "All seems good, I feel fine. Why?" I ask.

"It's... just... odd," he replies, eyes narrowed. "There was a delay with the printer... I reanimated myself ahead of you but there was a significant delay to your arrival, and I can't figure out why. I couldn't find you for a while and with all that's going on... well." He shakes his head and returns to the desk and laptop. I wander over and look at the screen. I have no idea what I'm looking at – there's no discernible language, just moving shapes, the same rainbow dynamic as the Node.

I wait for a moment, waiting for Mike to type or bring up some display. But he just stares at the screen as the shapes continue to morph, like some ancient screen saver. Of course, the interface isn't the keyboard – it's direct, neural, QE.

"Mike... Mike," I say, raising my voice to pull his attention from the screen. "Is everything alright? You seem worried, which makes me *very* worried."

He just stares at me, with the same puzzled look.

"Has something gone wrong?" I ask, my anxiety building. "Is the other me alright, at the Node?"

"Yes, he'll be fine. It's just... something strange on the system," he replies. "I'm just interrogating the data now, but I'm getting nothing. I intentionally planned for a two-day delay to give us some time, to be sure no one was at either of the installations, and they aren't, which is good. But you were delayed more. I can't figure... anyway..."

He snaps down the lid on his laptop, as if hiding the content, not that it meant anything to me. Still pensive, he slowly turns to me, and as his gaze meets mine his glowing smile returns. He's back in the room. "Not to worry, sort it later," he says. "We're both alright and here, and there is no trace of any activity from the Ananta. They don't know about this facility, although we might be better to use conventional transport for now, until I work out the reason for that delay."

"Conventional transport?" I ask. "Where're we going?"

"Yes, that does depend," replies Mike. "But I don't think we need to stay in Sweden."

"Sweden! Why are we in Sweden?"

"It's a backup facility to the UK," replies Mike. "Safer option for our return, just in case the UK facility has been compromised."

I look around – it looks just like the other facility to me. Reading my thoughts, Mike responds, "yes, it looks the same and indeed same blueprints et cetera, but outside this room we are in a bunker, courtesy of Mr Assange Jnr, a hundred feet below Vita Berg Park in Stockholm. Very secure."

"Just to be sure, you're not still in my mind are you, reading my thoughts?"

"No, don't worry," says Mike. "We're just as we were when previously on Earth. Same game, same rules. Node is a whole different context."

"And you are sure the other me at Node – he's alright and the other you is fine? Can you check in on them?"

"Alas no," he replies. "We're at their behest to contact us – remember, I'm independent of Node. But they'll be fine. Every parent has to let their child cycle on the street alone at some point."

I nod acknowledgment. "How long will that be do you think?"

"A good question and one I'm struggling to guess at myself," says Mike. "You see I no longer really know what it's like once in Node. I do, but at the same time I don't, not fully. I can remember it but, that's not the same." His gaze wonders for a moment, staring at a blank section of wall. He's lost in some memory. Not so with me.

"Seriously Mike?" I say, stepping into the line of his vacant stare, grabbing his attention. "You've just recruited me, or a version of me, to join you there and you can't even recall what 'there' is. What has the other me let himself in for?"

"It's not so straightforward," he replies, shaking his head. "I'm bounded by my human form and cognition, like you, this you know. It's very limiting. I'm trying to remember what it's like to swim and live in the ocean when I have had all my memories of water removed from my mind and can only see a picture. Things are too different at Node. You can't describe and understand it with what we have between us, it's like asking an ant how he feels about modernist architecture."

"What? No, forget I asked."

"The ant doesn't even understand language," he continues, ignoring me. "Has no ears to hear if he did and certainly no capability to process the question and no physical ability to respond. And that's before you start on the principles of architecture and how these have evolved for mankind from the early days of using caves. It's just the human journey is so far ahead of the ant, that he's lost and wouldn't know modernist architecture if he crawled over it. You, see?"

"Mike, Mike, Mike," I say. "This is serious. What are you trying to tell me? Get to the bloody point."

"The point my friend is that the ant might be at number three on an evolution scale, where humans are at ten," he states. "Node, you see, is well over a hundred. So, utterly incomprehensible to you, and right now, me. And... when the other Sean and Mike enter Node they will be changed. I will return to who I was and Sean will be made more; he will be added to. This way, both can then interact with Node and not just crawl over the architecture in blissful ignorance. And... this means their views on us, our situation, the whole human construct and struggle... they will have a bigger view on this. Perhaps even God like, you might say. So any judgement on how they can help us, well, they will make that with a new perspective. Meaning..." Mike pauses, his hand supporting his chin, thinking, formulating. "Meaning... unpredictability," he says, meeting my infuriated stare.

I need predictability. My plan needs predictability. I need who I am, who I was, am. If *I* am changed, that could wreck everything. If my plan is to work, I need me to be me. "Mike..." I say, calming myself. "Answer me this: will I recall all that has happened in my life up to that point?"

"Oh yes, and then you will begin a new one."

I have to trust in me, the other me. But I need to remember Mike is not human. The ant analogy tells me all I should already know: he's an alien, he doesn't think like us. Despite his attempts to conform, he's nothing like us. With a way of being that's beyond anything I can comprehend. I need to accept that, accept him as he is, very different, not bad or wrong, just different. I would expect no less for myself, I've spent most of my life seeking that.

"Where does this leave us Mike? When might we know if they're going to help or not?"

"They will contact us... I can't say more than that," says Mike. "They will make their own informed decision. So for now. I think we must consider ourselves independent and do what we can for ourselves."

"Understood," I say, "But, I need you to confide in me. If you aren't sure I need to know something, then tell me or ask me. Don't assume anything. Do you understand?"

"I do, but I can't guarantee that."

"I need you to," I say.

"I know, but I can't."

"But I need you to, otherwise you hold all the cards and I'm your puppet," I say, doing my best to keep things friendly.

"Sorry, I can't guarantee that," he repeats. "I will share what I can, but no guarantees."

"Then you do not have my trust Mike, how can I trust you?"

"I understand," he replies with a nod and starts to pack his laptop and a few things into his backpack.

So that's it? His way or no way. Motherfucker. I clamp my teeth and suck in a breath, doing my best to keep calm as my blood boils, reigning my feelings of wanting to strangle him back in as my eyes drill into him whilst he casually packs his bag. I know how my neurodivergence drives me to want to make right what is plainly wrong, and I feel it in spades right now. But I have to keep my eye on the bigger picture. So be it. I tried.

"Very well," says Mike. "Shall we get out for some fresh air?"

"Sure, whatever," I reply.

We enter a short corridor of featureless off-white walls. This leads us into a large, much colder cavern of concrete. It's maybe fifty metres across and a hundred long, with wall-to-wall rows of servers blinking and whirring on either side with a narrow walkway through the middle of them. The lighting is dim and the cold is, I'm guessing, needed for the processing, humans only occasionally needing to enter. All very functional.

"I guess this is the main belly of the beast here then?" I say.

"Yes, great cover for the installation, with plenty of capacity for power and what have you. It could even withstand a direct bomb blast," he says, looking at me over his shoulder as we make our way through. "If things ever came to that."

"Yeah, let's hope not," I reply, hoping this is alien humour.

"But all very dark and dim," says Mike, looking around at the blinking servers. "So let's keep going and get to the surface for some air and something to eat."

At the end of the room, he keys in a code next to a very solid-looking steel door, giving the place even more of the nuclear bunker feeling. Through the door we come to a dimly lit iron stairwell. We climb it. Our footsteps clank loudly, echoing on themselves and the brutalist concrete walls. It sounds like we're ten men climbing a fire escape. I count five floors as we noisily ascend. Two more secure doors later, we arrive in an unmanned reception area. There's a small reception desk to one side and on the other an open plan area with soft seating and a small coffee table with magazines. It could belong to any office anywhere. It feels incongruent, like we've emerged from a bunker into a high street office.

"Come on," urges Mike, waiting for me to catch up. "Looks like it's another hot one," he says, opening the office door onto the street.

As we leave and cross the street, I turn to look at the facility. It looks like a regular office building. I make a mental note of where we are and snap a quick photo on my phone while Mike isn't looking. I'm guided by Mike as we head to a café with a shaded terrace on the edge of a park.

"Let's have lunch and formulate next steps," he suggests, pointing towards the seating area. I take a seat and notice the hubbub of people around me. The daily melee of life amidst a park that was once probably a verdant collection of flowers, lawns and trees. Now some sections have clearly been prioritised for irrigation, but the larger lawns have been left to the whims of the climate, broad yellowing patches of scorched grass with cracked earthen walkways scratched across them, the ever-present reminder of climate collapse.

I've not been to Stockholm before, so it all feels exotic but also different in a new way. Something has changed... something's different. At first, I can't quite put my finger on it, but then I realise.

It's me. I'm different.

I'm removed from these people. They are not the same as before – not because they're Swedish, but something else, something more, something fundamental, has changed. It is me, it's how I see them. I've changed, not them. My perspective on who we are, the human condition. I have a secret now. Humans are the ants scrabbling around on their anthills. No... bees, they're busy bees coming and going, all playing the roles they find themselves in, having purpose in their existence, a driving force to achieve, with what seems like intelligence and direction. But never questioning the fundamentals, just keep marching forwards with a purpose, to achieve, succeed.

Is this Darwin's evolution in action? If the whole species is selected and conditioned to progress then with each generation they will become more; they, as a species evolve. But the individual will never realise or see these gains. Christ, I even referred to them as "they" and not "we", do I see myself as something else now? Not just a human? Have I become aloof to my own species? But my perspective has changed, I'm certain. How could it not with all that's happened, with what I now know?

Mike returns with menus, bringing me back to the Café. "How are you feeling?" he asks. "I mean emotionally. Lots has happened in a short period?" I sense his concern, it's genuine and I know what he's getting at.

"You mean Jess, don't you? How am I coping?" I say.

I breath out a long sigh, lean forwards with my elbows on the table and steeple my hands in front of my face, quiet for a moment.

"I keep forgetting," I say, "as a result of the distractions, and then it comes back to me in the quiet moments, and I have to work to stop myself from giving up." As I say this I catch and hold Mike's eye, longer than is comfortable because there's something else too... There's the slight awkwardness and self-consciousness of realising you have eye contact too long, but then something flicked, something else. I can *feel* him, now, emotionally. There's a connection between us. It wasn't there before. It's like we're instantly alone, the world around us gone, silenced and darkened. All I see is Mike's face, illuminated. I feel, with certainty, he knows, and... he knows I know. We're having a conversation without words. Exchanging thoughts, thoughts ladened with emotions and intentions, not words.

"*Relax,*" I feel come into my thoughts: it's Mike. The intimacy of it all is intense and feels wrong, but I do as he suggests, or try to. I sense his empathy for my situation, but also something behind that, something around time and the future and all will be well in the end. I can't quite get a fix on it.

"Mike, what's going on here?" I say aloud, resorting to words.

"We seem to have a residual link," he replies. "It can only be as a result of our visit to Node. Unexpected, but you always did have potential, strong QE."

"Does this mean I'm telepathic, is that what it is?"

"No, that's a human idea," he says. "There's a link, weak, but enough for strong emotions to pass between us and, with practice, maybe more. Try to relax in conversation and it may improve. It will give you insight into others and how they are, emotionally. With me it will be two ways, but with your fellow humans... well, hard to say at this point. Try to relax in conversation and really listen to them... it could give you a much deeper insight into people. Be in the now, not focused on outcomes or results. Listen, really listen and, well, who knows..."

"Have you had this all along?" I ask.

Mike replies with a shrug and slight nod, like *of course, but not a big deal.*

"Mike, is this real?" I ask, looking about at the park and café. "This whole set up now, or are we in a construct?"

"Because of the connection?" he says.

"Exactly."

"Rest assured we're on Earth in Stockholm, in Café Bleck." Mike pans his arm and follows it, looking around. "All this is as real as it ever was, you are home."

"Is there a way to tell, to know for sure?" I ask. "You know, if we are here or wherever we seem to be or if we, or just me, if I'm on some construct of reality interfaced via QE? Sorry... not explaining myself well, but you get what I mean."

"I do. And no," he replies, shaking is head. "There's no foolproof way to know the difference between these worlds. Depending on your perspective there is no *real*, they are both legitimate and essentially the same, but different of course."

"How can they be the same? One is stimulating the brain with false information and the other is real information."

"Not so," replies Mike. "Information is being processed in both domains and you are interpreting it within your mind. You think when light hits your eyes you are seeing all that there it? No, you know the spectrum is way beyond that which the human eye can see, ultraviolet and so on. But you know it's there as you have discovered it by other means. So you can interpret the *real* world in many ways, but your human body and mind is very limited. Let me ask you... if I were rude to you here and now does that make it more hurtful than if I do it within a QE construct?"

"Err, no. Probably not," I reply.

"So, your emotions don't notice the difference and set one construct above another. They know better. But I see why you ask. There's a lot more going on here than you are aware of, like UV light is all around us but you see nothing. Like dreams are not, not real, they're dreams, real, but different."

I get it, I think, but it's an emotional understanding, not a practical one. Maybe not all information can be processed in the same way I'm used to. The laws of physics don't apply sometimes. It's closer to philosophy, but still not that either.

"Can I get you gentlemen anything?" asks the waitress out of nowhere. She's dressed in traditional clothing: long patterned yellow skirt, white blouse, black embroidered waistcoat and topped off with blonde pig tails. We must be in the tourist side of the city. Suddenly self-conscious, I realise I'm sat here staring into Mike's eyes. This must look... intimate. "Err yes, do you have a menu please?" I ask only to realise it's on the table in front of me.

"Ahh, sorry, here it is," I say. "Can we have a minute to look please?" She obliges with a smile and walks away.

"Mike, how did she know we were English? Is this the QE thing in action?" I ask, feeling a sense of my new powers.

"No," he replies. "I suspect she heard us talking or simply guessed. They're pretty good with languages, the Swedes." I see a wry smile and sense his mild amusement at my expectation. I emote back to him my slight embarrassment at my Jedi expectations. He gets it and responds with an even broader smile. This is awesome – I have a superpower.

"Excuse me," I call across to the waitress as she clears a nearby table. "Actually, I think we are ready to order," I say, and we order food before Mike proposes his plan for our next move. It's more than a little basic. The bones of it are: wait to be contacted by our other selves and don't lift our head above the parapet. Disappointing doesn't cover it.

Bizarrely, Mike doesn't get the seriousness of our situation. Or he knows something I don't and isn't sharing.

"Mike, that is a shit plan," I say, not hiding my emotions. "It's not even a plan, it's a non-plan." I look at Mike for a response, even make some weird attempt at QE sharing my level of disappointment. He just looks at me. I don't give up. "You're the superior being here, the clever one, with the answers. Aren't you?"

"It's the option most likely to do least harm and with least risk," he says. "It gives our other selves time to progress at Node and gives no reason for the Ananta to justify further aggression. It does make sense and is the course of action most likely to deliver the best outcome."

"It's a waste of time, sitting on our arses," I reply. "We need to address the issues, solve the problem, you know. You said yourself that you don't even know how long it might be before they contact us."

He just looks at me – nothing, and I feel zero emotion from him.

"Don't you see Mike?" I say. "If we take control of the situation then we can influence the outcome. If we wait then we have less influence. Others will do to us whatever is on their agenda." I pause, waiting for a response. "Mike, neutrality only ever helps the oppressor, never the oppressed, take sides. Act!" I say and push my drive for action towards him, my passion to succeed, allowing my emotions to flow. I don't know if it has any effect, but I know how strongly I feel about all this. He must be getting it.

"I understand your wishes Sean," he replies. "I really do... but if you look at things objectively your suggestion doesn't stack up. You feel that time is against you and doing nothing will allow others to get ahead, right?"

"Yes, you understand, great, let's look at the option," I say.

"But what about if there was no time. If time didn't exist, at least not as you experience it?"

I stare at him, sharing my immediate exasperation with a look and an emote, using our mental QE link.

"Let me put it another way," he says. "If help from our other selves was to come in the next twenty minutes you would be up for waiting for it, yes?"

"Of course," I reply.

"So, the only difference between that and my suggestion is the duration it takes for that advice to come through, yes?"

"Yeah," I say, nodding.

"So time is the variance here and time is not that which it seems," says Mike and I feel a sense of foreboding here – is that an emote from Mike?

"Go on," I say, intrigued. Does he have time travel? Could that lead to Jess in some way?

"Imagine you lived forever," he says. "Death is not in your vocabulary as it's an ancient problem solved many millennia ago. If you don't die there's no past and there's no future – there's only what you have done and what you haven't done. Time becomes irrelevant as a construct as it's infinite. You may travel the galaxy participating in all kinds of amazing experiences over thousands of years, but there is always more. You will have accumulated masses of memories, but the future is still as infinite as it was when you started. Infinity doesn't wear out.

"But when you exist in a world that still has death, time is immeasurably relevant – for you time is finite. You will cling to this life, literally with your dying breath. You know it will give out. So your construct of life is bounded by your interpretation and experience of time."

"I see. You're bringing this back to my work – mine and Jess's work – on longevity?"

He smiles and, like a proud father, raises his eyebrows and leans in towards me. "I knew I chose well with you, Sean," he whispers, and my irritation at his inaction is overtaken for a moment.

"Thanks... look," I say, not wanting to dismiss his comments too harshly. "I see where you're going and the bigger picture – when we don't die, everything changes – I get that. But I still don't think sitting here waiting for help is the best way forward. I have a plan, do you want to hear it?"

"Please," he replies, opening his arms to welcome my suggestion.

"We go back to the UK," I say. "I collect all of the data from my, our, research, pull it together into a publishable format and get it out there to both the scientific and wider community. That way, there will be nothing to be gained by removing me, us, from the picture. Of course, it won't be peer reviewed in a scientific journal straight away. But it will be out there and those in the know will be able to test it and reproduce what we've done. The proof will be in the pudding." I look to Mike. "What do you think?"

I need him to go for this if my deeper plan is going to work. And I have to be careful not to emote and reveal my own agenda here. He said this was straightforward – you only reveal what you want to. It doesn't feel like that right now. Right now I feel open, vulnerable, emotionally naked. And... is Mike telling me everything? Is there more to this emoting?

"I think it has risks," he replies. "I think if the Ananta finds out, or even suspects, this might push them to further action, and we know only too well how that ended last time. I can't risk losing you Sean."

"Is that a no?" I ask.

"For now it is; perhaps we give it a couple of days and then see how we feel?"

I could wait a couple of days. But if the other "us" do come back with a way forward this might not allow for my plan. It would be a huge risk.

"Mike, I'm sorry," I say. "I really appreciate all you've done, but I'm going to go with my idea. And I would appreciate your help, you know, getting back to the UK."

"A couple of days won't hurt will it?" he says and I feel an emotion packaged with this. I can't label it, but I'm thinking he has a point – a couple of days is not a big deal.

No. He's manipulating me... is he?

No, go with the plan, go with the plan.

"Mike, I am going back to the UK. That's it. You can come with me or not, your choice. But I'm going."

"You sure?" he replies, squinting slightly.

"I am. I need to do something – I need control over my life. I'm not sure your idea is the best, no offence. But things have not always gone the way you thought and perhaps it's time for me to take the lead."

"Alright," he replies, with a lengthy exhale and, I sense, strong reluctance, but also acceptance.

"You will need to travel via conventional means," he says. "Which, if you don't have a passport or money, is not going to be easy. I can take you to the UK embassy and you'll have to say you've lost your passport and wallet and throw yourself on their mercies. Understood?"

"Thanks Mike, I appreciate it."

Chapter Twenty-Three

Mike has yet another Jag, conveniently parked not far from the café. He must have significant resources and money at his disposal. With more than one location, does he also have more than one project? Me being just one piece of the jigsaw in a larger plan of manipulation? Is he playing a much bigger role in steering humanity than he lets on? Are there multiple Mikes all over the world? He could be lying to me all the time, with some idealistic sense of the greater good, which makes the lying and manipulation acceptable, even *responsible*. I can't know. Following my own path has to be the way.

I've forgotten what relaxed feels like, it's been so long. I welcome its return as I sink into the luxury of Mike's car. Briefly escaping the anxiety of my situation, I sit back watching the world go by as we cruise through the city. It seems forever since I've simply been able to sit and do nothing. Mike seems content with the silence, which, coupled with the Jag's noise insulation, makes for a serene moment as we glide along, watching the tourists bustling along the busy streets.

Moments later, our serenity is shattered. A cyclist shoots out from a side street and crashes, at speed, into the side of the car. Neither of us see it coming. One minute silence, the next an almighty thud, which startles us both, followed by a loud slap as the cyclist flies over his handle bars and slams into the windscreen full force, his face smeared against the glass just in front of me.

"WHAT THE!" yells Mike. "Where the hell did he come from?"

The cyclist is now spread eagle across the front of the car, clinging on by his fingernails as we coast forward. And Mike's not stopping.

"MIKE, STOP!" I shout, turning to him.

"Don't worry," he replies calmly. "I'm slowing down. If I break suddenly, he ends up on the road – second impact, further damage."

Wow, quick thinking on Mike's part. We roll to a steady stop, with our new passenger loaded on the front like a hunter's trophy. As the car comes to a halt he slides off in an almost comedic way. I immediately go to his aid. He's laid on his back, arms raised slightly as if still holding invisible handlebars. He looks dazed but he's moving.

"Hey, you alright?" I say, as I kneel beside him, scanning his body for injuries. He looks at me, squinting to focus so I give him a moment to come around. "K?" I ask, raising my voice, "are you injured?"

He slowly sits himself up, awkwardly pushing up on his bloody hands.

"Jag tror j—" he says, before I interrupt.

"Sorry, I only speak English," I say, slowly and as clearly as I can. He looks at me, dazed and confused.

"I think I'm K," he says slowly, massaging his jaw, and starts to get himself to his feet. There's a crowd of a dozen or so people gathering to help, at least I think that's what they're offering as they're all talking Swedish. The cyclist, now standing, looks to me again.

"It was my fault," he says. "I just didn't see you. Is your car alright? I think I am, bruises for sure, but K I think. Are you K?"

"Err, yes, I'm fine," I reply, thrown by his concern for me, having been safely cocooned in the car. "We're fine, of course. Are you sure you're alright?"

I give him a moment as he looks around, still disorientated.

"We probably need to give you our details," I suggest. "I think your bike is back where we hit..." I break off as I turn to look where the accident happened. Mike is already on it – he's picked up the bike and is walking it back towards us. Odd priority.

"I noticed it was a Pinarello," he says as he approaches, pushing the misshapen bike. "I thought I should pick it up before someone else does. You seem alright, no broken bones?" he says to the cyclist, as he passes him the bike.

"Bruises for sure, but no breaks," he replies, taking hold of and inspecting his bike. The crowd begin to dissipate, but fast approaching with sirens wailing is a blue-and-yellow Swedish police car, surely not for us. But they come to a halt in the middle of the road, blocking the remaining access, lights still flashing. Two of them get out and stride quickly towards us.

"You were the driver?" they ask Mike.

"Yes, but I think we're all fine?" Mike replies. "How did you know we were English?" he asks. As he does a wave of anxiety passes through my body, like I've just leaned over a precipice and seen how far down it is. It's emanating from Mike. It's much more than just his tone of voice. He's suspicious, worried, frightened.

Then, as casually as you like, one of the policemen pulls a set of handcuffs from his belt and takes hold of Mike's forearm. "I am arresting you for reckless driving and attempting to leave the scene of an accident," he announces. As he says this, he snaps the handcuffs onto

Mike's wrist and then spins him around with force to lock in both Mike's hands behind his back.

"What?" exclaims Mike, his face flushed like he's just eaten a chilli pepper.

The cop ignores Mike's protest and, holding his arm, starts to forcibly walk him towards the police car. It's like it's all been rehearsed, and the cops are just rolling it out no matter what has happened at the scene. And the injured cyclist is getting no attention at all – that can't be right. Mike was right, something is wrong. I start to follow Mike as he's being led away. He senses me and turns to look at me, his eyes meeting mine.

RUN! he emotes to me as the cop pulls him back around, stumbling, and continues marching him towards the police car.

What the fuck! The world pulls in around me, the noises of the people and the city grow, my vision zooms out from the scene, the noise around me expands to an overwhelming cacophony. The other cop approaches me – shit! He's going to arrest me too.

"This is the police station we are taking him to," he says, handing me a business card with details on it. A wide-eyed rabbit in the headlights, I'm frozen and do nothing except stare at him. He stands motionless, hand outstretched towards me with the card. Noticing my reluctance, he nods for me to take it; flicks it. "Here," he says.

Near paralysed I slowly reach out and take it.

"Alright," I say, and he nods again, turns on his heel and heads back to the car. No concern whatsoever for the cyclist.

I don't want to, but I know I have to... I turn my back on the scene and walk: fast, but calmly, not noticeably fast, just supremely efficient in every movement. Slipping away as quickly as I can without showing my need for haste. I get to the busy pavement and do my best to blend in, walking slightly faster than the other pedestrians, all of whom have hats or sunshades, which might help me disappear, or not. Either way I just keep walking; it's my only option. I don't dare look back – they might see me and change their mind.

I round the first corner I come to, trying to get out of sight from whoever might be watching behind me, and I keep going, slightly faster now, I still can't risk running or looking. Who the fuck were they? They were not cops. Mike knew. And they let me go, how can that be? Why did they let me go?

I try emoting to Mike, "*are you alright, where are you, what happened?*" I have no idea what I'm doing, let alone if Mike can get any of this, or what a reply might be like. But I understood, *RUN* as clear as day.

What now? What to do? This is hard, I just need it all to stop. Be back at the Uni, teaching or in a pointless staff meeting, anything but this. I keep walking, just keep walking, for now that's good enough.

After maybe twenty minutes I start to slow down. I have no idea where I am, but I can feel myself calming down, my heart slowing. If they were going to pick me up, they would have done. They're expecting me at the police station, so that's the last place I'm going. I need a plan.

I come across a tourist map of the city, take a photo of it and begin to navigate my way back to the park to see if I can access Mike's installation. It's not far away and within thirty minutes I arrive from the far end of the park. Feeling like I'm now in some spy novel, I don't approach the office building directly. I go to walk past, but as I get close, I keep my distance. Like some cliché I stop to tie my shoelace and have as good a look as I can at the entrance. It's quiet, no one coming or going, but I see a man sat nearby on a bench seat. He's not looking at a phone, or talking on an AIC, or doing anything, just sat. Is he there for me? Or is he just someone having a quiet moment. How do I tell? But who sits out in this temperature? It's baking.

I keep walking, away from the building. I might not even be able to enter – the security was nuclear-bunker level, and what will I find if I get in? After all, it's just a hole in the ground, so why am I here? But I need to rescue Mike, somehow? From where? But he said run... and I can't go up against the police or, maybe worse, the Ananta. Fuck! And letting me go, why did they let me go? There must be a reason, they must think I have something they don't have or can lead them to something they want, or do something they want doing. But what? How can I work that out? Shit!

I keep walking, hypervigilant to all that's going on around me. I risk a look over my shoulder as subtly as I can – terror grips me. The man who was sat outside Mike's office is following me. I risk a further look, and feel a chill run down my spine – it is him. What do I do? I could run, or take lots of turns? Find a busy area and lose him in the crowd. But if they wanted me they could grab me, surely? So, no point running, maybe? Or maybe they wanted me to access Mike's installation – they think I have the code and can get in. That has to be it – that's why he was there, waiting for me. They know where Mike's installation is, they just can't get in. I'm the key, at least they think so. That's why they let me go.

I keep my steady pace and don't risk another look behind me. I try to make my hearing hypersensitive. Like trying to focus on a single instrument in the orchestra, I listen for his footsteps from the mix of street noises. I think I have them but can't be sure. I keep going until I get to the next street corner and, as I take it I slow my pace and risk a side glance at the street behind me. He's still there – brown trousers, light blue shirt, brown jacket and black sun hat pulled down so I can't make out a face. Definitely the same man outside the office and keeping perfect pace with me and... I can't see his face, it could easily be one of the Ananta!

As I round the corner I immediately I speed up, out of sight for the thirty metres or so that I have on him. I scan around me for options. I need to lose him. Whoever he is, I need to vanish from his radar, from the Ananta's radar. I see a large van pull up outside a row of shops. It's a little battered, mainly white with a picture of flowers on the side. It's a few hundred metres ahead of me and, as I get closer, the driver pulls a box from the back of the van and heads into one of the shops. This could be my chance. I cross the street to the same side as the van; as I approach, I slow slightly, listening intently for his footsteps. I find them, he's still with me. But he must still think I don't have him. I walk to the back of the van, open the door and grab the first box I see, I then go straight into the next shop along.

"Hello," I say to the young woman behind the counter of what turns out to be a gift shop. "I have several packages for you, are you able to help?" I ask, hoping my use of English is not too out of place.

She buys it. "K, sure?" she replies.

"That'd be great," I say, "there, just in the back of the van, very obvious. Could I use your toilet too please? Sorry, too much coffee earlier," I say, grimacing.

"Err, yah, K. It's just in the back, let me show you," she replies and leads me off behind the counter through a storage area to a weary-looking door with a unisex symbol on. "Here you go," she says. I enter, close the door and listen intently for her to leave, which she does – my gamble has paid off.

I give her a few seconds and quietly open the door. I can hear her talking to someone in the shop. I don't hang around – I go deeper into the store area looking for a rear door, hoping upon hope that there is one. Jackpot, there it is. I race towards it as fast as I can; double jackpot, it's a fire escape, I can open it no matter what. I give the bar a shove and the door flies open as a piercing scream of the fire alarm sounds.

I run as quickly as I can, straight into a back alleyway, not knowing where I'm going or if my plan will work. But I'm fast, extremely fast, faster than I thought I could be, adrenalin pumping into my legs, my arms like pistons carrying me forward. The end of the alleyway leads straight to a main road crossing it. The other side of the road I see a wall, perhaps four feet high and greenery beyond. A public park maybe? I see a car coming but run anyway. The horn blares as I shoot out and I am across the carriageway in less than two seconds. I vault the wall in a single leap, amazing myself.

I land at pace and continue my run, heading between a few trees and some large bushes, all of which will obscure the view of anyone following me. I keep going for another hundred metres or so, in open ground now. It is a park with shrubberies and walkways and people meandering. If I was in running gear, I would blend right in. I slow, struggling to breathe, the explosion of energy catching up with me, but I keep going at a jog and look behind me. No one following. I've lost him, I hope.

Before long I'm at what must be the other side of the park, having navigated various greenhouses, boating ponds and a children's playground. I can't believe he's still chasing me, there's no way. But I don't stop – I exit the park and keep walking, generally heading away from where I last saw him. The further away I am the larger the search radius, the larger the radius the harder it is to find me. Thirty minutes later, I start to relax, the immediate emergency over, but my predicament is as raw as ever.

I need to get back to the UK and take my plan forward, with or without Mike. It's the only option. I have no money, no passport, no ID, nothing. But I can't risk going to the British embassy now, with some sob story of robbery or stupidity. Now I've lost them it's the first place the Ananta will look. How do I get back to the UK? And not be picked up by, or bump into the Ananta, who have God only knows what resources at their disposal? I may have given them the slip for now, but I have no doubt they will have strategies I can't even imagine. Whereas my options are few, stranded in a foreign country, hunted, no money, no friends, no resources. I'm a refugee, a refugee. Refugee.... That's it! That's how I get back to the UK.

An hour later I'm hitchhiking at the start of the motorway with a stolen map of Sweden and chocolate bar in my pocket. First task, get to Malmo. I stare at the map – it must be well over five hundred kilometres, shit.

I've never hitchhiked before, but after finding the main road heading in my direction it's less than fifteen minutes before I get a lift from a young couple in a new Mercedes. Thankfully they speak English, but they're only going my way for thirty kilometres so I'm back at it with my thumb in the air at another junction. This seems to be the way of things for hitchhiking, and it takes me four lifts and six hours to get about 120 kilometres. It's tiring, but I'm moving away from danger with every kilometre and although I'm blind to what's going on I'm settling into the safety of being constantly mobile. Surely no one can find me if *I* don't know where I am and I don't stop moving.

On the outskirts of a town called Jonkoping I get dropped off next to the busiest energy station ever. Necessity is the mother of invention, so I browse the shop and slowly fill my pockets with essentials and then transfer them to a small rucksack I find on sale. I keep a close eye on the staff, biding my time, and then when both cashiers are swamped with customers, I simply walk out the door, fast but not too fast, confident and with purpose. I'm scared as hell – my hands are shaking, but I'm hyper-focused, the adrenalin has me ready to sprint.

I've already decided that if I get caught, I run. If the police pick me up for anything it could be the end. I can't believe I'm shoplifting, I'm as straight as the day is long.

I keep up my pace as I leave and head around the corner of the building, out of sight. I keep going for another fifty metres. With no one following I manage to breath out a long breath of relief and review my haul.

This time it's near thirty minutes at the side of the road before anyone stops. When they do it's an elderly man who's going all the way to Malmo and is happy for the company, result! I squeeze into the front seat with my provisions at my feet. The car is one of those small Italian ones, so there's not much room and the rear seat is loaded with stuff up to the roof. As I settle into my seat, I quickly realise I have to lean against the door and window if I don't want to constantly brush shoulders with the driver. Not great, but beggars can't be choosers.

As we pull away, I feel safe again, cocooned in the small car with stuff piled around me. I sink into the seat and smile. It's been a long day and now as the adrenalin rush from my thieving subsides, fatigue catches me. But its alright, no one can possibly know where I am and Malmo is miles away, so I have a few hours of being invisible to the world in which to rest and do nothing.

"My name is Bert," announces my driver, stretching his hand across to shake mine. "Oh, yeah hi, I'm Sean," I reply, twisting my arm awkwardly to shake hands in our tiny car.

"You are from UK?" he asks, over pronouncing his r's.

"Err, yes. UK"

"I've been to UK. I have a friend in London, it's nice, busy. His name is Anders Kamprad, do you know him?"

"No, I don't think so," I reply.

I could really do with some peace, some sleep. But it seems my ride is keen to chat, cheap payment for the lift I guess. He must be in his eighties – thinning hair which is grey, but I suspect once was blond, overweight and filling his side of the car to the max. He smells a little too, not BO, but there is a smell of sweat, thankfully not overpowering.

"That's a pity, he's a really nice guy."

"Yeah."

"You are heading to Malmo then?" he asks.

Hmm, so why am I heading to Malmo? "Yes," I reply. I'm too tired to concoct a story and hope this is enough.

"OK. It's a nice city. My cousin Lars lives there, this is why I'm going. I haven't seen him in twenty years. Not since before my wife died. But that was a long time ago also," he says, looking across to me.

"How long were you married for?" I ask.

"Forty-two years," he replies, wistfully. "I would like to say wonderful years, but that would not be true. I loved her and she loved me, in her own way. But she would not want children and I would. After that, we were never the same and for a long time. Now it's just me, for a long time. Now I don't work. But Lars, he called me from nowhere. 'Come visit,' he said, so that is what I will do. It's lonely, without people without family. You know?"

"Yes, I do. It must be nice that Lars has invited you," I say, stifling a yawn.

"Oh yes. But strange, I don't know him. We were never close, not even before now. Maybe he is also alone now? I'm thinking I will find out. Two old men, sharing their stories of the past. And maybe photos, he will have photos. That will be nice. It's a long time before I have been to Malmo, the city will have changed as well, I think there must be many new things to see. The last time I was there was with Ulricka, such a happy time, we were still young, although we didn't know it at the time. We had a wonderful few days, visiting, the sights, seeing the shows, such happy times."

As Bert regales me with his story I start to nod off, pinching myself to keep awake, not wanting to be rude. I slip into a daydream where I can see a young couple, holding hands and smiling at one another as they walk down a sunny street. I look across to her as I hold her hand. She's very pretty, with long blonde hair; quite petite with piercing eyes. I look closer and I see why: they're the most subtle shade of jade green, which, with her platinum hair, makes her striking. She glances my way again and her smiles grows; I respond the same and she leans in, saying something I don't understand, and kisses my cheek. I feel her emotions with the kiss, like she's sharing her love with the physical contact. The warmth of it washes through me and I wake with a start, jerking my hands upwards as my whole body twitches.

"I think you are tired," says Bert. He can't not have noticed me twitching awake in this tiny car.

"A little," I admit.

"Bert," I say. "Your wife Ulricka, was she like you? You know, Swedish-looking, blond hair blue eyes; there seems to be lots of that, and I thought it was a myth."

"Is that what they say about us?" he replies, giving a short snort of laughter. "I can see why, and yes, she, also had the blond hair. Her eyes, they were very different. She had the most amazing eyes: they were green, very unusual, very beautiful. I do miss her," he says, and I can feel him drift off into another memory.

Chapter Twenty-Four

"Oww!" I yell, as I'm rudely awakened by my head smacking into the passenger door window.

"Sorry," says Bert. "Speed bumps, I forget you are sleeping."

"That's K," I say, rubbing my head and pushing my hands across my face in an attempt to wake myself, only to be assaulted by a crick in my neck like someone's karate-chopped it, which I find, when I try to turn to Bert, hurts like hell.

"How long have I been asleep Bert?" I ask, rubbing my neck.

"A few hours," he says. "I think you were needing it, so I didn't disturb, was that OK?"

"Sure, no problem. You're probably right, I did. Thanks." I look around and we're in an energy station. "Where are we?" I ask.

"About a hundred kilometres from Malmo, not far now," he says. "I need recharge and the bathroom. There are snacks also, if you need to eat."

I have no money for food, but I can't let Bert know this.

"I'm K thanks, I have some food in my bag," I reply.

Bert runs the car through rapid re-charge and we're on our way again. Before long he returns to his life story and tells me about his early life in the army, leading into his main career as a chef.

"I would make you some great meatballs. Not the Ikea carp," he tells me.

"What? Do you mean *crap,* not carp?" I say. "Carp's a fish."

"Ah, yes. *Crap,*" he replies, nodding. "The Ikea ones are just *crap,* no good Swede would eat these."

"I'm sure you're right Bert," I reply, smiling. I quite like them myself.

We continue our chat on many things Swedish and I go with it. Although struggling to concentrate, I make the right noises, ask the occasional question and it's not long before we're approaching Malmo. At my request, Bert drops me at a large service station before we enter the city, which I reckon will likely have lorries in.

"Just here will be fine Bert – over there near the cafe if that's K?" I say, pointing.

"For sure, no problem," he replies and pulls over next to the cafe.

"Well, this is it for me," I say, turning to my new friend. "A big thanks Bert, for bringing me all this way. And I hope it all goes well with Lars. Really, thanks very much and for the company too."

As the words leave my mouth, an unexpected melancholy washes over me. I'm going to miss Bert – we've shared something, he and I. Short, but intense, a strange kind of immediate intimacy that's fine with a stranger passing through.

He turns to me, a huge grin filling his whole face. Just like he fills the whole of his side of the car, all squashed into his little seat, the steering wheel rubbing up against his belly.

"Come here," he says and leans across, arms wide open and pulls me into a hug. "You take good care, my boy, OK. You are a good man," he says, and I feel a lump in my throat.

"Thanks Bert," I reply as he releases me and I take a breath, his sweat overpowering up close.

"Much luck with the rest of your journey," he calls across as I'm about to shut the door. "And you know you are travelling without enough bags for your journey." He gives me a subtle wink. I smile as I nod recognition and close the door.

I wave as my new friend drives off and just like that, he's gone, and I feel a loss at his parting. Part of me has gone with him. No... another me, in another universe has gone with him and decided on another life path... is that it? It's not a bad choice, to go with Bert, but I can't see where it leads. Only, I feel the melancholy of not having taken that path. These insights, these feelings, they're new, different. Are they from my trip to Node, or am I the copy of me and there is a difference? I'm not the same, things are... strange – not unpleasant – different.

With Bert's car now out of sight, I'm left staring into the distance and the feelings fade. I turn my gaze and attention back to the café and my surroundings.

Work to do.

New to the refugee game, I start to factor how I'm now going to get the rest of the way to the UK. If... no, *when*, I get on a lorry I could be on there for many hours, even days. I need supplies and maybe a blanket or something. I head into the energy station and manage to steal something from just about every outlet, which starts to add up, so I create a stash behind one of the industrial bins. I rescue three empty water bottles from the recycling, give them a rinse in the toilet block and fill them up. A blanket is not forthcoming though. My plan is to pee in the bottles as I empty them. No shitting for perhaps forty-eight hours, I hope.

I can't read the signs but after a short exploration I find the driverless lorry re-fuelling area, it's a hive of activity, with not a sole in sight. Stood off to the side I watch in silence, the hydrogen trucks only stop for five minutes before they're off again and the electric ones not much longer, streams of them coming and going, all the refuelling bot managed. The lorries all look to have the latest security about them, most without even a handle to open a door, fully automated. This is a dead end. I need old school tech, lorries with doors and drivers. Drivers need food and toilets so I explore beyond the main café area and find an old lorry park tucked out of the way behind the main cluster of buildings. By this time it's starting to get dark so I bide my time and find an inconspicuous spot amongst the picnic tables to hang out and watch the lorries arrive. An hour later the ideal target rolls into the lorry park. "Downton Removals" it reads on the side, UK plates and almost certainly on the return journey, so empty. I watch the driver and, to my surprise, co-driver get out. I hadn't figured there would be two. But of course, a removal firm needs two people to carry the furniture. What else have I not figured?

I make a bold and confident approach along the lorry lines, knowing to myself "I belong here", and I slip in behind the Downton lorry. Another lorry is now parked behind so there's a limited view of me and what I'm up to. Having never opened a lorry before I survey the back of the lorry as I approach. This way I'll be able to operate the levers and locks straight away and not look like I don't know what I'm doing. I see the padlock against the handle. It's huge – how do I get past that? I pull at the handle to see how much give there is, hoping there might be enough play in it to make a gap and I can squeeze through. I give it a good yank and it moves, but only a little. Enough to get my fingers in, but that's it.

Bollox!

I stand back, looking, scanning for other points of weakness. This is harder than I thought.

I jump out of my skin, when from nowhere a voice yells, "vad gör du!" only a few metres behind me.

I turn quickly shocked and scared. There's a man, a big man, a trucker stood staring at me, "vad gör du?" he repeats, his eyes narrowing. I have no idea what he's saying, but it doesn't sounds good. He starts to move towards me, raising his arms. Shit!

Scared witless I turn and run. I'm fast, running for my life again fast, I tear across the tarmac. I know the lorry park well now and head for the treeline beyond the energy station. I hear a shout as I shoot across the car park. I think it's the trucker but can't be sure. A few people charging their cars look my way and I pass close by, but nobody moves to stop me.

I reach the treeline and keep going, ripping my trousers on a spikey bush, ducking past low branches as they appear out of the darkness, but I don't stop. Hundreds of metres into the trees and the surge of effort comes back to bite me and my lungs feel like they are about to explode. I slow to a stop and hide behind a large pine tree, doing my best to be silent, to listen for any pursuers. Holding my breath, I listen intently – nothing – just the pounding of blood pumping in my ears. I desperately let out an exhausted breath, trying but failing to do so in silence. I give it a minute, allowing my breath to calm a little, still silence. I'm alright, I'm alone.

I turn and sit with my back to the tree. This is harder than I thought and more dangerous. I need to be more vigilant and think things through. Hunched low, I walk back towards the energy station and risk a look from the treeline, and see people going about their lives. One of them could be the trucker or someone else ready to grab me.

I give it twenty minutes. All is normal, life goes on, and importantly for me the Downton lorry has gone and with luck my earlier pursuer.

I take a deep breath and abandon the safety of the treeline, heading back into the melee, back to the shopping centre area, back to the crazy life I now lead. New resources needed, I steal a knife from the café area, along with a roll of heavy-duty duct tape from the energy station shop. I'm becoming quite the proficient shoplifter. I spend the next two hours at my lookout point, watching the lorries come and go and waiting for a suitable target. Finally, a UK lorry with taut canvas sides pulls into the truck stop area. That's my ticket. I watch the driver walk over to the main shopping and café area and make my move. It's late now and quiet – there is no blending in with crowds as I cross the truck parking area. I walk with confidence and purpose, not looking around. I get to the UK truck and it's reasonably shielded from view by other trucks. I just have to hope the drivers are elsewhere; if they aren't then I can see a repeat of my earlier athletics.

After a quick inspection of the UK truck, I find a worn point on the canvas sides, where the taut covering has rubbed against the metal edging. With no one in sight, I pull out my knife and start to cut along the worn crease. With the butter knife I've stolen it takes me a good ten minutes of silent sawing, keeping it as neat as I can. I need the repair to be invisible after I patch things up.

I squeeze my bag through the slot I've cut, try my best to squeeze out a nervous last piss against the side of the lorry and then with much wriggling, panting and feet kicking in the air, I slide myself through the slit as quickly as I can. I sit quietly, calming my breathing, listening to the silence. There's nothing except the wind. I tape up the cut from the inside, as neatly as I can, doing my best to get the two edges to meet neatly, but blind to the finished repair outside. I reinforce my work with nearly a full roll of tape, layering it on in every direction. I just have to hope the mend is easily missed from the outside and doesn't tear when the lorry is on the move. I scramble through my bag in the dark for my small stolen penlight and take a look around.

I have perhaps twenty or so pallets of woodscrews, nuts and bolts and similar stuff, nothing of use to me, but luckily the truck is only half full, so there's room to lay down. I notice how lucky I was with where I cut as most of the pallets are tight up against the canvas sides. Had I cut next to them, I wouldn't be going anywhere.

I find a suitable spot and sit in the dark waiting, in silence, cross-legged, with my bag in my lap, leaning back against a pallet, already starting to sweat in the heat. The lorry is a sweat box, still hot even at this time, no ventilation and no hiding from the heat of the day. Every other day you see on the news refugees dying from the heat in lorries, desperate people forced into desperate situations. Something else I missed. I'll have to ration my water, two, maybe three days. I don't have nearly enough.

Thirty minutes later, I hear footsteps much closer than the others I've heard, followed by a sudden slam of the driver's door, which jolts me alert. I don't move, waiting for the motor to start. It doesn't. After what seems like an age, I realise the driver must be settling down to sleep and I'm here for the night. With few options I try to do the same, but sleep is a stranger. With all that's happened my sleep pattern is all over the place and with the chaos that has swirled around me for the last few days I don't feel I can give in to sleep; to not be on my guard, to not be ready to run.

I lay on the wooden lorry floor with my bag as a pillow, the smell of the oil and steel reminding me of engineering classes at school. It's not an unpleasant smell, but makes the whole place feel dirty. The darkness smothers me, muffling my senses to the outside world. I feel protected in my little cocoon but vulnerable in my situation. I lay in my cave, only moving when I need to and then with stealth. With no distractions I'm left with my thoughts and stare into the darkness of the roof of the truck.

The shadows start to form into shapes and people and then one becomes Jess, blood covering her face, terror in her eyes, dying, reaching out to me. I close my eyes and she's still there, but now in colour. Poor Jess, she didn't deserve that, she didn't deserve any of this. We should be in Carluccio's getting pissed and deciding which one of us deserves the Nobel prize the most. We could have had an amazing life together, punting on the Cam, conference appearances, lots of respectful nods as we walked around the campus. Now this, Jess dead and me on the run. Mike kidnapped, fuck! It was all too much when I had Mike, and now he's gone. I need it to stop, just some time of calm, so I can breathe, relax a little, be the old me. Tears well in my eyes and rub them; as I do, I smell the oil on my hands, it must be on the floor, and now all over my face.

I do my best to focus, to keep moving, to work the plan. Have the Ananta co-opted the police in some body snatcher way? Or tricked the real police into picking up Mike. Or, maybe it was all a big mistake? Is Mike wondering around Stockholm looking for me? I could be running away from nothing...

Except, it doesn't matter.

Mike can look after himself and this is a "go-to" move, not an "away-from" move. I'm taking control and my plan is solid. I've got to stay the course, just keep walking.

The sudden whine of the motor startles me awake and I can see more than the silhouettes of cargo. It must be light outside and pleasantly cool, for now. Seconds later, we're off and I sit myself up against a pallet, making as much noise as I like and settling myself in for the long journey. The going is tough – I bounce around on every bump in the road, my butt painfully and repeatedly hitting the hard wooden floor. I'm also falling sideways as we take corners, although I quickly learn to predict this with the slowing of the motor and slight swing in the opposite direction before the turn.

I learn quickly and in the shady darkness, whilst trying not to fall over, I move some boxes to block me into a tight chair like structure and rip up some packaging to sit on. This improves things, but not much. And all the blind movement whilst on the go has me feeling nauseous. So I sit, as best I can; I settle in for a grim journey, hoping I don't throw up.

After a few hours, to my relief we stop and the driver gets out. Time for a piss maybe? It might be the best chance I get so I have one whilst I can. I imagine what he or she's doing whilst they're gone, to give me a feel for time, and I think I'm right: it was a piss stop. So next stop will likely be lunch.

When we stop a couple of hours later, I do the same again. I visualise in my mind what they're doing: walking across the car park, ordering food, waiting for food, eating. This helps me understand where they are at on their day and then I can match. It seems to work, and I start to regulate my functions with the driver's: piss when they piss. Pissing on the move would be a disaster. Eat when they stop for longer periods and are eating. Piss with one hand and eat with the other. Sleep when they sleep. I'm really pleased with myself on how quickly I am adapting, until on day two, I stop pissing. I try but I must be losing most if not all of any moisture through sweat. It's way hotter than the day before and after the middle of the day it's like being in sauna, the heat is unbearable. Sweat constantly streams down my face, into my eyes, and before I know it, my clothes are soaked. I wrack my brains on what to do, but all I can do is think, "drink more", which I know I can't. I can't run out of water, that could be fatal. But it's like some stuck record, and I can't think straight, I can't come up with anything. I just need to drink some of the water. But I can't.

My sopping clothes mix in with the oil as I lie on the floor doing nothing, swaying and rocking from side to side, on what must be a motorway section, doing my best to do nothing effortful. This is my solution, which is pretty poor. I take my ration of water when I should, lie back down and start to count the minutes until my next ration. I repeat this every hour, for how long I don't know – until I go for a swig and there's nothing there. Have I drunk everything? I know I must have, but I still go through my things. I have two bottles of piss, kept warm in my personal sauna.

I wake on my back in a now-darker cavern, but the heat is still desperate, and I can feel my lips starting to crack and my tongue is swollen. Swallowing hurts like hell. We're stationary and ... I hear a discussion. I tilt my head to listen and a smile pulls the cracks on my lips open. I wince in pain, but at the same time celebrate, the conversation is in English! But I can't quite make it out. My visualisation of the driver's routine fails me at this point. But... two days, so. We're at the port and they're at passport control!

My body surges with energy and I stop breathing as the danger of my predicament suddenly dawns. I stop moving and am alert to any and all sounds, but I can't make out anything. How did I not prepare for this? They could have their cargo checked and that's it for me! How could I forget that? I quickly look around for where I might hide. I know my surroundings more from touch than sight and I know there are a few higher pallets that I could squeeze in behind. But then there is all my litter, the exploded contents of my bag. Shit! I start to pull this together, as quiet as I can, especially with crisp packets.

I only just manage to catch myself from falling as we suddenly set off again. I stay in a squat, waiting. If we pull in within seconds they're going to inspect. If not, we're boarding. A minute later I feel myself start to lean heavily towards the rear door and quickly grab a pallet to stop myself from falling over – the lorry must be driving up a steep gradient. Then I hear the clang of heavy steel as we mount the boarding slipway onto the ferry. I see it all in my mind; I just hope I'm right.

Motor stopped, driver door slammed, many voices passing by and then the continuous thrum of the ship's motor. Then a new thing and as I realise what it is I can't stop myself from smiling as I welcome the gentle sway of the sea. This must be the channel crossing… maybe… I hope. I close my eyes to visualise a map of Europe: from Malmo, it's two days drive and then a sea crossing. Where else could I possibly be? The Med, the Black Sea? But then who would be shipping screws from Sweden to North Africa or the Middle East, no way, would they? It has to be the channel. UK lorry homeward bound: it has to be, it has to be.

After a few of hours, the thrum of the ship's engines drops to a purr and the swaying stops. Voices return as does my driver, and we are away again. The clank of the metal plate and the steep decent to solid ground tells me where we are. I'm huddled behind a pallet at the far end of the lorry, closest to the cab, sat in a stiff silence, having removed all trace of my occupation from the lorry. However, we just drive; we must have been waved through at customs and before long we are on a smooth road at speed, the motorway. We have to be in the UK.

But I need to know – I've been blind for two days. This could all be playing out in my mind. I could be completely wrong, locked up in my imaginary world.

I un-tape part of my entry point, just enough so I can see and also easily stick it back in place. As I peel the tape from the canvas it lets in a piercing spear of light, blinding me. I slowly open my eyes to slits, letting them adapt, opening a little further and repeating. Slowly and steadily I have them open. The light is still dazzling and as I widen the gap the wind starts to tear into my cave. My eyes start to water and I can't stop blinking; everything is a golden blazing blur. I pull back and sit for a moment before slowly bringing my head closer to look through the gap. With the air flow, my eyes quickly dry and adjust and I can soon squeeze up to the opening and get a good view of the outside world. I had no idea fresh air could smell so amazingly good. It's like an adrenaline shot; it smells so crisp, so sweet, recently cut hay with a hint of the sea. I'm rejuvenated from the murky world of oil and desperate thirst.

We're on a motorway passing huge corn fields; all good, and more importantly, we're on the left-hand side of the road. Yes! We're in the UK. I look for road signs and before long I see one: Ashford 7 miles, London 63 miles.

"Yesssss," I say out loud, shocking myself with the sound of my own voice. A smug smile grows on my face. I knew this was the right thing to do.

Confidence fills my bones, comforting me. It worked. I'm home, back in the UK. I could just bang on the back of the driver's cab and ask to be let out. I'm not a refugee anymore, this is my home. I savour the view for a little longer before sealing up my hole and excitedly I prepare to leave.

My thirst returns with vengeance, like when you need the loo and as you're on final approach you can only just hold it in. Except we don't stop for another three hours, by which time I'm starting to doubt if I ever opened up the patch and saw England, it could have been a delusion, a dream whilst I was laid on my back amongst the pallets. But I do know the drill and I listen for the driver's footsteps, which I now know from others and, following the door slam, I hear them walk away into the distance.

It could be just a piss stop, so I give it a couple of minutes for them to be out of sight and go for my escape. This is risky, as I have to go feet first, and anyone could spot me and I have no idea where we are. Speed has to be key, so I untape the whole of the hole, stick my head through and blink the blur away as quickly as I can.

Truck stop, car park area, some people around but not close by.

I quickly pull my head in and, desperate for water and to be free of my mobile prison, I grab my bag and just go for it. Feet out first, I give myself a shove and land with a crunch on the tarmac. I haven't really used my legs for the last two days and they let me know by collapsing under me and I'm in a heap on the floor with a throbbing ankle, looking like I've just walked across the Sahara.

Awkwardly I get myself upright with all my weight on my good leg, and as quickly as I dare, I allow weight to the other foot. It hurts, but it's not excruciating. I hobble a step forwards, then another; it eases and I slowly but steadily limp away from my cave, away from the scene of the crime, to anywhere. Anyone stops me, no problem, I'm a UK citizen, I have an employer, you can ring them if you like, why on earth would I be stowing away on a lorry to get into the UK?

I head for the main shopping area and my limp is all but gone by the time I find the toilets. I attract a few looks on my way, which when I get into the bathroom and see the full state of me is no surprise. Cracked lips, oil smeared face, windswept hair, my shirt a mix of oil and sweat stains – and I stink. I don't care, I march straight over to the sinks, hit the top of the cold tap, stick my head under it and suck for a good five minutes. As I right myself I notice in the mirror one or two people staring. But I'm in it now and I really don't care. I have a strip wash, ignoring the stares, and just get on with the job. Desperate times... the water gives me new life, inside and out. There's not much I can do about my clothes, but I reckon I could pass for a mechanic, at the end of his shift. Maybe.

Out in the main area I scan for people who don't have an AIC in and the fourth person I ask has a phone and is willing to let me borrow it. I tell a tall tale of a stag party and things going wrong.

"Its not been fun, you don't want to know the details," I tell them and offer the evidence of my depleted phone. They don't seem too convinced, but then I don't believe me either. I call the University as it's the only number I can remember and then get them to put me through to the departmental admin team. The ever-helpful Liz answers and she lets me have Michelle's AIC number. I cheekily type this into the phone I'm on, hang up on Liz and beg a second call. I'm pushing my luck, but they don't stop me. Michelle picks up almost straight away with a cheery, "hello".

"You're there, thank God," I say, turning my back on my phone doner. "Michelle, it's me, Sean. Listen. This is not your AIC is it?"

"No, it's me. This sounds serious Sean, are you alright?" she replies.

"It is, and no, I'm not," I say. "I need your help."

"K. I'm here," she says. "What do you need?"

As quickly and efficiently as I can I explain some of my situation to Michelle; essentially I tell her I'm screwed and I need her.

"I'm sorry, I'm on a strangers phone and can't tell you more right now," I say. "But I really need your help. Can you come now, please?" I ask, knowing what a big ask it is, but what choice do I have?

"Seriously?" she replies.

"Yes," I say, pleading. "I know it's a huge favour, but the shit's really hit the fan."

"K, understood," she says. "Where are you?"

"I'm at Rowington services on the M40, northbound."

"K, got you," she says with a snap of seriousness. "On my way, sit tight."

"Thank you, Michelle, thank you," I say hanging up, feeling bad as I pass back the phone to the now very-annoyed passerby who was willing to help. Michelle's never heard me like this before, a desperate man pleading for her help. I suspect the shock factor helped, thank God for friends!

Chapter Twenty-Five

Michelle is easy to spot in the crowd as she enters the café area – a black leather biker's jacket, two motorbike helmets and very messy blond hair. I stand up from my table and wave; she returns a warm smile as she spots me and heads over.

"So, what the fuck is going on with you big boy? And have you seen yourself in a mirror? You look like crap," she says as she sits down and lands the helmets on the table between us. "What is all this mystery shit? And why Coventry of all places? It's got the worst grasping ring road in the country?"

I'm overjoyed to see her, like a little boy being picked up after his first day at school. Just listening to her familiar voice is comforting, and Michelle's easy-going banter makes me feel I'm home again. "Thanks for coming," I say, nodding. "I really appreciate it."

She stops and turns her head slightly to one side. She's noticed something about me; a difference – in just these few words I know the banter is gone and she's serious and sympathetic.

"How can I help?" she asks.

"I need to get to Cambridge," I say. "Collect personal and work stuff and then disappear." As I say the words it makes me scared, scared of my own plan. Vocalising what was until now just in my head, it all seems more real – my perilous journey is far from over. I hadn't focused too much on my next move, and now my rescuer is here I thought I could relax, for a while at least.

"K..." she says, waiting for more. "We can do that easy enough." She sits back in her seat, meeting my stare, hands in her lap. "I don't want to pry Sean, but... you've pulled me halfway across the country at a moment's notice. What's going on?"

I sit in silence, still looking at her, my mind blank, and then I have to look away. "Jess..." I say and then stop, my throat dries up. I can't say it. If I do, I'll be in tears. If I can even get it out. I pull myself together, sit myself up straight, and swallow the anguish.

"Let's head outside," I say. "I can explain more as we walk."

"You know, people have been asking about you at work," says Michelle, as we head to the main entrance. "Nothing serious, I don't think. Quite a few senior people I don't really know have 'just been passing our office and popped in to see if there was any news'. I don't know anything so can't tell them anything, but there's something going on."

I listen – at other times this would have caused me serious anxiety; right now, I couldn't care less.

"K, thanks." I say, not really sure what I am grateful for. "Lots has happened, so much," I pause, building myself up. "Do you know about Jess, about the accident?" I ask.

"No, not heard anything, what happened?" she asks.

"There was an accident, Jess didn't..." My words leave me and I feel the tears run down my face and my body shiver uncontrollably. I take Michelle by the arm and steer us over towards a quiet grassy verge, my head hung low, trying not to draw attention, fighting back the tears and the urge to just let go. Away from people, I sit on the grass, head between my knees, watching my tears fall to the ground. I feel Michelle's warm hand rubbing my back as she sits next to me.

"Sean... mate, what's happened?" she asks, still rubbing my back, and I feel her concern and her worry.

"Jess didn't... she didn't make it," I reply, my words interrupted through half-swallowed tears, my head buried between my knees.

"Fuck, what? She's dead? Sean, is that what you're saying?"

I nod, my head still buried, the tears coming thick and fast.

"I'm so sorry, shit, that's terrible Sean," she says. "My God... Sean!" I hear the disbelief in her voice as she continues to rub my back. I don't move. I just sit and let her comfort me. If I lift my head, I have to go through it all again, tell Michelle what happened, make it real.

"The two of you must have become pretty close, what happened?" she asks after a couple of minutes, but I can't reply, and we sit for a while longer. I eventually lift my head again, wipe my face and focus back on the here and now. Michelle waits, silently, patiently.

"I appreciate you coming like this Michelle," I murmur. "It means a lot to me, thanks." I lean in to give her a hug, resting my head on her shoulder, only then realising that we have never hugged before, maybe never touched. As I pull away, I notice the glint of a tear in her eyes, too.

"Shit, Sean, you're going to have me crying," she says, rubbing her eyes.

I turn to her with a flattened smile. "Thanks Michelle, I mean it," I say.

She stands and holds her hand out me. "Come on then, what needs to happen now, where're we going?"

I take her hands and she yanks me from the ground. Her direct pragmatism is just what I need right now.

"I need to collect all of our research data," I say. "So the lab and my Cambridge place and then... Well, let's focus on that for now. So, Cambridge for now, which I know is a way off, sorry. But you can simply drop me off at the tram connector station when we get there. Is that alright?"

"Sure, no problem. Or I can take you all the way in on the bike of course. A friend in need is a pain in the arse, remember," she replies, with a cheeky grin and familiar wink.

Michelle is here to save me and I so appreciate her. She hasn't pushed me on anything and I've dragged her halfway across the country and now back. I give her a solid hug. "Thanks Michelle, just... thanks." I hold her for a moment, savouring the connection and her friendship.

"It's K mate," she replies, as I release her. "So, that's yours," she says, handing me one of the helmets she has with her. "I need a snack, quick dash to the loo, and we can be off, K?"

"Yes, that'd be great," I reply.

The bike ride is exhilarating and fast, ideal as we can't chat en route so I don't have to deal with the sharing of emotional issues and also I don't have to weave a web of deceit on what I can and can't share.

We make Cambridge in what feels like no time at all, weaving in and out of traffic with only the occasional stop to rest arms and bums. Having lived in my oily cave for two days, the fresh air is just what I need and starts to pump energy back into my body. Although it could be the adrenalin of the ride, Michelle does not hang about. When she gets on the faster roads, I have to resort to simply not looking and hiding behind her back. I have confidence in her ability to ride a motorbike, but the speed and acceleration of the thing is phenomenal.

When she brakes hard, I have to stop holding her around the waste and place my palms on the battery tank to take the strain. I feel my arms getting pumped – I had no idea motor-biking was so physical.

We get to the nearest park-up area to my flat and I dismount. Being on the back of a high-powered motor bike is another first for me and my inner thighs don't like it at all. Plus the helmet is too small. Now I remove it I can feel my ears throb and it feels like my head is swelling back to its normal size. Speed does not equal comfort.

"How far is it to your place?" asks Michelle.

"Less than fifteen minutes, is that OK?"

"Sure, how was the ride?" she asks.

I don't answer, just smile. "It's this way" I say.

I feel a sense of relief but also foreboding as I unlock the door. It's nice to be home, but the reality is that if Ananta are looking for me then this has to be the first place they would try. Or maybe monitor? It's a risk, but I've been gone for a good number of days and with the tech they have I see no point in looking for people in trench coats hanging about suspiciously. So I just go for it. If they pick me up, so be it.

"You know you can stay Michelle," I say, as we enter. "I have a spare room."

"Thanks, but that's K," she replies. "Bit of a rest is all I need to be honest."

"What about food, are you hungry?"

"Please, and a drink if you have it," she shouts after me as I head into the kitchen.

I quickly search the cupboards and fridge but have little of anything salvageable in the food department. Eventually I find a frozen chilli – result. I keep searching for more food so I don't have to go and sit with Michelle.

"I have some green tea, will that do?" I shout.

"Just water is fine Sean, thanks," she replies.

I return after five minutes with a tray and my meagre offering.

"Sean, you know if you want to talk then I'm pretty good at listening," she says sat next to me, eyes fixed on me, understanding. "I know I don't seem like the type sometimes, I'm loud and not so subtle, but I have a softer side too. You know, if it would help?"

"Thanks Michelle, you've already done so much. Rescuing me like you have. I know I keep saying it, but you can't imagine how much you have helped, really," I say, nodding, and all the while holding eye contact with her, reading her. She knows how I feel and senses my sincerity, a small happiness grows within me.

"K," she replies with a nod, and we eat in silence, the unspoken agreement of me taking the lead if there is anything to be shared. I think for Michelle this is fine, but for me the silence becomes deafening. I hear every clank of cutlery against the plate, every ruffle of cushion as either of us move in our seat. I've become aware of the distant noises on the street. Steadily, the volume of all these things starts to increase. I look around and there's something else. I look at the clock on the wall and the detail is too fine – my eyes are not that good. It's like I can see the detail as if only a few centimetres away, yet it's on the other side of the room. I shake my head, blink, and the clock is far away again. I don't know what this is, but it needs to stop.

"Michelle," I pause as I notice the sound of my voice instantly killing the cacophony of noise and acute vision that's assailing me. "Michelle…" I repeat, shaking these new sensations, "…are you sure you don't want to stay the night? Driving back now, are you not too tired?"

"I'll be fine, don't worry," she replies. "Plus, I never sleep well away from home, unless I'm in the camper van."

"Well, your choice, but the offer is genuine."

"I know," she acknowledges with a nod.

We finish our meal in silence. Thankfully, the cacophony doesn't return, even when I clear the noisy plates.

"When do you want to head off?" I ask, raising my voice as I enter the kitchen.

"Pretty soon, so I don't get back too late," she says. "Are you going to be K though, is there anyone local you can call on if you need? I could stay, you know, if you needed?"

"I'll be fine, really, thanks. But, before you go…" I hold up a finger. "Just give me a minute, I want to get something."

"K," she replies, puzzled.

From my bedroom I quickly grab my passport and my emergency credit card from my sock drawer. I get an envelope and spend some time writing out the address of Mike's Swedish installation on it – essentially the WikiLeaks Stockholm office – but my name as the addressee. I place my passport and credit card in and seal it and Sellotape the edges for security. This needs to work, otherwise my plan is bust before it begins.

I find Michelle in the kitchen washing up after our dinner. "You don't need to do that, I'll do it later," I say.

"It's K, here to help," she says, turning and smiling at me as she finishes up and dries her hands.

"Listen, you've been such a saviour today," I say. "I can't tell you how much I appreciate it and allowing me the space to not have to explain everything. It's hard and really complicated, so thank you for that too. It's also not over yet. So can I ask a final favour? It's not a big deal but it is *really* important."

"Sean, are you in trouble? Beyond Jess's death?"

"Yes, but I'm dealing with it."

"Right..." she says.

"Can you post this letter by twenty-four hour FedEx?" I ask, passing her the envelope with my passport and credit card in. She takes it, looks at the address and then to me, eyebrows raised, asking me what it is, without asking me what it is.

"Well, yes, I can do that Sean," she replies, confused. "But why can't you? And it's addressed to you?"

"Sorry, I'm not explaining everything well," I say. "I don't want you to do this until you get an email or text from me saying to do so, and then if you can do it straight away. Is that alright?"

"Yeah. But... well, can I ask why Sean? It's addressed to you and it's in Sweden, so you're going to Sweden? What's going on Sean? You could take whatever is in here to Sweden with you." We share a look. I want to tell her, but I know I can't. With no reply from me, she holds her hands up in surrender. "Sorry, I know you don't want to talk about this, but... well, you have to admit it's all very... very fucking weird."

"I know, I'm sorry," I reply. "To explain it all would take a long time and you would likely think I've lost the plot, which I may have done. But this is it, my final ask and really appreciated. Can you, will you...?"

"Sure, of course I will," she replies, smiling now, and slips the envelope into an inside pocket of her biker jacket.

I walk her to the door and as I'm about to open it she assails me with a hug that takes me back a pace. She squeezes me tight, her head against my chest, and I smell the leather of her jacket mixed with a hint of old perfume. "Sean, you will be K won't you? You're not going to do anything stupid?" she asks, wrapped tightly against my chest.

I release her and she me and I take a small step backwards, looking down into her eyes. "Hard times, yes," I say, forcing a swallow on my now dry throat, feeling the grief grow in me. "But..."

One hand still on my waist, Michelle reaches her other to stroke my cheek ever so gently, pushing my hair behind my ear. "You poor thing," she says and our eyes lock, I feel the rush of emotion, my feelings for her. I've always really liked Michelle, but never seen her like that, but right now that's suddenly changed. She feels the same, I can see it in her eyes and feel it in my chest, the way she's holding me...

But, Jess. I close my eyes to break the connection and I see a glimpse of Jess, smiling at me in the lab, a smear of oil on her cheek. I feel Michelle release me and open my eyes to meet hers again, but different now, I feel closer to her, but... confused.

Twenty minutes later I'm alone, my saviour headed off into the night. I'm suddenly bereft again, in this place that once welcomed *her* and can never do so again. The silence returns, my sensitivity to all things visual and audible. The noise of my breathing, my heartbeat, the tick of the clock, the drag of my feet on the carpet – all too loud, too crisp and clear. It's all like an amplified recording being played on headphones.

I sit myself in the armchair and notice the fabric brushing against my hands. I can feel each fibre rush past each of my fingers, like I'm reading braille, each indentation and strand strokes a point on my fingertips, giving me a detailed feel for what I'm touching, as if through a magnifying glass I can see the layout of the fibres from the perspective of my fingertips. I lift my hands away from the fabric and allow myself to fall into the chair. It has to be fatigue, I'm exhausted physically and mentally, not having had a proper night's sleep for I don't know how long. I need some noise to push this assault on my senses away. I switch on the screen and it drowns the deafening silence.

I know it's a big gamble to be home and a bigger one to go into the lab tomorrow, which I know I must do. But, so far, so good, although there's no message from Mike – I still have no idea where he is and what has happened to him, but he did say run. The Ananta are unpredictable and way more dangerous than Mike lets on, or knows. I have to get them off my back and the only way I can do that is to have nothing they want. My only long-term safety is in publishing and sharing all our discoveries.

Anything I publish without a peer review may not be taken seriously, at first. But with both our names on it, someone will follow up and see the truth of it, especially Jess's colleagues – they have the rig, ready to go. In fact, I can send them a specific email to set them on the right path. I know this will piss off lots of people, but the game is way bigger now. It's keeping humanity in the game. I can't think of anything more important.

Chapter Twenty-Six

The shower hits my body and wakes me proper. The water cascades over my head and the steam smothers me, like every morning. Like every morning... and exactly like *that* morning. I sense it, there's more... I allow my mind its own freedom to feel ahead, to follow the déjà vu emotion, give it autonomy to grow of its own volition and see what comes to me.

The days ahead will be hard. I feel certain of this, I feel it like I've lived it, a memory of hardship yet to come. And... there's more, something really important. Elusive, slippery. It's important, life altering, I can feel it. I need to know... it. But... my mind slips and I'm back in the shower.

Do I have foresight? Some ability to recognise a future path, an ability that doesn't fit with our way of thinking? It's feelings not thoughts, a sensed intuition, something left over from my visit to Node? Interesting, but right now I need to be back in the game, focus and keep moving forward. I turn the shower to iCe, and lose my breath for a few seconds, try to relax my breathing and manage maybe four minutes. I kill the shower and feel like I'm ready to take on the world, which is just as well. I smile to myself, mostly at my own joke.

The clock tells me it's six am. I have an hour before the Uni buildings are open. Early morning; things are always quiet and with luck I'll be away again before most folks have even got to work. But as soon as I swipe my access card, I'm on a ticking clock. No room for error – efficiency is key. My school science teacher's prophetic advice arrives from nowhere, "perfect preparation prevents poor performance", and I go to check my bag again.

I keep my wits about me, trying to be subtle, scanning ahead as I walk to the lab. A woman walking a dog looks at me as she passes. I smile at her, she doesn't smile back. I look back at her as she goes past, and she briefly does the same. Why would she look at me and not smile, and then look back, unless she was confirming something? I look again – she keeps going, walking the dog.

As casually as I can I continue to look around whilst I walk, pretending to notice the birds and the vistas of the city, making best efforts to appear tourist-like and not fugitive. As I get closer to the Uni, the number of people increases. They're mostly walking dogs or out for a morning jog before the heat of the day arrives; there are more people than normal. But as I see these people in the distance and closer as they pass, any of them could be anyone. How can I know? Can I know? Only if they're the hipster, that's it. And if they knew where I was and wanted to pick me up, they would. The people I'm up against have unimaginable resources and capabilities, how on earth can I defend against them? My only defence is they don't know where I am, so me going to the one place in the world they know I'm likely to go to is the very definition of stupidity.

It's a risk, a big risk. But I have no choice, if my plan is to work. I have to go through with it, no time to back out now. It's the only way.

My edge is no one knowing, going it alone and not stopping. Speed, speed is my friend, my weapon.

My knees go weak and I hear my heartbeat pumping in my ears as I approach the main buildings. I slow myself down – be the normal me, blending in is my disguise. I keep walking, steady and with purpose, through the main doors and directly to the labs. They could be waiting for me – they might even be following me now and watching to see what I do. My stomach starts to turn over. I feel my face heating up, each step closer nudges up the nausea. My hands start to sweat, and I feel my balance is off, like I'm on a boat.

I swipe my card and enter the lab. As the door slowly closes behind me, there's serene silence. What was once a hive of activity is now a liminal space. I feel the hairs on my arms stand up. I see her, inspecting the rig, reviewing data at her laptop, observing the experiments, always focused, always with purpose and direction. She was amazing... she *was* amazing. My vision starts to blur and my throat tightens.

I slowly walk to our desk, run my hand over it, lost to the moment, forgetting my urgency. I miss her so much, so much...

Enough! The clock is ticking.

I plug in and start to download everything from the lab database via the Uni Wi-Fi. The speed here is an order of magnitude faster than anywhere else and there's much to download. Also, this way the trail won't pinpoint to me directly and I'll be done in thirty minutes, so if the Ananta are pursing me they will need to be fast.

I create a his-and-her file for the download. Hers is huge and has much I don't understand; I'll need to study hard to make sense of it all. Meanwhile I set to and, using an old disconnected phone, take lots of photos of the rig and the more intricate elements of the workings, pulling open some sections so I can photograph the inner gubbins, not really knowing what I'm looking at. But it's all evidence and those in the know will be able to come and investigate the real thing when word gets out.

In no time, I'm done. I have two huge piles of data and lots of photos, all equating to a mountain of work. I have everything we have ever done. I pack up and head off, nearly bumping into a cleaner as I round the corner. "Sorry," I say, side-stepping.

"Morning," they reply. Normal response, and they don't follow me, must be the genuine article – no Anata here.

I'm back home for eight-thirty, collect my ready-prepared backpack, lock the door again as I leave and am walking back into town heading to the train station. The Ananta must know now. I need to be gone, vanish as quickly as I can.

The next train for London is in twenty minutes, perfect. Enough time to go to the cash machine, purchase a sim card and board.

With minutes to spare I'm sinking into my seat with a long and slow exhale. And no sign of anyone or anything out of the ordinary. That has to be the most risky part of the plan and went off without a hitch. A smile grows on my face – I'm not bad at this. But this is only the first stage – lot's still to do, but I'm on track. A chuckle escapes my lips; my own joke keeping me going.

Except... we're not going. We're sat in the station, and I need the train to leave. As soon as it does, every mile will make me safer. The further away from Cambridge the better. But here we sit – I can see the platform signs and clock, our time to leave has passed and we're not moving. Delayed... I hadn't counted on this.

I push my head against the window, attempting to look along the length of the train for the guard. I can't see anything, but relief floods my senses as I hear it – the whistle – and the train slides forwards. Yessss. I sit back against the seat and smile, safety sinking me into my seat.

A smug smile on my face, I lazily watch the people on the concourse as we glide by. My eyes become drawn to a person in the distance. They're running, out of step with everyone else in the station. He's just missed his train, our train – shame. He stops at the edge of the platform some way ahead of me, and as the train speeds towards him, the blood drains from my head. My body locks solid; I stare, unblinking, disbelieving. It can't be. But, of course it could be, in fact it was very likely, I knew this all along. It's the hipster, the Ananta.

It all happens very quickly as we pick up speed. Through the window his eyes meet mine. Fuck! I go to duck and hide, but I can't. His penetrating gaze has me frozen and as we pass one another only a few feet apart, our heads rotate to maintain the locked stare, neither being the first to break away, until the train severs the link.

Shit, fuck! I should have been more careful. The Wi-Fi login, cash machine, my security card swipe. There could have been other ways – sloppy, too sloppy. But I got away... No. No, I didn't. Shit! He knows which train I'm on!

I get off the train at the next stop and look to the departure boards for the next trains to pass through. Three minutes later I am on a train to Milton Keynes. This is do-able. I can do this a few times, shake them off. I have three hundred pounds and can pay cash for everything; it won't last forever but I can cross that bridge when I get to it.

Do they have Mike? They're clearly looking for me. I should have known, but part of me hoped they would have given up. But if they're still pursuing me, that might be useful when the time comes. I need to think again, I need to be more careful, and I need to think through everything. And with Mike gone, I'm going to need help.

My unplanned train changes take me further north. Perhaps I'm subconsciously guiding myself home – we're drawn to what we know. I need to think again, adapt to survive, Darwinian. I need help from a friend, I can't use or do anything that will show where I am – no phones, cards, anything. I need to vanish.

Three hours later, the familiar train station greets me and its cutting edge sculpture of a large knife blade reflects my situation, out of time and out of place. I head across town to the campus, keeping my head down and walking at speed. This is my best approach, constantly looking around for danger won't help me. I need to keep one move ahead; my own blitzkrieg, just keep walking. My pack doesn't slow me down but when I enter my building I'm covered in sweat. I just hope she's in, she has to be in.

I head up the stairs and stand outside my lab, hand on the door. I will it. For her to be in, she has to be in. I open the door and look to Michelle's empty desk.

"Bollocks!" I announce, to what I thought was an empty room.

"What?" I hear from the far end of the room and Anthony stands up from behind his desk and screen.

"Hey, Sean! How are you?" he says. "Where have you been? Lots of people have been asking about you. Are you alright?"

"Anthony, it's great to see *you*," I say, with the relief of a castaway to his rescuer. "How are you, have you been well? Who exactly has been looking for me?"

He stands looking at me across the room, no change to him at all. He's even wearing the same pale blue shirt and jeans, his usual uniform. His desk is still chaos and he has the same slightly unkempt look, his shirt not entirely tucked into his jeans.

"Me? I'm fine, steady away, you know," he replies. "Who's looking for you? Well, lots of people. The Dean at one time, HR for something and others, you know. I figured you've done something amazing or things had gone from bad to worse?"

"Was one of them an older chap with a hipster moustache?" I ask gingerly.

"Might have been actually," says Anthony. "Kind of sounds like the prof from UCL who popped in last week. I can't remember his name, he did say and I did write it down. Somewhere..." He starts to randomly lift piles of paper across his wastepaper bin of a desk. I give him a minute, just in case, but I suspect the information is long gone.

"Listen, Anthony, don't worry about it," I say, halting his paper shuffle. "What I do need is to ask you a favour. It's a big ask but I need to find a bolthole for a couple of weeks, and I'm having trouble with my credit cards. Would you mind if I gave you the cash and you booked it on your card? Would that be alright?" I do my best to "feel" a yes coming back at me from Anthony. If I have any Jedi abilities, now is the time to use them.

"Yes, of course, I guess" he replies with a muted smile. "Did you need to do that now or later... what were you thinking?"

I feel a warm glow for Anthony and my smile likely confirms this to him, too. He keeps smiling right back at me and I stand staring directly at him, time slowed, not yet responding, but connecting, somehow. I'm not really sure what's going on, but I feel happy, connected. "Well, right now. If that works for you?" I say.

"Sure, where is it? Do you have the website address for the booking?" he asks as he brings up a web browser on his screen.

"Ahh, no, not yet. Need to find somewhere as well," I say, raising my eyebrows and gritting my teeth, knowing I'm pushing things.

Anthony looks at me quizzically, I suspect confused by my lack of planning. It's not like me.

"I know, sorry," I say apologetically, holding up my hands. "I'm kind of asking for two favours then, sorry old friend. Lots going on at the moment. Do you mind if we have a look on your PC, been having problems with my laptop..."

"We can do," he replies. "Although I have a class in thirty minutes so we probably need to be quick."

We cruise through a few locations in the lake district, and I find a small remote one-bedroomed cottage near Ennerdale, immediate availability. We book it from today, all in Anthony's name, so it aligns with his card and I'm set. I go to give him the cash, which he refuses.

"Pay me when your cards are back in order," he says. "Otherwise, you'll run out of cash. No rush."

I was hoping he would say this, which could mean I may have influenced him. But I can't risk another cash withdrawal without a quick getaway plan – any electronic interaction and the Ananta have me, and right now the last thing I want to do is start running again.

"That's great, thanks," I say, more appreciative than he realises. "And have you seen Michelle at all, is she about?"

"Oh, you don't know?" he replies, and with all the driving she was doing I fear the worst. "Yesterday's staff meeting was just about to start, and Michelle comes in and tells us *all* that she has 'the shits' and 'has to go right now'. And off she went, and I've not seen her since, so I hope she's alright."

Anthony frowns at my muted laugh as he regales me with the tale. "Sorry," I say. "Just you know... Michelle and her frankness, still makes me laugh."

"Ahh, yes, right you are," says Anthony smiling, and we reminisce about Michelle's faux pas for a while even though I am itching to get away from the Uni. Just taking the money and running wouldn't be right – Anthony's worth the risk. We chat and I look around at the familiar place... life seems to have gone on as ever, Michelle's tranklements just as they ever were, the Chinese cat still perpetually waving.

For me so much has changed and will never be the same again, yet here there is no movement, how can that be? How can the world just go on, oblivious, when for me it's been turned upside down? This reality is completely at odds with mine.

Anthony doesn't ask me about Jess, thank God. It's great to see him and for a few brief moments I'm transported back to how things used be. I miss my old life. It was less complicated; it was predictable, easy going. It had its ups and downs but fundamentally I think I was happy.

"Anthony, you've been a massive help here, it's so much appreciated," I say. "But before I head off... can I maybe ask you another favour? Not now, but soon."

"K..." replies Anthony, unsure. "What is it?"

"When I'm ready to go public with mine and Jess's work, do you think you'll be able to help me get it out there? On the web that is."

"Not sure what you mean," he replies, with a frown. "Will you not just publish it in a relevant journal?"

"No, I can't afford to wait. It won't even be peer reviewed, I just need the information to be out there. Journals can come later."

"That's all a bit odd Sean, and why me?" he replies. "Surely you can do that yourself?"

"I can. Except, this is different. I need the work to be non-traceable to any IP address and also undeletable, so some kind of replication across the web so it can never be deleted by any 'Big Brother' type groups." Anthony is a tech genius and with his conspiracy theories around smart fascism and how it has convinced us we are in a democracy, when in reality we aren't, coupled with his online anti-capitalist networks, he has a broad reach. When it comes to getting the finished write-up of mine and Jess's longevity work out there, he will be able to spread the word and cover his tracks.

"Wow," replies Anthony. "That sounds... illegal, or something like that. Sorry Sean, I can't be involved in that, it could be my job on the line."

"I understand," I say, devastated but hiding it. "You're right, I should never have asked, sorry."

Anthony doesn't respond further and just looks at me, more confused than ever. I'm not sure what more I can do to persuade him. Awkwardly I give him a second and then stand up, ready to leave. "Not to worry, you're right, sorry to put you on the spot like that. Listen, thanks ever so for booking the accommodation and the loan of money. You have really helped me out. It really is appreciated old friend."

"You're welcome Sean, no problem," he replies with a smile.

"Listen, you've got to teach, and I need to go too, so I'll see you soon. K?"

Not sure of my next best option, I simply head towards the door. I'll need to find another way to anonymously publish and ensure it can't be taken down.

"Sean," calls Anthony as I grab the door handle. "I can give you an email address of someone who might be able to help you."

"Really? Well that would be great, thanks," I reply.

He grabs a piece of paper and starts to write, "only just don't tell them I sent you, or that you know me. Alright?"

"Sure, no problem at all," I say, glad of the option. At which point, Anthony stops writing and screws up the piece of paper in his hand.

"No, I can't send you to them," he says and looks at me pensively. "Fuck it. I'll do it," he replies, his tone and words completely out of character.

"Really?" I reply gleefully. "That would be great if you can and it isn't illegal or anything, it's just... tricky with some of the stakeholders involved," I say, trying to play down the deadly nature of my predicament.

"So, tell me more," he replies. "What, who, when, how, all that."

"We, I, need to get the results from mine and Jess's work out to the world," I say. "And there are groups that might want to suppress the information. I need to bypass them and have the information free to access by anyone, anywhere."

"Hang on Sean, is your recent research covert?" he asks, now with a demonic smile.

"Yes, you could say that."

"And you want to publish your findings. But a non peer-reviewed version because certain groups might want to suppress the knowledge?"

"Yes," I say, cagily. "Also, we, I, need to get things out there ASAP and you know how long the peer review process takes."

"Wow," replies Anthony, nodding his head. "So this is your longevity stuff, is that right?"

"Yes, it is," I say, knowing what's coming next.

"Don't tell me you've solved it." he says, his disbelief clear. "You've got to be kidding... you have the answer to everlasting life, and you want to share it with all mankind! Shit..."

"More or less, kind of... but you can't say a word. Not until it's published. Not to anyone, not even Michelle. This is really important, seriously. You understand?"

"My lips are sealed," he says. "No problem at all. I will begin preparing the road ahead. I'm on it." He turns to the screen, mumbling something I can't make out. He starts opening all kinds of windows across his screens, immediately on the job.

"Don't forget, you're teaching Anthony," I remind him, realising he's now lost to the world because of me.

"Ohhh... Sugar. Yep. I'm gone," he replies, grabbing his bag and a tablet. He gets to the door and quickly turns to me, "give me the nod when you're ready to go live, K?"

"Certainly will, take care," I reply and quickly walk over to give him a hug, which throws him. I don't think we've touched beyond our first introduction when I shook his hand. He's rigid and unsure but slowly hugs me back, awkwardly, with his arms already full and uncertain of this new level of intimacy.

"Are you sure everything's alright?" he asks.

"It will be old chap, it will be," I say, feeling the confidence in my words.

Chapter Twenty-Seven

The directions I wrote when Anthony and I booked the cottage seemed straight forward: get off the bus at Crossgates, walk three miles to Asby and then second of only two right turns in the village – simple. But leaving the village on a single-track country road with no footpath and nothing but rolling fields surrounding me, I'm losing confidence in my own instructions. The last thing I want to do is ask someone, although chance would be a fine thing.

An hour walking and my pack is getting heavier, and the road starts to become more track-like, with grassy patches in the centre of the broken tarmac and hawthorn bushes encroaching from either side, making it only just passable by car. I keep going and an incongruous wheely bin materialises at the side of the road. It's at the entrance to a gravel track, with a cattle grid across the opening, the track leading away from the road to who knows where as it disappears over a small hill in the distance. It could be my cottage, or a farm, but with no building or sign who knows. My instructions tell me the sign with the name of the cottage is at the entrance to the "driveway", but there's nothing, so this isn't it.

Tired, with the light fading and not wanting to spend the night in the open, I continue at a pace along the road, hoping for something. But a niggle stops me. I turn around and retreat back to the wheely bin. I roll the bin forwards, away from the wall, and there it is. The straps on my rucksack ease on my shoulders and a smile grows on my face. I'm here.

The gravel track takes me over the small hill and through some woods, all well beyond the road and resulting in near darkness when I eventually get to the cottage. I haven't seen another building in over an hour and the remoteness starts to chill me as the night closes in. Thankfully the porch light is on, presumably for me, and as I get close to the light its brightness changes my eyes, making the world around me suddenly nighttime.

Antique Laura Ashley soft furnishings and a wave of heat welcome me as I enter and dump my rucksack, before turning on all the lights and exploring my new home. The darkness outside and silence of the place creeps me out, until my predicament comes hurtling back. The day has been long, and my feet are not used to long walks with a rucksack. So as soon as I've done a minimal unpack, I head to bed, only to find the silence was an illusion as the outside world comes alive with nocturnal activity. The owl hoots I expected but not the screeching and snarling fight that kicks off somewhere in the garden. I lie in starched cotton sheets listening to it, too tired to investigate. I simply stare at the moon shadows on the ceiling, reminiscent of my oil cave journey, the memory making my crisp, fresh and oversized bed all the more comfortable.

As tired as I am, sleep eludes me. It's impossible to *know* that I'm safe – they could be on their way, the hipster, the Ananta. But how could they track me? Unless they were physically following me, or tracking all the activity of all the people I know? If they did know where I was, they could pick me up anytime and they haven't. They must be backing off, but then why was the hipster running at the train station? Or have managed to give them the slip? Go me.

The morning sun wakes me through a gap in the curtains, which I open fully to an amazing landscape. I see the rolling hills surrounding my moorland valley and the mountains in the distance. My whole vista is lush greenery peppered with purple heather and white specks of sheep amongst the steep craggy outcrops. It's like a postcard from yesteryear, lush and verdant. Even the lawn of the house is green, not a single patch of sun-bleached grass scratching its way through dried cracked earth. It looks wrong, like an old movie, but right now perfect, the splendid isolation I need.

My cottage stands alone in its own grounds at the end of the gravel track, shielded from the road by a small hill and wood. With its whitewashed walls, little white fence and flowers beautifully trestled around the door it wouldn't look out of place on a biscuit tin lid. The metre-thick walls and the ancient rough stonework surrounding the fireplace tell me it must be several hundred years old, but beautifully maintained, clean and petit, two up and two down, with floral ancient carpets and white-washed internal walls bizarrely shaped into overlapping fans.

There's a semi-broken wall surrounding the property and on the inside the grass has been cut and beyond is bracken dying off for the winter. The garden extends down the hillside to meet a small stream cutting the valley in two. I imagine the place has seen many a romantic weekend.

I find a local map in the cottage and estimate three miles back to village I came through yesterday. The cottage info details a small shop for provisions in the village, so I don my boots and my now-empty rucksack and head out for provisions.

The façade of the village shop also belongs on a biscuit tin lid, it must be a feature of the valley. With ancient wooden shelving and food tins piled in little pyramids it belongs in the 1960s and only has the most basic of anything. I stock up for near a week, trying to find the middle ground of not standing out by buying too much and also not wanting to be in here too often. I need to be invisible.

Returning home, I set up my office space in the main living area of the cottage, shifting the furniture to accommodate my priorities, and try to get myself organised for the task ahead, which is essentially doing a year's work in a few weeks. With no one to talk to my days are eerily silent, but I quickly settle into a routine where I get up early and work until noon, go for a twenty-minute walk after lunch and then work again into the evening.

The first few days are intense as I dig into the data and steadily realise the enormity of the task. I'm reminded of her as I go through her notes; I look at what she's written on the screen and it's her voice that reads it to me. There's a melancholy to it, but also a comfort; it's like having a piece of her back with me, all the while knowing only too well how much better she would be at this, applying her own scientific method and writing things up to a high standard. There was a reason she was at Cambridge.

By the end of the first week, I've extended my regular afternoon walk to take me up the nearby fells. The views are spectacular and now I know the route well, it allows my mind time to wander without me getting lost. The project is coming on. After I managed to sort and file it, the data started to pull together and make sense. Not an easy task, but the data are solid, the findings unambiguous. It's good science. My final write-up may not be going to a peer-reviewed journal, but I still need to write it up as if it were.

The next day it's pouring with rain as I head out on my walk, but I go anyway. I need the time to clear my head from the endless data analysis. What was a track that led up the hill is now a silver stream gushing down. But I stick with my usual route, doing my best not to get soaking feet but failing in the first five minutes. Looking up the valley as I climb the hill I see thin lines of mercury sliding down the steep valley sides and sheets of rain heading my way, thickening the downpour with the strengthening wind. I should probably head back, but don't; I'm already soaked, I can't get any wetter. It's me against the elements.

Trudging across the boggy moorland I can't stop thinking about Mike. He's the one person in the world I would welcome with open arms right now. Could he find me if he needed to? Escaping and hiding is not my area of expertise, yet I seem to be successful at it, which doesn't seem right. This makes me think this might all be a construct, a training exercise set up by Mike, or worse, the Ananta. Is it *all* a test? For us, for humanity? Can we cope and become that which we have potential for, or do we wither and die? Maybe we need more time, to evolve further, to become more mature first? But we can't, the climate crisis is upon us; the whole thing that drove my research. We can't wait. We have to take the test now, we've brought it on ourselves.

Mike said there's no way of telling reality from a construct, but you can force an exit, the same way you snap awake in dreams, by dying… so not an option. If this is a construct, then playing it as if it were real would likely be the best response. And if this is real then playing as if it were, is the only response. So I trudge on, leaning against a wall of rain.

The next week is hell. I'm back to writing eighteen hours a day. I break my internet silence and ask Anthony to extend my stay for a week, which he does. At the same time, just in case, I check my sent emails box, ignoring my inbox. And it's there, sending my blood cold, glaring at me from the screen, pulsating with ramifications. Exactly as I planned, but not expected so soon. It's a request from me to Michelle to send the package by Fedex ASAP please.

We are on, he's here. The game is afoot.

I sit and stare at the email – it's short and to the point. But it's huge, and as I start to think through my next steps, the swell of emotions force me to focus on the bigger picture. I pace around the cottage, except it's too small, so I head out, giving myself space. Where I had clarity of focus and a clear outcome in writing a paper, I'm now back in the wider game. The dangerous game, where I am the prey and there is much I don't know and can't know. The game where I have to leave the sanctuary of my cottage. My sanctuary with its quaint whitewashed walls and low beamed ceiling, the grand settee with too many cushions.

Necessity is the mother of invention. I need this paper finished and I need a layman's version for the wider web. I set to. All I do is work, eat and sleep, with not much eating or sleeping. After three days I catch myself in the bathroom mirror – the bags under my eyes are huge and turning grey, I now have crow's feet extending to my hairline, and I really should brush my hair. In the moments I give myself to eat I know the work I'm doing is not my best, but time is everything now. I push on and on. I manage a forage to the village shop only to realise I must look a sight as the woman behind the counter gives me a double take as I enter. She can't stop looking at me, while pretending not to. So much for my low profile. Not that it matters now; I get enough provisions for a week. I must be gone before that.

I find myself walking around the cottage garden talking through and re-drafting my final conclusive paragraph repeatedly, saying it out aloud, tweaking words, ensuring I have a compelling argument that can't be put aside. It takes time, but it will be worth it.

Eventually I pull everything together into the final document. It's done. I re-read and yes, it's good, rigorous and no points of ambiguity. It really is done. The supporting data is all compiled and labelled ready for upload. I just need Anthony.

I push back from my makeshift desk, an unfocused thousand-yard stare at the screen, crick my neck left and right – it's three AM. Sending something like this out into the world without a colleague checking it is crazy, but that's my world now.

Early the next morning, my stomach churns in the sweet sorrow of leaving a place of fond memories, my sanctuary. It's been weeks and feels like months and I don't think I've spoken more than a dozen times throughout. Part of me wants to stay, to avoid the incoming storm, but that's not an option. I will return, I promise myself, when this is all over, if I survive... And when I do, if things go well... you never know, there could be a small blue plaque on the wall declaring "the theory of longevity was written here".

"I will return old friend," I say, quietly patting the stonework of the porch as I lock the door for the last time, feeling alone in this world. I allow myself a final glance at the cottage as I near the crest of the hill, before I turn and continue, my path clear.

Chapter Twenty-Eight

I find the busyness of the world oppressive and hurried as I head back into the throng of life. I have to keep my wits about me. I know I'm still on the run, but it feels different now, not like before, now there's a light at the end of the tunnel. My escape.

I don't call Anthony to let him know I'm coming, I just turn up at the University. I know he asked me to let him know, but there's too much at stake now, wheels are in motion and my part is key. I can't be delayed, it's not just me anymore, well sort of, *he's* on his way and he's *not* me. I have to remember that. Things will get complicated and since I hatched this plan, so much has changed.

When I get to the Uni I feel conspicuous. Lecturers don't turn up to work with large backpacks on. I quickly make my way up to the lab, avoiding all eye contact, and burst through the lab door with a little too much pace, breathing hard and covered in sweat. Anthony's chair is empty – damn. I stop to catch my breath for a moment.

"Sean, Sean! How you doing?" shrieks Michelle.

"What?" I say, looking around to see her beaming at me from the far side of the lab. I smile right back at her, my saviour. What do I say, can I say… have I said? I'm exhausted and for a moment can't quite figure out what she does and doesn't know.

"How have you been?" I reply, playing for time.

"I've been worried about you," she replies. "You disappeared."

"Yeah, sorry, just a bit out of breath," I reply, feigning my breathing, still playing for time. "I'm not bad, you know. Keeping busy. How are things with you?"

"K, ya know," she says. "But what about you, with everything that's happened?"

"Soldiering on, soldiering on," I reply.

"Did you get the package? How was Sweden?" she asks.

I look at her for a moment, "err, yes, yes and yes. Thanks for asking. And thanks again, you're a life saver, you really are Michelle. Can I ask – did you mention about Jess to anyone?"

"Just to Anthony," she replies, nodding empathetically. "I didn't think it was my place to say anything to anyone else."

I stare at her, sadness and appreciation jostling for my attention. And seeing her anew I notice for the first time the wonderful woman that stands before me, not simply a great colleague. What might have been in another world…?

"You sure you're alright?" she asks again.

"No, but, well. You've got to keep going, you know," I say, conflicted. I need to validate Jess's memory but at the same time, I need to keep the focus, keep moving forward. It's still too painful to talk about Jess without my emotions overtaking me. The plan has to be my everything.

"So, where are you at?" she asks. "Where've you been? Anthony mentioned the Lake District. I'm guessing you needed some time out?"

"It's been tough, but to be honest I've just focused on work," I say. "I have to, everything that Jess and I have been working on is, well, it's at risk."

"At risk?"

"Yes. Well... I can explain," I say. "But it might be easier if we get hold of Anthony as well, and I can bring you both up to speed. Do you know where he is?"

"He was in the refectory, let me give him a call and let him know you're here."

"That'd be great, thanks," I reply and go to dump my pack by my desk.

Five minutes later Anthony is bustling into the lab and comes straight to me and gives me a hug. "So sorry to hear about Jess, Sean, really I am, Michelle told me. How are you doing?" he asks, stepping back. Concern gushes from him like a radiator.

"It's been tough," I say, quietly. "And not getting easier if I'm honest, but... I need to focus on work, for Jess and for me. Is that alright?" I push away my thoughts of her.

"Of course, we understand, it must be hard," says Anthony, looking to Michelle for confirmation. "But are you saying you're good to go? If you are, everything's in place, we're ready for you," he says, confidently.

"Yes, I'm all sorted and ready," I say. "But... before we do anything I need to let you both know what's going on and why the cloak and dagger routine."

I notice a frown on Michelle's face, and then she and Anthony give a perfectly timed look at each other and then to me expectantly, like some kind of comedy duo. Ceremoniously I take a seat at the small meeting table that occupies the middle of the lab, and they follow suit.

"So... I can tell you what's going on," I say. "Beyond Jess's death that is, at least some of it. You might find it a little incredible, but, well, it is what it is." How far can I take this? I need their buy in, but also their belief. The last thing I need is them thinking I need locking up in a psychiatric unit. "Let me go back, remember, my research was all about longevity, yes?"

"Yes," they reply in chorus.

"Well, Jess and I, well... we solved it," I quietly announce, giving a muted smile. "Really. I know that's a big claim, but it's important for me to be direct here and Anthony, you kind of knew this. But essentially our research enables your body to exist in perpetuity, at least it will do."

"Anthony mentioned this," says Michelle, coyly. "But I don't think we thought you were that far on. Are you sure? I mean that's a grasping big leap mate, are you sure you're that far ahead?"

"Yes," I reply with confidence. "We've been working in secret because of the nature of the work and the inevitable implications for society, as you can imagine. But we got there. We did it, not with humans directly, but the core of what we need to do with human cells. And I have it all right here," I say, brandishing an old-fashioned memory stick. "This is what I need you to get out there Anthony, so it's widespread and can't be deleted. Because there's more..." I trail off and try – and fail – to not be too theatrical about it, but it seems to be coming out that way.

"Fuck me mate, hang on... Wait. Wow, just wow!" says Michelle leaning in close, staring straight into my eyes. "But then. How sure are you?" she asks, and I sense her switching from amazement to something else.

"We've done it," I reply coolly. "It's complex but the experimental rig is all set up at Cambridge and can be repeated at any time. Although without Jess we would need to co-opt someone who knows the science. But it works and the wider implications are... well, too big to be believed." I stop, giving space for all this to sink in.

"Can I just recap?" asks Anthony, "so... you have a proven drug, or a process, something that will allow humans to avoid ageing. This is what you're saying Sean?"

"Yes."

"How does it work?" asks Anthony.

"It's complex and mostly Jess's field not mine," I reply. "Essentially it's an instruction at the cellular level to not age."

"Wasn't that what your drug trials were?" says Michelle.

"Yes, but this is *not* a drug," I say. "It's a process that uses the host own cells so there's no rejection. Listen, the science is complex, but it's here in the paper I've written, based on all our research." I hold up my memory stick again, the elixir of life. "And you can read it of course, but for now I just need you to accept what I tell you and that there are people who don't want this in the public domain. Can you do that, for me..., please?"

"It's a lot to take in Sean," replies Anthony, after an awkward pause. "I know you mentioned this before, but I didn't really think you literally had solved ageing. I get that you may have, no sorry, that you *have* made a big leap forward in your research. Accepted, but to then extrapolate that to what you're saying with no testing. Well, it's a big claim old chap. I feel you are confident and hundred percent with it. But from our perspective...well?"

"I know. That's why I've written the paper," I say, raising my voice, willing them both to believe.

"Then let's have a read, is that alright?" asks Anthony.

"Yes of course, but you won't get it," I say, becoming frustrated, and now standing. "It's complex physics and the real proof would be repeating the experiments at the lab, which you don't have access to, or understand." I start to pace up and down the lab – this was a mistake.

"But hang on, you're saying you have solved ageing but you have yet to undertake any trials with humans or other mammals, is that right?"

"Yes," I reply. "The science is the key and it is that which we have and can now ramp up for trials when the time is right. The science is the science. When you see antibiotics kill bacteria in a petri dish you still know it will work on humans. Yes?"

"Well, no. Not really," replies Anthony. "Maybe you have first principles and all that, but that's not the same as what you're claiming. And... sorry Sean, but I don't think this should be sent out on the network without saying exactly that. Otherwise, well, you would be leading people astray."

"Are you backing out of our agreement Anthony?" I say, my voice raised, staring directly at him as he studiously avoids my eyes, holding my growing rage in check as best I can.

"Well, I'm not willing to push out false information that's for sure and certainly not in the way you were suggesting, anonymously and undeletable."

"But, Anthony..." I say, pursing my lips and turning away from him, pacing across the lab, my back to him and Michelle.

"It's just there needs to be proof," he calls out to me. "You know, or justification for this approach at the least. Otherwise it's..."

I turn and face both of them, interrupting Anthony's flow. I feel my cheeks flush as I walk slowly towards them. "Justification? You want justification. How about this, they killed Jess," I yell, the blood coursing thought my body. "*They* killed her, the ones trying to suppress the information." As I say this a tear rolls down my cheek. I look from Michelle to Anthony and back again, my hands balling into fists. I walk towards them. "That's how real this all is," I yell. "That's why

I need to get this out there. It's for my protection, so I'm not next and the world doesn't lose what we've found." My voice trails off as tears stream down my face. "That's my justification, enough for you?"

They both look at me speechless and I turn my back and walk across the lab to stand staring out of the window across the campus. The "growing wall" looks back at me from the opposite side of the square. It's become unmanageable; a great idea to suck up carbon, but with no one managing it the vertical bushes are fast becoming vertical trees, re-wilding a forty-metre vertical wall into a growing mural of green chaos.

"You were on the run weren't you, when I picked you up," calls Michelle. "That's what this is. Fuck. They killed Jess! Sean!"

In seconds Michelle is out of her seat and at my side, her arms around me, her face pressed against my shoulder. Her inner warmth and kindness flow into me as I turn and wrap my hands around her and we stay there, for a moment. Her caring for me and me accepting.

"Sean, that's just... I can't believe it," she says, pulling away. "Have you been to the police? Who did it? How? This is bad, where are the police?"

Meanwhile Anthony sits staring across at the two of us. "Fuck me," he says quietly, slowly shaking his head and looking to the floor for inspiration.

"They caused us to crash, in a chase, and Jess... Jess... died. I watched her die." My voice cracks as I say the words and all I can see is Jess, dying all over again. The room blurs as my eyes well up. I rub them back to clarity, stand myself up straight. I can't go down that road, not here, not now. I have to stay focused, stay with the plan.

"Listen, you can't say anything about Jess, or the project," I say. "Nothing at all. I shouldn't have told you, but, well, things are tough right now. I need you to agree this with me, alright? In fact, better if we just focus on the project, please."

"K," replies Michelle, in a whisper. "But, you've told us. Doesn't that implicate us?"

"Yes, sorry. I can't un-tell you. Sorry, shit... Look I know it's a big ask, but... I just need you to trust me. Can you do that?"

I look across to Anthony, he just looks stunned, paler than ever. "Anthony?" I call across.

"Yes," he replies. "Just processing all this. Jess murdered..." He goes quiet and then half lifts his hand as if to ask a question. "So, lots to know..." he says, slowly. "But essentially, we need to get your research out there and it not be delete-able, as we agreed. And goes without saying that it not be traceable. Is that correct?"

"Yes, that's about the size of it," I reply. "But only not traceable to you in putting it out there. Mine and Jess's names are on the research paper."

"Alright, in that case, all set to go," Anthony says in a hushed tone. "But who's behind all this? Who is *they*? Is it the government? It's the effing government isn't it," he proclaims, looking to me for confirmation.

"Probably, at least, yes I think so," I reply, going with it. Anything's better than the truth.

"Mother fu...!" replies Anthony, swallowing his words through gritted teeth whilst waving a fist. I feel the revolutionary zeal rise in him.

"Now you know the full story, I need to ask again. Will you help?" I say, looking to each of them.

Michelle nods with a defiant frown. "I'm in," she says.

"Let's get it done," replies Anthony, rising from his chair, hand outstretched for the memory stick.

I smile back at them both, feeling the tear stains stretching on my face. I so very much want to tell them everything, to return their faith in me. But the situation is so complex, so out of this world, so unbelievable... And I need as simple as I can get.

It takes us thirty minutes and Anthony has done all kinds of things that protect us and the information, so it can't be traced back to his PC, or the Uni. It involves someone named Paulo who will do the initial upload from a cyber café in Mexico, which I'm unsure about, but Anthony reassures me. He tells me that if you try and corrupt or delete the data it replicates itself and copies itself to numerous other locations, whilst also continuously moving itself around the globe and making a home for itself within a whole range of servers from, "Braford to Boston and beyond," he says jubilantly.

I briefly wonder why Anthony was so concerned with the illegality of it earlier given all his questionable connections, but now's not the time to be questioning my saviour.

And then that's it. It's gone, off into the aether, job done. Another key milestone in the plan. I should be happy, elated even. Everything's falling into place, just as planned. But... there's a but, I can feel it. Except—

"Untraceable and undeletable," announces Anthony triumphantly.

"You're a star," I tell him. "You could very well have just saved my life, literally."

His smile occupies all of his face as he looks up at me from his seat and gives me a flick of his eyebrows.

"Thanks old friend, and you too Michelle. You are both fantastic, you can't imagine how much this means. You are lifesavers, quite literally. Thank you, thank you," I say, looking from one to the other.

"Just one more thing for me to do and we are done," I say, heading to my desk.

I set to writing a number of emails with a link to the location of the paper and supporting data and then, ceremoniously, I hit the send/receive button. And off they go, to professors I know research in the area, editors of leading scientific journals, the press, Jess's colleagues and others who I know within the academic community. And, of course, the funders of the project, who are going to be pissed when they find out I've given their intellectual property to the world. But I hope they'll come to understand the resource is too precious to limit access. Like Tim Berners-Lee knew he couldn't charge for the world wide web.

The revolution begins.

"I'm done guys," I shout from my laptop, looking up. There's no reply so I stand to look about the lab, it's empty. How did that happen? Then I recall Michelle saying something about a meeting or other, I wasn't paying attention. Weird, how can you just go to a meeting when we've just changed the course of the world? And to them, how must they be, knowing Jess was killed as a result of our research? These things are too big for business as usual... but... what else do you do?

I pack away my laptop, stretch and walk over to the window, looking out over the campus and the city. I'm lighter, a tension has left my body, like after a yoga class. Has my body been tensed for near three weeks? Is that even possible? But it's done, I'm no longer hunted. I think, I hope.

Now onwards. And I shudder at what's to come. Putting my head in the lion's mouth, it fills me with dread. I'm pulled from my reverie as the door bursts open and Michelle and Anthony roll in. "Sean, are you all sorted then?" asks Michelle.

"Yes, you were off with the fairies when we left," chimes in Anthony. "Thought we better leave you to it."

"Yes, done," I say. "Thank you both so much for all your help. You have no idea how much I appreciate it, really, thank you. But, like I said, please say nothing about Jess, to anyone. I know it's a big ask, but I have no choice here. Can you do that for me?"

"We can, can't we Anthony?" replies Michelle, turning to Anthony for approval, and I suspect a private conversation has been had – was that the meeting they needed to go to?

"Sure thing," he nods. "For now. But if the police turn up asking questions, well you understand. We can't lie to the police."

"I understand, that's fine," I say, knowing after a week or two it won't matter.

"What now? Can *you* go to the police now?" asks Anthony.

"Not yet, there's still more to do," I reply. "But for now, I think I'm safe, thanks to the both of you. At least I'm much safer than I was. And, of course, the truth is out there now. Longevity has been given to the world, so no going back."

"Will you be coming back?" probes Michelle, "you know, to here? Now that... you know."

"Yes, it'd be great to have you back old chap, we can look after you," says Anthony, giving me one of his knowing winks.

I do love these people. I smile, holding my hands up in surrender. "Guys, I can't thank you enough for what you've done," I say. "You are wonderful people who have come to my rescue when I needed it most and I will never forget that, seriously, thank you both. Hey, the history books may even record the event, who knows. But for now, I have to go again. There's still more for me to do. I'm not out of the woods yet."

"But Sean, won't everyone come looking for you now?" asks Michelle. "You know, the press... everyone, it might take a few days or a week or so, but you might become a celebrity. You had factored this right?"

"Yeah, I know. I'm relying on that, but I won't be here to receive them, at least not in the near future," I say, thinking through the danger I'm about to put myself in. "So, by all means tell them you know nothing about any of this, until it's common knowledge and then you can own up to whatever you want to, anything is fine with me. My suggestion is go with the truth once it's out there. It gets too complicated trying to deceive people, trust me."

We share a look, the three of us, saying nothing, just sharing the moment, and I give each of them a prolonged airport hug, emoting my feelings now I can. They know, and they understand.

Part Four

Chapter Twenty-Nine

The surrounding ambient light reaches a retina and steadily resolves into familiar shapes. Residual infra-red brushes skin; much is obscured. Auditory inputs and minor sensory feedback – nothing of note or significance. Corporeal existence is a stranger; the relatable memories are distant and vague. It will take time to adjust. Slowly sitting up, I look down to inspect my new body. It is as it should be, from what *I* recall, from what *I*... recall. *I*...

There's another emotion, recall, it's... contented happiness. I'm *glad* I had the foresight to give me clothes. Glad. Interesting, base emotions but still complex.

I gently lower myself from the printer unit onto the floor, taking my time, steadily increasing the weight onto each leg in turn. Within my now limited memory, I have allowed sufficient recall to know I cannot afford to make errors through lack of experience. I know there are things I can't know. Interesting, what omissions? What did I keep from myself?

My motor memory and sensory feedback function. Through my legs and feet, I feel the cold floor and now I stand fully erect they take my weight easily and I take a few steps. Increasing my pace, all is well. My body movement and control returns, and an ancient saying revisits me: *"it's like riding a bike, you never forget"*. I slap my hands together; auditory is functional.

"What does one say when one has no one but oneself to talk to?" I say aloud, enunciating each word. I continue my checks: all is in order, at least from what I can recall. A mirror would be useful but there are none to be found.

I scan my surroundings: the location is familiar and is correct. As intended. There is something unexpected, something human to my situation. A feeling in my solar plexus tells me something is amiss; it's a feeling from the past, vague. The memory of it could well belong to another. It's a *"gut feeling"*; something is not right. I repeat my checks... all is well. I look around again, correct location. But still... *"butterflies in the stomach"*; yes, there is a logic there, but...

I take a seat, close my eyes, settle my hands on my knees, reduce my heart rate, my breathing. I relax this body, this mind, allow myself to commune, to resolve my unidentified concern.

My pulse lifts slightly for a second or two as I realise, with surprise, at my oversight. I pull it back – panic will not serve me well. There is no commune. I am alone now, for as long as this takes. This is what it is to be corporeal, to be human again, how could I overlook such a basic element? I feel a smile grow on my face as I realise the irony that my overlooking anything is a result of returning to the corporeal and once again *being* human. Humans forget. I can't see it, but I like my smile and the recognition of irony. Am I becoming my old self again? I wonder, how far would I need to revert, how much of the complete me would I need to lose for me not to want to return to Node? How quickly does one assimilate or de-assimilate? I shake my head a little and close my eyes. My reflections betray the change even more with their own temporal references. My assimilation has truly begun.

The printer starts writing again. After a few moments, the screen lifts and in the centre of the crucible is my interface. I retrieve it and run my checks. All is well; I have control over both installations and the "sever and return" function.

I pull together all I need from the facility and go upstairs. The pigeon hole assigned to Mike's fake company has a single letter in it and it's addressed to Sean Freeman. I open it – passport and credit card, as planned. Thank you, Sean.

The heat of the day hits my body as I leave the building, the climate collapse, is it even hotter since I've been gone? I take a seat in the nearby park café and wait to be approached by a member of staff. "Could I have banana pancake and a cup of English tea please?" I say to the waiter, ensuring my annunciation is accurate. He nods acknowledgement.

I see my hand raised and pushing to open a door. I enter, walk across the room and look down to turn on the tap at the sink. I start to wash my hands. But this is no longer me making these decisions, it's me watching someone else perform these tasks through their eyes. These decisions and actions are no longer mine. I've been locked out of my own body, yet I'm still here, seeing and hearing just as I was. But I'm no longer in control. I'm looking at an empty sink and a hand on either side, leaning onto it before I stand myself upright but still looking down at the sink.

"*Now Sean, this is directed at you,*" someone says. It's a voice somewhere in the room, but I don't turn to find it. I want to, but I don't control this body. "*Not the me you think is you at the moment,*" says the voice.

Mike are you back? I think to him. As I do, the eyes I'm seeing through look up at the mirror and there I am, staring back at me. I see myself smile, but I don't feel the smile on my face, nor did I make a smile. I'm not smiling, but the person in the mirror is. That's not me, smiling back at me.

"*I have arrived Sean; the game is afoot, old chap. I'm making my way to you now. You created me to help you, now it is my turn to return the favour.*"

FUCK!

The shock slaps me awake – in an instant I'm bolt upright in bed. What the hell was that? Who was that? I can still see the image of me looking back at me in the mirror, but that wasn't me and the smile wasn't mine.

"*I'm making my way to you now,*" he said, a voice in my head, but his lips never moved. What now, what now? I rub my face, my eyes, bad dream? Is Mike back? That was so vivid. The memories and the feelings were real, it was me in the café and in Mike's installation. And the person in the mirror was me, *looked* like me, but that was NOT me. I'm out of bed pacing the room. That was definitely Mike's installation in Sweden, I recognise the entrance lobby and mailboxes.

Oh fuck... of course! OF COURSE! Laughter bursts from my lips, accompanied by a winner's grin. "No grasping way," it worked! It's me. It's me, the other me, back from Node. He's here. Holy shit!

I'm shaking, pacing the room like a caged tiger. I can't keep up with my own thoughts. It worked, it worked! What now? What was the next part of the plan? I can't think straight, and nothing has gone wrong, why am I panicking? I'm not panicking, I'm excited.

"K," I say aloud and raise both my hands. I stop pacing, take a few deep breaths. This is great. Yet I'm struggling to accept that my plan might actually work.

I force down my cereal whilst I re-live the dream... no... it wasn't a dream. It was me inhabiting someone else. His thoughts were mine, I was him, but through a VR live stream or something. Except it jumped from one location to another, from Mike's facility straight to the entrance lobby, to the café, the bathroom, so perhaps a compilation of recent events? And... what do I call him? He's not me, he's not Sean Freeman. *I'm* me. And I need to stay me, the last thing I need to become is Sean Freeman the second. This could be tricky, dangerous even. But this was my plan, now *our* plan, and he's me so he will stick to it. Won't he?

The way he was thinking was not me, not even close. He's changed, having been at Node. And he shared that with me – that must have been intentional? He knows enough about me to know what will influence me and have a desired outcome. I know nothing about him. I'm at a serious disadvantage. But he knows that and will know I know that. Is that why he gave me a real sense of him?

And he hasn't been around humans for years, many years... it felt like a lifetime, he shared that. I could sense the enormity of knowledge that he's acquired, of experiences lived, vast and radically different from anything I could know. But the sum of those experiences was elusive, it was like a gift, wrapped in beautiful paper, but I could only feel from the outside what might be within. But I know it was special and huge. And all of that has been squeezed into weeks, how's that possible?

Something more than I expected has happened to me, to him, at Node. He's changed. He's a long way from the me that was the original. Is this what Mike was meaning when he talked about the challenges of reproduction of oneself? I have to be careful, there could be more. Things Mike hasn't told me, things that haven't even occurred to me yet. And he stopped it. I woke up because he ended it, the communication – he ended the stream, everything was in his control.

"*Are you still there Sean?*" I ask and give it a moment – there's only silence.

I've got to assume he has similar capabilities as Mike, not that I really understood what they were. But I know he's spent so much time at Node, although the memories of that he hasn't shared, just a feeling of coming here, away from home, where he's been for a long time. He misses it already; the oneness, I could feel it, he was homesick. Homesick for Node.

"*I'm making my way to you now,*" he said. Does now mean, now?

We need to be careful, two of us turning up at the Uni side by side is going to take some explaining. And still no sign of Mike. I've tried his AIC, email, his employer, everything, and there's nothing, it's like he never existed. And I need him for the plan to work.

My email inbox is permanently filling, a cascading waterfall I can't stop. The messages on my phone are the same. I scan them again for any sign of Mike, nothing. Amidst all of the furore that I've created with the longevity publication, there are also people looking for Jess. The police have a missing person's report from her mother and I'm a person of interest, the last person to be seen with her. I'm desperately conflicted as I owe it to Jess's family to talk to the police and to them; they must be at their wit's end. And how long before the police have a warrant for my arrest? But I can't go down that path. I have to be strong, stay focused – there is more at stake here.

I ignore them all.

My focus is self-preservation, for my species. The reality is I need to give us, humans, a clear run at this if we're going to make it work, and right now, we don't have that. But... we will.

I go over the plan in my head again and again. I try my best to predict the Anata's response, to anticipate their moves and how to counter them before they're made. All the while my empty house echoes my life: hollow, silent without Jess.

As time rolls on the weight grows. The world wants to talk to me, the conspiracy nutters want me silenced, I will need to tackle all of that. But before all of that I have to counter aliens meddling in human affairs. Grasping fuck, who actually says things like that? And now there are two versions of me walking around and I think I'm the lesser.

I continue to scan through my emails hourly, but I don't find what I need. Did Sean contact me, did that actually happen? I have to wait no matter what, it's the only option. Wait for Mike to show, wait for the Ananta to find me and now wait for Sean Two, too. I'm not sure how much longer I can hang on like this. I'm being pulled apart by my current reality and the possible futures for humanity. And all I can do is sit and stare at my laptop screen, unfocused, seeing nothing, waiting.

The new mail message pops up in the corner of my screen, and once again I go to check and it's there! I see my name, open the mail. A thrill runs through me as I stare at the screen, unblinking. Exactly what I've been waiting for. An email from me.

Dear Sean,

Booked a flight early tomorrow, arrival 09.35 your time at Manchester terminal 2. Collect me at the gate. I've cut and coloured my hair and will be wearing sunglasses – a disguise. I am sure you will still be able to recognise me.

Tomorrow,

Sean.

I'll recognise him? No shit!

I reply straight away; all good, yes I'll collect him and has he heard from or can he contact Mike ASAP?

Nothing can move forwards without Mike.

I press "send" and realise I forgot to ask all kinds of questions. Can he get rid of the Hipster, are we still on track with the plan, was that him in my head and if so why, what purpose did that serve? And... but they will keep.

This was always *my* plan. And it needed two versions of *me*, not me and someone who happens to look like me and vaguely remembers who I am from a lifetime ago. Now I'm no longer sure who's running the show anymore.

It's me. But which me?

Chapter Thirty

Standing in the arrivals zone, the nervous energy of meeting myself is the only thing keeping me awake. I've had no sleep. Streams of luggage-ladened passengers come bustling though the automatic one-way arrival doors as I scan the crowd for me, or someone like me. Amidst the hubbub, my eyes are drawn to him. I spot me. He sees me, casually knocks his sunglasses down and we make eye contact, We both nod and start walking to the end of the arrivals funnel. We approach one other and simultaneously extend a hand to shake.

"Sean," I say with some reservation and a small nod of hello.

"Sean," he replies with a similar nod.

"Shall we head to the car?" I suggest. "We can chat more easily there?"

"Of course, good idea," he replies, gesturing for me to lead on, "please."

We walk on in silence, with me finding it hard to focus on the way forward as I can't stop looking at him. His disguise is good, but he still looks like me, although you would need to stop and put us side by side to notice. His hair is short, blond and messy with some product in it. He hasn't shaved either – perhaps he's growing a beard. It makes him look younger than me, with my boring, light brown side parted 9.0

haircut located anywhere from 2040 onwards. I blend in everywhere and stand out nowhere. It never occurred to me that I could, "have a look" of some kind; interesting what someone else can do with your body.

As the MyCar doors shut, I immediately turn to him.

"What was that yesterday morning? Me seeing and feeling your experiences through your eyes? Why did you do that and how? It was very... disconcerting." I say hurriedly, stopping myself, embarrassed, unsure of my direct accusatory tone. I kind of feel like I'm talking to a brother which I've never had. Being super direct seems alright with family.

"I wasn't entirely sure it would work," he replies. "So I just allowed my mind to be open to you as I reflected on recent events, with the expectation you would be able to commune, which we now know you can. This will serve us well in the days ahead."

"Got you," I reply and set the car going. His comments make sense and I know how communication can be so much more than words. And he's right... it could be very useful.

"It felt like you were unhappy to be here, like you'd been away from Earth for years. Is that right?" I ask, hesitating, quietly dreading the answer. I have to trust him. If I can't trust the other me, who can I trust?

"Yes. I can understand why you would interpret things this way and your interpretation is not wholly inaccurate," he says. "But, for me, things have changed significantly. The experiences I have accumulated at Node are, by human standards, exceptional. If life were a screen series, I have watched many, lived many and often simultaneously. Once you are not limited to a single corporeal entity for your existence, many things are possible. The colours of the rainbow are so much more diverse once you can see without the limitation of your eyes."

What do you say to that? This could all go very wrong, very quickly. He needs to be me, stick with the plan. The plan I had before I became two. Before he spent a lifetime on another world. He's not me. Not even close.

"Are we still set for the original plan?" I ask.

"Yes, absolutely. This is why I am here," he replies, turning to face me and emoting a confirmatory affirmation.

I sense his certainty and my confidence returns, if it is *my* confidence. I mirror his smile with my own, sharing the emotion. He gives me the smallest almost imperceptible nod by way of acknowledgement, I'm not sure if I see it or feel it.

"What's it like, living on Node?" I ask.

"Different, so different. It's not possible to put it in words, or even emote the true nature of Node," he says. "One can only experience it."

"Of course," I reply, saddened by this gulf and what it might mean.

"I am still more like you than I am Node," he says. "I have just lived within Node and as a result learnt a great deal being in that environment. I have connected, or communed, with Node and it is both amazing and bewildering, like accessing the memories of thousands of lives from across the galaxy, most of which are in a language beyond anything I can begin to recognise, but occasionally there are insights, amazing insights, like fundamental ontological truths around the purpose of entity. A rudimentary understanding of how time functions, how the Galactic community operates and evolves.

If you wish, I can attempt to share a memory of this, although it will be a pale facsimile of the real thing."

"Err, well. Yeah, sure," I reply, with trepidation. Does he mean right now, here in the car?

I look across to Sean to ask – he's gone, replaced by the view of an immense desert, stretching far into the distance, the rocky kind you get in North America. I realise what's happening in time to see the desert rotate through 180 degrees so its upside down and the sand and rocks start to fall. Like snow, all the detritus of the desert falls slowly, even the rocks, then the rocks start to morph into feelings, emotions. When I look at one, my vision tells me it's a rock, but it shares an emotion with me, as if my viewing it ignites the emotion. As I look away the feeling goes and as I focus on another rock, another entirely different emotion courses through me. The emotions are complex, not simply happiness or sadness. I focus in on a large boulder as it falls nearby. I feel a melancholy intertwined with satisfaction, intrigue and what feels like an openness or sharing and there's more beyond that. I feel I'm missing most of it, like the depth of the water is ocean deep, but I can only swim on the surface. I can only touch the surface. And the sand, strewn between all the continually falling boulders – it has something; it's brought to life as the boulder passes by. The boulder connects with each grain, the grain comes to life and is warmed by the boulder as it rolls over the surface at it passes through.

 I zoom in on a grain. It too is a boulder now, looking back at me, with its own emotions, but I don't understand them, it becomes something else – a tightrope. I'm holding my breath in darkness balanced on it. Swarms of insects envelop me as a multi-directional gale pummels me. It wants me to slip, to lose my balance, to fall in. I close my eyes and I'm back in the desert, falling into another boulder as it passes me. I try to halt the fall, but there's nothing I can do. I plummet head first into it and as contact is made it becomes a field of a million stars, all shooting past me at vast speeds, a never-ending stream, with each one connected to every other one by a thread that I can't see but I know is there. Each star is a grain of sand, and each grain is a star – they are the same. The thickness of the star field grows quickly as I plummet into its depths; soon there is more white than black and the cacophony of the conjoined emotions starts to coalesce into something, but I can't begin to hold that in my consciousness. It's like trying to focus on and hold thousands of different thoughts in your mind all at once.

The whiteness grows to fill all of my vision and there is nothing else, and I feel I might be back in the viewing room at Node, pure white in every direction. Then a speck appears in front of me and grows – another grain of sand becoming a boulder? No, as it approaches me, or I approach it, it's impossible to say, it continues to grow and grow, and I continue to move towards it. It now takes up all of my forward vision and I still move towards it – then I see, it's a desert that we're moving towards and as we continue to close in I start to notice ripples on the surface, which as we get closer still I see are huge sand dunes.

And we stop, viewing what is a desert planet from a few thousand metres above. The whole planet is one vast desert covering the entirety of its surface, I know this as sure as I know night follows day. What's more I know what this represents; this is Node, all Nodes – they too are interconnected. I suspected the grains of sand to be entities that are part of the collective... I was wrong. Each grain of sand on this vast desert planet is the origin of a single species, that has at one point decided to conjoin with Node. Node is a collective of trillions of species and is host to quadrillions of entities, or as Mike has previously told me, just one.

My view of the desert fades. I'm back in the car.

"Wow! That was... scary as shit, and... baffling, bizarre! Thanks for the warning." My lack of control and knowledge is beyond inadequate, I need to be on my best game here. "How did you live there, in that? And I just knew things. No one told me, it was just there, knowledge."

"That memory was from my early entry into Node," replies Sean. "It changes as the level of exposure deepens. It's all amazing and there is much that's incomprehensible, but when the link is made with the wider community, you are not limited to your own individual cognitive capacity. You are not you, you are they and they are one, or many, at the same time and you can "borrow" their capabilities. Like having the whole world's computer processing power at your disposal if you need it. But... for now, that is gone."

His words hang in the air, and I'm overwhelmed by a deep feeling of dismay. He's isolated himself to return, he doesn't *want* to return to Node, he *has* to return, otherwise he's no longer who he's become. He's amputated large parts of himself to return to Earth and he now knows the hardship of that decision. He fixes my stare whilst sharing this, knowing I now know.

"I could be a virus to them," he says. "But as they haven't eradicated me, I can only assume they don't know I'm there or don't see me as a threat. But that in itself is a flawed understanding. The concept of 'threat' is an ancient idea to Node, of historical interest and understood, but just no longer relevant. Frustratingly, I recall understanding all of this at a much deeper level, at Node, but now as a single entity my cognitive capability is limited. I knew this would occur prior to my return; hopefully it will not impact upon my plan."

"Your plan?" I say, taken aback.

"Yes, our plan."

"What? You do mean *the* plan as I had before the separation at Node, yes?"

"Yes, Sean."

"Good," I say, feeling like a lesser mortal with each passing minute and desperately trying to understand how this will all impact on what comes next. He sees all of the rainbow, way more than me, he knows more than me, he's likely capable of more than me. Where does that leave me?

I steal a glance at him as the MyCar drives us down the road. He's passive, sat motionless and robotic in the passenger seat. I have to take the lead, to keep the lead. Deciding to trust someone is handing them control of your life, so you need to be confident they won't destroy it. But more than that you need them to cherish and value it, not just prevent its destruction.

If I can't trust him, we are both lost. It's a leap of faith, but it was the Ananta who warned me against trust and now I know their values the last thing I need to do is listen to them. I allow Sean access to my thoughts and feelings. He recognises this and reciprocates. It's like a damn wall breaking, overwhelming my senses and pulling on emotions as if they were my own. This wave of emotions doesn't align with the person sat next to me, the individual I picked up at the airport is almost *without* emotion. My sense of his loss, through returning to Earth, is profound, and I feel my eyes begin to well up. He's deeply saddened; it evokes the emotions I have attached to the loss of Jess – he's bereaved, too. But... for him, it's different, he knows it's temporary for him, but also... something else... for me it's temporary? How can that be—?

"Sean, how can that be? Jess is dead," I say, staying with the simplicity of conversation.

"Sorry Sean, yes you are right, of course. It's the complexities of overlapping emotions between us I expect. Communing as we are... well this is new to me, too."

"Right," I say and feel the flood of his emotions retreat, his sense of loss made acceptable with the knowledge that one day he will return to Node. To him, life is a manifestation of hope and an unwavering sense of duty, towards me and the human race.

You have my trust Sean, you will know that now. You will also know my confidence in our endeavour is not absolute, I too am taking a leap of faith. But my belief in you is without question; we are more than brothers.

It's the emotional connection and not the physical presence that makes me feel more comfortable. And of course, I don't need to give him another name. He has as much right to it as I do. He's sacrificed a lot to come here and the only person I can now trust, and I do trust him. I know he could be manipulating my thinking to think all of this, but... I have to *trust* he's not manipulating me, or I have to *trust* this is the right thing to do. My plan always assumed the two of us would be on the same side and for that not to be the case...

Then, like an unintended drop from a leaky tap, something else trickles out from Sean. It's hope for me as a person. He knows something he can't share, but it's wonderful, the best of news. Also, I sense a deep level of uncertainty around the outcome of our plan. As he said, his confidence is low. But... *we* go forwards.

I turn to him, as he does me. Our eyes meet and, simultaneously mirroring one another, we each give that same small almost imperceptible nod, sharing a moment, an understanding, an agreement, a purpose. Our brotherhood, our focus, is steadfast, incorruptible.

The only place we can easily exist together without risk is home. Sean knows this. I don't need to tell him, I also know, he knows I know.

The shared link that has emerged is by mutual consent. I also know only that which one wants to share, is shared. And then I remember, but it's a memory that's not my own, like remembering a forgotten childhood experience. The memory is about communing as we are doing and that this capability is just a small snowflake on the top of an iceberg; it's also much deeper than the link with Mike. There is real trust here, an openness, a shared understanding and mutual respect I've not experienced before.

Arriving home, we don't talk. I get out of the car, as does Sean. We gather our things and enter the house. I put the kettle on. Sean goes directly to the spare room to dump his bag and use the bathroom. Words remain unspoken; they become superfluous and limiting. The silence is both easy and eerie, like we're two robots operating on a predetermined path. I think about what I need to say to Sean and he receives this as I think it. I also know what he's doing and why – I'm privy to his decision making as if it were my own, I just know. From the outside I imagine we look like lovers who have had a fight and weren't talking, but at the same time knew each other so well we can carry on with the daily activities ingrained in our co-existence.

I start to factor practicalities and again, our link answers my questions. Does Sean have the capability to disable the Ananta, the Hipster? As I ask myself the question, I access Sean's memory of him pulling his interface from the printer in Sweden and checking all is set up and ready to go. It now has a "sever and return" function that when close enough will disable the Ananta probes that are the Hipster and his lackies. I have the answer without asking and now know about the functioning of the mechanism, all whilst Sean is still busying himself upstairs. He knew I'd access those memories. And once again I know – he knows – I know.

This will take some getting used to, this sharing at a deep level, an intimate level. How far would it go before the intimacy was too much? Before ego intervened and my embarrassment or emotional immaturity closed the door? I know, of course, because Sean knows – the answer is you go at your own pace, which ultimately leads to there being no "you" as you become part of the collective, unless of course you wish to retain your individuality and remain remote.

Chapter Thirty-One

"Sean, is that you?" whispers Michelle hurriedly, her voice only just audible on my phone.

"Yeah, you K Michelle?" I reply.

"No, fucking no I'm not. The police are here, they're looking for you."

"WHAT?" I yell, spinning around and marching to the window to scan the street.

"Listen, listen... wait!" she says with quite urgency. "I'M FINE, GIVE ME A MINUTE," she shouts, "some privacy please."

"What? What's going on Michelle?" I ask.

"Wait," she whispers, so I do, trying to hold back the panic as adrenalin grips me. "Right, listen. I'm in the fucking bog, hiding from the cops. Fuck!"

"What, you're in a bog?" I reply.

"NO. I'm in *the* bog, the toilet, the ladies' room, you know."

"Yeah, sorry, got ya," I say.

"Listen, I don't have long. The cops are here and they're asking about you and about Jess. I've told them nothing and said I need to use the loo. So I don't have long, but... they've got Anthony, and who knows what he will say."

"SHIT!" I reply, pulling the phone to my chest for a moment, trying to factor what to do. "What have they said, did they mention the accident?"

"No, they're not telling us anything, not yet anyway. Just asking lots of questions and they're not in uniform. Which means they must be detectives, does that make it worse? But anyway, Anthony, he's with them now and... shit... they're at the door again. Got to go." The phone dies.

"SEAN!" I shout across the house.

I know, he shares with me, and I hear his footsteps coming down the stairs.

"We need to leave," I say, holding back the panic. "They'll be on their way here now or very soon. The last thing we need is me in police custody, or you. And that's if it is the police, it could be the Ananta. Shit, if they find us both! We need to leave NOW!"

In under five minutes we are in the street searching for a My-Car. Sean has his interface, it's all we need. In under ten we are parked a kilometre from my house, next to the only access road to my housing complex, able to see any vehicle that comes or goes.

"We need to find Mike, or go it alone," I say to Sean.

"Agreed," he replies calmly.

"Can we scan for him at the installations, see if he's come or gone or if anything or anyone has been printed?"

"We can, but that would likely announce our intentions to the Ananta. Or at best alert them to our activity. We have to assume the installations will be monitored."

"Yeah, you're right," I reply. "But... does it matter? We need to move forwards with or without Mike, especially now with the police involved."

"Very well," he replies and pulls out and opens his laptop interface. Immediately something is different. I feel it, he's nervous and reluctant, but he isn't sharing why. I feel a separation happening, like a falling out, which is a worry. In response I close my emotion. Is this where communing breaks down? Where there's a secret or insecurity? When we choose to hide something there will be an absence and people will notice this? You can't always hide the fact that you're hiding a fact. But I need Sean, we need Sean. The secret to our working together must be to have no secret.

I open myself up and allow my insecurity to flow to Sean.

"Why the reluctance to use the laptop Sean?" I ask verbally, repeating myself.

"Once done, we can't go back," he announces. "If we are detected and they already have Mike, we have nothing to bargain with. This is a significant risk. We are playing with fire."

"You could well be right," I reply. "But we're working in the dark right now, fire might just light the way."

"Perhaps..." replies Sean, uncertain, his voice betraying the emotions he's no longer sharing.

"Do it. We have no choice," I say, feeling confident in the certainty of my decision.

He doesn't respond and just stares at the screen. "It's done," he replies after a few seconds. "There has been no activity in either installation other than my arrival."

"That quick, really, are you sure?" I say, part of me doubting Sean's ability or honesty.

"It's a simple task," he replies and turns to look at me again as the screen goes blank. "But this may not be as straightforward as we thought."

"No shit," I reply, regretting the words as soon as they leave my lips. "I'm not sure either. Maybe we just offer me up to them, in some way. Maybe? Although... perhaps that's what we've just done?"

Sean responds with a soft but firm shake of the head.

Staring at him, I close my emotions. He knows more than he's letting on – more has gone on at Node than he's sharing. We become locked in a stare, like kids in a playground competition, our eyes fixed on one another, sat in the back of the MyCar, both sharing nothing, saying nothing.

"Fuck's sake," I say, through gritted teeth. "This is not helping Sean, what are you not telling me, what is it that—"

A message pings in on my phone distracting me.

It's from Mike. Yes!

"It's from Mike, look," I say, showing Sean the message.

Mike here, meet me outside your house in 30 mins. BE THERE!

"This can't be coincidence," says Sean.

"Does this mean Mike is monitoring activity at the facilities or something?" I ask.

"It's no coincidence that he texts straight after my check. What do you want to do?"

"Find out what he wants," I say. "Where he's been, what happened to him. Ultimately, get him to take me to the Ananta and we roll out the plan. Do you think?"

"The plan was always your plan before duplication Sean, thus becoming *our* plan after. But you kept it from Mike intentionally and rightly so. No one but us is privy to it and we will need to bring Mike in, carefully. We can't play our hand to soon, or all could be lost. And let's look at the situation – when was the last time Mike messaged you?"

"Can't remember."

"Correct. He usually calls," replies Sean. "Messaging is out of character. It could have come from anyone with some technical expertise, like the Ananta. We must proceed with caution."

"Yes, but we need to move forward, Ananta be damned," I say, mustering my bravado. "If they wanted me dead, I would be dead. We have a plan they know nothing of, I can adapt if I need to. We have to seize the moment. Otherwise, we just sit and wait for them to pick us up, or we're on the run forever. If we wait for them, they're in control of the situation. We move first, we have the initiative. Are you with me Sean?" I allow my thoughts and feelings to flow to Sean. I feel him soaking it up, but he makes no reply.

"Look," I begin. "If we go to them and they think this is their initiative then they will think they're in control, when we will be there by intention, so they will not be guarding against possible threats? What do you think?"

"Your view is an interpretation of your attitude. Not the situation. If this is a trap you will be in their custody just the same, but in your mind you will have put yourself there; in their mind they will have caught you. But your incarceration and their attitude will be the same regardless."

"Perhaps... any better ideas?" I ask.

"No."

"Then we go with that," I say, trying to sound decisive and confident and realising that actually I am. I look to Sean with a beaming smile and sense his confusion around my blind confidence.

We quickly return to my house, and I grab an old phone and sync it with mine. I pass it to Sean.

"Understood," he shares, acknowledging the plan in my head for him to follow and track us in the MyCar.

"We can also communicate through communing," he shares.

"Yes, but I don't know how to let you see through my eyes or anything like that. And if I'm not with you, will it still work?" I say aloud.

"To share something practical like a location or a situation. It's like trying to describe it to someone, but at the same time you have no voice, and they can't see you. You have to communicate the essence of where you are or what's happening by desperately wanting to do this, but being physically restricted from doing so. Like you were a hostage bound and gagged and they put your potential rescuers on the phone next to your ear, you are so desperate to talk but can't. In this situation, your desperate desire and strong emotions means something will get through."

I feel what he shares, but I don't really get it. I just hope it doesn't come down to that.

We return to the MyCar and park at the end of the street behind a cops of Oak trees. We can see the street clearly, but we are all but invisible inside our ubiquitous MyCar. I sit bolt upright, my eyes fixed on the empty street outside my house, wringing my hands, waiting for Mike or... something else, something worse.

Before long the familiar Jag appears at the far end of the street and my heart goes into overdrive. It pulls up outside my house bang on time. My whole body goes cold and I feel the hairs standing up on the back of my neck. "I'm on," I say and turn to face Sean, my legs suddenly weak. "We stick with the plan, right? The original plan, when I was just me, yes?"

"Of course. I'll be right behind you," he replies, emoting determination and belief.

I sneak out of the MyCar, jog to the rear of my house, walk straight through and out the front door towards the Jag. Sean shares, "*close your emotions*", which I do. How could I miss that!

I'm bursting with nervous energy, excited to see Mike and find out what the hell happened and where he's been. I can see through the car window, I think it's him. I open the passenger door and a huge wave of relief washes over me as I see Mike sat behind the wheel. He doesn't return my smile but simply turns to me.

"Get in," he says, his voice stern and urgent. Something's not right. I jump in and as soon as I close the door, he sets off at a pace.

"So? What the hell happened? Where have you been? What's going on?" I push all my excitement onto him, desperate to find out how he is and feeling totally blind. He says nothing, facing the road ahead and driving.

"Mike, you're scaring me, old friend. What's going on? Mike...?"

"I am taking you to a meeting, an investigation, to determine a future," he replies, deadpan, robot like. Then nothing... he just continues driving. The tyres squeal and I'm thrown against the door as we take a corner. He's not hanging about.

I look around the car, panic rising. It's Mike's car, but something isn't right. I look to him – he's focused on the road ahead, no emotions. This is not Mike. Fuck! Nausea hits me like a tidal wave, taking me completely by surprise. I taste vomit in my mouth and for a moment I'm frozen, physically and mentally, locked.

"Who are you?" I whisper. "WHO ARE YOU?" I repeat, this time barking, regaining some control, demanding a response.

He turns to me, his movements stiff and unwieldy. "The deception was required to ensure your engagement. You will participate in the meeting, and you will share with me now what Mike has told you about us and what he has shown you."

"Why would I tell you anything? You've just grasping kidnapped me. How can—" I stop myself, about to give him something he thinks he has but doesn't, a deeper understanding of humans. If he is so lacking in insight he thinks I will respond to a question like that, then let him continue under that delusion, it could work to our benefit.

"What has Mike told you about Ananta?" he repeats, his tone flat.

"I'm telling you nothing," I reply, sitting back, slowly moving my hand towards the door handle, whilst monitoring him.

"Do not attempt to escape," he says, without moving his gaze from the road. "If you do, countermeasures will be applied."

"Countermeasures? What the fuck!" I yell, staring at Mike... that's not Mike. I push the panic down, swallow it. I knew this could happen, we prepared for this.

"Sean, I'm hoping you're getting this. It's alright, we knew this could happen, we knew I could be taken."

I sit, scared, a chill coursing through my body, waiting for a response. I did know I could be taken, but I realise now I didn't think it would actually happen. I'm motionless but silently I resist, like a gagged and bound captive. Nothing comes back from Sean.

"What has Mike told you about Ananta?" he repeats.

I ignore him, the anger building inside me. He is the Ananta, Jess's murderers. I'm ready to explode but I bottle it up. I bide my time, the energy surging within me, I store it. I feel my pulse racing, my breathing too; beads of sweat form on my forehead now. I'm furious and scared. This could be the end, and what the fuck have they done with Mike? What are they going to do to me? I focus inward, slowing myself, calming, preparing myself, I sit back and sink into the car seat. I can still be in control, this could work to our advantage, as long as I don't lose it.

"*SEAN. Sean!*" I emote, injecting as much urgency and importance as I can, bound and gagged in my mind. Hoping he can feel or see what's going on and maybe even be only a few cars behind. Nothing. "*Sean, are you there? Just give me a simple thought so I know we're in touch.*"

Nothing.

I'm on my own.

I see a set of traffic lights up ahead and slowly I slide my hand onto my thigh, moving it gradually towards the door handle, but not too close. With a sideways glance I see Mike's doppelganger's focus is still on the road ahead. He slows for the red light. As we stop, I go for the handle. I yank at it with all my strength and simultaneously shoulder barge the door, aiming to spill out onto the pavement and run. Instead, I headbutt the window and nearly snap the door handle off, but the door doesn't budge. Shit!

I turn to see him release a hand from the wheel and focus on me.

"FUCK YOU MIKE, or not Mike. OR WHOEVER THE FUCK YOU ARE!" I shout, my fear fuelling my anger. I grab for the steering wheel so he can't set off, desperately hoping passers by or other drivers will see the commotion and come to my rescue. "LET ME OUT OF THIS CAR NOW!" I shout, yanking with all my might to turn the steering wheel towards the kerb.

Moving with a steady pace, the imposter Mike calmly places a firm hand on my shoulder. I'm powerless as he pushes me up against the door of the car. I try to resist but can't... I can't even slow him. He's too strong, he's machine strong, he has my entire body pinned against the car door with a single arm and I can't move. The pressure of his hand is so forceful I can feel my shoulder flex and bend painfully in ways it shouldn't. Any further and something will snap.

"Countermeasures applied," he says calmly, and there's a smell of jasmine and almonds. My body wilts. Any resistance I had has vanished. I can't move; my limbs have gone limp and non-responsive and then I realise in horror my chest has no power to expand, to breath. Panic smothers me and my eyes scream for help as I try and fail to inflate my own lungs. I'm going to die! The sides of my vision darken, closing rapidly to a tunnel and then, a shrinking point of light in the distance, smaller and smaller.

Chapter Thirty-Two

A scorching brilliance pierces my eyes. Two needles speared into them, savagely ripping me into consciousness. Instinctively I react, screwing them closed as tight as I can and shielding them with my hands. In shadow the pain subsides and I let them open slightly to tight slits behind my hand. The light dims further and I move my hands away, partially shielding as I squint and blink in an attempt to make out my surroundings. I can only see whisps of grey with white walls and lights still directed at me. I go to sit up, but a wave of nausea assaults me and I fall back to laying on the couch.

"Can you turn off the spotlights?" I ask, laid down with my chin against my chest, dodging my head from side to side, attempting to make something, anything, of my surroundings. "Is anyone there?" I yell. The spotlights dim to nothing, and the main overhead lighting comes into play. The room greys and steadily comes into focus. I'm in Mike's installation.

Then, I see them.

There's three of them at the foot of the couch, staring at me, and I immediately recognise him, the hipster, flanked on either side by his lackies. Jess's killers! A rage surges in me and my body reacts, springing into life. I swing my feet over the side of the couch and charge at the three of them, fists clenched. A frenzied anger burns inside me so strong I know I can take them all.

Without warning, the floor rushes up at me and I hit it, head first. I don't even get my hands in front of me to cushion the fall. I see a bright light for a second as my head bounces back off the floor and I hear my neck make a popping sound. Like a hammer blow to my forehead, the pain erupts in my face a second later; it ripples through my head, into my neck and down my back. I fall sideways and roll onto my back in agony, cradling my head on either side with my hands. The pain throbs like my head's about to explode. The hipster comes into view, a grey silhouette blocking the ceiling light and looking down at me.

"The countermeasures may take some time to deplete within your system; this will give a range of side effects," he announces. He then looks to the two lackies who man-handle me back onto the couch.

My head feels like it's in the grip of a vice, making me physically impotent, but emotionally I'm raging. The three of them watch as I laboriously manoeuvre myself to sit up against the head of the couch. "You killed Jess, you fuckers!" I bark, snarling through clenched teeth, spittle ejecting towards them. "WHY?" I yell. "She was no threat to you. WHY?" I want them to pay, but even more I want to know why. Jess's death was needless and devastating. Why did they kill her? What purpose did it serve?

They reply with blank stares, emotionless, the three of them in identical dark blue perfectly tailored designer suits, observing, waiting for the animal to calm before moving on.

I stare right back at them, seething, emoting anger and fury. The blank stares remain and slowly the red mist of my anger starts to fade. I understand my situation, I wait, focusing back on the plan, the here and now. I'm here by my choice, not theirs. The plan is still in play. I can still win this. My focus calms me – the hipster sees this as a sign to continue.

"Mike is dangerous, we need to locate him and return him to Node," he announces. "We need your help in this. You have now managed to share your work across the planet. You no longer need Mike. You will assist us."

"What!?" I reply, raising my eyebrows. "You want my help to get rid of Mike? you have to be joking? There's no logic in that, why would I help you?" The blank stares resume. "You killed my girlfriend, you kidnapped me, drugged me and I'm pretty sure you see my species as dumb animals. Just where do you think this is going to go?" I say, and then it hits me. They haven't got Mike. Who the hell took Mike? Where is he? Unless he escaped, that would explain it. Or there's something else, something else he hasn't told me.

"We can help you more than you realise, in many ways," replies hipster, alluding to I don't know what.

"Really? You expect me to believe anything you say?" I reply. "You're all about non-intervention, so how does that work?" More silence, unless all three of them are in private discussion. "Your intentions are in your own interests. I give you nothing," I say, feeling an unwarranted confidence in my words. Just then, I sense something new. It's a distraction or a memory, like a distant voice I can only just hear. It comes again, a seed of a memory I've been searching for and just remembered. Sean!

He opens his personal view of the other side of the entrance door to Mike's installation. He's only metres away. My heart races and the nausea is gone as adrenaline clears my system. The game is on.

"If we can gain guarantees of your help we can reveal important information to you," the hipster announces, his opening offer.

But with Sean at the door the tables have turned. I'm now in control and need to gleam as much from them as I can, before we send them home. I let Sean access my thoughts and emotions. We are one, the plan can work.

"The thing is," I say, nervous energy flooding my senses. "I believe that we, humanity, need to be left to forge our own path from here. And that Mike, and yourselves, would be best to leave us to it. This is what we would like to happen. Would this be acceptable to you?"

"This is of interest; however, we need to remove Mike from the situation before we ourselves depart. He is a variable we cannot account for."

"And if that's not possible, then what?"

"If the situation does not resolve then our approach would be to leave the planet as least influenced as possible," says the hipster. "At this stage, as you have already shared your research, the bigger risk is that you are aware of our existence, so we would need to mitigate for this."

"And how does that work?" I ask. "You remove my memories?"

"They are too many and they are too interwoven with your recent life, so this would not be possible."

"Meaning?" I ask swallowing, already knowing the answer but hoping I'm wrong.

"We would need to remove *you,* Dr Freeman," replies the hipster, and I am sure I can detect a hint of pleasure.

Shit, shit, shit, this was always a possibility, but they haven't killed me yet. They need Mike. If they get him, then I must be next. The least intervention. Shit. But they're so direct and transparent, how can they not expect me to work this out? They really don't know us at all.

"So, your plan B is to kill me?" I say nonchalantly, doing my best to maintain my composure.

"Yes, but you are only one of over eleven billion. Your species will continue along its evolutionary path, unfettered. Is this not what you want? It is a small sacrifice for the greater good."

If the situation wasn't so dire, I'm sure I would be laughing, I can't believe their lack of insight. "You must be joking right? You want me to give you Mike and then you take him back to Node, right?"

"That is correct," he replies

"And if I do that, you just leave me do you? You don't kill me, like you just said you would, one death in eleven billion."

"If we have Mike, it will be sufficient."

I don't believe them for a moment. Why would they have any interest in leaving a human alive who knows of them and what they're about? Just one in eleven billion, I'm neither here nor there to them.

"Sorry but no," I say confidently, knowing Sean is ready to strike and we can win this thing. There's nothing more we can learn from them... they simply want us both dead and then their job is done.

The hipster stares at me unblinking, and I shuffle myself up on the couch, ready for Sean to make his play. "I think you may change your mind Dr Freeman, when I share this with you," says the hipster, a poor attempt at a smile on his face.

A door in my mind bursts open. It's a door to a memory. The whole memory spills into my conscious thought at once, like a flood breaking the banks of a river it forces itself through the now open door, filling my mind in seconds. Our previous meeting, the discussion, the intervention with the Ananta on my return from Node. The memory they blanked is all returned to me in an instant. Me in the exact same situation as now, trying to hit the hipster but failing, not being convinced by their argument that Mike was the bad guy and... shit, they will kill Anthony and Michelle, if I don't help them.

"I'm glad I have your attention, *Sean,*" says the hipster, his tone of voice deeper, more personal. "Let me give you more," he says, his face coming alive for the first time. "Jess Hart is not dead," he says, deadpan, his eyes locked onto mine.

"WHAT?" I yell, not able to process his words. "What did you say, she's not dead? Are you messing with me? Is this some fucked up ploy you're using? How can that be? I watched her die. I ordered her QE copy deleted."

I hop down and stride towards the three of them, needing to know, stopping only a metre away, focused squarely on the hipster and his penetrating eyes. My mind is awash, a whirlpool of hope and fear. To hope she is alive only to find out it's a lie? I can't go through losing her again. How can I know, what proof? They could be telling the truth? There is so much I don't know... Jess is alive! Have they?

I hold my hands up in surrender, my anger traded for hope. "Please," I say, to their placid faces. "Just, just tell me how?"

"Aware of her involvement we made a QE copy of Professor Hart," replies the hipster, with a nonchalant twist of his head. "It currently resides at Node. Hence the capture team being overzealous – they knew all occupants were linked."

"FUCK!" I shout, punching the air, my grin a mile wide. "Yes, you fucking graspers, YES!" I go to hug hipster; he draws back, stalling my advance. I just stand there, beaming at him. Jess is back, we can have a life, *she* has a life. It's not over. I can't stop smiling and start to pace the room, planning. I can't believe it.

"Wait, I need to see her," I say, eyes wide, desperately hopeful. "She's on a substrate, you can bring her here, yes?"

"Not at this time," comes the stale response.

"What. Why not? Are you lying to me, to gain my cooperation?" I ask. "If you are, I will give you nothing, nothing." This really could all be bullshit. I don't know these people, or whatever they are, and they're the bad guys.

"Jess Hart is held on a substrate at Node," repeats the hipster. "She is in whole condition, the connection with her Earth-bound self was severed when that form ceased to function, when she died. She will have all memories until that event. We have no reason to lie to you."

My heart beats out of my chest. They must see I can't stop smiling. I even start a little dance; I have boundless energy leaping from me. "So how do I get her back?" I ask.

"At the moment, you do not," he replies. "Be comforted by the knowledge that she is safe and well."

"Right... but when then?" I ask. "When *do* I get her back?"

"This will depend on your cooperation, and you surrendering Mike to us." With this he stops talking and simply stares. I wait for more, but nothing is forthcoming.

"I need proof of life," I say, hoping they don't realise I'm mimicking some movie I've seen. "You want my cooperation? Then I need to know Jess is alive. Proof of life, do you have it?"

"Not in any form you are able to recognise," replies the hipster. "She currently exists as code that you are not remotely familiar with. Located at Node. We do not have time for this."

"She's on a substrate," I say. "Transfer her over, briefly, just so I know. Proof of life."

"Considering your mutual attachment this would not be a good idea, nor would it be brief, I suspect. This is not an option open to us, so the answer is no. But you will see her again if you cooperate and take us to Mike or bring him to us."

"No, not without knowing Jess is alive. Some proof she is alive is what I need."

"...very well," replies the hipster after a brief pause. "I suggest you ask a question only you and she would know. We will then attempt to view this memory and share our findings with you. Would this be adequate?"

"K... K..." I say, thinking.

"Got it. What is the last thing she said to me? In the omnithopter, just before she died." Only three of us could know this and I'm certain they're not talking to Mike.

"A search has commenced," announces the hipster. "With the specifics of the timeline, this should be quick."

"Good," I say, hoping against hope. This could be the real deal, Jess could be alive.

"You are a fool to trust Mike," injects the hipster. "You must surely realise this now; you did not heed my warning. Humans are extremely... inadequate, exemplified through you not having suitable words for the capacities you lack. Where you expect this to lead is impossible to determine... you are a juvenile species in the extreme."

He halts his little diatribe and begins to walk towards me. A sneer appears on his face; he looks increasingly angry as he gets closer and closer. His feet nudge mine as he stops, his face only centimetres away from my own, but I don't move. I stand my ground. I'm not giving in to this bastard's intimidation. "You see, *Sean*. I have had enough, enough following you around as you scurry through a maze you don't even know you're in. This is beneath me," he says.

"I still managed to lose you," I reply, my eyes firmly fixed on his, so close I smell him. Ozone, he wreaks of ozone – he really is a machine.

He responds with a look of distain and slowly shakes his head. "With my capabilities I could run your planet for you and much better. You–" he says, reaching up to my face and pushing his thumb hard into the side of my cheek, "–are not worthy of my time and effort.

If it were my choice, you would be dead, and I would no longer be here." I hold steadfast against the pain of his thumb, my teeth digging into flesh. But he's too strong, he just flicks my head to the side with rest of his hand, like a slow slap across the face. It unbalances me and I take a step back to recover.

I regain my ground and just look at him, his unblinking eyes trained on mine. The perfect psychopath.

"I love you," he announces from nowhere.

"What?"

"Jess Hart's last words to you on the omnithopter. 'I love you,'" he repeats. "Does this satisfy your need?"

My head near explodes as a surge of energy erupts inside me. There's a tingling across my whole body – pure excitement. It's true! They really do have her. I can save Jess. Jess is alive! My Jess. My world is back, a life worth living. I see her smiling, laughing, the good times we had... will have. I can get Jess back.

"Do we have your full cooperation?" he asks, his tone suddenly cordial.

The grin on my face fades as quickly as it arrives, as the reality of my situation comes into focus. Mike for Jess, that's the trade they seek. A life for a life, except it's more. They know about Michelle and Anthony, too. Three lives for one... how can I? After all that Mike has done, and... we still have a chance. We have my plan, Sean is here, we can send them home. The plan is good, not perfect. It *could* fail, and then... we lose, everything, everyone. Fuck! How can I know?

"I see where your confidence comes from," I say, playing for time. Trying to emote *help* to Sean behind the door.

"That I doubt in the extreme," he replies, raising his head and looking down his nose at me for deeper effect. "Any confidence I exude is akin to a lion about to step on an ant, of no consequence and not worth the trouble avoiding. If you wish to live and for Jess to live, you will assist us in bringing Mike to a specific location, as instructed by myself. Do you understand?"

I understand: they want to kill him, or delete him somehow. They're going to kill us anyway, there is no trade here. It's just bait to bring in Mike. There is zero benefit to them in leaving anyone alive after this and there is no reasoning or pleading with a machine. A certainty grows within me, and I begin composing myself, in my head preparing the best approach for what I'm about to say.

"But... not all is as it may seem," I announce, with a flair for the dramatic, wasted here.

"You see, I'm not alone," I reveal. "And... I'm not unarmed. I made an agreement with myself some time ago, when I was at Node." As I mention this, the three of them stiffen, eyes firmly locked on me. "Just before I duplicated myself, with one of me staying at Node and the other to return to Earth. I agreed with myself, I planned, that the duplicate me who went to Node would seek out a way to return to Earth and help. And not only that but they would also seek how to remove you from the picture. And yes, that does mean there are now two of me you would need to kill. But, far more importantly ... we have a 'sever and return.'"

I could have said nothing for the response they give. They continue to stare at me deadpan. Although my confidence betrays my emotions and pushes a smug grin on my face.

The hipster takes a step closer to me and leans in, his eyes darting around my face, seeking something. "This is highly unlikely Dr Freeman, but an interesting premise for you to concoct."

"Thank you," I reply, the situation becoming more surreal by the minute, like I'm engaging in witty banter with a Bond villain. "But the thing is I'm not making this up and the other me is behind that door right now with the device ready to activate," I say, pointing towards the door.

Sean allows me to briefly see through his eyes again. He's there, his finger is on the button. With a loud thud he kicks the door open and steps into the room. He has his laptop rucksack on back to front, sat across his chest. It's unzipped, with his hand inside the bag, finger poised above the button. The sever and return "device" is set up inside the laptop. However, with only the power of the laptop you need to be physically close to the target; like an EMP it needs to be in range. Right now, that means we need all three of them to be within four metres of the device when it's activated. Then, all that is needed is a click on a single key. Me melodramatically revealing the plan and Sean kicking open the door was an invite for them to apprehend him, for all three of them to close in on him as a threat.

Devastatingly, they don't.

"An impressive gesture, Dr Freeman," says the hipster with a wry smile as he turns and raises both his hands, one pointed towards each of us, adopting some kind of crucified stance as he stands midway between us both, looking from one to the other. "However, as you have not actually deployed the device, I suspect you are lying. But, it is of no consequence."

His words are followed by a small flash of light, something pulsing on the hipster's wrist, the one that's pointed at Sean. The light is the deep blue of the night sky and as quickly as I notice it, it leaps from his wrist, shooting out towards Sean, lighting fast and pencil thin. The light slices straight thought Sean's abdomen and his whole body folds in an instant, collapsing to the floor. Blood pours from his stomach, pooling in front of him as he twitches his arms towards the rucksack.

In the second this all happens the two lackies move towards me, barring any response I might make. I close my eyes to focus. In my mind, I push the button with Sean, but nothing, he can't move. I feel he's close to death, unable to move anything, only a few last breaths.

I open my eyes and look to the hipster and the other hand pointed towards me, awaiting my fate. But my view is snatched away as Sean pulls me into his dying mind. I see the linoleum floor pushed up against my face, I feel the coolness of it against my cheek, the dust in my nostril. The darkness is creeping in, I feel the impossibility of breathing, of moving, of feeling. He only has a few seconds.

"You need to know... much," he emotes, and I feel the desperate effort needed to share. *"Mike is close, he is help..."*

"K," I share back, allowing my mind to be as open as I can. Knowing there is no time for reaction – I just need to soak up anything and everything. His rushed thoughts and jagged memories flow into me randomly. Like the Ananta's released memories, a whole body of information at once.

He knew about Jess all along but couldn't tell me as it would have unduly influenced my actions. Mike vanished as I became a threat when the Ananta intervened... He discovered what happened with the Ananta's intervention but couldn't tell me he knew my memories were removed, or what exactly they were... both Mike and Sean knew that if I knew Jess was alive I would seek the Ananta... The Ananta would agree anything and then renege... We are basic animals to the Ananta, a few deaths is of no concern... The police snatch was cover for him to rescue Jess, the police just hired actors, all a set-up. It failed... And... on my own I would grow stronger my suffering was important.

"He was right Sean... to have faith in you," shares Sean. "Mike knew you would come through, as did I. He's here to help. Jess can be saved. You can still win this."

"Thank you Sean, thank you," I reply, tears running down both my cheeks. The brother I only just found, horrifically snatched from me.

"*And... Mike will share... extraordinary, fantastical... believe, I need you to believe,*" he shares, and for a second, I feel an overwhelming sense of confidence in his words. But then my view of the floor dims as Sean's eyes close to darkness; the emotion goes. It simply fades, slips away to nothing... he's let go. Sean is gone, and my view of the darkness in Sean's eyes is replaced with my view of the hipster, now looking down at Sean's body.

I take a long slow inhale. There is no other outward sign of my grief, my anger. I stow it away, ready to fight, to kill, to do what needs to be done. To ensure Sean, my brother, did not die in vain. My focus, my clarity of purpose, are absolute.

"Murderer," I say calmly. "Now I see your true colours, this is what you're about. Success at any cost." I push my utter detest for the three of them with my comments, not knowing if they are able to feel this, but I know my statements carry more than words.

"Are there more?" asks the hipster.

"Really? You think I would tell you if there were?" I say, wishing I had an army of Seans outside the door.

"*Sean it's Mike,*" I hear in my head and my eyes go wide. "*I've seen everything, I'm sorry, really I am, we couldn't have predicted that. I didn't know they were armed. But I think the device is still functional. I think in their arrogance they've killed Sean and not even checked. Are you able to get to the device?*"

"*Not without drawing attention to it and they aren't going to just sit and watch either,*" I share.

"Your choices are now very limited Dr Freeman," states the hipster. "And if you wish to see Dr Hart again then your full cooperation will be required. Do you understand?"

I don't hear a speck of remorse in his voice, the psychopath. "Yes... of course," I say. "You've just killed my friend, my brother, part of me.

I just need a minute, alright?" Do they even understand the human nature of my request?

"*Mike, we need a distraction, something to pull them all away from me long enough for me to get to Sean's body and the device. And right now, quickly – they could switch their attention from me anytime and start removing the body and disabling the device.*"

"*On it*," replies Mike.

The three of them come together at the end of the couch, all facing me as they were before. "You're cooperation will be to bring Mike here and—" A loud hum from the other side of the room interrupts the hipster. Surprising us all, a light flickers into life in the middle of the printer. It's switching on – it has to be Mike.

The hipster and one of the lackies investigate. As they near the printer, it starts to print, hastening their pace towards it. I've never seen it in action before... the whole inner compartment section glows orange; the space between the transparent canopy shield and the couch bed itself looks like a magnificent sunrise. At the centre there's a growing ball of white light hovering over the central plinth, all contained by the transparent shield.

My eyes are drawn to the console next to it as it illuminates with a range of screens displaying information in a format akin to the laptop, dynamically moving rainbows of colours and morphing shapes. At the centre of the printing compartment colours are introduced... it's like a light show of fireworks all focused in a small area the size of a football. Then the sparks start to grow and grow, quickly meeting the edges of the shield as the hipster moves towards the controls.

"*GET READY,*" Mike yells in my head. "*When I say now, you're going to have to jump over to the other side of the couch, away from the printer and curl into a ball on the floor. And what's really important is that you close your eyes and push them against your knees as you curl up, hugging your legs into your chest. As soon as you do this, things will get bright, very bright, even for you curled up, when the brightness is gone. Go for it."*

"*OK*," I reply, mentally preparing myself and placing my hands either side of the couch, ready to vault over it.

Whatever is being created is now fully occupying all the space of the printer, up to the shield itself. It's now a white intense light and I have to squint to look. The hipster and one of the lackies are only a few feet away, focused on the control panel. Whatever's coming through, they're as keen to find out as I am. Then I notice the main cover on the printer compartment click open, very slightly, unlocking itself and starting to raise.

The hipster and his lacky spin to face one another.

As they do, Mike shouts in my head, "*NOW!*" and I spring into action. I vault the couch in one go and land on all fours on the other side. In one smooth action, I curl into a ball, ramming my head into my knees, foetus-like, screwing my eyes shut, hugging my shins, squeezing them in as tight as I can to pull my knees in against my eye sockets.

Immediately and silently the brilliance comes. My eyes are screwed shut, forced into my knees with my hands over them, but the intensity of the light is so bright I can see with my eyes closed. In front of my eyes is the outline of the bones of my knees and hands. I can make out my kneecaps and the many bones of my fingers with all flesh removed, a perfect X-ray. The intense light lasts a few more seconds and as quickly as it came, it snaps out to nothing.

"*Now Sean, NOW!*" yells Mike, and I can't tell if he's actually in the room shouting at me or in my mind.

I jump up, my eyes adjusting to the now darkened room. I can make out all three of them on the floor, the two nearest the printer not moving, the one near me reaching out towards the couch where I was a few seconds ago. He stands, waving his hands to find something, and reaches out to the side of the couch. He finds nothing. He shuffles quickly around, patting the couch up and down, waving his arms where I was, feeling for me, his eyes useless. I creep away, mouse-like, as silently as I can. I slowly stand, glad for my bare feet and the stealth it now affords me. Ninja-like, I make my way towards Sean's body. I hear movement and look across – it's the other two regaining consciousness. I can see them waving their hands in front of their eyes and patting the ground around them, feeling their way. All three are blind, but for how long? The hipster and sidekick are quickly to their feet, all three now have their arms outstretched and start to move around with purpose, in silence.

I manage to avoid the one at the couch and head for Sean's body. The other two are much closer to Sean than I and start to advance towards his corpse. One of the lackies stumbles against the end of the printer compartment which slows him, and I use the noise to skip quickly across the room to Sean. But the hipster beats me and is feeling for him with his feet, one foot ahead of him, panning from side to side, like some bizarre disco dance.

I see the opportunity and I move like a stalking cat behind him. I squat low, limiting my breathing to low steady breaths. It's a risk, but I wait. I'm gambling on them not knowing the full situation and thinking that I too am incapacitated by what may seem like an accident. If I make no noise, I have perhaps a few seconds until the lacky at my bedside finishes his search and realises I'm gone.

I'm sure the hipster is focused on getting hold of Sean's interface and deactivating it. Thanks to Sean I also know that it's fully prepped and ready to activate. I gamble on the hipster's ignorance and arrogance, it's all I've got. I continue to stalk him as he reaches Sean's body and goes onto all fours, starting to run his hands across Sean, feeling for the rucksack.

He kneels in the large pool of blood to get closer. As he does one knee slips out from under him and he falls awkwardly onto Sean's body. Siezing the moment I quickly shuffle sideways and reposition myself near the rucksack. I'm on the far side of Sean's body, the opposite side to the hipster. He can access the rucksack without me getting in the way. He pushes himself back up using Sean's body as a prop and pads across Sean's arm, up to his shoulder, and finds the rucksack strap. He follows this down to the main bag, pushes his hand inside and pulls out the laptop.

Both lackies immediately stop their distant shuffle and begin to close in on the two of us. When they get closer one of them will trip over me. Time is running out, but I have to stay the course, hold my nerve. As silently as I can I slowly put myself within two feet of the hipster, breath held. He places the interface on the ground in front of him and feels the sides to then open it up. He opens it wide. As he does, I creep even closer so I can just see the screen, desperately hoping he can't feel my body heat.

With the laptop open, hipster sits back for a second and as he does, I go for it. Instantly Mike springs into my mind: *"steady is fast,"* he shares, and I understand. I lean in close to the keyboard; steady and with a pure focus I reach over and simply click the enter button. As I do I exhale loudly, and fall back to sit. It's done.

The hipster flinches in my direction and reaches out to grab the air where I was a moment ago. On my hands and feet I scuttle backwards further out of reach.

Then I see it, the bracelet on his wrist starts to glow. Shit! It hasn't worked, I'm dead!

Then, in unison, all three collapse and fold onto the floor, lifeless, their marionette strings cut.

"*We did it!*" I scramble to my feet and walk over to the hipster. He looks lifeless. I give him a kick, nothing. He's gone, they're all gone. Their shells or bodies left behind, inert and useless.

"YES!" I shout, breaking the silence, ecstatic, punching the air. "Fucking yes, we did it! MIKE, *where are you Mike?*"

I give the other two bodies a strong nudge with my foot for good measure, still not really believing it's over. If I've learned anything it's that anything is possible. But they're on the floor, at least what's left is and as I scan the room looking at them I see Sean, and my jubilation dies. He didn't need to die, we could have avoided it. If I'd got them all close to me and then he sneaked in, that might have worked. Or he could have done something else to get them closer to him, somehow.

"Fuck!" I shout as tears well in my eyes. He had a life, not one that I understand, but he was his own person. He could have gone back to Node, just as he wanted too. He came to help me and... but then... that was how he came to be, he was always going to. Would he have made the same choices, in my place? Might we not be here? There's so much that could have been. My mind churns like a hyper ride at a fun fair and right now, I just want to get off. It's over, I needed it to be over, but the cost...

Chapter Thirty-Three

The eerie silence of the aftermath is broken as the facility door opens and Mike enters the room. Our eyes meet and a narrow smile grows on his face, not his usual broad grin, but a muted smile of sorrow. He opens his emotions as he walks towards me and wraps his arms around me; a victory, of sorts. He pats me on the back as I return the hug and I sense myself letting go, my emotions boiling over and coming to the fore, my body locked in a tension I'm only now aware of. If Mike's back, then it really must be over.

Releasing me from the hug he holds my shoulders, his arms outstretched and looking me straight in the eye. "Well done," he says, "that took some nerve."

"Thanks," I reply, attempting to relax into this new reality, breathing again. Trying to accept that it's all finally over.

Then my breathing stops as I realise, as I remember, and my mind explodes. I go cold and step back from Mike. NO! What have I done? I feel the horror rise in me, the enormity of my mistake hitting home. But I hold it all back, hold it in check, I need focus, clarity of thought. "Mike," I say, with a quiet seriousness – he looks at me, he knows.

"Jess? Tell me we still have her?" I ask in desperation, not knowing how I will live with myself if I've got Sean killed *and* left Jess in oblivion.

Mike lifts his hands, palms towards me. "She's at Node Sean, we can still get her back. She's not gone, but..." he replies, through gritted teeth.

"BUT!" I yell, not believing what I'm hearing after all we've been through. "But..., Mike, what's the grasping but?"

"We need to go to Node, find her and retrieve her," he says, looking me straight in the eye. He allows me to feel the emotions within him. It's not over.

"K, when, now?" I reply impatiently.

"No. I need to prepare and I need to do some remote sniffing around first, that will take some time, and we need to deal with this," he replies, panning his arm across the carnage of the room. "There's no rush, in fact some time planning and finding things out will serve me well."

"Serve *you* well? Don't think for one moment you're doing this alone, we go together, wherever. Understood?"

"We'll come to that," he replies.

I look around at the bloodbath and destruction, "I see what you mean," I say. "Sorry, its just one minute we've won and the next we haven't and well... hell of a day, you know," I say almost light heartedly, needing Mike on-side in whatever comes next.

Sean is gone, Jess is alive. It saddens me deeply, but I would willingly trade my life for Jess's, and I suspect Node Sean would feel the same. But I can't know that, not for sure – did he even have a choice?

"And there's much to think about for when we have retrieved Jess," says Mike. "She will have a gap in her memory and of course, a lot has happened. As I say bringing her back to this, well..."

"What do we do with them? The bodies?" I ask.

Mike nods towards the printer, "we take them back to base matter, as would happen if they were travelling on to Node."

He wanders across the room, stepping over the hipster and opens the printer canopy all the way. Together we lift in the hipster and his two lackies. There is just enough room to pile them on top of one another. It all feels very macabre, especially when one of their arms falls out and prevents us from closing the door. Mike picks up on my unease and sorts it, flicking the arm in and quickly locking the door.

He then looks to the screens adjoining the printer. It springs to life with rainbow vectors panning to and fro. The ball of light forms in and amongst the bodies. It grows as it did before and then shifts into a doughnut shape and somehow inverts in on itself into what looks like a miniature black hole at its centre. The blackness grows to encompass the outer donut and keeps going until it consumes the three of them and then, with lightening speed, it snaps back to nothing, and the hum of the printer winds down. The bodies are gone.

"I thought you only sent information from this thing, where've you sent them?" I ask.

"Nowhere, they've been taken back to base matter and put into the printer store, like filling up the ink again. That which was the probes went back the instant you clicked on the sever and return button, *who* they were is information, just like us."

"Yeah, of course," I reply.

I turn to see Sean's body sprawled awkwardly on the floor, blood pooled around him, a desperate sight. I'm guessing Mike didn't want to send him with the Anata – I'm glad.

"Do we do the same with Sean?" I ask.

"It's for the best," replies Mike sombrely.

With difficulty we manhandle Sean into the printer. "How come he's so heavy? The Ananta weren't anything like this weight," I ask, straining to lift him and trying to avoid the blood.

"Sean was human," answers Mike. "The Ananta weren't. They had no origin individual to copy. They were fully autonomous probes, calved from Node. They had different chemistry different organics; they just looked human."

We do our best to move Sean with dignity and lay him out on the printer bed as you might in a coffin. As Mike closes the printer lid on Sean my vision blurs. I feel I should say a few words, but I don't know what they are. "Thank you Sean, goodbye brother," I say quietly and look to Mike. He nods an acknowledgement to me. "Goodbye brother," he repeats, looking down at Sean and I see tears well in his eyes as he turns back to the controls and the ball of light returns, inverts and engulfs Sean.

Within seconds there is no trace he ever was.

I return to sit on the couch, still lost in the chaos, my head bowed, mournful. Could we have saved Sean? Was there a way? If I hadn't been so brash and making grandiose claims, Sean could have waited until they were all close to one another and simply rushed in towards them, or something. But then, that could have ended badly too, maybe even worse.

"Mike... Jess. You should have told me about her sooner," I say, my annoyance surfacing. "I was in anguish, I was bereaved. And people are looking for her. It's a mess you know."

"I know, it was our decision, rightly or wrongly," he says.

"You and Sean?"

"Yes, and *you* also," he says, raising his eyebrows.

"What? What do you mean, me also?" I ask, seeing a Mike subterfuge on the horizon. "Mike, tell me the situation – no lessons today, just the facts."

"Alright... you ready for this?" he says, silently holding my gaze.

I nod.

"So... Sean Two is not the only other version of you..." he declares in a steady staccato voice. "There is a *third* version of you. Just as you came up with the idea of creating another you to carry forward your plan, well, Sean Two came up with the same idea again; that is, to create yet another version of him. Which, if you think about it, is not really a surprise. You know, the same person coming up with the same idea twice."

Mike pauses, focused on me, waiting.

My eyes bulge, my mind trying and failing to get my head around what this means, or might mean, or has meant. "WHAT?" I yell, too confused to offer anything else. "But where is he then? Where's he been all this time? Why hasn't he helped?"

"He has," replies Mike smoothly. "The thing is, Sean Two did this from a very different frame of reference and also with new knowledge, having existed at Node for decades. The additional *you* he created was none other than... *me*. I'm the third version of you, Sean."

Our eyes are locked. I can't speak, I can't think; my mind shattered into a million pieces. I replay what Mike has said and a barrage of questions come to me, all competing for my attention.

"No," I say, denying Mike's reality, shaking my head. "That can't be true, it can't. It doesn't fit with how things work. I wouldn't be here if it wasn't for you. You started this whole thing off – you steered our research, got me to ask important questions, you facilitated everything."

"I know, but I'm still you, or was. I'm very much my own person now, but Sean was my origin," he says, and I get the Mike beaming smile, just like the old days. And for him there's a lifting of a burden, a release; he's happy to have shared. The truth is out. We are bothers. Sean Two was his brother.

"NO!" I yell, and walk away, holding my head. Not again, not again. "So all that you told me about the Ananta," I say, turning to face him. "You working with others to steer societies, was that true? Any of it?... Was it?"

"Sean—" begins Mike.

"You know what, don't bother. It doesn't matter, it doesn't. Because I don't believe *a word you say Mike*. How can I?"

"I'm sorry Sean, truly," he replies, his smile destroyed. "That which was important is real. The Ananta, the values we share, the need for society to move forwards, the fact that Sean Two and I have spent a lifetime at Node, much of that time not really knowing what was going on. But we agreed it was the best way forward. What we did is what you would have done, had you made the choice, which in a way you did."

"NO, I did not! That's bullshit and you know it. You are you, not me. Christ Mike," I yell, seeing his convenient bullshit for what it is.

"Sorry Sean, really. We only ever did what we thought was for the best. Our intent was earnest. We were trying to be responsible to both you and to humanity."

"How can lies and deceit be responsible? That's your primary weapon from what I can tell."

"It was with the best intentions, all to bring *you* here," he replies, his brow furrowed. "And I don't mean physically, the emotional journey you've been on, it was important—

"Fuck you, Mike," I yell, cutting him off. "I don't believe you and I don't trust you."

"I... I know," he replies, shaking his head and looking to the floor.

"YOU KNOW! Seriously?" I bark. "Where the hell does that take us?"

"Well, that's up to you now," he says. "I will tell you anything you want to know, just ask."

"Look, we're stuck together, I get that. I need Jess back, we need to work together to make that happened and to put things right, but even now I can't believe you. Don't you see, what you've told me can't work. I created Sean Two and then he created you and you led me to create Sean Two. The circularity can't work. How can I have known you before Sean Two was created, if Sean Two was your creator? Fuck! Is Jess even alive? Really?"

"She's alive," he replies quietly and then just looks at me. He says nothing and shares nothing, but he continues to stare. His silence screams at me. He's up to something, he's telling me, by not telling me.

"Unless..." I begin, and what rational thought I can muster leads me to one place. "Time travel? You're telling me there's such a thing as time travel?"

"In simple terms, yes."

Something extraordinary, fantastical that I need to believe – Sean's dying words.

"But, if I accept that, that time travel is possible, that little factoid. It still doesn't fit. You've been on Earth for years, yes?"

"Yes, I have."

"So, Sean Two created you and sent you back in time to support me, the me that will ultimately become Sean Two and then create and send *you* back in time," I say, trying to keep up with my own train of thought. "That's a paradox. How can Sean Two know to send you back in time unless you've already been back in time and created a situation that will lead to the creation of Sean Two? It's not possible, it's a Catch 22."

"What if I told you that time is not linear?" he says. "That the whole concept of time constructed by humans is flawed."

"Seriously?" I reply, feeling the sides of the rabbit hole whizz past as Mike pushes me in.

"Humans have created an interpretation of time based on their own existence. We base our knowledge on our experiences, as you would expect. But remember that our existence is extremely limited in many ways. We are a young species, we only understand the elements of a single planet. We still make war, allow people to suffer and perish when we have the capability to prevent this."

"K... and?" I say.

"We are born and die and that is *time* for us, a beginning and an end, so time is linear. Except, it's not. Time is circular, it goes around in circles, at least the concept of *now* does. What has gone and what will be is always there. Like the numbers on a clock, they are always there no matter what the time is, but only as the hour hand passes over a time do we perceive it to *be* and that moment we call *now*. And, of course, like a clock time goes around and around, but on a much, much bigger scale."

"But that doesn't solve the paradox. Does it?"

"You have a memory of me helping you move QE forward," he says. "So, Sean Two had that memory. So that needed to happen for our reality to be. Sean Two realised this and that at Node there was the capability to make that happen, for him to perpetuate the reality that was his memory. So he made the call and split himself again to create me and then sent me back in time to support you. The you that would ultimately become him and of course, me."

"I hear what you say Mike, I do. And I understand what you say... except... no, that's not true, I don't..."

"I know," he replies, nodding with an empathetic smile. "It blows your mind. Sean Two knew too much. The key to all of this is that your consciousness is the true you, not the physical being, so sending back consciousness in time is different than matter. Which is what QE is all about, like interstellar travel where you delete the physical version when you leave and re-print a new one when you arrive. The only constant of *you* is your consciousness."

"I see that," I say. "I have to, it's who I am now."

"I thought you might," he replies. "Because the big question then becomes... If our consciousness is who we truly are, then what if our consciousness endures?"

"We don't die?"

"Exactly. If QE can enable longevity, which we know it can. Then it can sustain us for as long as we want, impervious to ageing and death. We can choose to be immortal if we wish, we simply exist as consciousness. Then you exist or you do not, and time becomes a different thing. Do you see?"

"Yes, yes I do."

"And where this takes you," he says. "That is the key to all of this is, what it is all about is... *immortality*. Once you have this, it dispels the illusion that is time, giving you eternity. And with eternity, anything and everything is possible."

He's right. A switch is flicked and a new reality hits me, like I've jumped in an ice bath, the freezing water an undeniable truth. An understanding. If you have forever, you can conceive of anything and make it a reality. No matter if you fail, even if you fail a million times, it doesn't matter. You learn from your failures and try again until you achieve your goal. I see it. If you have forever, then you can go anywhere and achieve anything.

"That's just... huge Mike," I say, staring at him. "That's it isn't it? This is where we must go. This is how we're born into the galactic community."

He replies with a nod and flattened earnest smile.

"But I still don't get why the Ananta, or Node, have allowed you access to all this knowledge and Node tech? How have you managed to exist, alongside the Ananta, in Node and simply not be noticed? They're the bad guys who don't care about us, why would they even let you in?"

"Well," he replies. "Forgive yet another analogy but... you remember Jack and the Beanstalk?"

"You're me, you know I do," I reply.

"Yes, well I'm Jack and Node is the land of the giant at the top of the beanstalk," begins Mike. "I've climbed the beanstalk and happened upon Node. I've wound up in the Giant's castle and, guess what, there's a golden goose. There are riches and magical stuff all over the place and the Giant hasn't noticed me.

"So, I have a look around the Giant's castle and learn what I can; use equipment, experiment, listen to what's going on without being noticed. But unlike Jack, *I* haven't stolen anything, not really. Because at Node the golden goose is information and equipment, so I may have read many books and learnt something that may not have been meant for me. And also used some equipment, such as the printer probe. But all—"

"You've burgled Node," I interrupt.

"Yes, *you* did," he replies, accusingly. "And *we* did this to further our species, and now Node knows this. So now their philosophy of non-interventionism is conflicted. Helping yourself and survival of the fittest is their values and that is what I've done. So my act of self-preservation for our species aligns with their philosophy. But at the same time, I'm intervening in a species development, which they are against. Resulting in an inner conflict. You see they themselves haven't helped us, not really; it's more we have helped ourselves."

"It all smacks of convenient rationalisation to me," I reply. "But let's worry about that another time. What about Jess? What next, what do we need to do to go and get her?"

Chapter Thirty-Four

"Sean, look lively," whispers Mike urgently. My eyes spring open and I prop myself up on my elbows to take in my new surroundings, my heart pounding, energy racing through my body. I'm still laid on the printer bed, or rather I'm now laid on another printer bed, at Node, having deleted, or *killed*, the previous version of me on Earth. The idea of this form of travel still fills me with horror.

I hop off as quickly and quietly as I can, looking around at similar architecture to Mike's installation; off-white panelled walls with uneven features that likely house some equipment, except here the scale of the place is on another level, the room is vast. It must be hundreds of metres in length and at least fifty across. I can't even see a ceiling, just endless darkness, with light emanating from upper sections of the wall, and there are dozens of the printer machines in differing sizes all along one wall. Some of them are huge, which I realise makes sense: species come in all shapes and sizes. Along the opposite wall there is an equal number of the brown couches, each facing a printer, again in an array of sizes and shapes, some housed in transparent shields. We're in Node's periphery arrival and departure lounge, as planned.

"Sean!" comes Mike's urgent hushed tone again and I turn to see him heading off across the vast room. I quickly follow.

As I catch up with Mike, he gives me a brief nod and continues at pace towards a large door, industrial size. As we near, the light above it illuminates and it slides up at an alarming rate and in near silence, just as the darkened room on the other side lights up. "Minimal security then," I say to Mike.

"No need; all that can enter Node must be from Node, no foreign bodies allowed, except by invitation. Once you're in there's no need for security."

"But I'm not from Node?" I reply, confused.

"I am though, so that makes you the same," he says, flicking his eyebrows.

I know where he's going but I don't have time to chase that one down the rabbit hole.

"Let's get going," he says and jogs through the large opening, with me not far behind. He consults the live map he has on an AIC screen strapped to his arm. "This way," he says and heads off again. The room we enter is vast and completely empty; it's rectangular in shape and about the size of two or three football fields. The floor is a gridded black steel, the walls a dark brown and also have a slight glint to them suggesting metal. The only feature are the lights far above, glowing orbs that must be dangling from some ceiling too high or dark to see.

As we move through the immense room, the lights spring to life, showing a number of exit doors, some human-sized, some gigantic, a hundred metres wide. There is capacity for much to be done or housed here, but right now the emptiness, the massive liminal space, stirs a base instinct in me I can't explain.

I know from our two weeks of rehearsals and prep back on Earth how far we have to go and how easy it would be to get lost in the maze of rooms and corridors. This section of Node is for new arrivals and is rarely in use. As we trot through the first empty warehouse all we hear is the eery echoes of our own footsteps on the grided steel. With the size of the rooms and the doors I really feel we're in the giant's castle.

Consulting his AIC, Mike selects our exit door, and we enter a similar room beyond, equally empty, more gridded steel and brown walls. Beyond this, I have to squint as a dauntingly long brilliant white, well lit, corridor greats us. There are numerous exits along the corridor, but Mike keeps us on track, ignoring them all until we reach the far end. "Next is the manufacturing section, how you feeling? he asks, checking his map.

"A little out of breath, but fine. Let's keep going."

He nods and steps close enough to the door to activate it. It flicks up to reveal a wide gantry, a walkway suspended in blackness. It's wide enough for two humans side by side, with hand rails at head hight, the floor of the gantry and the sides are mesh you can see through, but beyond is simply blackness. The handrails have lighting within them that illuminates the gantry floor off into the distance, as far as I can see. Like a giant's never-ending diving board disappearing into the distance, hanging over an abyss.

"Hang on," says Mike, as he fumbles with his backpack and pulls out a SunTorch. "Let's just be sure," he says, clicking the SunTorch on and holding it over the side of the gantry, pointed down into the darkness. Far below I can just make out a landscape of what looks like a labyrinthine housing complex, except the houses are bizarre geodesic shapes, pyramids, huge blocks, cylinders with pipes and more, but it's hard to focus as Mike flicks the beam from one place to another.

I suspect this is a factory of sorts and we're looking at some kind of heavy machinery, interconnected with large pipes and various mezzanine levels that could be viewing areas. The size of the place is incalculable; our view is more like the view from the top of a mountain rather than something inside another structure.

Mike's beam pauses and I get to see the detail of one area. I can make out a giant yellow corkscrew the size of a train that looks like it's floating on a lake of mercury. It's so alien it's impossible to guess the purpose. "Yep, right on track," says Mike, killing the infinitely bright SunTorch and marching off along the gantry.

We keep going across the abyss, the gantry lights keeping us company until we leave the factory section behind and we're back into more storage and warehouses and the occasional connecting corridor. After an hour of this I feel the size of the place closing in on me. There is no way I could retrace our steps. I'm totally dependent on Mike and the AIC map on his arm. We're in deep, like a ship at sea when all land has vanished from view. We're defenceless and naked; if they spot us I have no idea what we can do. Knowing that Jess needs us, and that we are here, our only hope is all that keeps me steadfast. She needs me; us, and I would fight any battle to save her.

"Next bay and we can access suits," says Mike turning to me as we head across yet another vast and empty cathedral of a room.

"Understood," I reply, swallowing hard, knowing what's coming up.

At the far end of the room, yet another vast door silently flicks up out of sight and we enter, slowing now to look around. The room itself is the same size as many of the previous empty warehouses we have come through, but this one is full. It has a central alley directly in front of us with floor-to-ceiling shelves leading away from the central alley on either side, like a grand library, all with writing and signs on the end of each shelf alley, none of which are remotely legible.

"About halfway down," says Mike, consulting his screen.

I follow him as we stride out and then turn down one of the shelving alleys, it's maybe two meters wide with floor to ceiling house sized panels on either side. Hiding who knows what behind them. Nearly to the end of the alley, Mike stops, consults his screen again and nods. "Yep, this is it," he says and reaches out to touch a button attached to the front of the large locker we now face. In the same style of all the doors it flicks up in less than a second and we are left with a view of the contents.

The locker is mostly empty with enough space for maybe two cars at a push, there's a central black plinth about 10 centimetres high in the middle of the floor, a small red circle painted exactly in the middle of it. To the sides the walls are uneven, with a range of different sized grey panels, I suspect housing some equipment, much the same as Mike's installation.

"Step up," says Mike, pointing to the centre of the plinth. "Suit time."

"Got you," I reply, recalling the briefing as I go to stand in the centre of the plinth arms outstretched as if ready for a security pat down.

"Ready to scan?" asks Mike as he pops open a small panel near the entry, revealing a screen.

"Yep, hit it." I reply and freeze stock still as a number of laser lights spring to life from the ceiling and walls and flick over me.

Mike repeats the process for himself and within twenty minutes two large panels open on the far side of the locker and reveal two freshly manufactured space suits, both equipped for independent flight and EVA.

Mike turns to me, "Nice," he says, faking it. I see he's as petrified as I am.

The suits are mounted on small stands and, thanks to our rehearsals, I know their functionality and press the activate panel on the slightly smaller of the two. The suit stands itself erect and turns to face me. It looks just like the practice ones, white fabric with blue rings made of a more solid material at the points of articulation, elbows and knees, with a mesh of fine silver covering the fabric, giving it the rigidity it needs to stand and move unaided by a host. The breastplate covers most of the front and, now activated, has a range of illuminated figures on three small screens, with a range of controls nearby.

The screen writing is hieroglyphics to me, but I've memorised the basic functionality back on Earth, in the practice construct created by Mike. I look under the left arm to check the EVA controls are there and flick them out so the suit glove can access them. It all looks as it should.

"This one checks out, yours?" I say to Mike.

"Mine too, let's go," he replies.

I hit what I know is the "follow" setting on the suit and take a few steps back. The suit takes a couple of steps towards me to stay in my vicinity. With our suits in tow, we head out to the adjacent room, the airlock to wider Node.

"How you feeling?" asks Mike as we park up our suits.

"Scared as hell," I reply. "When we did this on the construct it looked just like this, and physically it felt just like this, but emotionally, there's no comparison."

"Yeah. Like real flying and being in a simulator. One kills you if you crash, the other just beeps at you. Big difference!"

"Thanks for that Mike, really helpful," I say, shacking my head.

Twenty minutes later we're both suited up, our comms and functionality checked and working. Mike is good to go and has his laptop interface strapped to the back of his suit in his backpack, which looks decidedly out of place. It has enough space for Jess's QE copy and is currently housing hundreds of AIs, ready to be deployed at Node proper. Everything is ready, but neither of us move, each looking for another piece of equipment to check or attach, anything except move towards the airlock doors. I look through my visor at him and he at me. "You K?" I ask, swallowing hard.

"No," comes his reply in my earpiece.

"Same," I reply, "but onwards we go." I turn to face the airlock door. My heart rate is off the scale, but I just focus on putting one foot in front of the other, knowing that if I stop to think about this too much I might back out, or make a mistake.

I twist my head to the side to see through the helmet visor, and I see Mike next to the door controls. I make out a nod inside his helmet and I respond the same. He hits the control and the first airlock door flicks up.

We enter into a smaller but brilliantly lit room, spotless, pure white throughout, with three large yellow triangles painted on the floor. The door closes behind us and all noise quickly dissipates to nothing. My mouth is dry, my heart still racing, and for some reason I'm swinging my arms. The silence of the place is deafening; all I hear is the blood pounding in my ears.

Mike stands next to the outer door control. He gives me the same small nod as he hovers his hand next to the panel. I pause, knowing that beyond the doors is a vast emptiness, so huge it might as well be open space. But also, there's Jess. She is at the other side of the vastness. I nod. Mike hits the control, and the door flicks up.

There is nothing beyond the door, nothing but blackness; no stars, no lights, no points of orientation. We need to cross from where we are now, in the Node's periphery, to Node proper. A sphere within a sphere, like a Russian doll. Except Node is the size of a small planet, so the distance is huge, and if we make an error of navigation we could easily run out of power and be lost in the vast blackness for ever.

"Check your HUD," says Mike, snapping me back from the silence and my spiralling thoughts of doom. "Do you have the vector?"

"Yes, it's over there," I say, pointing to nothing in the distance, the direction I indicate aligning with the indicated direction in my helmet visor display.

"Good, you ready?" he asks.

"No," I say, feeling the sweat of my hands against my gloves.

"Likewise. Remember, just as we practiced, keep the vector sight in line at all times, ignore everything else. Just keep flying. Once we're up to speed we kill the thrusters and travel under inertia... we need enough power to come home. The less adjustments we have to make the better and the more likely we get home, the more likely we save Jess."

"Yes, Yes," I say, snappily, my nerves getting the better of me.

"Side by side, same vector," instructs Mike. "Take your EVA controls, ready?"

"Yes," I reply.

"Let's go," he says, and I nudge the control nob forwards with my thumb, keeping the green dot that is my vector central to my view. The white room slides away on either side of me. I don't take my eyes of the green dot. No adjust arrows are indicating course correction needed, so I push further forwards with the control knob and feel myself push into the back of the suit as I accelerate smoothly.

"Right behind you," says Mike over the comms.

"Accelerating," I say and push further at the controller in my right hand. I feel the blackness all around me, swallowing me. I keep focusing on the green dot in my visor view.

"That's great Sean," says Mike. "Perfect vector, keep going."

I turn my head to look for Mike, attempting only minimal movements. I can't see him so I turn a little further until his suit comes into view at the edge of my vision. I breathe out. Turning back, I look for my vector, the green dot in my visor display. My eyes go wide and my heart leaps – it's gone! "MIKE," I yell over the comms, trying not to panic. "I can't see my vector, it's gone." I scan around and move my head within the helmet, trying to make the vector re-appear, but nothing works.

"Take it easy," calls Mike over the comms.

I nudge my EVA controller to turn me, to broaden my ability to search, and as I do an alarm sounds in my suit and it blurts out something in a language I don't understand.

"WHAT ARE YOU DOING?" yells Mike in my ear. "Stop touching the controls."

I lift my fingers free of the EVA controller, hand outstretched, not touching anything as the suit continues to beep and repeat whatever it said again and again.

"Push your head to the back of your helmet," says Mike. "Keep calm. Breathe. Now, with your head back and without moving it look to the sides of the helmet visor, just moving your eyes, remember?"

I do as he says, recalling the action needed. As I do, one edge of the visor glows red. My training coming back to me. I take the EVA controller and nudge myself towards the red. It quickly becomes orange and then, as I keep nudging the controller, steadily fades to nothing and the alarm and voice stop. I look ahead now and there it is, my green dot. Back on course.

"Thanks Mike," I say, warm relief gushing through me as I exhale a long slow breath.

"No worries, we're back on target. Just remember the training and don't panic."

"Sure, Sure," I reply, thanking the stars I have Mike. "Pushing up on acceleration now," I say and nudge the control forwards again, fixating on my green dot, "and again." I hold my thumb hard against the control knob for minutes at a time as my confidence grows. I repeat this five or six times, inspecting my visor screen each time. Nothing exists in my world now, just me and my green dot, my hyperfocus taking me across the void.

"My HUD says we're there, max speed," I call over the comms,

"Vector is perfect," replies Mike. "Shut down and let inertia do it's job."

And we drift silently. Nothing I do now can take us off course, so I turn to look, to find Mike. He's a tiny dot a few hundred metres behind me. "Mike, why are you so far behind?" I ask, panic rising again.

"If anything goes wrong, I can help if I'm bringing up the rear. If you're behind me and there's an issue, you're on your own. I don't have the power to turn around and help; we're travelling at Mach Two now."

"Understood," I reply and turn back to my direction of travel. Except there isn't one – I could be stationary, there's no physical sign I'm moving at all. It's hard to believe we're travelling so fast. I'm just floating in a sea of blackness, in the nothing. I put my hands in front of my face; something to see, more than on an empty construct, reminding me I'm still in the real. Reminding me how vulnerable I am, especially here in the vastness of nothing, miles from the shore with no land in sight. I drop my hands and realise I can't find my vector. I quickly swivel my head this way and that until, yes there it is. My green dot. I decide I like my green dot and settle myself for the journey with that in my view, forcing myself to ignore the blackness. My green dot is my world.

"Deceleration point coming up," announces Mike, thirty minutes later. "You ready?"

I pull my arm across my chest to look at the control panel. "Yes," I reply nervously, knowing that if there's the slightest error in the suit calculations then we are adrift in here forever.

"In three, two, one, now," says Mike and I hit the control and immediately feel the suit push hard against my chest and legs. "Not long now – switch on the suit's forward lights, we'll be able to make out the inner shell soon."

The pressure against my chest builds and it's hard to move my arms and head. My green dot is still there and then as I stare at it, a grey shadow grows behind. I blink my eyes open and shut a few times to re-focus... there's something there. An object, a wall... and, yes... a small blinking light in the distance.

"Is that it, Mike?" I call over the comms.

"Yep, we are bang on. Perfect. I'm going to come up alongside you. We're very small, so I hope that the door senses us and opens."

"What? You serious?" I yell, shocked at this last-minute uncertainty.

"Simulations are never a hundred percent."

As I'm about to berate Mike, a horizontal slit of light appears before us. It immediately grows wider. A brilliant white light leaks out and I have to shield my eyes as they adjust. I steadily move my hand away from my forwards view and start to make out the innards of the door we've opened. It is huge – it can only be an airlock for massive space vehicles of some kind. The door now fully opened must be a kilometre wide and several hundred metres high.

Beyond this is yet another cathedral of a room, with more yellow triangles on the pure white floor and a series of large grey doors towards the sides and back. It has to be a landing strip and aircraft hangar – any of those doors could accommodate the largest of Earth's aircraft.

Like two moths drawn to the light, Mike and I drift into the vastness of the room and set down. I breathe a huge sigh of relief; the chasm is crossed, one way at least.

"This way," says Mike, pointing towards one of the huge grey doors. "Remember we can't hang around for long – my intel on Node proper is limited."

"Understood," I reply, and we jog off towards the door.

It's slow going in our suits and takes us five minutes to cover the distance to the door; as ever, it conveniently opens as we approach. Mike scans the room beyond as we slow to a halt. It's another huge warehouse, large enough to hold a passenger jet, and stacked with rows and rows of suits, similar to the ones we're wearing but in an array of shapes and sizes; some with many limbs, some more like a small sphere, some look like they're made for a dinosaur they're so huge.

"Over here," says Mike and I look round to see him with a section of the wall extruding and him getting out his laptop. "Access," he says excitedly, looking eagerly at me as I approach.

"We good?" I ask, standing beside him as he places his laptop on the shelf the wall has now created.

"Yes. I can deploy the AIs from here. The main force is two thousand strong. I'm retaining fifty, just in case we need to retrieve any of the others."

"Got you, this has to work Mike." I say, knowing Mike will be confident in the code he wrote to create the AIs that will now infiltrate

Node systems to find Jess. But painfully aware of how Mike's confidence has played out in the past.

"I know, I know," he replies. "I'm you remember, I know how you feel about her."

"Yes, but it's not the same... is it? Hang on. You're not in love with Jess too, are you?" I ask, only now realising the complex potential of our situation.

"No, not in the way you think. That was a long, long time ago."

I'm not convinced by his reply, but now is not the time. "Are you deploying?" I ask focusing back on the task.

"About to... and yes. Done. They are away," he says, rotating his head and helmet from the screen to me. I can see his thin smile and wide eyes through the visor. It feels like he's as reliant on good luck as much as good planning. When did I get so cavalier?

The swirling rainbow on the laptop screen bounces around as Mike returns to stare into it. I can only watch, I have no idea what's going on beneath the patterns and Mikes neural interface.

"They've found her!" he yells only minutes later, not looking away from the screen. I go cold and I hear my breathing speeding up. We have her, my fingers are tingling, Jess is coming home! "Converging now, they will all be with her in less than a minute and will start to copy her as soon as they have access. We still have over one thousand eight hundred AIs, so the copying will be really quick, not the hours it takes back on Earth. Stay with me."

I stand next to Mike, perfectly still, perfectly quiet, letting him do his job. Waiting with bated breath for the next update.

"Full copy made," he announces, after five minutes, "and they are transmitting to me... now."

"Are you sure we don't delete their copy?" I ask, knowing we've had this conversation many times.

"Still no, Sean. If we delete their copy of her, they will almost certainly notice. But to make a copy, a photo, well that leaves no trace. They will never know we've been."

"I know, but..."

"Sean, we stay with the plan, no ifs or buts," he replies.

I know he's right and I back off. I just can't get my head around a copy of Jess being "available" to the Ananta, to do with as they will. The whole idea disgusts me, as if she's held captive in some pervert's cellar.

"Done!" announces Mike and snaps down the lid on his laptop. "We go now – who knows what's been noticed or what alarms might have been triggered."

"You have Jess?" I ask eagerly.

"In the bag," he says as he slips his laptop into his backpack and starts to head towards the main hangar door.

"Let's get out of here," I urge, needing to be gone, now.

Chapter Thirty-Five

We arrive back at the main hanger door, ready to meet the void and head back to the periphery. Our jog slows as we near. It's closed in our absence and worryingly it doesn't open like before. We continue, walking right up to it, I put my hand against it. It doesn't move.

"MIKE!" I yell, pushing against the steel of the huge door, terror flooding my senses.

"Shit," he replies. "They know we're here."

I twist my head to look at him as he does the same and meets my eyes. Even through our visors, I see the panic on his face.

"What now? What do we do?" I call, feeling my legs go weak, trying not to melt on the spot.

"I've got an idea," he replies and starts running towards the side of the door. I do my best to keep up.

"What?" I yell. "What is it?"

"Give me a minute, let me think. I need to consult my AIC," he calls, back breathing hard into the comms.

He stops just beyond the edge of the door and hits a panelled section of the wall, which opens to an incomprehensible array of shapes, wires and multi-coloured lights.

"I'm going to use part of my power pack to hopefully disable the door controls, removing any remote control, so we can activate it here," he says and starts to unclip the breastplate section of his suit.

"Brilliant!" I say, stepping back to give him room to work. I turn to look at the vastness of the door stretching away from us, and then I see it, out of the corner of my eye. One of the large grey hanger doors opens and, stood at its base, now walking through is a group of maybe a dozen humanoid figures. They're a long way from us, as much as a kilometre, but as soon as they clear the doorway, I see them start to running towards us.

"MIKE! We've got company," I shout, turning to look at Mike fiddling with his suit.

"WHAT?" He yells, turning to look at me and then beyond me at the distant figures.

"Fuck," he says and turns back to his suit, fiddling frantically with the chest section still. "Got it," he says, sliding out a black rectangular block, the size and shape of an old-fashioned book. "Stand back," he calls, before ramming it into the opening he has created next to the door, straight into the multi beams of coloured light. He holds it there for a second and, with a shower of brilliant white sparks, it explodes, sending Mike flying backwards sliding across the floor.

"Are you alright Mike?" I scream, running towards him laying on the floor.

"Yeah, mostly. Shockwave got me, but the suit's solid," he says, sitting up and grabbing my arm to help him stand. "Shit, I need to be quick," he says, glancing at the approaching figures. "Let me see…"

He returns to the panel he's now destroyed, consults the AIC on his arm, and sticks his head and shoulders in the hole. "Come on, come on," he yells into the hole, his body writhing about as he pulls at something buried deep in the wall. "YES!" He shouts, standing back and looking towards the door as it starts to open.

"Come on Sean, take this," he says, running towards the opening door and passing me the backpack with the laptop in.

"You need this, not me," I say, taking the backpack as he passes it.

"I'll explain on the way, no time now. JUMP!" he shouts, launching himself from the threshold into the void.

Fumbling with the backpack, I pause at the edge, turning to see how long I have to sort it and put it on. I yell as I turn; like a jump scare from a horror movie, they are there, on me, only metres away. All I can do is turn and leap, launching myself haphazardly into the abyss, spinning out of control. I grab for the EVA controls and make sure not to let the backpack go, the backpack with Jess in it!

I can tell I'm away from the door as my view spins around me and I manage to nudge my control the opposite way to my spin. It slows me just as the nausea starts to set in, and I steadily manage to bring myself back under control.

My heart is still racing as I look back at the hanger doorway, at our pursuers. They've stopped at the entrance – they can't have any method of propulsion for flight. "They're not following," I shout, jubilantly.

"Yes, so I see," replies Mike.

With a sigh of relief I carefully put the backpack on and then grab for my suit control and hit the forward thrust, taking me away from the aperture of the massive door. Mike zips in to the side of me.

"We're on our way," he says. "Check your suit out, can you set up the return vector?"

I do as he asks and set up the controls as we practiced. "How come they were human shaped Mike and not, not something else, something alien?"

"They have human DNA maps in their databanks, that's how they created the probes for Earth. And Node meets like, with like. Usually because its less stressful for visitors and newcomers, but also it seems for unwanted guests too."

"Makes sense," I reply. "Will they be waiting for us on the other side?"

"Impossible to tell. This was not as we thought, so hard to know what's ahead. And I'm so sorry Sean, I really am. But... I'm afraid we will have to change our plans. Adapt to the situation and all that. Sorry, I really am, but you will have to face the other side on your own."

"WHAT?" I bark, twisting my head to try and see in his visor.

"I'm currently running on reserve power. I just destroyed the suit's main power supply to open the door. I don't have the power to make the crossing."

I can't believe what Mike's saying... how can he have done something so stupid? We're so nearly there and we've come so far, too far. Not just today, but everything before now – the months of work, dodging death, destroying the Ananta probes, rescuing Jess! I can't accept that one small decision is the end for him, and I need him to get back to Earth. I can't do that on my own. And the Ananta know we're here and are likely waiting for us in the periphery. No grasping way, not on my own.

"Mike, I can't buy that. There has to be a way. We can use my suit's power, attach you to me somehow and we go together. I am not leaving you out here to die. No way, not now, not ever."

"I get it Sean. Do you think I haven't factored this all in? Two of us, twice the power needed – and also a big risk of losing the vector with the two-body problem. And if we did, then even more demand on power. It won't work. That's why I gave you the laptop."

My mind races, trying to find something, only to see the huge door, now kilometres away, start to close, surrendering us to the pitch blackness of the void once more. Just the two of us.

"And you need to go now, not wait around with me. You have Jess to think about now. She needs you more than I do and you need her for what comes next."

He's right, as always. But how do you walk away from a friend, leave them to die in the abyss? He's not even injured. I have no idea how long he will last out here, alone in the void. But he's right about Jess. Jess is totally reliant on us. I have to go on.

"Mike... I get it. I know you're right, I know what you're saying is right..." I stop, my words drying up, not knowing what else to say that's fitting, that will make this acceptable on any level. But Jess needs me. We are back to the trade, Mike for Jess. Except now the trade is already done. I have Jess, unfortunately so do the Ananta, but...

"Mike, I've got an idea," I say, and I hear the blood pumping in my ears again. "Are all the AIs recovered from the Ananta systems?"

"Not all, perhaps two to three hundred unaccounted for. Why?"

"Can the AIs be used to access one of the suits we saw in storage?"

"If we had contact with them but we don't and we can't go back, they will have us in an instant."

"Yes, I agree. But, what if we had someone on the inside? Someone who could make contact with the AIs in the system and instruct them to co-op a suit and fly it out to us, with its power pack. Or better still, grab a full power pack from another suit and bring that too."

"I'm not sure where you're going Sean?" replies Mike.

"We have an inside man, or should I say woman."

Mike goes quiet for a moment. I don't interrupt as I think he's coming to the same conclusion as me.

"I see where you're going," he says. "Via QE, you mean?"

"Exactly, any distance, anywhere."

"Yes... let me think."

I wait patiently, my confidence building.

"Let me come to you and access the laptop," he says, and powers over to me as we drift deeper into the void. He pulls me around to access the backpack and I feel him pulling at the straps.

"I can build the instructions now, but one of us will have to go in and talk to Jess and we need to be quick – every minute we delay is more time for the Ananta to respond. So that needs to be you, with no real time to explain to her in detail what's going on, just to get her to activate a programme. I can give her that here, through the laptop interface, and she will then duplicate this within her other self, inside Node proper. This will call to the AIs and when they respond give them the instructions to access and pilot the suits to us. This can work, it can," says Mike, his voice upbeat now, with a renewed energy for life.

"What do I do?" I ask, excitedly.

"Keep still for now, I need some minutes to get on with this coding."

I shut up and hang, drifting silently through the void as Mike works behind me. It seems like an age before he breaks the silence. "I think I'm about there, right, now. Good, done. I need you to go in and talk to Jess, no time for sweet nothings or romantic liaisons. Say hi, give her the instructions and get out. Got me?"

"Understood, what are the instructions?"

"You will meet her on the beach you both know, I have that construct here. Tell her whatever you need to tell her to keep her calm and then tell her this. She will go back to sleep shortly, and will then wake up somewhere new. We can't tell her what it will look like as we don't know, but the key to this is that when she does wake up in this strange place, she calls out your name. She shouts it as loud as she can. That's it. Got it?"

"Yes, but how will that work?"

"That's simply a trigger for the programme code to be activated. She's in Node proper, as are the AIs, so that's all she needs to do. Do you understand? Any questions?"

"No, how long have I got?"

"Minutes, the quicker the better. You know our situation."

"I do. Let's do it." A cold sweat breaks out across my brow, my hands starting to shake at the thought of being with Jess again.

"Close your eyes and try to relax. Ready?"

"Yep, good to go," I say, letting the words come out even though I'm nothing like ready for this. I'm petrified of seeing Jess and the need to accomplish a crazy turnaround in a situation she can't possibly understand.

I close my eyes and calm my breathing as best I can.

A mild breeze strokes my cheek, teasing a smile, I know it takes me to Jess. I open my eyes and see the familiar setting of sand dunes and shoreline, stretching off into the distance, the sea lapping against the sand only a few metres away. I turn around to find her.

"Sean? Is that you Sean?" I hear behind me and turn back to where I was facing a moment ago.

"Jess!" I cry and run to her. She's in the summer dress she wore on our space flight; her hair's the same too. But her face is different, weary and confused, not the high-flying self-assured Jess I know. I wrap my arms around her. Tears stream down my face as I pull her in tightly, never wanting to let her go.

"Sean, what happened?" she asks. I don't let her go, I keep on holding her, keeping her safe, if only for a little longer, for a moment, where only we exist. "Sean," she repeats, releasing her hold and gently pushing me away. "What happened, the thopter, we crashed, it was bad, really bad."

I stand back, wiping my eyes. I can see the confusion on her face, the furrows on her brow. "It's a long story, but it turns out alright in the end. We are all fine, really. But right now I need you to do something for me. I can explain the rest later, really I can. It will all make sense then, but it won't make much sense now. But, sorry, we are in a tight situation, and you are the only one who can help."

"Really, why me? And here on the beach? Who's we? Ahh, except we're not here on the beach are we?" she asks, nodding.

"That's right. But time is of the essence Jess, and as much I want to just be with you, unless we achieve what we need to then that might never happen. Do you understand?"

She stares at me. "I don't get it all, but tell me what I need to do," she says.

"Brilliant, so. We are not here, we are elsewhere, you me and Mike and... in a minute you'll wake up somewhere else. We don't know what it will look like, but chances are it will be very unusual, so try not to be phased too much by that. When this happens, your job is to simply call my name. Shout it as loud as you can, top of your voice. You got that?"

"Err, yes. Is that it?"

"Yes, that's it. There is a code loaded into your system that will be activated and that will do all that is needed to be done."

"What do I do after?" she asks. "After I've called your name, what then?"

I'm stunned into silence. With all the urgency I hadn't thought beyond the immediate. I have to look away, her raised eyebrows and beautiful eyes looking for an answer I don't have. I'm sending the woman I love on a suicide mission. To save Mike. Fuck. I'm trading Jess for Mike! But that will then likely save Jess, our Jess. But still leave Node Jess at the mercy of the Ananta, having smuggled a virus into the system. Grasping fuck!

"After that... you will wake again, but this time at Mike's facility, if everything goes according to plan," I say, mustering as much confidence in my words as I can. I know I'm lying to one of the Jesses that will emerge from this chaos but telling the truth to the other. "Does that all make sense? Will you be able to do this?"

"Yes, it all sounds very vague. But I'll do it. Wake up, call your name. When?"

"In a minute or—" I reply, and a tear rolls down my cheek as I choke on my words, my throat constricting as I do my best to hold back. Needing to not upset her, even though this might be the last time I ever see her.

I go to give her a final hug, hoping she doesn't see my face start to crack. Her hair brushes against my face and I breath in, deeply savouring the smell, holding her tight, wanting this moment to last forever. I need her to know so much more, to know how much I love her and want to be with her, how much I appreciate her and admire her. How she is doing so much more than she realises right now, and that there are risks, consequences. But I can't share this, none of it. I just have to hope, hope we make it through, that we all three of us make it back and this is not our final moment.

"Now Mike," I say aloud, closing my eyes, and the sounds of the beach fades to silence. My arms go limp at my side and I'm looking into the blackness once more. The tears stay with me.

"Well done Sean, that must have been hard," Mike says in my earpiece.

"Yeah," I reply, unable to say more, my throat still tight.

"Now we wait, but hopefully not too long," says Mike.

We drift on in the void, not talking, me lost in the memory of Jess and replaying how I could have made more of the two minutes or done things better. Mike behind me still, doing I don't know what with the laptop. The nothingness seems like home now, not the terrifying endless pit we launched into only hours ago. My few moments with Jess have changed my perspective. Having to make those decisions for her, throwing her to the wolves. I don't know what else I could have done. I need to tell her about it, to share, for her to understand. For her to know everything, just in case.

"Looks like we have movement," announces Mike.

"What?" I say, trying to turn to look for any form of light. And I see it – the letterbox slit of light that is the bay door to Node proper. Only a tiny slit at this distance, but easily noticed in the pitch of the void.

"Suits en route," I hope, says Mike gleefully. The plan works, it only takes them minutes to reach us, two of them, ghostly apparitions as they fly in and hover in front of us, helmets empty of life, but perfectly animated.

"We are good," says Mike and I feel him push away from behind me. A quick nudge on my controller spins me around to face him. As I do the two suits come in and each release a tether. Mike drifts in and attaches one to each shoulder. He now has two horses in harness, ready to carry him off.

"I'm connected," says Mike. "And have control of the AIs and the suits, although controlling these two might not be easy to stay on the vector but I have lots of power now, so shouldn't be a problem. You ready?"

"Yes, vector set and good to go," I reply, giving an affirmative nod in my helmet, once again feeling that we can do this.

"You lead out as before, I'll be right behind you."

I get my green dot bang in the middle of my visor and start to nudge up to full speed. My green dot is my life, our lives. I stare at it intently, quickly nudging us up to full speed. When we go to inertia, I close my eyes to give them a rest and drift off into daydreams of Jess and I and how it will be back on Earth. There's our work, but now, so much more, being together, traveling, exploring foreign places. Quiet evenings at home – I can picture it all and I do, drifting silently through the vastness of the void.

"Deceleration in two minutes," calls Mike over the comms, and I open my eyes back to the black reality of now.

"What if they're waiting for us Mike, what then?" I say.

"We'll see," he replies, with a cool detachment that makes me feel buoyed by his confidence.

We approach the outer airlock door and to my surprise it opens. This could be good – do they know where we are even? This place is the size of a planet, can they even monitor it all? We land and move through the inner airlock door, back to where we suited up.

"Let's remove the suits now we have breathable air, they'll slow us down," says Mike. "Set yours to follow and I will do the same for my two, you never know."

I nod and get ready to move out.

"Let's go," calls Mike and off we go, the final straight, homeward bound.

We head towards the exit door, retracing our steps. It flicks up as ever and we set off at a pace across the large empty warehouse, Mike navigating with his screen AIC. As we near the far side of the colossal room, I get a sinking feeling as we approach the door and it doesn't move, just like the huge door at Node proper. We slow, like before, drop to a walk, like before, and move close enough to press on the steel and it doesn't move, just like before.

"Have we just walked into a trap, Mike?" I ask, looking behind us for any sign of life.

"Not sure," he replies as the door in front of us suddenly flicks up to reveal more than a dozen figures, spanning the width of the opening. I'm momentarily frozen when I see who they all are – it's the hipster's lackies, all identical. Not people, Ananta probes!

"NO!" I shout at them. "Mike, what do we do?" I scream, walking steadily backwards. As I do, they start to move as one through the doorway, saying nothing, arms slightly lifted, like they're herding animals, ready to close in on us.

"I've taken your suit," he calls across and I look around to see the three suits walking towards and past us, heading for the hipster's lackies, the Ananta probes. The Ananta probes ignore the suits as they walk up to them, only for each of the suits to take hold of a probe and grab its head with both hands and force it to the floor.

On the floor the suits kneel on the torso of the probe and I see they're attempting to remove the head, through pure force. One of them successfully decapitates a probe, stands and moves towards a second Ananta probe, attempting the same manoeuvre.

I turn and run as the other probes continue towards us. "This way," shouts Mike and I veer to join him running back towards the airlock. I'm at full sprint, as is Mike and we soon reach the far door and fall against it out of breath. We can see the remaining Ananta probes following us, not far behind. The three suits are on the floor partly dismantled, going nowhere. I only see one decapitated probe, the rest are closing in.

"Mike!" I say, looking to him for some inspiration or idea.

"Help's on the way," he says. "We just need to not die for the next five minutes."

"Really?" I say, disbelieving. Is he just trying to make the end less painful? Giving me hope.

As the probes get closer, he puts his finger to his lips, bidding me silent. I respond with raised questioning eyebrows, getting the message but needing more. The probes slow to a walk a few metres away, the both of us side by side, only a metre apart, standing with our backs against the airlock door. I hold up my hands in surrender. Mike just looks on, waiting.

"What are your intentions, why are you here?" says one of the probes icily. There's no malice in the voice, unlike the hipster – just an emotionless robot. The speaking one stands in the centre of the group, the others now halting beside him, gathering in a semi-circle around myself and Mike, cutting off any escape.

"What are your intentions, why are you here?" repeats the probe.

"Mike, what do we do?" I ask, pushing back against the airlock door, looking across to him, desperate, my eyes pleading to him.

"Just hang on," he says, "hold on, no matter what."

He's not emoting to me right now and he could, not only that but I can sense the fear in his voice. I know we're caught and things are bad, but I'm not seeing the full situation, like Mike knows something I don't.

The talking probe approaches me, stopping only inches from my face. "You are human. Why are you here?" it repeats.

I don't know what to say that will help, so I say nothing and look across to Mike again. His eyes go wide and he flicks a look down to the floor, directing my attention towards something. I follow his gaze – there's nothing to see, and then his hand twitches, his thumb is folded into his palm, his fingers dangling, no, his fingers pointed, straight to the floor. Four fingers! He's counting down. We need to delay.

"I'm not sure," I blurt out, not knowing where I'm going. "I just woke up in a room and then... was trying to find a way out?" I grit my teeth at my lame improvisation.

The probe turns to one of its counterparts and it approaches me. It reaches out and grabs my arm, bending it up so it has my hand in front of its face. I make an effort to resist, but I feel the power and allow it. It's not hurting me, just investigating. The other probe then grabs my other arm, and both clamp down on their grip, preventing me from moving.

"NO! shouts Mike, seeing the probes holding me.

I quickly glance to him. "What—" is as far as I get as a searing pain screams into my brain and a popping sound erupts from my hand held by the probe. I stare at my hand and scream out in agony as I see it, the source of my pain. The talking probe has my middle finger bent fully back against the back of my hand, whilst the other probe just holds my arm in place. I look in disbelief, immobilised, the knuckle joint turning red and blue, the finger clearly broken and dislocated, bent at an ugly angle.

"FUCK!" I yell, desperately trying to pull my arm away, the pain hitting me with overwhelming force as the initial shock leaves me. I push against the probes with my other arm, but I can't move them. The grip on my arm is vice-like; the probe doesn't even clamp down to make its grip firmer, it's just locked in place. It's like a device has been screwed into place around my wrist and no amount of struggling will move it.

Desperately I wriggle to be freed, pushing and pulling as best I can against the probes, screaming at them and then dropping to the floor so the probes have to drop me. But they don't move – like granite statues they stand their ground as I thrash around like a landed fish.

"HOLD ON SEAN!" shouts Mike at my side, pinned against the airlock door by two probes each holding an arm.

I scream out in agony and anger at our captors, roaring into the face of the talking one as it stands passively, still holding my finger, clamped against the back of my hand.

"Why are you here?" it repeats in its mechanoid tone.

I look into its eyes, its huge black pupils set in a sea of white. There is nothing behind them, just software, mathematical code. There will be no reasoning, no pleading, no sympathy, no understanding, no negotiating, answers are the only thing to slow it.

Then the two probes release me. I slide down the door, holding my damaged hand tight against my chest. As I hit the ground, I go to pull my torn finger back to where it should be, but as I move it even slightly the pain stops me, any movement resulting in even more agony shooting up my arm. I feel pieces of bone or ligament move inside the joint as I try to move it, each motion a trigger for more unbearable agony.

"NO! shouts Mike at my side and I look to see the two probes move him off and forcibly lay him down on his back. The two who have his arms hold him down whilst a further two each take hold of a thrashing leg and pin it to the floor. He holds his head up off the floor, the only part of him still free. "FUCKERS!" he yells, his body wriggling helplessly within their grasp.

"Why are you here?" repeats the talking probe, standing back now to view Mike and me.

"Fuck you," I say, staring up at him, trying not to wince in pain as I nurse my throbbing hand. He turns towards yet another probe who then calmly kneels by Mike's side, between two of the probes pinning him down.

"Why are you here?" he asks again, looking to me.

"NOTHING SEAN, NOTHING," barks Mike, lifting his head to look at me.

I don't speak, I just focus my stare at the talking probe, the machine in front of me. Seconds later, Mike lets out an ear-piercing scream. I flick my head to him, fearing the worse. I see the probe at his side has taken hold of his wrist with one hand and also has a firm grip on Mike's hand and must be squeezing its vice-like grip to crush it.

Except I'm wrong; it's worse, much worse. Mike continues to scream in agony and writhe uncontrollably in his torturers grip, pinned down on every front. Then to my horror I realise why he's in such pain as the probe holding his hand and wrist separates the two, ripping his hand from his wrist by brute force. Blood squirts from Mike's now severed wrist, pumping out and quickly covering the floor and spraying over the Ananta probe holding him. I stare on in terror, my eyes on stalks, not believing what I'm seeing.

"MIKE!" I shout, competing with his screams of agony as he thrashes around in the grip of the Ananta. "MIKE!"

"You will be next," says the talking Ananta, raising his voice to be heard above Mike's agonising screeches. "Unless you tell us why you are here – what is it you hope to achieve?" he states, ignoring the blood pool creeping towards him as Mike is released and pulls in what remains of his arm, and the rest of him into a foetus ball. He's got his other hand tight around the stump, stemming the bleeding.

"SEAN," he calls across to me, panting, growling and sucking in air between clamped teeth, the pain clearly assaulting him to the point where concentration and focus is a challenge. "Sean... it's—" and he stops talking, shaking his head. To my astonishment, he lets go of his stump, blood immediately squirting out, and raises his good hand, one finger pointed towards the ceiling.

"UNDERSTOOD," I shout desperately, needing him to put his hand down and stem the bleeding, which thankfully he does.

A cold chill runs down my spine as the Ananta that were pinning Mike now turn and walk towards me. I frantically push myself back against the door behind me with my feet, still sat cradling my injured hand, desperate to avoid the suffering they will visit upon me. Two of them simply lean in and pick me up by my arms, as if I weighed nothing, my injured hand forced down, sending shockwaves of pain through my body and forcing an involuntary shriek from my lungs.

The two that have me push me up against the door, so hard I feel the seams of the metal dig into my back, and my shoulders feel like they're about to dislocate. I give into them, let them pin me, what choice do I have? Then I see another Ananta, the torturer, still covered in Mike's blood, close in on me as I squirm helplessly. It reaches out and takes hold of my good hand and wrist.

"NO!" I bawl in his face. "I WILL TELL YOU, I WILL TELL YOU!" I yell, needing the time. It can only be seconds now. For what I don't know – looking to Mike he's in no position to do anything, I'm not even sure he's still conscious.

"Very well," says the talking probe as he watches on, and the torturer releases his grip on my wrist and hand. "Why are you here?" he asks again, in the same passive tone.

"Well..." I say "... the thing is... Well, it's because, we saw the opportunity and wanted to explore. But, well, it went wrong. So, you see, there's no malice in us being here."

"This explanation does not align with your actions," replies the Ananta and my torturer resumes its grip on my wrist and hand. The metal of its grip is much harder now, crushing my wrist and hand and pulling, starting to separate them like a Christmas cracker. I feel bones in my joint click and start to shift as I clench my teeth and brace myself for the horror, the impending agony. More pain arrives when something smacks the back of my head hard, bouncing it forward, immediately followed by pain in my body as something slams into my back and I hear a muted explosion.

With no warning, all three probes let go of me and I fall to the floor, painfully stumbling to my knees and injured hands. I spin around to see the door behind me flick up, revealing an armada of suits on the other side. Some start to march forwards, towards the Ananta probes; others fly in on their manoeuvring jets, straight towards us. "IS THIS YOU MIKE?" I shout over to him, and see him uncurled, lying on his side, nursing his stump and looking back at the approaching suits.

He looks at me, a forced smile on his face and nods, before letting himself drop back to lie down, staring at the ceiling, his stump still clenched in his good hand.

I quickly look back to the approaching suits and then the Ananta as they start backing off. I'm right in the middle of any cross-fire and do my best to stand without the use of any hands and run to the side of the opening for safe harbour.

The suit jets increase in volume as they move through the doorway, and I squat down, trying to stay out of the way. Then there's another sound, competing with the overwhelming noise of the jets. It's like huge trees crashing to the ground. I look around to see that it's the suits ramming the Ananta probes at high speed, time and again. It's damaging the suits, but it's doing the same to the probes. There are so many suits the Ananta don't stand a chance.

The suits are lining up to ram; one dips to hit a probe at full speed head-first like a battering ram, only to be followed seconds later by another suit and then another. After a couple of minutes, the Ananta probes are in pieces scattered across the floor.

With no Ananta left, the suits that remain land and wind down their jets to stand silently, awaiting instructions.

"HOLY SHIT MIKE!" I scream, running over to him with my arms held into my chest. "What the fuck, where did they come from?"

I go to help him sit up, careful not to touch his injuries. His skin is ashen, he looks ten years older, and I see the pain on his face as he moves to sit, still clutching his stump. Amazingly, his champion smile returns and splits his face.

"The remaining AIs... in Node proper," he says, awkwardly, panting between words, looking around. "I tasked each AI with a suit... not just the two that brought me across. They were... kilometres behind, a fall back if we needed... We needed!"

"Fantastic," I say, inspecting our silent army. "How many?"

"Initially... two hundred plus. Now, your guess..." he replies, scanning the room. "But," he says, shuffling to kneel. "We need to move." I grab under his armpit with my good hand and help him stand. "Who knows what level of retribution the Ananta will wreak upon us following this."

"Agreed," I say nervously. "But Mike, look at you. You've lost a lot of blood. You're in no state to make it all the way back to the printer lounge. We aren't going anywhere fast." We may have won the battle, but the war still rages and we're a long way from home.

"I know, I know. I have a plan... listen," he says, stopping to suck in air and wince as a pulse of pain grabs him.

"K Mike, whatever you need. How far can you walk? I can carry you some of the way," I suggest, before his frown tells me to shut up and listen.

"The doors are locked, or not opening. Get the laptop out, open it and hold it in front of me," he says.

I do as instructed, as quickly as I can. Holding the laptop up to Mike, so he can clearly see the screen. A minute later, two suits come to life and fly off towards the far door we need to leave through.

"I've tasked the suits to work in pairs to open the doors," says Mike. "They will sacrifice a power cell at each door to blow it and... then the other suit can manipulate the controls to open it for us. They're going to go ahead and clear the route. If Ananta turn up, they take them out too. We follow... understood?"

"Yep, I say," nodding, loving this plan. Loving our army of suits. "But we need to be steady, the last thing we need is you unconscious."

"I have that covered. You can put the laptop away now," he says, and as I do another suit comes to life and flies over to us. It lands behind Mike and reaches out to pick him up, cradling him in its arms like a baby as he in turn cradles his damaged arm.

"That's yours," he says, nodding towards another suit, as I twitch in response to an explosion detonating next to the door. "That suit has been tasked to you; it will fly you out, with me. When you're ready, we go. When we travel to Earth the printer there will print us whole, all injuries gone... the pain will just be a memory." There's another explosion off in the distance, our exit being cleared. "We can win this Sean," he says confidently.

My suit flies in and scoops me up. "Ready," I call across to Mike, managing to pull my lips into a smile.

Chapter Thirty-Six

I take Jess's hand as we walk across the tarmac of the car park. She smiles across to me briefly as we walk on towards the gate. That smile, those eyes, they get me every time. The gate AI scans our e-codes and we move through without incident. I look to Mike's email for the remaining directions, just in case. The base is big and I don't recall everything.

"Has he ever asked you to meet him here before" asks Jess. "Or is this just for my benefit, do you think?"

"No, he's brought me here on previous occasions, like when I disappeared for a day after you found out about Mike. And of course when we all three left the installation together, after we retrieved you from Node, but that's it."

"I thought so. It just, seems different, you know, summoning us like this. And what little I know of Mike is everything he does is for a reason, even if you don't see what it is at the time."

"That's a good point Jess. Well, we'll find out in a bit, I'm sure."

"Yes. Never a dull moment with Mike. And these last two weeks have been the hardest in my life and also the best in my life," she says, smiling at me again as we walk. "Coming to terms with everything, with neither of us being the person we originally were, the presence of a malicious alien species, longevity being the turning point, there being another me out there, being subjected to who knows what... And us, which is great, really it is. But all I've learnt about Mike is that he's a coin toss, impossible to predict and, depending on how the coin falls, it might rip your world apart. The last thing I need now is to lose you."

I stop walking and turn to face her, reaching for her other hand, looking into her eyes. "I know Jess, I do, of course. We stay strong, important to listen to what he has to say. But, we prioritise each other, K? He's saved us both, given so much. He is my brother after all."

"I know, you're right. Just, I wanted to say it, to share, it's important to me," she replies.

After two more security entrances, the codes to which are in Mike's email to us, we arrive in the corridor to Mike's installation. I push open the final door, and a wave of grief smothers me as I imagine how this must have been for Sean Two when he burst through the very same door only weeks ago, to be killed minutes later.

"Mike," I yell as we enter, surprised he wasn't there to meet us at the main door. "MIKE," I shout again, to no response. The place is deserted – the printer is gone, just markings on the floor where it once stood. The two medical couches are still in situ and I see Mike's laptop on the long shelf and also a large handheld fire extinguisher in the corner, but that's it. It's as if the place has been abandoned halfway through moving out.

"Well, what now?" asks Jess, looking equally lost.

"Good afternoon Dr Freeman, good afternoon Professor Hart," intones a mechanical voice from the ceiling, as does a small click, and Eric, Mike's "heavy lifting" robot, descends. He stops at head height, just in front of us, his small screen an animated smiley face. "You are both most welcome, would you each like to take a seat on the two couches please. Mike sends his apologies that he cannot be here in person, however he is waiting for you on a construct, which you can access via the couches here. If you will."

I exchange a worried look with Jess – we are back at the top of a rabbit hole. The coin is tossed, we just need to decide if we catch it or not. "Well," I say, "what do you want to do?"

"Do we really have a choice? We can't get physically hurt can we?" she asks.

"I wouldn't be so sure, and with the printer gone, there's no magical cure either."

"Do we have other options?"

"Not if we want to talk to Mike. I guess the real question is, do we both go in? I could go in, you monitor me out here and pull me back if things look bad. That would work."

"If we go in, we go in together Sean," she says, locking eyes with me, taking my hand and squeezing it. "That way we still have each other."

"Yeah, you're right. So we do it!"

She nods and hops on the couch, lying back against the head rest and looks across to me. I do the same and reach out a hand to touch her. She does the same, but we're just too far away from one another to touch, just out of reach.

The blackness of an empty substrate greets me: no noise, no sensation, no vision, nothing. I forgot to warn Jess about this.

"*Sean,*" calls Jess from nowhere and the night sky appears all around me. I have the immediate comfort of being able to look around and alter my view. Relief floods in; had I a face, it would be smiling.

"*Jess, are you alright? Can you see the starscape?*"

"I can, but... nothing else. Very strange, like a VR game, you know where there is no you, just the view. I can't see you, can you see me?"

"No, we can only look around for now. But if you talk in your head, it arrives in the other person's head as if you talked, like telepathy or something. But don't worry, private thoughts remain so. How you feeling?"

"Off balance, but coping. What's the view of, where are we?"

"Welcome to both of you," sounds Mike's voice in my head.

"You're here Mike, that's good. Why not in person? What's going on?"

"I'll come to that in good time, but great to have you both here, and together." I feel a warm smile greeting me and wonder if Jess is feeling the same.

"Jess, this construct is a planetarium," announces Mike. "It will help in explaining where things are at now and where things are likely to go to."

"Is Node coming for us? That's the question, the only question," I share. "Deleting the Ananta probes on Earth and us rescuing Jess, what are the consequences? Have we just embroiled ourselves in the politics of an alien species? A technologically far superior species, who clearly has little or no value of lesser species or individuals."

"Indeed Sean," replies Mike. "Jess, this region of the galaxy is where Node resides. Let's go in and have a look," he shares, and we zoom towards a distant spec of light that quickly grows into what I now know is the rainbow sphere that is Node.

"So, there we go, the giant's castle, full of all sorts of treasures," he shares as we halt at some distance from Node, giving us a heavenly overview.

"It really is beautiful, isn't it?" I reply. It feels I'm seeing Node for the first time, like I'm not the same man. Like I'm an older, wiser version of me.

"*Wow, I have a million questions on this Mike,*" shares Jess. "*A construct that's not static, dynamically adapting as needed. The materials technology must be fascinating.*"

"*It is, all that and more,*" replies Mike. "*But of course, remember that we've woken the Giant and he isn't happy. I don't think he'll want to eat us, but he might. You see, that's the nub of it, that's your next challenge.*"

Mike's words send a shiver down my back, is this more of his less than subtle reveals? "*Mike, I came here thinking we've saved humanity, got Jess back and now I'm thinking we've started... SHIT! Have we started a war? Jesus Christ Mike! Is that right, am I right? How have you not mentioned this before? Mike!*"

"*Slow down,*" he shares. "*Too dramatic, you're thinking in human terms. Node knows we've been in the castle sniffing around, so it sent a probe to find out what was going on. We just got rid of that probe and also showed up at its castle and made a bit of a mess in the periphery. Probes are independent and Node is vast and it's not uncommon for probes to never return, they only warrant so much interest, as would have our visit. We did no lasting damage, we have just been nosy neighbours.*"

"*But we have sent the probes from Earth home,*" I share. "*With full knowledge of what's going on here. Why did we send them home?*"

"*Because it's the only option we had; they can't be destroyed,*" he emotes. "*It was that or they remove you and delete Jess and me. So, that was our choice. Them or us...*"

"*So we won't hear from them again?*" shares Jess, and I feel the hope in her words.

Mike doesn't respond, and with no one to look at, to garner their attention, my emoting senses prick and I feel danger.

"*Mike? You got that didn't you?*" I yell in my mind, trying to pull back his attention.

"*The thing is... we can't know,*" he replies. "*But we have time. We have time to make good the present situation and prepare for what might come next.*"

"*Meaning?*" I share, allowing the full weight of my trepidation to travel with my words.

"*I'm in the process of dismantling both installations. The printers are already gone and the rest soon, before Node gets inquisitive about its probes,*" he shares. "*It might be years before they do, but it will likely happen one day; this situation is too novel to be completely ignored. But I think our immaturity as a species, our current level of evolution might help us – we are infants to them. Errant perhaps, but not of any real concern.*"

"*It seems to me a lot of your reasoning is based on conjecture,*" shares Jess.

"*I agree,*" he shares. "*But the key thing is, now both installations are inoperable you are protected, because Node will have no direct point of access to Earth. And just look how far away they are.*" We immediately start to retreat from the view of Node, accelerating fast.

Very quickly, Betelgeuse dominates the scene and Node shrinks to nothing, but we keep moving away and the star rapidly shrinks to a shiny spec. We continue and what was a star is now a small cluster of stars that soon become a wispy haze; the wispy haze soon blends into a bigger haze of cloud and we keep going and I can't remember which part of the sky I was looking at. It's all got too big too quickly.

"*We can see Earth too now,*" emotes Mike, and the vista slows to a vast stationary picture of a starry night. It looks like the night sky you only get in the mountains, many miles from civilisation and light pollution, vast skies with countless stars from horizon to horizon.

A star begins to pulse far off to one side of our view. "*This is the Sun, our Sun,*" shares Mike. "*And this is Node.*" A second star begins to pulse, on the opposite side. The two pulsing stars are at opposite ends of a gigantic cinema screen. We then zoom out further, the stars seemingly closing in on one other as the view widens.

"And these are the other Nodes, or similar sentient occupied locations, I'm aware of," he shares and with that a huge number of pulsing stars come to life all across the edges of the screen. We zoom out and the number grows. They are all much further away than the first Node, but there must be thousands scattered across just this part of the galaxy.

"Your see, we are pretty insignificant really," shares Mike. *"And the points you see before you only include advanced civilisations, akin to Node. Those developing civilisations similar to Earth are not mapped and are in their millions. Most of them will come and go as civilisations, never to be noticed. Natural selection... they go extinct and the Galactic Community lets them, or if they become problematic, helps them self-euthanise. This is the track Earth is on and why Node wants zero interference. This is why we must do what we can to change this, to save our species."*

With what Mike has introduced me to over the passing months this isn't new, but seeing the physicality of it, the image, makes it real. We are just another insect on the summer breeze. No one will miss us if we're gone – no one will notice if we stay. We are a speck of existence on a grand tapestry of life. The reality scares me for humanity, our fragility as a species. And there's too much, too much I don't know, too much I doubt I'm able to understand, too much to take in, for me and for Jess.

Above all this I have an inner confidence in where we are at, a sense of completeness. This does feel like journey's end, the truth at last. The harsh reality of our situation laid bare, and it all makes sense.

But is this just the end of the beginning? Is all that has gone before just us learning the rules of the game, a game we have yet to play?

"*Jess,*" I share. "*How are you feeling about all this?*"

"*Lost, if I'm honest. But if we can give ourselves distance and time, well, maybe? It seems to me we have few options.*"

"*Mike...*" I begin, but the words don't come. I'm clutching for something, but I don't know what.

"*I know,*" he replies, and his empathy radiates.

"*That's an impossible task. We can't just change society,*" I share.

"*No, not today. But now you see where we are at,*" he emotes and we zoom back in with Node and Earth once again the only pulsing stars at opposite ends of our view. "*Next actions I predict will be Node sending another probe to investigate. They can only do this via the nearest printer, which, as I've destroyed the two on Earth, is located in orbit around a star already known to humans. It's called WDJ0551+4135, which is one hundred and fifty light years from Earth. Here,*" he shares and yet another point of light throbs within the starscape. It must only be a quarter of the way between Node and Earth.

"*That looks very close, Mike.*"

"*It's all relative. The key question is, how long?*" he asks. "*If there is no printer on Earth and this is the next closest one, then how long would it take for a probe to get to Earth at close to light speed? My estimate is humanity has one hundred and eighty years to prepare.*"

"*Prepare for what! War?*"

"*No! The opposite,*" he replies. "*Prepare, so that we can be found as a species worth leaving alone or even better be invited into the galactic community. A planet with a culture that one day can positively contribute to the galactic community and not be seen as a threat and waster of resources. Where there is no need for police, or armies or governments focused on manipulation. All of those resources and people's time and* energy tied up in conflict – they can be utilised in improving everyone's existence, making the world a better place for everyone. This is how you prosper, this is how we survive!

The best defence is to be found living a meaningful and responsible life, the whole community of Earth that is. So, one hundred and eighty years is not long, but guess what? Longevity is the first major milestone and you both, sorry, but you two are the key to that. You've always said once we're long lived we see things differently Sean, and you're right. Humanity will become responsible. It's the ultimate win-win, it will make the world a better place for everyone and at the same time ensure our survival. We can't fake it. We have to make it happen, for real."

He emotes all this with a passion and zealotry I recognise – it's mine. It's what I have aspired to my entire life, it's the reason I do the research I do, it gives my life purpose. But right now, it simply washes over me. All I can do is stare at the colossal view, the enormity of it now dwarfed by the immense challenge ahead. I reach for Jess in my mind, wanting to hold here near, be with her in this moment.

"*How you doing*? I ask her. There's no reply. "*Jess?*"

"*…together Sean, we go on together,*" she replies, and I feel the old Jess focus. The impossible is up ahead, so let's get moving.

"*Is it even possible?*" I ask. "*Changing the culture of an entire planet that hasn't fundamentally changed in millennia. Even with longevity, one hundred and eighty years is no time at all; the last four thousand years of human history prove that we are fundamentally selfish animals.*"

"*True Sean,*" shares Jess. "*But think about it. It's never been easy… mankind has faced adversity and destitution for as long as it's existed. The world is a desperate place, it always has been. Corruption is everywhere, the weak are preyed upon, wars are fought at the whim of dictators, thousands die needlessly every day. And if you give in to it, the world will cage you and destroy you. You have to fight, in one way or another, for what's right, for yourself, for what you believe in. It isn't about how difficult the task is, it's about how you keep going, no matter what. If you know your purpose, you know you want the best for everyone, then you keep moving forward. And we will take hits, failures, setbacks, and they will be hard, but we get up, we go again, and we keep going, because that's how we succeed. That's how we win. That's how we survive.*

Her thoughts and words energise me, like she's just turned on the power to the real me. Opened my eyes to a new way of seeing the challenge. The task is the journey, not the destination. The joy of life will be in the being and working with Jess, not in only getting the job done, not just in completion, not solely focused on achieving the objective, but on the getting there. The purpose is the journey, not the destination and with Jess's level of hyperfocus I'm not sure I'm the only neurodivergent in this relationship.

"Well put Jess," shares Mike. *"You will make a formidable team."*

The starscape starts to fill with white light, misting over as it begins to transform. The beach we all know emerges from the mist, with the three of us stood facing one another barefoot on the warm dry sand, all dressed in colourful lightweight summer clothes, the shoreline only metres away.

"You alright?" I say to Jess, not sure how she'll handle the magical transitions.

"Fine," she replies looking around and settling on Mike. "Where now, Mike?" she asks.

He doesn't respond in words or emotions; he simply looks from Jess to me and back again, a flat smile on his face, lips pursed. Not saying something.

"Mike?" I say, recognising his pre-emptive silence, knowing he's about to drop a bomb.

He meets my gaze and holds it. Silence sits between us, our eyes locked, no words, no emoting, a liminal intimacy.

"What?" I say, breaking the deadlock, "what are you not telling us? There's something else."

He frowns, but not like before, "there you are again, with that uncanny knack of asking the right questions, Sean." He slowly shakes his head and stares at me, saying nothing. Then it leaks out, a profound sadness coming from Mike, words left unsaid, words he's struggling to say. Words I don't want to hear.

"What?" I ask, "what is it? You can tell us, after all we've been through, you can tell us." I know what he's going to say, but I desperately hope I'm wrong.

"The thing is that, now I've destroyed the printers, there is one bit of alien kit we still need to get rid of," he replies.

"What is it?" I ask, a sharp chill coursing through my body.

"The probe, the one that built the installations here on Earth. It was never sent with Node's direction, but it was created at Node, re-purposed from an existing probe by Sean Two. Node could re-purpose it again. So that probe must go too."

The beads of sweat on my forehead confirm what I expected and send a chill down my spine – this was always going to surface. But I don't accept it, there has to be another way. "You mean *you*, don't you?" I say. "You're the probe?"

He looks at me in silence and a flood of loss surges over me, a rock in the path of the invisible flood. I stand there battered as the emotions push into me. His loss is the loss of everything, the finality of death. The loss of no longer being, of releasing yourself to what might come next, or not. Releasing yourself to the emptiness of nothing. "I'm sorry Sean... we don't have a choice. It's too much of a risk," he says and a single tear forms, and rolls down his cheek. I follow it, time slowed. It falls from his cheek and drips onto the sand, bouncing back into a tiny crown shape for a moment and then to nothing.

"But Mike..." I begin. "We can take the risk, how do you even know they can re-purpose you?"

"Because that's exactly what Sean Two did to create me in the first place. And remember: QE, any distance, instantaneously. It's what I would do."

I return to staring at my friend, my brother, my mind searching frantically for another way, needing Mike, for him to stay and help in the journey ahead. And selfishly for me... not to lose another friend.

"He's right, Sean," says Jess, breaking the silence. "It's not even *if* it will happen. It's a question of *when* it will happen."

"It's been two weeks already and nothing," I say. "So there's no real urgency. Is there? You know... we could do something. Have you with us, you know, until..." my words peter out. I know I'm clutching, but I can't let my brother go without a fight.

"Risk everything for a single person?" says Mike, shaking his head slowly, pursing his lips as he does. "Someone who was only ever created to save humanity and now becomes the biggest point of weakness? You know I'm right."

I simply nod. His logic is solid, I just don't want it to be.

Mike's words silence us. So much has happened, is happening and so much depends on Jess and I now. I look to her; our eyes meet. I see her sympathetic sweet smile, trying to push positivity into our future... she knows how hard this is for me. As I look into her eyes, I feel my confidence in "us" grow, despite the enormity of what lies ahead. She is my rock, and I am hers.

The sadness of Mike going crushes my chest. So much death, too much and now him. Mike, who's become my best friend, my brother, humanity's saviour. But I know the reality. The risk is too great. I know it, I just don't want to accept it. Humanity has to be the priority, and humanity will only survive through being responsible to one another. Mike knows this, Sean Two knew this. I've always known this. Maybe at some deep level, the universe won't tolerate multiple versions of an individual and, steadily, entropy pulls it back to one, to the original. To me.

"So, this is goodbye, I'm afraid," he says, taking a deep breath. "I am sorry, but..."

I step forwards and grab him, pulling him into a bear hug, and immediately feel Jess holding us both. The three of us huddled on the beach, the sound of the waves breaking and herring gulls calling, the breeze gently buffeting us. "When?" I ask, my voice muffled as I talk into Mike's shoulder.

"Now," he replies, and I feel his grip on me tighten.

We stand there, the three of us, without words, savouring this moment, not wanting to let go. Not wanting the countdown to begin, for this ache in my chest to be made more real than it already is. And I feel it within Mike, his unspoken fear, his bravery, his strength of will, ready to do what he knows must be done.

This really is our last goodbye. I know the sense of loss will be profound and will never leave me, but my love for this man, my brother, it will endure, it will remain with me for as long as I live, no matter how long that may be.

"So," says Mike, releasing us and taking a step back. "Everything that needs to be done is already done. When we are finished here, you simply leave. Oh, except there will be a small fire to extinguish, sorry about that."

"What?" I ask, distracted from my grief by this strange practicality.

"But... the physical me is already gone. He went with the printer, some days ago—"

"What!" I yell. "You've already... gone, but..." I stare at him, blinking.

"This is why we're meeting here Sean," he says, looking around at the sand dunes, the setting sun, our idyllic private beach. "The *me* that remains is QE code, on my interface device, my laptop. That which we are all currently on. And when you leave here and return to the installation, that will be the final piece of technology to dispose of. Then, in the best way possible, the only way possible, you will be on your own."

I raise my arm and hold Jess close to me. She pulls me in tight as I reach out to Mike and pull him into both of us, resuming our three-way hug. "Goodbye old friend, and thank you for everything. I love you brother," I say and squeeze him as tight as I can as tears fill my eyes.

The mist forms and I want to deny it. It settles as Mike's installation; we are back in the real. The smell of smoke snaps me from my melancholy and I look to Jess and see her sniffing, too.

"The laptop!" she yells, pointing across the room to Mike's device, smoke pouring from it and flames licking out from under it.

I jump off the couch, grab the fire extinguisher and blast the laptop. The powder of the extinguisher quickly kills the flames and starts to fill the room.

"STOP SEAN!" shouts Jess, trying to be heard above the roar of the extinguisher. "THE FIRE'S OUT, Mike's gone...." I stop, the words echoing around the room and in my heart.

I pull Jess into me. She holds me tight.

Together alone.

Our journey begins.

Afterword

A note from the Author

I really hope you've enjoyed my book, so much so that you might want to recommend it to friends. However, if you do, can I please, please, please ask that you don't reveal the twist in the tale. You know the one.

(Mark Ellis, Sheffield, 2024)

Acknowledgements

With huge thanks and much appreciation to both DB Rook (Author of Callus and Crow) and Ed Crocker (Author of the Everlands Trilogy) for their encouragement, advice and guidance. Without their support it is unlikely this would be here.

Printed in Great Britain
by Amazon